THE BOOKS OF SORCERY, VOL III
OADENOL'S CODEX™

By Conrad Hubbard, Lydia Laurenson,
Peter Schaefer, Dustin Shampel, John Snead

CREDITS

Authors: Conrad Hubbard, Lydia Laurenson, Peter Schaefer, Dustin Shampel and John Snead
Comic Scripter: Carl Bowen
Developers: John Chambers and Dean Shomshak with John Masterson
Editor: Carl Bowen
Art Direction: Brian Glass
Artists: Newton Ewell, Andrew Hepworth, Jeff Holt, Imaginary Friends Studio (with Aramia, Jho, Kiat and Yina), Saana "Kiyo" Lappalainen, Pasi Pitkanen, UDON (with Joe Ng and Chris Stevens) and Melissa Uran
Cover Art: HOON
Book Design: Brian Glass

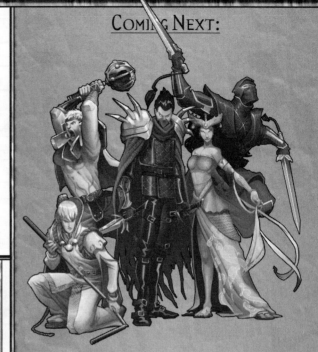

COMING NEXT:

THE MANUAL OF EXALTED POWER — THE SIDEREALS

$31.99   224 PAGES

Gifted with power by the Five Maidens, the Sidereal Exalted were once the trusted advisors to the Old Realm's Solar masters. However, believing the Curse-maddened Lawgivers' irredeemable and unshakably convinced in their moral duty, the Chosen of the Maidens persuaded the Dragon-Blooded to rise up and slaughter their masters in order to end the Solars' depredations. Since that time, the Sidereals have influenced events behind the scenes in order to safeguard Creation from its myriad of enemies. But with the return of the Solars, the advent of the deathknights, the Dragon-Blooded Realm nearing civil war, the tribes of the Lunars threatening war and the Fair Folk massing for another assault on the shaped world, will the Fivefold Fellowship win the day or will its many sacrifices have been for naught?

COMING NEXT IN THIS SERIES:

THE BOOKS OF SORCERY, VOL. IV — THE ROLL OF GLORIOUS DIVINITY 1: GODS & ELEMENTALS

$24.99   160 PAGES

In this fourth of **Exalted**'s five **Books of Sorcery**, elementals and spirits finally get their due. This supplement outlines both the little gods of Creation and the Terrestrial Bureaucracy, as well as the elementals and their many courts. In addition, it also reveals the many spirit Charms available to these divine beings (as well as to enterprising Eclipse and Moonshadow Caste Exalted).

1554 LITTON DR
STONE MOUNTAIN, GA
30083
USA

WHITE WOLF PUBLISHING

THE BOOKS OF SORCERY, VOL III
OADENOL'S CODEX™

TABLE OF CONTENTS

INTRODUCTION

Welcome to **Oadenol's Codex**, a supplement in the **Books of Sorcery** series for **Exalted**. In the world of **Exalted**, supernatural power comes from manipulating the universal force of Essence. Charms, by which Essence augments the ordinary talents of mind and body to supernatural extremes, form the basis of Exalted power. The **Exalted** core rulebook and the various books in the **Manual of Exalted Power** series describe the Charms of the various sorts of Chosen. Sorcery and its dark reflection necromancy enable stranger feats of greater power, as described in **The White and Black Treatises**. In the First Age, the Exalted developed a third way to wield power: Essence-fueled magitech that the Second Age duplicates with difficulty, if at all. The magitech described in **Wonders of the Lost Age** did more than either Charms or sorcery to make the elder world an Age of Splendor in contrast to the current Age of Sorrows.

But Creation also holds other forms of magical power, which the Exalted did not invent. Sometimes Essence naturally concentrates in certain locations called demesnes, and in particular plants, animals and minerals. Long ago—before the gods Exalted their chosen champions—mortal creatures learned to tap and control these natural sources of Essence.

Oadenol's Codex describes four of these ancient modes of magic. They lack the portable raw power of Charms and sorcery, or the flash and dazzle of magitech. Nevertheless, the Exalted use them all. Just as the mightiest combat Charm grows from the sweat and blood of mundane weapon skill, some of the greatest feats of Exalted power depend on paying attention to the Essence already at large in Creation.

WHAT'S IN THIS BOOK

Each chapter of **Oadenol's Codex** describes one source of magical power.

Chapter One: Artifacts and Artifice tells of the enchanted wonders whose magic comes from craftsmanship and mystically potent ingredients rather than sorcerous science. Artifacts range from writing-brushes that take dictation to mighty weapons any Exalt would fear to face in battle. Not only does the chapter describe dozens of artifacts, but it gives a thorough discussion of how to create them—from the perspectives both of a character and a player or Storyteller.

Chapter Two: Demesne, Manse and Hearthstone expands upon the core rulebook's discussion of demesnes, those places where Creation's Essence wells up in superabundance, and the manses built to channel that power. This chapter discusses new ways that characters can gain power from demesnes and give power to their manses. It also explains the techniques of geomantic construction that produce manses, and can create or modify demesnes—or destroy them. The chapter ends with more than 100 hearthstones, those magical jewels that channel Essence from manses and confer other strange powers.

Chapter Three: Thaumaturgy discusses the 11 magical Arts that mortals can use. The rituals of thaumaturgy may seem slow and weak compared to Charms and sorcery, but they are powerful enough that the Exalted should not take them lightly. This chapter reveals the history of thaumaturgy and describes the people and groups that practice it.

Chapter Four: Magical Flora, Fauna and Phenomena collects a sampling of creatures and substances that magical forces have shaped. Some of these phenomena are deadly threats to all who encounter them; others are natural artifacts waiting for anyone brave and strong enough to collect them.

HEROIC MORTALS AND MAGIC

The subjects of these four chapters have something in common: they don't need the Exalted. People who can't even perceive Essence on their own can learn thaumaturgy, collect magical plants, craft the weaker sorts of artifacts and even build manses. Exaltation *helps*, but it isn't completely necessary. Therefore, a few topics about mortals and magic deserve special discussion here since they have relevance for more than one chapter. But first, a word about heroic mortal characters in general.

ESSENCE AND MORTALS

Mortals typically have Essence 1 and no Essence pool. This might change two distinct ways, though a character could potentially benefit from both.

Increased Essence: Rarely, heroic mortals gain a higher permanent Essence score. The mortal attunes to Creation and feels some degree of its Essence flows. By itself, this does not grant the mortal an Essence pool. However, having an Essence rating of 2 or 3 does give the mortal the other benefits that come to the Exalted, such as an increased Dodge DV, greater minimum damage and higher minimum dice pools. Mortals cannot have Essence 4.

Essence Pool: Mortals with the ability to actually manipulate Essence are called enlightened mortals. Unless the Storyteller makes the differences between sources of enlightenment an important part of her series, pools of (Essence x 10) motes will serve as a "quick and dirty" rule. The character can use the first (Essence x 3) motes easily. If the enlightened mortal spends a Willpower point, he can access the remaining (Essence x 7) motes for the rest of the scene.

Chapter Three includes a ritual by which mortals can gain Essence pools. **Scroll of the Monk**, pages 17-20, discusses several more. Half-mortal characters, such as the God-Blooded, Ghost-Blooded or Half-Castes (children of powerful Exalts) can have Essence pools, too. A mortal with an Essence pool can increase his Essence rating, and his pool with it, through experience.

ATTUNEMENT

Enlightened mortals can use their Essence to attune artifacts, manses, demesnes and hearthstones—but they need thaumaturgy to do it. The thaumaturgical Procedures are easy, though; see Chapter Three. Once an enlightened mortal attunes something magical, she gets all the normal benefits from that item. She can swing the daiklave that's bigger than she is, gain Essence from a hearthstone, and so on.

With so little Essence, though, *keeping* an artifact or manse might become a problem…

THE ENLIGHTENED MORTAL SORCERER

Much has been made of the fact that mortals cannot normally learn the powerful spells of sorcery and necromancy. However, Creation is vast enough to permit exceptions. A mortal who achieves a permanent Essence of 3 and Occult 5 can learn the Terrestrial Circle Sorcery Charm and sorcery spells, provided she could endure the trials of initiation. The same goes for necromancy. A mortal cannot become both a sorcerer and necromancer—but even the Exalted find that difficult.

Even if a mortal somehow gains the prerequisites, learning sorcery takes longer and requires more effort for a mortal than it does for any of the Exalted. As such, mortals must pay 15 experience (12 experience if Occult is Favored) for the Terrestrial Circle Sorcery Charm and for each spell learned.

FOLK RESOURCES

Crafting artifacts, building manses and performing many thaumaturgical rituals costs a lot: as described in **Exalted**, most of these activities demand that characters muster considerable Resources. The high expense of workshops, tools and materials might seem to place artifact creation beyond the reach of tribal shamans, village witches and other folk savants, while building manses would be unthinkable. How do they even afford the higher-Degree rituals?

Remember that Resources measure more than cash. For folk magicians and savants, Resources indicate direct access to raw materials and accumulation of time and effort.

For instance, a barbarian shaman might chant prayers in a hut while he kneels on a mat and scratches symbols on a talisman of wood and feathers… but the hut is made entirely from the bones and sinews of tigers. The mat was woven from hair of the shaman who trained him, the shaman who trained *her*, and so on back six generations. He scratches the symbols with the claw of a gryphon his grandfather slew. The feathers come from birds that nest in the tree of a forest's ruling god. Even though by most standards the shaman and his people are desperately poor, the shaman still has a master's workshop, because a civilized artisan would need to pay a fortune to obtain a similar panoply of mystic tools.

Folk magicians usually limit themselves to the talismans and minor enchantments of thaumaturgy. Nevertheless, the wise folk of barbarian cultures can sometimes craft artifacts as powerful as any from the Realm.

Even manses are not beyond the reach of a determined tribe or village. Building a manse takes years. They *have* years. If a community doesn't have large numbers of skilled artisans, well, it takes a bit longer—but they can do it if they really want to. The chief limiting factor is knowledge… but knowledge has a way of getting around, especially in a world of magic where shamans can summon spirits and priests can talk to gods.

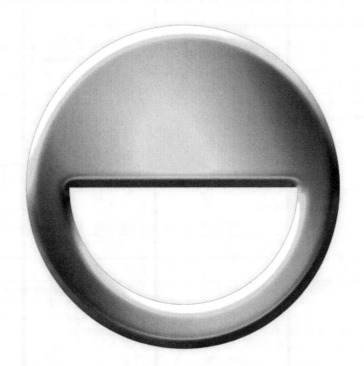

CHAPTER ONE
ARTIFACTS AND ARTIFICE

Artifacts are the tools of the Exalted. As a sword is to a soldier, so a daiklave is to a Dragon-Blood. One of the Chosen *can* shift earth with a mattock and shovel, but why would she when she can wield a fabled singing staff? Artifacts range from tools of convenience, such as animate brushes, to true world-changing wonders, like a blade that cuts time. This chapter discusses the creation and use—for players, Storytellers and characters—of artifacts for **Exalted**.

A BRIEF HISTORY OF WONDERS

Tools of power first entered the hands of the Exalted as gifts. The Incarnae's servants and the machine-god Autochthon created artifacts, mostly weapons, in preparation for the first rebellion and gave them to the gods' Chosen. Most were magnificent wonders, the like of which are seldom seen in the Age of Sorrows. The gods considered small artifacts unimportant in their quest for freedom. As beings of magic, they didn't think to bind with artifice the small miracles that accompanied their every breath.

Exalted craftsmen changed that even before the first offensive of the Primordial War. Almost childlike in their exploration, they created toys, minor useful tools and other things unnecessary to war. Eager to explore the nature of Essence, they crafted the most basic equipment as experiments. Some daiklaves and suits of enchanted armor crafted then, the simplest of artifacts, still exist today.

Lesser wonders existed before the Exalted created them. The vegetative artifacts of the Dragon Kings, greened-copper wonders of the Western princes and other objects of power were already in Creation. But these people did not bless humanity with their cleverness, instead treating them as slaves or lesser beings. Gods Exalted humanity, and humanity invented anew.

The War changed everything. Uncountable artifacts of tremendous power were lost in battle along with the heroes that bore them. Others took their places as the gods forged fantastic new weapons for the Exaltations' new hosts. Unique wonders disappeared forever during that period, their powers never again to grace Creation.

Combat with the Exalted's alien foes spurred creativity. Capturing a Primordial's tooth or ligament opened infinite possibilities to Exalted artisans. Even in wartime, they took opportunities to forge wonders from their spoils. Traveling inside foreign worlds defined by Primordial Essence, where natural laws became unnatural, made unheard-of marvels possible.

When the war ended, the Exalted turned their attention to governing Creation, and they gained time to engage in research for its own sake. Artifacts became varied in purpose, origin and appearance. First Age craftsmanship had no equal, before or after. The best artificers of the Age surpassed their instructors by far.

ARTIFICE IN THE SECOND AGE OF MAN

A large portion of Creation's wonders disappeared in the Usurpation, effectively forever. Many resources were destroyed by defeated but spiteful god-kings or by fearful Terrestrials and Sidereals. Even the Lunar survivors lost some of their equipage to the Wyld.

Burial of the Solar Exalted caused an enormous depletion of the First Age's artifacts. Rightfully afraid of hungry ghosts bloated by "Anathema" powers, the usurpers did everything they could to mollify the dead spirits. They interred the slain with full regalia and the Exalted's favored weapons and tools. Some burial parties threw in artifacts that had no connection to the Exalt in question, simply as a safety precaution.

The artifice of Creation dwindled rapidly. Even in the early Shogunate (called the Low First Age by some), the weapons and tools that the Exalted created were of a lesser sort. Though skilled, the artisans could not approach the level of sheer ingenuity that existed in the previous Age. Very occasionally, a wunderkind would arise among the Dragon-Blooded, or one of the Sidereal or Lunar Exalted would find the leisure and resources to craft an object of great power, but even those could not approach the height of the First Age's wonders.

Today, great artifacts are legacies of a time lost more than things to be made. Scavenger lords rarely consider that their treasures could be made rather than found. The Great Houses of the Scarlet Empire pass down arms and other artifacts carefully from parent to

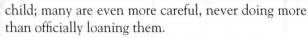

child; many are even more careful, never doing more than officially loaning them.

The returning Solar Exalted, however, have the most reason to see artifacts as tokens of vanished glory. Dragon-Blooded, at least, have the time and resources to create new wonders—if only of a lesser sort—in a world gone dusty and gray. Solars spend their time surviving first, and pursuing their visions second.

Very soon, that will change. Everything is coming to a head, and very soon, Creation may see new artifacts that have never before graced the world.

GRAVE GOODS

Anything buried with a person may manifest in the Underworld along with the person's ghost. No one can guess how many First Age artifacts now have spectral duplicates—which might exist long after the originals were destroyed. Their arsenal of grave goods no doubt helped the nascent Deathlords' rise to power. Now they turn those artifacts against the descendants of their murderers—and the rest of Creation.

USE OF ARTIFACTS

This section focuses on using artifacts in your game, from both players' and in-game perspectives.

WHAT ARE THEY FOR?

Artifacts play many roles in **Exalted**. You can approach artifacts' roles from the *character's* perspective and the *game's* perspective. Several approaches are given below as extremes, but none of them are exclusive of any others.

Artifacts as equipment. They are magical tools, and that's about it. To a character, this makes a daiklave just a better sword and a tireless brass horse just a way to get there faster. This sort of Exalt doesn't need to be buried with his equipment, and probably also won't respect the equipment of others, which might leave some unsettled spirits behind him.

When a series follows this standard, artifacts are things for players to pick out and give to their characters. There may be an *excuse* for that wavecleaver, but there's no real *reason* for it: players don't care much about their tools' origins or destinies. And that's okay. You can tell a thousand different stories in **Exalted** without tying them to the character's artifacts.

Artifacts as legacies. Remnants of a greater past lure characters to greater heights and sadden them at what was lost. Every artifact tells a story. This motivates

a character, driving her to seek out lost treasures not (just) for power but for their legends. It colors the way she uses artifacts, because each has a special meaning to her and to history.

Games that use this role make artifacts' histories important to the story. Where it came from, who wielded it in what battle and when it was buried or lost are all relevant, perhaps clues in a grand mystery. The group can also use artifacts to play with themes on loss.

Artifacts as objectives. Acquiring them is a goal in itself, or an important means to another end. A character can have many reasons to make an artifact an objective. Seeking something that belonged to a previous incarnation is common. Artifacts can be mysteries to be discovered and solved. Characters can also seek an artifact that will help them defeat enemies or keep them safe. This applies equally to characters on a mission to create or repair an artifact.

This is one of the easiest roles for a Storyteller to invoke, but it works better when the players are also interested. Artifacts can be classic, plot-driving MacGuffins—find the (fill in the blank) to save the world!—and tied to Creation-spanning quests. Take care not to overuse this role, though; one "treasure hunt" after another can get old.

Artifacts as companions. They have a character all their own that comes out in play. This doesn't refer to automatons and magical intelligences (both covered by **The Books of Sorcery, Vol. I—Wonders of the Lost Age**), but to artifacts that color the way they are used and affect the nature of their wielders. A warrior might pull steel at the drop of a hat until she recovers her First Age incarnation's daiklave—and then learns that it was only drawn in order to kill. A gleeman might go to great lengths to recover his stolen sitar because it is as dear to him as a sister. Many characters of legend had tools that became as famous as the characters themselves.

Most games need to apply a special level of importance to artifacts in order to give them character. Some players do this on their own, and some do not. It's not a problem unless you want to establish an overarching theme involving artifacts. Because the nature of an artifact is reflected in the character that bears it, players can easily make an artifact a special companion without assistance; they only need to make it a part of the character's attitude.

Most games mix and match these different roles for artifacts without a thought. Thinking about what you want artifacts to be *about* in your game allows you to fine-tune artifacts' involvement and themes until you're satisfied.

SCRIPT IMMUNITY

A Storyteller is usually free to arrange the theft of a character's assets, kidnap his family and kill off friends and allies, all in the name of story. Many players feel more protective about their characters' artifacts. Maybe they like having "stuff," or maybe they resent the loss of something they paid points at character generation to have. So, what's a Storyteller to do?

Figure out which artifacts mean something to their players and which don't before you start messing with them. Don't start a new campaign and yoink daiklaves from the players' hands—play a few sessions (at least) to see which players (characters also, but players especially) feel strongly about their artifacts. All you *really* need to do is make sure that anything you do with an artifact is reversible. Create a story: hunt down the thief, or find a First Age workshop to start repairs.

This applies more to artifacts purchased at the start of game with Background points than to artifacts found during play, with exceptions. The weapons and armor the heroes lifted from the failed Wyld Hunt are easy come, easy go. (Unless someone becomes *really* attached to one as a great trophy.) After the infiltration of a Realm armory to 'liberate' an earlier incarnation's weapon (in addition to any earlier buildup to the theft), though, a player may be less willing to lose her new acquisition.

GAME IMPACT

An artifact is only as useful as you let it be. A gauntlet that drains living plants for Essence is worthless in the desolate South, on board a ship in the West or in the Underworld. A daiklave is only useful in battle, and in a few additional circumstances (like intimidation or blowing your cover). Who needs a folding boat when the entire game takes place in a landlocked kingdom?

Players and Storytellers should both be aware of the game. Players should know better than to spend all their points on armor and weapons in a series about court intrigue. Storytellers should warn players against taking useless traits. On the other hand, Storytellers should also recognize that putting points into combat means the player wants to see her character kick butt.

A player might intend to take an artifact she never uses—like being the bearer of the Tzaddik Key but sworn not to use it, which is a story hook that the Storyteller should seize like a pit bull. If there's no such intention, then something should change to bring unused artifacts into play.

Conversely, artifacts may be very, very useful. This can be a case of a man with a hammer seeing only nails, but it's also up to the Storyteller to make sure that no single artifact dominates the game's conflicts. If a single artifact solves all the characters' problems, either it is too powerful or the characters are meeting too limited a range of challenges. A daiklave can't make the maharani fall in love with you or repair the dikes before they burst.

COMMON TRAITS OF ARTIFACTS

Unless noted otherwise, all artifacts share a number of general traits.

• **Artifacts register as magical.** They may be detected by their flows of Essence. All-Encompassing Sorcerer's Sight (see **Exalted**, p. 222) and similar effects detect artifacts instantly unless concealed (by Stealth Charms or other means). A ritual using the Art of Geomancy also enables a character to identify objects as artifacts (see p. 138).

• **Artifacts are eternal.** Wonders do not wear down, wear out or break accidentally. A very few artifacts are, of necessity, fragile enough to shatter or tear if not well treated. Even these artifacts never just wear out, assuming they are not ill-used. The power of an artifact is bound into it forever and does not need maintenance, unlike the "magitech" found in **Wonders of the Lost Age**.

• **Artifacts are difficult to break.** Creation of a magical wonder solidifies Essence flows in a harmonious manner, making artifacts difficult to break. The base (Strength + Athletics) needed to break an artifact equals that of a normal object of its type *plus* its Artifact rating. First Age artifacts increase this value by another one, due to techniques now lost. Also, use the mundane equivalent's soak and health levels, adding two to each trait per dot of the artifact's rating. Artifacts that are more or less difficult to destroy say so in their descriptions.

• **Artifacts require Essence, committed or spent.** Most artifacts' Essence patterns are quiescent. Only when attuned with Essence, through a lasting commitment or an instant expenditure, can it function as designed.

• **Artifacts do not count as Charms.** Activating an artifact's powers does not interfere with the use of an Exalt's Charms, except inasmuch as the actions conflict (one cannot use a simple Charm and a miscellaneous action simultaneously). Likewise, bonus dice gained from an artifact do not count against the limit of dice gained from Charms (see **Exalted**, p. 185).

POWERS VERSUS POWERS OR CHARMS

When an artifact's definite, unrolled power contradicts another unrolled, definite power, resolve it by referencing "Unstoppable Force, Immovable Object" in **Exalted**, p. 179. If either qualifies as an attack and the other a defense, the defense wins. If neither is an attack or defense but both originate from artifacts or other, similar inanimate sources, the higher-rated artifact wins. A tie means that neither effect takes place.

When an artifact's power goes head to head with a Charm, the player whose character activated the Charm rolls whatever is appropriate at a difficulty of the artifact's rating. Success means the Charm effect overrides the artifact's effect; failure means the opposite.

DESIGNING ARTIFACTS (FOR PLAYERS)

A new artifact should begin in the mind of the player before it ever becomes dots on paper. Here are some suggestions on how to do that. Consider the following before you even go so far as to assign a dot rating to a prospective artifact.

• **Artifacts do things mundane items cannot.** The hammer that adds two dice to all Craft (Fire) rolls *could* be an artifact, but it could also be a well-crafted mundane hammer. See **Exalted**, pp. 365-366, for the limits of non-artifact equipment. If an artifact's magic can be duplicated without enchantment, reconsider its powers.

• **Artifacts should do more than add dice.** More than anything else, an artifact should be *fantastic*. Daiklaves are larger than life, befitting the heroes who wield them. Spell-capturing cords are interesting and duplicated nowhere else. But no one fits an arrow to a bow and exults that it adds two dice. Excellencies can do that, and better. Artifacts should do wondrous things that leave normal rules behind.

• **Artifacts should be more than just powers.** They should also be history, plot hook, signature equipment and a lure for trouble. If you're not interested in getting anything from your artifact but its special effect, and *especially* if you would hate it were that power suddenly stolen from your character's hands, consider making the artifact into a custom Charm (or set of them) instead.

If you still want an artifact, summarize it with a brief concept much like you might a starting character. In the same way, you should find the concept interest-ing or engaging. Why would one of the Exalted make something that was *boring*?

From the concept, you should have some idea what the artifact can do in a mechanical sense. Reference the scale below for a sense of what level the artifact should be.

THE FIVE-DOT SCALE

As a game where nearly all traits are rated on a 1-5 scale, **Exalted** cannot help being imprecise at times. The difference between a two-dot and a three-dot artifact is often little more than a gut feeling to the people involved. Of course, it often matters only at character generation, when players distribute Background dots and bonus points for their characters. Once the game starts, it only matters what an artifacts can do—not its point value to a starting character.

That said, this section makes an effort to clarify what each dot of the Artifact Background means. Each dot has a description of the power scale, including a list of the maximum benefits an artifact of that level can bestow. Just as the description is a guideline, so are the "hard caps." If it's clear to you that an artifact should be rated Artifact X, go for it. Each level of artifact also lists standard Essence costs. The number before the slash is standard commitment; the number after is the standard expenditure for instant effects.

Hard caps disappear after artifacts rated at three dots. Four- and five-dot artifacts are extremely potent, and their powers should be difficult to quantify. A five-dot artifact *could* add 10 dice to every Athletics roll, but it would be an exceptionally boring use of a five-dot artifact. Artifacts should probably not exceed the bonus limits for three-dot artifacts, displaying their power in more interesting ways instead.

Required commitments and expenditures of Essence can vary both up and down. This flexibility helps to balance artifacts; when you disagree on the relative usefulness of two artifacts of the same rating, adjusting their relative commitment or instant costs is an easy way to readjust on your own.

Hearthstone sockets are another way to fine-tune arti-facts. Having a hearthstone socket *is* a power for lower-level artifacts (see the hearthstone amulet, **Exalted**, p. 380), but after Artifact 2 or so, the sockets become secondary. Most arms and armor have at least one, and some have two or more. Adding one or taking one away is an easy way to slightly increase or decrease an artifact's power.

In the end, assigning a dot value to an artifact re-quires understanding and compromise between players and Storyteller.

• **Toys and Minor Tools:** *One-dot artifacts have minor effects with limited influence on the game.* One-dot artifacts are weak. They might amaze a mortal, but a one-dot artifact should not much impress an Exalt; they do cooler things themselves. Such artifacts are often tools of convenience: writing brushes that take dictation, or cups that create limited amounts of water or ale. The least of the artifact weapons and armors are one-dot artifacts because they improve only slightly on the mundane weapon.

Most magical toys are one-dot artifacts; some of these may have an incidental ability to aid a very limited set of tasks. Very *large* toys may have greater artifact values to represent their grand scale and that they required more effort to craft. Artifacts with minor benefits may require less committed or spent Essence. One value of toys (versus the more effective minor tools at this level) is that they are more easily sold. Rich lords may spend money for an animate soldier; fewer care to own an aid to surviving the wilderness.

Maximum benefits: Attributes +1, Abilities +2, Soak +2 and Hardness 2, Damage +2, Rate +0

Standard Essence (C/E): 2m/2m

Examples: A brush that paints as its owner mentally directs, enabling it to include details smaller than most humans can manage. This decreases the difficulty of appropriate rolls by one and works while the character performs other actions. A drum that slowly beats through the night without a player, keeping wild animals away. Toys: A toy soldier that animates and moves as directed. A Gateway board that plays out its own games. The first might aid in increasing the War skill if used in numbers, decreasing the untutored training time by one day. The second might similarly reduce training for a Gateway specialty under War or Lore.

• • **Effective Tools:** *Two-dot artifacts are quite useful in specific circumstances or moderately useful in a broader range of situations.* An artifact falls at this level if it has significant effects on the game by eliminating certain worries or strongly aiding a range of actions. These artifacts allow a character to surpass certain obstacles with relative ease. A two-dot weapon might make beating a mortal opponent easy but only provide a small advantage against other Exalted. Two-dot artifacts are common enough (especially as daiklaves) that their advantages generally balance out when they go up against each other. Two-dot artifacts may mimic the powers of Charms with Essence minimums of one or two.

Maximum benefits: Attributes +2, Abilities +4, Soak +4 and Hardness 4, Damage +4, Rate +1

Standard Essence (C/E): 5m/3m

Examples: A pair of sandals that increases the character's foot speed is somewhat useful in combat, in competition and when every second of dashing counts, making it generally useful and a two-dot artifact. A chair that makes the person seated in it aware of all who approach is a two-dot artifact, because it doesn't automatically defeat Stealth Charms and is conditional. A lantern whose glow illuminates the undead is handy only when such creatures are concealed. A whip that gives those struck by it a -1 MDV penalty toward the wielder is not tremendously potent, but useful no matter what sort of order the character wishes to give.

• • • **Wonders:** *Three-dot artifacts confer a great advantage in a single discipline or a significant advantage in a broad range of circumstances.* These powerful items give their owners significant abilities denied to people who lack such artifacts. A character with a grand daiklave, facing a character with no artifact weapon whatsoever, gets all the bets. Although truly clever or powerful characters may be able to best the effects of a three-dot artifact in its area of focus, it's rarely a sure thing.

Three-dot artifacts may change the way certain aspects of the game are played. Artifact weapons are common enough that possessing one, even a three-dot artifact weapon, only escalates combat rather than changing it. But a knot that captures sorcery and paper that becomes any contract, written and signed, provide entirely new solutions to the game's conflicts. Three-dot artifacts can be equated with Essence 3 or 4 Solar Charms, but it's a rough balance.

Maximum benefits: Attributes +3, Abilities +6, Soak +6 and Hardness 6, Damage +6, Rate +2

Standard Essence (C/E): 8m/5m

Examples: Anyone would fear, and rightly so, the warrior who wields a grand goremaul in battle. A belt of bat wings that grants the ability to walk as a shadow confers a matchless power. An enchanted mirror that allows a character to speak through other mirrors is extremely useful, especially in Exalted's world of limited travel and communication. A staff that places objects (not people) it strikes Elsewhere, and can call them back just as quickly, has a myriad uses in a clever character's hands.

• • • • **Greater Wonders:** *Four-dot artifacts provide overwhelming advantages in their spheres of influence, or great advantages in many situations.* These wonders perform feats that are flat-out impossible to most inhabitants of Creation, letting the character travel miles in the blink of an eye or shape the earth with a melody. A character equipped with a four-dot artifact has an advantage over anyone else in the artifact's realm of effect—even four-dot weapons rarely cancel

each other out, as their unique powers are not easily predicted or countered.

Four-dot artifacts almost inevitably change some aspect of the game. Characters who wield them have very attractive options open to them that are closed to nearly everyone else, which can avail them with a variety of problems. A character with a singing staff (see **Exalted**, p. 392) can use it to shape the course of a battle, provide irrigation or break into a vault just as easily. This broad usefulness suggests a diminished focused power, and it's true: the singing staff is hardly insurmountable by opponents—but it opens possibilities a character might not imagine otherwise. Four-dot artifacts are roughly on par with high-end Essence 4 and Essence 5 Charms, or Celestial-circle sorcery.

Standard Essence (C/E): 10m/6m

Examples: A clockwork bird that can lead its owner to any named person or object in Creation. A shield that protects its wielder completely from all physical harm as long as the owner harms no one. A seed that grows a forest overnight. A needle that, when used to pierce the eardrum, allows a character to eavesdrop on anything he can imagine.

●●●●● **True Marvels:** *Five-dot artifacts offer unbeatable advantages in their areas of focus, or overwhelming advantages in many situations or in a few potentially vital conflicts.* Whatever powers an artifact of this level possesses, they are usually unique and often impossible to counter. A daiklave of conquest (see **Exalted**, p. 392) makes a character a supernal general who will nearly always rout her enemies. Memories cut from victims of the Forgotten Edge can never be regained. A Dragon-Blooded warrior with the Eye of the Fire Dragon should be a true nightmare to the Solar Exalted.

It is hard to quantify a five-dot artifact's range of power more precisely than above, but they may be likened to higher-Essence Charms (6+) or Celestial or Solar Circle sorcery.

Standard Essence (C/E): 10m/8m

Examples: A key that opens any door and allows the owner to step out through any other doorway he wishes. A great orichalcum staff that can deflect any attack toward another target, including overtly magical attacks. A knife that severs committed Essence and ends lasting enchantments permanently. A prayer strip that ensures that a single object will never again be found by anyone.

N/A: World-Shaking Wonders

Some artifacts are so potent that they transcend the five-dot rating system. This *actually* means that they cannot be purchased at character generation and that only Storytellers can introduce them into a game. They have vast powers, such as granting wishes wholesale or allowing unhindered travel and spying across all Creation. They also inevitably come with associated (and grandiose) drawbacks, like granting wishes in perverse and malicious ways that loosen the bindings on the Yozis.

Example: The Eye of Autochthon is Creation's most notorious N/A artifact. In each of its three appearances since the Great Contagion, this indestructible relic of the Great Maker sparked wars that shook Creation. The sorcerer Bagrash Köl conquered an empire in the North that eclipsed the fledgling Realm, until it all vanished. The Empress' grandson Manosque Viridian used the Eye to usurp control of the Realm's war manses. He was three days from the Imperial City when his army fell into the sky. The prophetess Ikerre led her Cult of the Great Maker in a rampage across the Southern Wyld that left a thousand miles of barren crystal behind her. When the Realm's top agents caught up to Ikerre, they found her entire caravan transformed to quartz, but the Eye was gone.

Games revolve around N/A artifacts. That's not to say you can't run a game where the Eye of Autochthon is just part of the background, but it would throw some people off. N/A artifacts have no standard Essence commitment or expenditures.

Drawbacks

Drawbacks are restrictions to a wonder's use or penalties commensurate with its power. They scale from one to five dots as a measure of how much they hinder a character who owns or wields the artifact. Drawbacks can justify decreased commitment or Essence cost for an otherwise expensive-to-use artifact. A drawback of an equal or greater level than the artifact that possesses it reduces the artifact's rating by one.

Examples: The four-dot clockwork bird above can lead its owner to any person, place or thing the owner names, regardless of sorceries used to conceal it. This might be an overwhelming power… except that anyone who seeks the character attuned to the artifact immediately knows exactly how to find him. The two-dot sandals that increase speed may only function if the owner has slain a woman and trodden in the blood in the past day. This drawback far outstrips the

artifact's two-dot rating, reducing the sandals to Artifact 1 and perhaps reducing commitment.

Drawbacks come in many forms. They may limit the artifact's power so it only functions in certain situations, on certain targets or once certain conditions are met in advance. The artifact may malfunction in predetermined *or* essentially random ways. It may also have unwanted side effects that occur with regular activation of the artifact, causing trouble after the fact.

In a player's design process, drawbacks are generally optional. Players should choose drawbacks that they think are exciting or will be fun to play out. In these cases, applying drawbacks may reduce the artifact's rating or somewhat improve its powers. The player and Storyteller should both be satisfied with the balance of an artifact's powers and drawbacks.

After a drawback is decided, that's just the way the artifact is (or will be). The drawback is not a flaw in the design; it's a natural part of this artifact. Such drawbacks cannot be corrected later. If it *is* a flaw, it may be a flaw the artifact had since the First Age or a flaw the player *wants* the character to let slip into the design. Either one is a story hook eager to land a story fish.

The *character's* design process (see p. 18) is an attempt to realize the player's ideas in-game. Drawbacks arise from this process when a research roll botches. These drawbacks are flaws in the design that manifest in the final product. Unlike intentional flaws, they can be corrected, though the process is equivalent to creating an artifact equal in rating to the drawback being fixed. Drawbacks that can be repaired, whether caused by the dice or the player's design, do *not* affect the rating or power of the artifact.

- **Minor:** The artifact has a restriction that rarely comes up or isn't difficult to meet, an annoying quirk or a side effect that causes little trouble.

Examples: The artifact is unusable if the character hasn't prayed to the Unconquered Sun within a day. The artifact doesn't function without enough light to read. The artifact targets the wrong individual when there are at least four redheads in the wielder's vision. The artifact makes the wielder dizzy (-1 internal penalty for two actions).

- •• **Moderate:** The artifact has a restriction that comes up regularly or isn't easy to meet, a moderate glitch in the way it functions or a side effect that causes problems.

Examples: The artifact only works if the character utters an audible prayer (miscellaneous action) to the Unconquered Sun before activating it. The artifact requires a dedicated hearthstone to function. The artifact only func-

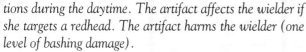

tions during the daytime. The artifact affects the wielder if she targets a redhead. The artifact harms the wielder (one level of bashing damage).

• • • Significant: The artifact has conditions that require significant effort to meet before it can be used, a very troublesome malfunction or a consternating side effect.

Examples: The artifact does not function unless the character has converted someone to the worship of the Unconquered Sun within the past week. The artifact only functions if the character has sacrificed a living creature to it within the last month. The artifact requires three dedicated hearthstones. The artifact only functions at the sun's zenith. The color red defends against or can banish the artifact's effects. The artifact drains the wielder's life (one level of aggravated damage).

• • • • Massive: The artifact's conditions may present great obstacles to its use, and its side effects can be devastating.

Examples: The artifact does not work unless the character has sacrificed a human to it within the last week. Only by sacrificing a family in the Unconquered Sun's name can a character activate the artifact. One mote attuned to the artifact must instead be attuned to a simple, fragile object, like an egg; destroying this object deactivates the artifact until it can be replaced. The artifact drains Essence of those around it for several hours after activation. The artifact causes widespread floods or droughts nearby.

• • • • • Overwhelming: The artifact cannot be used unless severely onerous conditions are met, and the side effects it causes can trigger entire adventures.

Examples: The artifact must bathe in fresh human blood before each use. The artifact must consume an orichalcum prayer strip to the Unconquered Sun (essentially Artifact 1) to be used. Activating the artifact opens a door elsewhere in Creation for a Second Circle demon. The artifact invents archrivals for the wielder out of whole cloth when used. The artifact rips Essence from its surroundings, draining demesnes for months or leaving plant and animal life for miles around to slowly die.

DESIGN NOTE: DRAWBACKS AS FLAWS

Drawbacks that are reparable flaws do not help balance an artifact's power because, somewhere, someone would use drawbacks to lower the artifact rating and then quickly eliminate the flaw. Yes, he ruined it for all of us.

OTHER SIDE EFFECTS

Nothing exists in a vacuum, especially in the very full world of **Exalted**. Every character worth playing has an enemy or six; likewise, any artifact worth having is coveted and makes people think that you, because you have it, are one bad mother.

Enemies: Two- and three-dot artifacts may have people following them. Some come without strings, especially forgotten ones, but many of them have people coming to steal them… or steal them back. It's just more interesting that way, and Exalted lead interesting lives. It might be an heirloom daiklave, or maybe your hero snatched it from the wrong tomb.

Four- and five-dot artifacts have reputations all their own, and there's nothing an owner can do about it. Unless these mighty wonders are kept secret (and that's hard to do), even the *suggestion* that they're out there will bring out the treasure-hunters, hopeful merchants and thieves.

Reputation: Having and using artifacts marks your character as one of the Exalted. Even the most average daiklave is a condemnation, proving a character more than mortal. There's no certainty that your character is Anathema (though orichalcum does tend to make the educated suspect), but there's no guarantee she's not, either. And that's just for the small fries.

Four- and five-dot artifacts give their owners reputations, just like they provide ready-made enemies. Even if the character wielding Soul Mirror (see p. 14) *means* well, people will fear him and his blade that consumes souls. Some artifacts are just that scary. As the character becomes associated with the artifact, he may experience bonuses or penalties on certain social rolls (for Soul Mirror, bonuses on intimidation and with a foul sort of people, penalties with goodly folk) and people simply treat him differently. By this point, even getting rid of the artifact may not be enough to shake the stigma without real effort.

Not everything incidental to owning an artifact is terrible.

Allies: There are people who aren't thieves in Creation, believe it or not. Some of them may respect a character who can wield such-and-such artifact, while others will want to manipulate that character. Either one manifests in the form of temporary allies, connected to the artifact rather than the character. Four-dot artifacts usually produce no more than two-dot allies, while five-dot artifacts can go as high as four dots. Whether or not the character can leverage them into true allies is up to her.

Followers: This is the watered-down version of allies and usually only kicks in for four- and five-dot artifacts. When the artifact has an expansive reputation, it can attract people who'd rather *follow* it than steal it. They may be cultists, worshiping the soul-drinking power of the blade, or musicians who wish to study the singing staff. Sure, they're following the artifact, but the wielder gets to use them. Four-dot artifacts may produce as much as two dots of Followers, and five-dot artifacts can go as high as three.

Influence: This goes hand-in-hand with reputation. The more people have heard of a given wonder, the more they expect the person carrying it to act this way and deserve yea-much respect. And so they give it: A character with a four- or five-dot artifact gains the equivalent of one or two dots in Influence, anywhere the artifact is recognized. In areas where the character already has Influence, this Influence increases by a dot. People listen to someone with the fabled veil that holds back time (for example).

All these qualities are at the Storyteller's discretion. An artifact lost before the First Age won't have much reputation and won't attract enmity or hangers-on, at least until word spreads. The nature of some artifacts (such as the Forgotten Blade) prevents them from becoming well-known.

DEDICATED HEARTHSTONES AND ESSENCE

This text assumes a dedicated hearthstone is one set in the artifact, which then draws in all the gem's Essence. The same Exalt must be attuned to both the artifact and the manse, and she gains no benefit from the hearthstone.

There are other sources of Essence for artifacts. Most don't need it, being completely self-contained, or they take it from the Exalt when necessary. Greater wonders of the First Age had Essence accumulators, which drew in ambient Essence so the attuned Exalt never had to spend her own. One First Age artifact drew its power from a cult specifically devoted to the artifact.

DESIGNING ARTIFACTS (FOR CHARACTERS)

Forging a work of wonder is not a simple task. It requires a great deal of effort, time and resources. The information from the **Exalted** book is summed up here. Before a character can begin creating an artifact, he must meet the required minimum Ability scores in Lore, Occult and the appropriate Craft (often Fire or Air, but any of the five is possible). See the table on this page. If the character meets that requirement, he may begin designing the artifact.

DESIGN

Before crafting an artifact, a character must first design it—deduce the materials and procedures needed to create patterns of Essence that achieve the desired effect.

The most difficult way to design an artifact is to *work from first principles*. The character has nothing from which to work and makes all decisions regarding the artifact's construction as part of the extended creation roll. About half the crafting time actually consists of research and experimentation, just as sorcerers must (often disastrously) cast their half-formed spells. Up to half the research (a quarter of the total necessary successes) can be done theoretically. A character doesn't need a workshop or tools while working theoretically, and he can retain all accumulated successes as long as he carefully records all his work (and doesn't lose these records). Discovering necessary exotic materials is a natural part of this process; seeking them out delays the extended roll without endangering the final project. Every five successes reveal one necessary exotic ingredient in addition to accomplishing preliminary crafting.

On the other hand, a character can *use existing plans*. First Age artisans could access complete design notes, including step-by-step instructions and comments on the process from millennia-old masters. Second Age artisans are rarely so lucky. Possessing complete plans for crafting an artifact reduces the cumulative crafting difficulty by *half*. It also saves time, because the character knows what exotic materials he needs before he starts. By definition, original artifacts can never benefit from this bonus.

Characters can seek out complete artifact designs in a number of places. Creation's most complete arcane libraries (in the Imperial Manse, Lookshy, Mahalanka and one or two other locations) hold hundreds of designs but are jealously guarded. Other artifact designs are recorded in ciphers now nearly impossible to crack. Still more reside only within the minds of surviving First Age Lunars and Sidereals, though persuading them to share such secrets would be a pretty trick indeed.

The disadvantage of using someone else's finished design is that you must also use exactly the same magical ingredients. If an artifact's design calls for nothing more exotic than jade or orichalcum, this is not much of a problem. If a recipe means you have to bargain with the Fair Folk for the love of a mountain for the sky, you may face greater difficulties. But such difficulties

ARTIFACT REQUIREMENTS BY RATING						
Rating	Difficulty	Required Successes	Ability Minimums*	Resources	Exotic Materials	Repair Difficulty
1	3	10	3	2	1	2
2	4	30	3	3	2	3
3	5	60	3	4	3	4
4	6	100	6	5	4	5
5	7	250	7	5	5	6

Rating: Artifact's rating.
Difficulty: Crafting difficulty.
Required Successes: Cumulative difficulty of the extended crafting roll.
Ability Minimums: Rating in the relevant Craft, Lore and Occult necessary to attempt creating the item.
Resources: Expenditure necessary for raw materials.
Exotic Materials: Number of exotic materials required for creation.
Repair Difficulty: Difficulty to repair damaged artifact.

make *stories*, so a pre-existing artifact design can be an advantage for the player and the Storyteller, too.

Partial information can reduce the cumulative difficulty for creating artifacts. Characters can find partial information in many sources. All the sources that can provide complete artifact designs can include incomplete designs or references to different methods. Libraries have torn-up books or fragmentary journals, and elder Exalted are "forgetful" (usually doling the information out or bargaining for a better trade). Tombs and lost archives may hold reference materials of use to artifact designers.

Relevant material adds to the accumulated successes of the crafting rolls by a constant number. The smallest dribbles of information add one success, and the standard range is 2-6 successes for a section of a sorcerer's workbook or diagrams carved on a lost temple wall. Despite the "standard range," information can add any number of successes. Finding a complete design is the equivalent of finding partial information that provides half the necessary successes to create the artifact. No amount of partial information, however, can ever provide more than this many successes.

If the character has access to a functioning artifact, he can attempt *reverse engineering*. By examining its Essence patterns and its physical form in minute detail, the character can puzzle out how it functions and backtrack through its creative process. The player makes an (Intelligence + Occult) roll at a difficulty of the artifact's rating. Add the roll's threshold to the Artifact rating; the character adds two dice to his crafting rolls for a number of rolls equal to this number. This only serves as a limit; the actual reverse engineering takes place during the time represented by the extended crafting roll.

Risk-takers may prefer to cut their time shorter. Dissecting the artifact allows a character to more intimately see how it works. If the (Intelligence + Occult) roll is successful, double the number of crafting rolls to which the dice bonus applies. This destroys the subject artifact. Botching a crafting roll using this method destroys the artifact prematurely and dangerously in addition to any other effects. The character (and anyone working with him) suffers a number of lethal levels of damage equal to the artifact's rating squared as its Essence explosively flows back into Creation.

Botching on a design roll introduces unnoticed flaws in the design, which negatively impact the final product. This could represent an oversight (not realizing the process must begin under a full moon) or sabotage from a rival. It may manifest by adding a drawback to the artifact (see p. 16) or increasing the severity of an existing drawback. Multiple botches may do both, or stack to create truly legendary drawbacks.

COLLECTING THE INGREDIENTS

Before the character can turn her complete design into a fully functioning wonder, she must obtain the proper materials. This usually includes one of the magical materials. These substances channel and store Essence much better than anything else in Creation, so they tend to appear even in artifacts principally made of other things. For instance, a wooden artifact might hold a sliver of moonsilver or jade in its core. Still, some designs call for very specific constructions and *cannot* incorporate one of the magical materials. In other cases, artisans simply cannot obtain the magical materials and must make do with substances of lesser potency.

DESIGN NOTE: ARTIFACT DESIGN

Roll intervals for artifact design are set to make choosing high adventure over research and dice rolls reasonable. If they were too short, even the travel time to distant locations would be prohibitive, let alone the exploration and research. Creation is huge, and many places to visit may not be right next door.

Finding or possessing a complete artifact design is a *huge* benefit, especially for greater wonders. Storytellers should make them commensurately difficult to acquire—but highly rewarding. If finding partial information for a handful of successes is a month's work, cutting the crafting time by half should definitely take longer.

The sheer power of the magical materials can make them difficult to craft, though. If a character works with magical materials not natural to him (a Solar working jade, or a mortal working any material), his player suffer a -2 internal penalty on each roll. First Age artisans circumvented this limitation by working together, a practice that would work just as well today. Having a single qualified Exalted assistant of the ideal type eliminates the penalty.

JADE

The most common magical material is jade. Each of its five varieties forms in a place most suited to its elemental association and works especially well for certain kinds of artifacts, though they see use in all manner of wonders. An artifact whose power can be associated with a particular Ability requires jade of the element associated with the Dragon-Blooded caste that favors that Ability. Stealth artifacts demand blue jade, for example, and Survival artifacts need green jade.

White jade occurs beneath mountains and near large deposits of dense stone. It is incredibly plentiful beneath the Imperial Mountain, directly over the Elemental Pole of Earth. The Realm uses white jade for its official currency because it resists wear and is so readily available. White jade is ideal for artifacts that manipulate earth and stone or restrain another being's mind.

Green jade looks as if it grew like a plant. It develops in regions of plentiful vegetation, such as thick forests or jungles, often entangled among the roots of the greatest trees. Wood elementals and forest gods often become protective of the jade that forms naturally in their domains. Green jade is best for controlling plants,

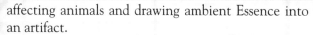

affecting animals and drawing ambient Essence into an artifact.

Red jade deposits appear in the hottest regions of the world—beneath active volcanoes and in the center of scorching deserts. Its location makes it difficult to harvest, sometimes requiring Fire Aspects, artifact-equipped mortals or summoned elementals to retrieve it. Red jade is warm to the touch and often flickers in the light. It is perfect for controlling fire or making people immune to it, as well as causing harm or heightening reflexes.

Black jade forms in deep lakes where water pools for a long time and in large seas. The floor of the Western Ocean holds astoundingly quantities, but most of it is so many miles beneath the surface that even Water Aspects cannot easily obtain it. Even a thin shaving of black jade seems to hold infinite depth, making it highly prized as a meditation aid. Apart from controlling water, this variety of jade works well for affecting or communicating with gods, elementals and demons.

Blue jade looks almost translucent with misty shapes that appear and vanish. Occultists and soothsayers sometimes use these shapes as an alternative to reading entrails or the constellations. This jade appears in areas of rarified air or great cold, such as the heights of the Imperial Mountain or the glacial wastes of the North. Artifacts that control the weather or sense or affect thought are usually best made with blue jade.

Acquiring jade is sometimes very, very difficult and sometimes surprisingly easy. Most significant jade deposits are under the direct control of Realm troops

led by a good number of competent Dragon-Blooded. For an outcaste or Anathema to access these sources of jade would require significant skill, luck and daring.

On the other hand, the Realm uses jade for money. Someone with enough financial backing could visit a few banks and come away with a good deal of white jade. Removing currency from circulation is an offense punishable by heavy fines that the Imperial Treasury treats quite seriously, especially in this time of dwindling taxes.

One pound of jade is a Resources 3 expense, up to nine pounds is Resources 4, and a Resources 5 expenditure can procure up to 25 pounds at a go. Even if the final artifact does not require 25 pounds of jade, the creation process often requires more than one would expect—jade can be ground, melted, distilled and alchemically treated in a dozen ways that reduces the quantity while refining the quality.

There are also many tons of jade extant in Creation, already part of artifacts. Although few mortals

YELLOW JADE

Yellow jade is a mistake. It doesn't appear naturally, and no one knows how to create it. Dragon-Blooded alchemists *try* to create it with different mixtures of regular jade, but none of their experiments ever succeed more than once. Yellow jade only appears when a thaumaturge makes an unrepeatable error when following an intended formula, such as spilling in unknown exotic ingredients or leaving a mixture to simmer a day too long. If any intelligent force decides when and where yellow jade appears, it certainly isn't the Dragon-Blooded.

This is a shame, because yellow jade has a wide variety of uses. Artifacts made with this rare material often require less committed Essence or none at all. It is a primary component of many artifacts that mortals can use.

JADE MATERIAL BONUSES

The standard bonuses for a Dragon-Blooded hero who attunes a jade artifact reflect the Terrestrial qualities of preparedness and strength. Jade is a superior magical material for reducing the Speed of a character's attacks. However, some Dragon-Blooded artificers treat jade to bring out other latent aspects of its elemental nature. Each color of jade offers its own suite of advantages to artifact weapons.

White jade adds +2 to damage and +1 to the difficulty of rolls to resist knockdown and stunning caused by the weapon.

Green jade adds +1 to damage and steals one mote of Essence from living creatures that take damage from the attack, transferring it to the wielder.

Red jade adds +3 to damage due to intense heat.

Black jade adds +1 to damage and adds +2 to defense.

Blue jade adds +1 to damage and +2 to Rate.

Each bonus is available to any Terrestrial Exalt who attunes the artifact (or other Exalted who make the effort), not just Dragon-Bloods of the appropriate element. Only one bonus applies, even when a weapon incorporates multiple types of jade. Bonuses apply equally to hand-to-hand and ranged artifact weapons.

would conceive of assaulting a Dragon-Blood for her panoply, other folk are less scrupulous (or scared). Jade in weapons and armor has been alloyed with steel, but that just means a would-be artificer must acquire more of it—after the reduction and extraction process, a character has about one-tenth the weight of jade as the alloy she had to start.

A workshop capable of working jade is a Resources 3 expense.

MOONSILVER

This magical material forms only in the Wyld. Beams of moonlight unpredictably illuminate a region of the Bordermarches or Middlemarches, boiling off the Wyld and distilling its Essence into the fluid, watery-looking moonsilver. Most Lunar Exalted believe this is a conscious gift to them from their patron.

Deposits of moonsilver look like normal silver, but they run through exposed surfaces in smooth, flowing patterns that veins of silver could never match unless melted and sculpted. They also move slowly, and twitch if you touch them. Under the moonlight, moonsilver reflects things that aren't there, like the images of dreams and memories sublimating from the observers' minds. Moonsilver is ideal for artifacts that emphasize fluidity, transience, chaotic change, sleep and dreams, among other things.

Raw moonsilver is unstable. An artisan needs special techniques to work it. Silver Pact elders pass down the necessary ritual by word of mouth. The Lunar Exalted also developed special Charms to help them work moonsilver. Any Lunar character with an interest in arcane artifice can learn them through that organization. Other folk might have more difficulty. Nevertheless, a few exceptionally learned artisans and savants know the procedure.

A few records from the First Age suggest that Exalted smiths then could create their own moonsilver using the Essence tokens from powerful demesnes (see Chapter Two) and moonlight concentrated by occult mirrors, rather like the ones used to create orichalcum (see below). The complete procedure, however, has been lost to all save perhaps a few elder Lunars and Sidereals, who either have no ability or no need for it.

ORICHALCUM

The golden magical material of the Solar Exalted is the strongest of all the magical materials. Its sheen bears the warmth and light of the Unconquered Sun, even when lit only by a candle or a caste mark. People mistake it for gold only when the light is dim or they cannot touch it to feel its inner fire. It is hard to mine and harder still to forge, almost as if it resists being worked by anyone but the Sun's Chosen. Once incorporated into an artifact, orichalcum represents strength, superiority, order, glory and (to a degree) perfection or striving for the absolute.

Artisans can find orichalcum where it forms naturally, or they can distill their own from molten gold. Natural deposits appear in areas where sunlight streams down upon an area heated by the blood of the earth—magma. Left there for centuries, gold deposits melt and distill naturally into orichalcum, which earthquakes and shifting earth eventually moves deeper or darker underground where it remains until mined. Alternatively, an artisan could distill his own orichalcum from gold, using a smelter heated by molten lava and sunlight concentrated using mirrors.

Orichalcum is in scarce supply in the Second Age of Man. The Terrestrial Exalted have guarded the natural deposits of orichalcum since the Usurpation. They fear the Unconquered Sun's wrath too much to destroy them, and fear the Solar Anathema too much just to bury them. And besides, a few Dragon-Blooded smiths *do* use orichalcum in their artifacts. In this Time of Tumult, the Great Houses have doubled the postings on the deposits that they guard, hoping to catch the demons there. It's cheaper than fielding a Wyld Hunt, and the Dynasts need all the legions they can muster back home on the Blessed Isle. As for making one's own orichalcum, gold is easy to obtain, but the occult mirrors are not. Both Guild factors and Realm agents might notice buyers of large, custom-made mirrors.

STARMETAL

Starmetal resembles mundane iron. Refined, it looks like clean steel that—in oblique light—reflects a faint rainbow of the Five Maidens' colors. In most other respects, starmetal can be worked like steel, though the result (once bound with the proper Essence patterns) becomes much harder than the mundane metal. Starmetal is the preferred magical material for artifacts dealing with choices, predictions, time, avoidance, mysteries and knowledge.

Erudite folk may know that when a star falls from the sky, it crashes into the earth and leaves a deposit of starmetal ore. These deposits are very rare, to the point where the sight of a brilliant falling star can set off a treasure hunt over hundreds of miles. Seekers are usually disappointed: The Sidereal Exalted, however, use their superior astrological methods to predict falling stars and collect the ore as quickly as possible.

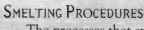

SMELTING PROCEDURES

The processes that smelt moonsilver, orichalcum, starmetal and soulsteel from their source materials are all Adept-level thaumaturgical rituals in the Art of Alchemy. In each case, the necessary foundry is a Resources 4 purchase (the reusable components for the ritual), while operating it long enough to produce a pound of the desired metal is a Resources 3 expense (the consumed material for the ritual)—not including the raw materials themselves. Characters may learn these rituals as Procedures. In each case, the Willpower expenditure represents the intense concentration needed to see the procedure through to a successful conclusion. To use these rituals, a character needs Craft (Fire) at 4.

Stabilize Moonsilver (2, Perception, 3, one hour): Raw moonsilver must be collected at night under the light of the moon. The raw moonsilver is still unstable with residual Wyld-energy. Through coaxing songs and careful taps and strokes with crystal hammers and probes, the artisan quiets the Wyldness remaining in the raw moonsilver so it becomes a stable metal. Pacify it too much and it freezes into silver; hit it too hard, and it shatters into drops of quicksilver.

Distill Orichalcum (2, Stamina, 3, one week): Purifying gold into orichalcum can only be done at a source of molten lava. It also requires large, high-precision mirrors to concentrate sunlight on the molten gold. Boiling the gold continuously for a week, using magma and sunfire, to drive out impurities, is not intellectually challenging... but the prolonged, constant attention to direct the mirrors and keep the lava from contaminating the gold is remarkably fatiguing.

Smelt Starmetal (2, Wits, 3, one day): Pulling starmetal from its ore should be easy. It uses the same smelter and tools used to extract mundane iron—but everything must be consecrated and purified: the clay and charcoal of the furnace, the tree from which the charcoal was made, the spade that was used to dig the clay... The small gods of the forge know the smith works on the remains of their kin, and will spoil the process if not suitably appeased. And then, the smelter engages in a frantic battle of wits to keep the furnace going and the forge uncontaminated as everything that could go wrong, does, driving the smith to his limits through sheer frazzlement.

Alloy Soulsteel (2, Manipulation, 3, one day): Hammering souls into the sooty ore from the Labyrinth involves more than strength. It is an exercise in cruelty and domination, breaking the will of the captive ghosts so they would rather accept an eternity trapped in black metal than the continued blows of the hammer, the scorching of bonefire and the bitter quenching in bile.

There's more to the story, though few humans know it. When a given god's existence is completely extinguished, that god's remains fall from the heavens as a shooting star and becomes a small nugget of starmetal. Gods' Essences may also be turned directly into starmetal, though doing so counts as murder and is severely punished by the Celestial Hierarchy. Instead, Sidereal Exalted who require starmetal arrange for an appropriate heavenly tribunal to audit, convict and execute a minor god. This creates a deposit of starmetal, at the light expense of morality.

Because of its rarity and great value to the leading conspiracy in Creation, starmetal is very difficult to obtain. The raw ore cannot be bought for any price in Creation or Yu-Shan, because the Chosen of the Maidens have usually requisitioned it for their own uses (and acquired legal ownership of it through the Celestial Bureaucracy). Starmetal artifacts are almost as rare and jealously guarded as unworked ore; almost

all of them are strongly claimed by a person or cause (though the ownership of many are subjects of ongoing disputes that will likely never see resolution). Dismantling a starmetal artifact for reconstruction into another artifact is sure to offend *somebody*.

SOULSTEEL

Once forged, soulsteel artifacts are a dull, matte black, much like dark iron. Only when in use, or when one looks too closely, do the faces and hands of those souls used in the artifact's construction become visible, screaming and pushing against the border of their dark prison. Soulsteel has no peer for artifacts dealing with all forms of death, although artisans sometimes employ bone or obsidian if soulsteel is unavailable.

Soulsteel has two primary ingredients: a black ore found only in the Labyrinth, and souls. Of the two, the first is more dangerous to acquire. The Labyrinth, that endless series of twisting tunnels and hideous chambers

that squirms between the Underworld and the Void, acts like putty for the undying nightmares of the Neverborn. Even ghosts fear entering the death-maze and often suffer something more terrible than death if they do, so even the Deathlords find mining soulsteel ore an expensive prospect.

Souls are easier to procure and far less dangerous. The skills and Arcanoi of ghosts rarely help them much against a driven Exalted opponent or the Deathlords' "press gangs." An artifact requires one soul in its construction for every 10 successes the artificer's player must accumulate when crafting it (one for Artifact 1 up to 25 for Artifact 5).

The Labyrinthine ore is brittle unless properly treated, and the smith must carefully fold the souls into the alloy many times to ensure that they cannot escape. The entire process requires a complex necromantic workshop. Ghostly sages know that, occasionally, passages in the Labyrinth open to reveal complete workshops perfect for smelting and forging soulsteel. None know whether these are remnants of dark enchantments worked by the Deathlords or somehow natural.

EXOTIC MATERIALS

Artificers use magical materials because they are usually ideal to contain the desired Essence pattern the artifact requires. But magical materials are fairly blank slates, and a craftsman must seek out other occult elements to complete the artifact. The natural Essence patterns of these exotic ingredients reinforce those desired in the wonder or serve as a mold to shape the artifact's Essence flow.

Artificers use exotic materials in various ways. These ingredients may be alloyed into the magical metal, woven into cloth (often through magic), used to fuel mystic fires for glassblowing or forging, sublimated into the material or anything else appropriate to the task. An ingredient might also find use in a tool used in creating the artifact, such as brewing other ingredients in the skull of a sage who confounded 10 gods, or wielding chisels made from a Second Circle demon's teeth.

In nearly every case, acquiring such materials requires an arduous search of some kind. The more powerful the desired artifact, the more rarified the necessary components. Ingredients may be conceptual, such as "the last dream of a fetus before it is born," but this requires dealing with Fair Folk nobles, demon princes or other powerful, dangerous entities that can blur the categories of reality and turn concepts into tangible entities.

Crafting powerful artifacts was once much easier. The preponderance of Exalted artisans and high

OTHER SOURCES OF MAGICAL MATERIALS

Each magical material's description suggests where to obtain or how to make that material. Other sources exist. For example, when a human prays to a specific god, those prayers materialize in Yu-Shan in the form of ambrosia, which the gods value highly. Ambrosia may be made into nearly anything (and is *always* of finer quality than the most expensive such goods in Creation proper), including jade. There is, therefore, a great deal of jade in Yu-Shan. However, only ambrosia created by prayer to the Unconquered Sun, Luna or the Five Maidens can become that particular Incarna's associated magical material. Acquiring ambrosia is a neat trick, but so is mining the Labyrinth, dodging Realm garrisons at orichalcum mines, or beating the Sidereals to a fallen star.

Another source, which the gods do not discuss for obvious reasons, is the gods themselves. Through special Charms, a god may be forged into artifacts of jade. They may also be forged into artifacts of orichalcum, moonsilver or starmetal, but they provide very small quantities of each unless they are direct servants of the relevant gods—in which case using their Essence for trinkets may not be a good idea.

Neither of the above methods creates soulsteel. In the First Age, soulsteel was a recognized and oft-abused magical material. It has many uses, and using it treads on no gods' toes. Only the walking dead objected then, and few in the First Age gave their opinions much weight. Execution in a manner to create a ghost, followed by permanent imprisonment in soulsteel, became a First Age punishment for criminals of the worst sort, such as serial murderers and traitors against the Deliberative. Lost workshops may still hold caches of soulsteel.

enlightenment in the First Age allowed the premier artificers to delegate some of their work. Creating an exotic component (an ingredient or tool) for an artifact is equivalent to creating an artifact one dot lower than the artifact for which it is intended. This includes the need for natural exotic materials… or reagents equivalent to still weaker artifacts.

A Twilight artisan, therefore, could have her apprentices working on Artifact 1 ingredients and tools for her advanced apprentices' Artifact 2 components. These would in turn fuel her journeymen's Artifact 3 handiwork, which might even be refined into Artifact 4 ingredients by the masters she trained in the past. The Twilight herself would then turn them into the final item, no doubt saving herself years of research, travel and exploration.

In time, even this delegation became considered inefficient. In the Old Realm's height, an Exalted master artificer could request time at an appropriate factory-cathedral outfitted to produce artifact components of the proper sort. Then, such wonders (Artifact 5 all by themselves, and bound to manses) could produce Artifact 3 ingredients for use in greater wonders.

The Usurpation reduced this industry of artifacts, and the Contagion almost completed its ruin. The sorcerer-engineers of Lookshy struggle merely to sustain the city-state's magitech arsenal. The Realm has built a few Shogunate-level workshops inferior to actual factory-cathedrals, which produce jade-steel weapons and armor for the legions. Reconstructing a true factory-cathedral would be a legendary feat worthy of the returning Lawgivers.

Selecting Exotic Ingredients

A Storyteller or player devising a list for artifact creation should ask, "What sort of objects does one associate with the artifact's purpose? What elements remind one of its focus? What might carry similar power or wonder?" More importantly, "What inspires a fun adventure to retrieve?" Ideally, someone reading the list of exotic items can make a reasonable guess at the artifact's intended abilities. The goal is to increase the adventure of creating an artifact—just having a well-equipped workshop and a pile of jade out back isn't enough.

Sample First Age Exotic Materials

The First Age of Man reached greater heights than most in the Age of Sorrows can dream, even the Dragon-Blooded. Its mastery of science and the occult enabled First Age savants to create fantastic components for their world-shaking wonders. Four- or five-dot artifacts require at least one ingredient comparable to these.

• **Essence of Pearl:** Exalted bred a species of giant oyster that could survive only in the farthest West, floating forever on the currents because there is no ocean floor. The oysters' tenders, often enlightened mortals, committed all their Essence to the air before them, creating a physical grain that they would place inside the oysters' shells. Over many years, an oyster so irritated would grow a pearl composed of the purest water Essence around the

irritation. The juxtaposition of such impossible purity being expressible only through the creation of impurity, given immense strength by the commitment of a being's entire Essence (which the enlightened mortal could not recover) made this exotic component perfect for eliminating flaws from artifacts during creation.

• **Heaven Leaf Fallen:** In the densest jungles of the East, Wood-aspected arborists grew massive, broad-leafed trees with canopies large enough to support palaces. Instead, the master gardeners planted over them, growing more than a dozen layers of trees on top of each other. When the topmost tree brushed the firmament with a single leaf, the god responsible for keeping the sky clear smote the entire series from the very top to the bottommost root. Only the highest leaf survives, charged with the pure quality of towering height and fecundity with a flavor of hubris.

• **Infinite Seeds:** Through miraculous alterations of vegetable life, Exalted gardeners designed a low but sturdy bush that grew a hard-shelled nut. Earth Essence made the hut's husk as strong as steel while Wood Essence ensured that the plant-to-be inside that nut continued to grow. The strength of the shell forced the plant grow to maturity confined within that small space. It would grow and die, leaving behind a nut of the same nature just small enough to fit inside. Another plant would grow inside that, and so on. Even the plant's designers were unsure when, if ever, the cycle ended. Artificers incorporated these seeds into their artifacts in order to lengthen its nature or incorporate infinity.

• **Neverdreamt:** Using captive or willing hekatonkhire and powerful sorcery, Exalted would merge the creatures into aspects of the Underworld's dead gods that even the Neverborn had not conceived in their worst or most joyous nightmares. Using multiple source entities, the resultant amalgams would be separated along different lines than they were first joined, creating altogether new hekatonkhire, which would be combined with the products of other such experiments. After repeatedly distilling more and more rarified qualities from the source hekatonkhire, a final process instilled this Essence into a crystal for use with an artifact. This component was much desired for creating wonders that would manipulate or change the Underworld and Labyrinth on broad scales, or one that might harm the Neverborn themselves.

• **Children of Breeding:** The Old Realm founded long-running eugenics programs in far-flung regions of Creation. Some administrators bred for selected qualities, others bred selected qualities out of the population. After several centuries, the Celestial Bureaucracy assigned a god to each program. With a small number of appropriate

bribes and blackmails, the Exalted behind the programs convinced these gods to procreate with some participants of the programs they oversaw, creating new populations inside the original programs—eugenics sub-programs, administered by members of the original and still ongoing programs. After another period, new gods were named for these internal programs. The process was repeated, and repeated, creating recursive breeding programs that bred selected traits into both the humans and the eugenics gods. Eventually, the humans in the programs and gods of the programs became indistinguishable—and useful components in artifice, though they were fairly useless as either humans or gods.

SAMPLE SECOND AGE EXOTIC MATERIALS

Without the sophisticated First Age methods and infrastructure, exotic objects take decades to build up the necessary Essence patterns required for greater wonders. Instead, arcane artisans look for ingredients that already possess occult power. See Chapter Four of this book or **The Compass of Celestial Directions, Vol. II—The Wyld** for potential ingredients suitable for lesser wonders. Artifacts rated three dots or higher require components that are correspondingly more rare and more difficult to obtain.

• **Frozen Lightning:** In the far, far Northwest, sea storms blow heavy and cold along westerlies into the North proper. There, a wind from the Pole of Air might instantly freeze the storm. The thick clouds sometimes become one with the frozen fog so rightly feared in the North, sometimes add a layer to the massive Northern glaciers, and sometimes fall on and kill unwary travelers. When a stroke of lightning leaps in the very moment that the cold front hits, the lightning freezes solid and falls to shatter on the ground. Artificers who recover a shard and keep it from thawing have very strong bottled energy on their hands.

• **Mournful Eyes:** Two eyes, which need not come from the same person, that have both *personally* seen all their owners' descendants die. This can be simple enough for a father of one, but the eyes from the patriarch or matriarch of sprawling clans acquire greater potency. The eyes of gods that have seen their purview completely and permanently eliminated are even better.

• **Spiritual Benefaction:** The approval of a god is no trivial thing. Should a god with the appropriate nature bless the manufacture of an artifact, the construction proceeds well. Craftsman gods are always appropriate, but they have grown jaded and rarely give their boons. The benefaction costs the god a permanent Willpower, which it recovers very slowly (over the course of years,

sometimes decades). For a benefaction to be effective, it must come from a spirit with a permanent Essence at least two dots higher than the artifact's intended rating. Demons can bless the process too, when it suits their own malevolent ends.

• **The Eternal Lord:** One to whom a people swear fealty gains a measure of power; one who has many subjects and keeps them (or their bloodlines) sworn for centuries has a great deal of power. The remains of a God-Blooded monarch or Exalted satrap who has ruled a province's people since before their grandfathers' grandfathers were born might possess enough power for a minor wonder. Sacrificing a monarch who ruled for at least a millennium could enable the creation of a greater artifact. A few savants whisper that the Perfect of Paragon was set up long ago for just this purpose.

• **Undrowned Losses:** An object lost at sea has a trace of occult significance. But such objects eventually sink, becoming lost forever, or float to the surface, symbolically found. Some objects do neither, getting caught in the currents of the Western Ocean, never touching the sea floor or seeing the sky again. After at least two decades, undrowned losses (which might well be corpses) collect enough power from that uncertainty that they become valid components. Every factor of 10 in the number of years spent circulating adds one dot to the level of artifact the exotic item can help create.

• **Perfected Water:** Anything from an elemental pole is sufficiently powerful to use in a minor artifact. Something that has felt the touch of multiple poles gains even greater power. For instance, water from that elemental pole can be carried to the Pole of Air, where it freezes solid. This gleaming ice is then taken to the Pole of Fire, which blasts the ice into vapor. The vapor, collected and condensed, then goes to the Pole of Air to freeze again. After 10 circuits of this brute-force distillation, the perfected water becomes potent enough to use for three-dot artifacts.

• **Life of the Dead:** When a dead spirit *willingly* volunteers to sacrifice whatever afterlife remained to it and become a part of an artifact, that is mighty. Willing nephwracks work even better as exotic components, if commensurately more rare.

• **Unseen Ingredients:** Something that has never been seen, that has never even been touched by the light that lets man see, has strong connections to both mystery and darkness. Such objects become exotic enough to be worth using in artifacts if they are finished products—a fully forged sword or porcelain teacup that has never seen light is an interesting acquisition indeed.

• **Vigorous Blood:** Blood from any mighty being carries power that might be transferred into an artifact. Gods and demons must offer their benefaction (above), but elementals, God-Blooded and a myriad of other creatures with magic in their veins may offer blood to aid an artifact's completion. The creature's Essence must be at least two dots greater than the artifact's intended rating. Exalted must have an Essence *three* dots greater, and they may not spend their own blood to power an artifact they create. Entities of such power often do not think highly of requests for a pint or two of their blood. Blood is an excellent ingredient to tie an artifact to an individual, and even the most skillful artificers may be unable to avoid giving an artifact some connection to the donor.

• **Stolen Virtue:** Any of the four Virtues make excellent ingredients for artifacts, but only a Fair Folk noble has the power to craft a stolen Virtue into a solid object. Artificers must deal with the noble to get what they want. The Virtue used tends to color the artifact's use, sometimes creating subtle drawbacks.

DOING THE WORK

Once a character designs the artifact and acquires the necessary magical materials and components, she may build it—assuming she has a proper place in which to work. The base difficulty to craft an artifact is equal to (artifact's rating + 2), and each roll represents a season of work. An improperly furnished workspace only makes it harder. In the First Age, Exalted built massive atelier-manses for their crafts, which provided an infinite variety of tools and workspaces while automatically rearranging the geomancy of the workspace for maximum harmony with the current project. Second Age artificers are not nearly so lucky. Fortunately, crafting daiklaves and other "no moving parts" artifacts requires less exotic equipment than does magitech, which cannot be built or repaired without a host of dedicated tools. On the other hand, relying on craftsmanship instead of motonic science and prefabricated components means that even the best workshops offer less benefit to artisans.

Workspaces range from ideal (the above atelier-manses) to rudimentary (a hut with a few scavenged tools). The quality of the workspace includes the existence, quality of and appropriateness of the tools within that space.

A *rudimentary workshop* is virtually free, but that's its only benefit. It applies an external penalty of -4 to all rolls to craft an artifact because of the great lack of preparedness. Shaping Hand Style (see **The Manual**

of Exalted Power—The Dragon-Blooded, p. 142) makes hands into effective tools of any mundane sort and allows a character to function at this level without any workshop at all.

A *basic workshop* is well-equipped but entirely mundane in its focus. This is a village blacksmith's forge, carpenter's shop, weaver's loom or other setup with all the necessary tools. It costs Resources 3 to build a shop and Resources 2 each month to maintain it. The basic workshop applies a -2 external penalty to all artifact-crafting rolls. A character using Craftsman Needs No Tools (see **Exalted**, p. 213) or Clay-Wetting Practice (see **The Manual of Exalted Power—The Lunars**, p. 149), both of which allow an Exalt to function without tools, operates at this level.

A *master's workshop* comes with every tool one could want for mundane artifice, whether the craft is weaving, gem-cutting or alchemy. It certainly includes several tools of superior workmanship, and maybe a few of perfect workmanship or preserved from the Shogunate or Old Realm. Such a workshop costs Resources 4 to build and Resources 3 each month to maintain, but does not penalize the rolls to create the artifact. Founding a workshop of this sort is sure to draw attention, unwanted by most returning Solars.

A *flawless workshop* is stocked entirely with perfect or First Age tools. The artisan has every mundane ingredient found in Creation, and a few exotic ingredients from demesnes, the Wyld, the Fair Folk or other arcane sources. The Dragon-Blooded preserved such workshops through the Usurpation, so contemporary savants and artificers call them Shogunate-style workshops. The Realm, Lookshy and a few other nations of exceptional wealth build and maintain a *few* flawless workshops; the Sidereals and the Silver Pact own a few more. A flawless workshop adds two dice to each crafting roll.

Assembling a flawless workshop requires a labor pool like that necessary for creating a three-dot manse, and the spiritual impact is significant. People sensitive to mundane or spiritual events must notice such a workshop's construction unless the artisans take extreme and supernatural measures for secrecy.

An *ideal workshop* consists of a First Age factory-cathedral or atelier-manse. Such facilities must be part of powerful manses (see the "Factory-Cathedral" manse power on p. 78). They also require *three* powerful, exotic components *every year* to continue operating. An ideal workshop adds four dice to artifact crafting rolls.

These wonders have all ceased to function since the Usurpation, and the Fair Folk and the Wyld destroyed many of their remains during the Contagion. Any that exist certainly need major repairs. If an ideal workshop could be built or repaired, all the powers-that-be from the Scarlet Dynasty to Malfeas would notice—and if they could not take it for themselves, they would try to destroy it.

Workshops may have *specialties*, indicating types of work for which it is particularly well-outfitted. This reduces the external penalties by one for lesser workshops or adds one die per roll for master's or better workshops. Specialties include silk-weaving, sword-smithing, gem-carving and the like. Refitting a workshop for a different specialty takes about a month of focused work or the equivalent of an Artifact 2 creation for a flawless workshop. Ideal workshops can mimic any one specialty at a time after one week of self-adjustment.

CHARMS

Exalted artificers surpass their mortal colleagues through Charms. The best of the best possess multiple craft-oriented Combos. In the Second Age, Combos of a Craft Excellency + Crack-Mending Technique and Excellency + Craftsman Needs No Tools allow Solars to dominate mundane artifice.

Exalted craftsmen can use Excellencies to improve the skill with which they create wonders, but an Excellency cannot provide mastery a character doesn't already possess. In short, increasing the character's Craft, Lore and Occult dice pools to the equivalent of 6 or 7 with Excellencies does not qualify the character to design four- or five-dot artifacts. That mastery must come naturally, or through other Charms designed for the purpose.

NEW SOLAR CHARM:

WORDS-AS-WORKSHOP METHOD
Cost: 16m, 2wp; **Mins:** Craft 5, Essence 4;
Type: Supplemental
Keywords: Combo-OK, Obvious, Shaping
Duration: Varies
Prerequisite Charms: Craftsman Needs No Tools

Creation is the Lawgiver's workshop. With this Charm active, as the character works he names whatever small things he needs—advanced tools, alchemical substances, common materials—and they appear in his hands, ready for use. Motes spent on this Charm remain committed as long as it takes to resolve a single roll. For artifact creation, this generally means one season, the length of a single roll interval. Words-as-Workshop Method allows the character to function as if he had a master's workshop.

NEW SOLAR CHARM: WONDER-FORGING GENIUS

Cost: —; **Mins:** Craft (any) 5, Essence 5;
Type: Permanent
Keywords: None
Duration: Permanent
Prerequisite Charms: Infinite Craft Mastery, Crack-Mending Technique, Craftsman Needs No Tools

As the premiere artisans of the Chosen, the Solars can achieve in a mortal lifetime what lesser Exalted require centuries to understand. Purchase of this Charm reduces by one dot each the minimum Craft, Lore, Medicine and Occult requirements to build or repair artifacts—to a minimum requirement of one dot for any Ability normally required for the task. Therefore, a four-dot artifact (normally requiring Lore, Occult and Craft at 6 to build and at 5 to repair) would require those Abilities only at 5 to build or 4 to repair. Purchasing this Charm also reduces by three the total number of dots the character must allocate among Craft, Lore and Occult to design manses. Characters may purchase this Charm up to two times.

AIDES

A master artisan can craft artifacts more quickly if she has a team devoted to carrying out her designs. Assistants must have minimum ratings of 3 in Lore, Occult and the appropriate Craft Ability.

Every five mortal assistants add one automatic success to each extended roll made by the principal artisan's player, to a maximum of the artifact's intended rating. Too many cooks spoil the broth, especially for lesser artifacts.

Supernatural assistants provide greater benefits. These include Dragon-Blooded artisans, craft-oriented Terrestrial gods, elementals and First Circle demons. Every *two* such aides add one automatic success, to a maximum of twice the artifact's intended rating. Such creatures still need all relevant Abilities rated three or greater.

Having master artificers collaborate for a superb project is tremendously effective. The work of each additional superior artificer (to a maximum of five *total* artificers) adds four automatic successes to each roll. Celestial Exalted, Second Circle demons, Celestial gods and the odd hekatonkhire or Deathlord generally represent this sort of assistance (though who's the assistant and who's in charge can become… debatable).

The assistance of a Third Circle demon, Incarna or the most powerful hekatonkhires adds six automatic successes. And beyond that? Having Autochthon or Gaia on hand to suggest improvements in method or Essence flow guar-antees success—but then, the character *definitely* becomes the assistant, merely serving as a Primordial's hands.

Teams of occult assistants, whether mere mortals or Third Circle demons, are neither cheap nor inconspicuous. Each member of such teams is a highly skilled professional whose expertise is strongly desired in Lookshy or Malfeas. The best of the best are mighty powers in their own right and have other things to do. Just like assembling a superior workshop, however, gathering a superior workforce attracts notice—whether it's a satrap who wonders why the best glassblowers of 10 provinces have all come to town, to a Yozi who wants to know why its subsidiary soul has been bound. The complications are left as an exercise for the Storyteller.

Workshop	+/- Dice
Rudimentary Workshop	-4
Basic Workshop	-2
Master's Workshop	0
Flawless Workshop	+2
Ideal Workshop	+4
Assistants	+ successes
Mortal Aides	+1 per 5
Artisan First Circle demons, Dragon-Blooded, Terrestrial gods, elementals, common Fair Folk	+1 per 2
Artisan Second Circle demons, Celestial Exalted, Celestial gods, Fair Folk nobles, Deathlords	+4 each
Artisan Third Circle demon, Incarna, powerful hekatonkhire	+6

REPEAT BUSINESS

Artificers who repeatedly craft a single artifact get very good at it. In the First Age, lesser artisans wrought many minor artifacts for the population's use, from light-emitting globes and magical ovens to practice or regulation daiklaves for official duels. The process speeds up after an artisan does it once or twice.

Example: Peleps Elise wants to equip all her close family with brand-new wavecleaver daiklaves. As a two-dot artifact, the first project requires 30 successes and takes some time. In the process, she learns shortcuts and puts herself in a perfect mindset to make more. Each subsequent wavecleaver requires only 10 successes from Elise's player: 15 because Elise works from a proven design, -5 because she's already done this task before.

Each artifact still requires exotic ingredients and a supply of magical materials, so a character who intends to make a string of identical artifacts must stock up ahead of time. When the character turns her efforts to other artifact designs or takes more than a full season away from crafting that artifact, her ideal mindset fades. The next time she makes that artifact, it will be at the standard cumulative difficulty (though she still has a proven design).

ARTIFACT REPAIR

All but the greatest wonders can suffer damage, sometimes to the point of malfunction. Repairing a nicked daiklave, however, differs significantly from fixing an implosion bow or the other magitech described in **Wonders of the Lost Age**. Magitech artifacts have multiple parts and were designed with wear and tear in mind; muscle-powered artifact weapons, singing staves and other "one-piece" artifacts were not.

Repairing a damaged artifact uses the same dice pool as to create one, with a difficulty of (artifact's rating + 1). If the artifact remains functional, each success repairs one level of damage. The time each roll represents depends on the artifact—small artifacts might take only a few days to repair, large ones might take as much as a month per roll.

Artifacts that suffer enough levels to count as *damaged* (see **Exalted**, p. 154) completely cease to function. These require significantly more effort. The artificer must completely realign the Essence patterns and flows to make the wonder properly channel magic again. Treat this effort as equivalent to crafting an artifact one dot lower than the artifact being repaired, complete with using exotic materials to reinvigorate the artifact's purpose. One-dot artifacts require the artisan's player to accumulate five successes to repair.

If an artifact suffers enough levels to be *destroyed*, it becomes highly exotic scrap. Such an artifact cannot be repaired. At most, it might be worth a few successes in the design process to craft a duplicate.

SAMPLE ARTIFACTS

The sample artifacts in this section serve both as examples of the system above and as possible additions to your games.

ARTIFACT •

BLESSING OF THE SUN

These slim rings of beaten orichalcum were common in the First Age, usually given by Solar daimyos to their favored enlightened mortal servants. It requires no attunement. Wearing it reduces the Essence cost of effects that evoke non-damaging illumination, such as Essence-fed lamps, by one mote, to a minimum of zero.

This is a very minor artifact, although Second Age Solars might still appreciate its effects. Even with no commitment, it's still on the low end for one dot.

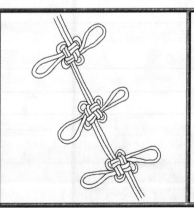

CORD OF WINDS

These knotted, blue-silk cords are common sights on all ocean-going vessels with any sort of sails. They usually hang from the central mast at head height. Each knot contains a slumbering air elemental, willingly bound at the artifact's creation. Untying a knot releases the spirit, which then blows in whatever direction the ship's captain desires for a night and a day.

Cords of winds contain elementals from Essence 1-4. An elemental increases the ship's mileage per hour by its Essence. Cords typically begin with a cumulative bound Essence of 40, generally containing four elementals each from Essence one to four, but are usually found with less.

In any game that spends serious time on the water, this is a useful power to have available. It can defeat both doldrums and pirates. The cord has finite uses, though—a restriction significant enough to reduce it from two dots to one.

The Fur Merchant's Gift

People call this minor artifact by the above name because of its appearance; it has no history to suggest anything else. It is a heavy fur mantle sized for a child of eight or nine. Any character may attune it for three motes, but it only offers protection to someone it properly fits. As long as it remains attuned, the person wearing it reduces all environmental damage from natural cold or heat by three, to a minimum of zero, before soak. The mantle is no more difficult to destroy than any well-made fur cloak.

Compared to the golden flame (below), the fur merchant's gift is superior: it reduces environmental damage further and affects both heat and cold. Its damage reduction might qualify it for Artifact 2. But it has a greater-than-average commitment, and being restricted to child-sized individuals is a drawback significant enough to ensure that it remains Artifact 1.

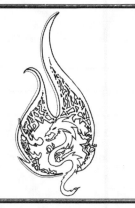

Golden Flame

This stylized flame is about palm-sized and made of normal gold except for a small core of orichalcum. Some are designed to be worn as pendants, others as broaches or clasps. It requires no commitment, and spending one mote suffuses the character with pleasant warmth for one full hour. It also reduces environmental damage from natural cold by two dice, to a minimum of zero, before soak.

Golden flames can be very useful in Northern series. They reduce damage by no more than two dice, marking them as Artifact 1. The lack of commitment and the low Essence expenditure balances the brief duration and minor protection, making this a solid one-dot artifact.

Heaven Thunder Leaves

Heaven thunder leaves are broad fans, reinforced with a magical material and painted with various scenes. They serve equally well for combat (treat as mundane war fans, see **Exalted**, p. 370) or courtly dancing. The magical fans add one die to ([Dexterity or Charisma] + Performance) rolls to use them for dancing, and when the fans are flourished properly, they tell a classic legend or fable. Each set of heaven thunder leaves tells a different story.

With at least three successes on the Performance roll, the dancer attracts the attention of local Terrestrial gods, and each success beyond that adds one die to the next social roll the character makes toward one of those gods. With two matching heaven thunder leaves, the maximum dice bonus becomes six. With only one, or with mismatched leaves, the successes necessary to attract gods increases to five and the maximum dice bonus is three. Heaven thunder leaves are Artifact 1 *each*. Commitment is two motes per leaf.

Heaven thunder leaves count as magical weapons, but their real strength lies in attracting godly attention. This qualifies the pair of heaven thunder leaves as Artifact 2. Separated, the difficulty to attract gods becomes high enough to reduce a lone heaven thunder leaf to Artifact 1, even though it can accomplish the same end. The maximum possible dice bonuses are higher than normal, but characters must work to get them.

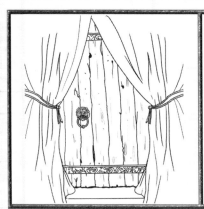

Privacy Veil

Privacy veils are curtains that come in a wide variety of styles. All are opaque—clearly designed for privacy. A character concerned also with being heard may commit one mote to the veil, levying a -2 external penalty to any attempt to eavesdrop through the barrier.

This power is limited in nature. The external penalty has limited impact, as it only applies to eavesdropping or being overheard, and characters with high Awareness, Perception or Investigation ratings can still hear through the veil. Considering that a character must activate the veil, this artifact has a limited effect on games and qualifies for Artifact 1.

SEVEN-JEWELED PEACOCK FANS

These war fans are half-again as large as normal and reinforced with a magical material. They are called "seven-jeweled" because their join is set with that many gemstones. Skilled warriors can use them to subdue by precisely lashing out with them when closed, to kill by closing the razor-sharp inside edges on veins, and to disarm by capturing or flicking weapons out of opponents' hands. They are Artifact 1 alone, but 2 for a matched pair.

Seven-jeweled peacock fans are more accurate and defensive than mundane war fans and gain the disarming bonus, but they are on par with other one-dot artifact weapons.

Speed	Accuracy	Damage	Defense	Rate	Minimums	Attune	Tags
5	+3	+5B/+1L	+3	3	Str •, Dex •••, Mrt •••	4*	D, M

* Attunement cost is for a matched pair; no offhand penalty to wield set paired.

SOLAR SEAL

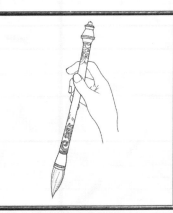

These seals have an edge of orichalcum in the engraving and can be two-inch, hand-held seals or signet rings. When a character seals a message with one, she may spend two motes to ensure its security. If the person who next opens the message is not the intended recipient or the author, the writing disappears instantly.

The artifact's owner can only indicate one individual as the intended recipient, not a group. "Members of the White Veil Society" doesn't count, but "the grandmaster of the White Veil Society" does. First Age seals recognize their masters' later incarnations, allowing reborn Solars to open secure journals that would wipe clean for anyone else. Dragon-Blooded in this Age use a version edged with blue jade called "auspicious secret seals."

The ability to ensure privacy is significant but comes at a large cost. There are many opportunities for others to open the message, and some people have slaves to open and screen their mail. With this enchantment, there is a decent chance that it will not reach the recipient intact, and the text cannot be recovered. This two-dot drawback makes the Solar Seal a one-dot artifact.

SILVER BRUSH

The mahogany handle of this writing brush conceals a thin core of orichalcum, but most people see its silver bristles immediately. The silver resists wear but is soft enough for good calligraphy. When a person commits a single mote to the artifact, the brush produces its own ink of any quantity, consistency and color.

Writing without the need to buy ink or replacement brushes is purely a matter of convenience. The lack of any additional powers set the Silver Brush squarely at Artifact 1—truly no more than a toy.

WINTERBREATH JAR

A winterbreath jar is a small urn or jug, finely crafted and inlaid with blue jade. Its enchantment of elemental air keeps its contents at a constant 45 degrees. Inside, perishables remain fresh and sparkling wine nicely chilled. Winterbreath jars rarely hold more than two bottles of wine or a small watermelon. They require no commitment.

As an object of convenience, especially with the limit on its contents, this artifact will not impact any game strongly—unless the players find some terribly clever use in some extraordinary circumstance. A clear Artifact 1.

AUDIENT BRUSH

Audient brushes are a more sophisticated version of silver brushes. The brush writes on its own, taking dictation from anyone present. It cleverly represents different speakers in different hands and colors, and makes appropriate associations (shades of gold for Solars, silver for Lunars, and so on) though it cannot identify people who conceal their identities. It effectively communicates mood and motive in its calligraphy, allowing readers to discern these with a (Perception + Linguistics) roll at a difficulty of half the speaker's (Manipulation + Socialize), rounded up (or a minimum of 2—figuring out a person's motives from brushwork is a good trick). The brush requires no attunement, but someone must feed it three motes to activate it for a scene. It can also acquire more paper for itself when necessary, as long as some is available. Whoever activates it may also indicate people for the brush to ignore and command it to strike out portions (usually in official proceedings).

The brush is not a powerful artifact, but it does provide characters the opportunity to record everything said around them and later examine the script for intent. Clever characters will find ways to use the brush for spycraft. It would be a very low Artifact 2 indeed if not for the low mote cost of using it.

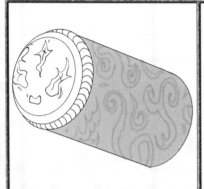

AUTHORITATIVE STAMP

This heavy seal includes all five colors of jade. When inactive, it bears the sign of a circle in a circle. Any seals, signatures or stamps a character attuned to this artifact personally observes, however, the authoritative stamp can duplicate perfectly. The artifact can only duplicate examples that its owner has seen while attuned to the stamp, and they turn out exactly like those examples. If the source has an unusual blotch, so does the duplicate. Attunement costs one mote; so does creating a forgery.

The authoritative stamp only forges signatures, seals and the like. While it's enough to fool many people, it won't fool everyone; one benefit is saving the time necessary for a mundane forgery. It's very useful but not superbly useful, making this firmly a two-dot artifact.

BRACER OF THE HAWK

This heavy bracer is entirely made from a single magical material, with a hawk boldly engraved on one side. It requires five motes to attune. At the wielder's command, the hawk steps out of the bracer and onto it, like a falconer's gauntlet. The hawk is made completely from the artifact's magical material and much larger than mortal hawks. It has the statistics of a strix (**Exalted**, p. 350) but with twice as many -1 and -2 health levels, 8L/12B soak and human-level intelligence. It can also talk, the only way it and its owner can communicate.

The owner of the artifact may return it to the bracer as a miscellaneous action if the hawk rests upon it. If the hawk is destroyed, the artifact loses its magic irreparably. Apply magical material bonuses to the hawk's attacks.

A talking, intelligent pet hawk provides no amazing advantages, but it has several useful applications. Able to serve as armed backup, messenger and guardian, it would be a low-end Artifact 3, if not for the danger that the hawk will die and be forever lost.

CHALCEDONY CHAMBERLAIN'S FLUTES

These two elegant drinking glasses of chrysoprase—green chalcedony—would grace any aristocrat's table. Committing two motes to the pair, they automatically neutralize any poison drunk from them.

Complete immunity to poisons would be a low-end three-dot power. The limitation that the poison must be in special glasses most appropriate at fancy parties is enough of a drawback to make it Artifact 2, even with reduced commitment.

COMPASS OF IMMINENT STRIFE

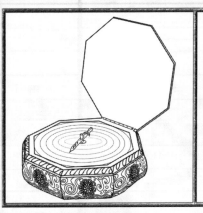

This orichalcum-and-starmetal compass only functions when installed at a ship's helm. Once installed and activated with a three-mote commitment, the compass points toward the largest battle within 50 miles. Size is measured both by number of participants and the power of those involved. A circle of Celestial Exalted tearing up the seas wins over a fleet of mortal pirates, for example. While the ship sails in the direction the compass points, its speed increases 50 percent.

The compass is not insignificant. Between its unfailing ability to pinpoint conflict and the increased speed, it could qualify as a three-dot artifact. The restriction that the compass must be installed in a ship's helm is also three dots, since the compass will never function without a working ship and simply can't be used on land. (At least not without a land ship, see p. 38). It also only points to the largest conflict. Usually, that doesn't matter. When your Circle-mate fights alone against a kraken and the compass leads you to some pirates attacking a merchant ship, though…

ESSENCE UNION DART

Essence union darts come in black and green jade varieties. All can be thrown by hand or fired from a blowgun (treat as a thrown needle with a +1 accuracy; blowguns have a 30 yard Range). They require two motes to attune. When the character successfully hits a living target with the Essence union dart, the dart creates a mystical link between attacker and target.

For the rest of the scene, the dart's user ignores cover, concealment and (his permanent Essence) points of the target's Dodge DV. This effect does not stack, but the character may affect multiple targets at once. Green jade darts can affect any living and material target; black jade darts pass right through living material creatures but strike immaterial living targets.

Essence union darts provide a significant advantage, especially against an opponent that depends on dodging. This could be a three-dot artifact, and would were it consistent. But the advantage depends on hitting the target first, and thrown darts can be lost (or taken) and are hard to use more than once per battle. This is a three-dot drawback, dropping the iffy three-dot power down to a medium-low two-dot artifact, which accounts for the low attunement cost.

GHOST-SUMMONING WHISTLE

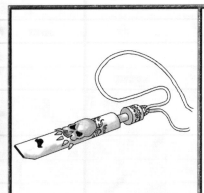

Ghost-summoning whistles are small silver and bone affairs strung with lanyards of braided white hair. During the day, they cause no sound. At night, they can be blown only three times. The first whistle sounds almost delicate, but all ghosts within three miles hear it and perceive it as a request to approach the user and present themselves to him. They may go if they desire. The second whistle is commanding, almost military in tone; ghosts within three miles must spend one point of Willpower not to obey the unnatural influence. The shrill and threatening final blast sets the whistle shuddering in the owner's hand as if it fears its own power. Ghosts must spend two further points of Willpower not to obey. After the third whistle, the instrument emits no sound until the sun has set 10 times.

Ghosts affected, especially by a third blow of the whistle, probably resent the user's interference. They arrive under no compulsion to obey or to treat the whistle-blower with kindness or respect. Dealing with the ghosts is the character's own problem.

On the one hand, forcing all the ghosts within a wide radius to approach the user is a three-dot power. On the other hand, letting all the ghosts in the area know where you are and making them angry is enough of a penalty to knock the artifact down to two.

THE GREENWOOD BLADE

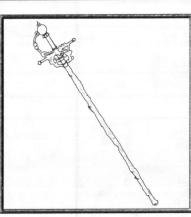

This artifact looks like a lightweight court sword, but the blade is a length of green sapling and its hilt is laced with green jade. The wooden "blade" is not sharp, so it inflicts only bashing damage (equal to a straight sword) to most creatures. But it can strike immaterial spirits without any additional enchantment and inflicts lethal damage against them. Material spirits suffer bashing, as normal. Each point of lethal damage the blade inflicts gives the wielder one mote of Essence. The greenwood blade requires five motes to attune.

The greenwood blade has one additional advantage. All the magic rests in the hilt. If the "blade" breaks, the artifact's owner can simply remove it and insert a new length of fresh-cut sapling, which then becomes steel-hard in turn.

*The greenwood blade has no numerical enhancements and simply mimics an Essence 2 Charm (Spirit-Cutting Attack, **Exalted**, p. 221). Inflicting bashing damage to material targets is a one-dot drawback that balances the small mote regain the weapon offers.*

THE HOUND'S EYES

The hound's eyes are a pair of golden orbs with stylized eyes engraved into one side. They were recently discovered sewn into a stuffed ragdoll of a dog, giving the artifact its name. Attunement costs cost four motes. A character leaves one of the two eyes in a location of her choice. Then, as long as she stays within 10 miles, she may put the other eye to her caste mark and look through the first eye for one mote per minute. The hound's eyes increase the difficulty for anyone not their owner to notice them by three.

Spying on distant locations is a useful power, but not incredibly so—not when you can only spy on one location. The artifact has reasonable attunement and expenditure costs, and the artifacts run the risk of being noticed and stolen during use. It's a solid two.

PERFECT TALON DAGGER

This steel-and-white-jade dagger resembles a large, curving tooth, especially with the red-dyed leather around its hilt. When attuned (two motes), it has the queer property of balancing on any point, from its tip to the rounded end of its hilt. It has the standard statistics for a dagger in hand-to-hand combat but reveals its magic when thrown. Its thrown statistics are below, and the character may reflexively spend additional motes in order to improve them. One mote increases the accuracy or damage by one or the range by five yards. A character may not spend more than three motes on any one quality, nine motes total.

Statistically, the perfect talon dagger is only slightly better than a normal throwing dagger. It got a one-point boost to accuracy and damage. Its real power consists of the ability to selectively increase its stats for a single, devastating attack, especially since an Exalt could combine it with Excellencies. It exceeds the maximum bonuses for a two-dot Artifact just barely, but accessing those bonuses costs more than the average expenditure—every time. On top of that, it's hard to throw the same dagger twice. That justifies it as Artifact 2, even with the low Essence commitment.

Speed	Accuracy	Damage	Defense	Rate	Minimums	Attune	Tags
5	+1	+3L	3	15	Str •	2	—

THUNDERBOLT SHIELD

Thunderbolt shields are broad shields crafted from a single magical material. They often bear symbols relevant to their wielders, such as sunbursts or stylized dragons. When attuned for five motes, they become lighter than a mundane shield of their size, and almost pull themselves into the path of oncoming attacks. The shield has no mobility penalty and increases the character's DVs against all attacks by two.

The magical material involved adds its own effects when the proper Exalted attune to the shield.
Orichalcum shields move more defiantly, increasing DVs by +3 instead of +2.
Moonsilver shields seem to push the Lunar out of the way, increasing Dodge DV by an *additional* +2.
Jade shields harden the bearer against damage, providing +2L/+2B soak.
Starmetal shields help the Sidereal avoid small bruises and cuts, reducing dice of damage by one before it is rolled in step 10 of combat resolution.
Soulsteel shields sap the momentum from attacks before they strike, increasing DVs by +3 instead of +2.

Mundane target shields add +1 to DVs and have a -1 mobility penalty. Thunderbolt shields increase that by +1 DV (about equal to two dice) and +1 die (for the mobility penalty). This would place them as a medium-low two-dot artifact. The magical material bonuses push it up to a medium-high Artifact 2, and the penalty of using one arm for the shield normalizes it.

THE UNSURPASSED SANXIAN

This sanxian is made of polished kauri wood and strung with silver and gold. The snakeskin covering its soundbox came from a serpent-god. The soul of an old master performer is bound into the strings, which never break or need tuning, and aids performances. When attuned for three motes, playing this sanxian adds two successes to Performance rolls. These add to whatever bonus an Exalted player can add through Charms. Any duffer can sound good playing this sanxian; a Solar musician could make Deathlords weep or call stars from the skies.

Two successes are about equivalent to four dice. The commitment is a little less than normal, but not enough to alter anything.

WAVE-STEPPING BOOTS

Wave-stepping boots are waterproofed leather boots with soles made of flexible black jade. With four motes committed, they allow the wearer to treat water as though it were solid ground. As long as the boots are functioning, his entire body (though not held objects, such as weapons) treats water as solid, so he cannot swim, and falling onto water inflicts normal falling damage.

The underwater society of Skyport, far in the Western Middlemarches, uses an amulet with similar properties to imprison people.

Wave-stepping boots provide a useful ability—walking on water. A character cannot swim while using the boots, but he cannot swim on land either, so they come with no significant drawback.

ARTIFACT •••

BLACK DEPTHS FORETOLD

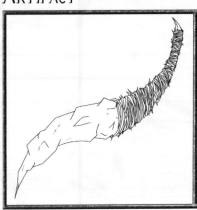

Black Depths Foretold is a very sharp dagger that looks as though it were roughly chipped from solid black jade. It is all one piece, and would cut the wielder as well as its victim were it not wrapped with tough leather, and even that needs replacement now and then. The weapon has the special quality of inflicting aggravated damage on dematerialized spirits. Its other special quality is that anyone examining the weapon's fate divines very clearly that the weapon is fated to slay the god of the Great Western Ocean.

*Inflicting aggravated damage on spirits is part of an Essence 3 Charm (Ghost-Eating Technique, **Exalted**, p. 221), but that Charm does more than this weapon. That's fine for balance, because the weapon has excellent statistics and can pierce a spirit's armor. It ends up being a high-advantage weapon against spirits and reasonable against everything else, but never overwhelming. Just right for Artifact 3.*

Speed	Accuracy	Damage	Defense	Rate	Minimums	Attune	Tags
4	+3	+4L/+4A	+1	3	Str •, Dex •	6	P*

* Weapon is only piercing against spirits.

CUP OF FLOWING BLOOD

This large, lidded chalice is forged of a blood-dark red-jade alloy. Any Essence-wielder may attune to it with a few seconds' concentration for three motes, even multiple characters at once. While attuned, a character cuts her palm and lets blood flow into the cup. Each health level of damage suffered is enough blood loss to fill the cup one-seventh of the way; the cup is much deeper than it appears when empty.

Drinking from the cup allows a person to instantly recover one lethal health level as a miscellaneous action, no more than once per action. Doing so removes one health level from the cup and lowers the blood level proportionately. The cup's magic does not disguise the salt-iron taste of blood but prevents gagging and retching. The blood heals bashing damage only if there is no lethal to heal. Only a character attuned to the cup can bestow health levels on the cup, a measure taken to prevent coercion or theft of life.

*This power has few points of comparison. The cup can rapidly heal a character of seven lethal wounds. This is incredibly powerful, especially in **Exalted** where quick healing is difficult to find. Call this a four-dot power. The drawback is equivalent: someone must lose all those health levels before a character can gain them. If this were potentially involuntary, it would be a three-dot drawback at most; some characters wouldn't hesitate to cut others open for their healing. That life must be volunteered makes the restriction much harder to fulfill, raising it to four dots and dropping the total artifact level to three.*

DARK RIDER

Dark riders are foot-high statuettes chipped from obsidian and attached to a thin base of magical material. The figures are humanoid but vaguely monstrous. They often show horns, large teeth or elongated normal features such as fingers or eyes.

A character activates the dark rider by committing six motes to it, making the statuette blur into the character's shadow. The shadow takes the form depicted by the statuette. From there, it watches the character's back, making it impossible to surprise him. The monstrous shadow also lends the character a frightening appearance, adding three dice to social rolls that benefit from the unnerving mien.

The dark rider can also be used offensively. A character mentally commands the rider and may insinuate it into another person's shadow, where it conceals itself near-perfectly. Rolls to detect the rider are difficulty 5. The character can see through the shadow's eyes at will, which causes both the character's and the rider's eyes to burn crimson (decreasing the detection difficulty to three). He can command the rider to return if it is within 10 miles, or to envelop a target. The rider then inflicts an eight-die clinch attack that, if the rider maintains it for at least two actions, forces the victim Elsewhere. The dark rider must then immediately return to its master and deposit the victim back in Creation.

Bright light (such as that of a Solar anima at the 11+ mote level) and fire both burn away the shadow instantly, ending the attunement and leaving nothing but a small statuette in its place.

No one of these abilities is very powerful, but all of them are useful. The shadow makes an effective personal guard, spy or kidnapper. It has a weakness against flame, but this is a two-dot drawback at best, perhaps accounting for the low attunement cost.

DUELING TORCS

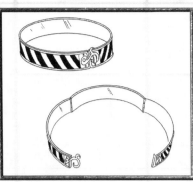

Dueling torcs are pairs of thin collars made of alternating bands of white and black jade but bound with an iron clasp. They were common in the First Age; less so in the Age of Sorrows. Two Essence-channelers put on the paired collars, and the iron clasps automatically seal once both contenders commit a single mote. The torcs end the effects of all non-permanent Charms and prevent the subjects from spending Essence. This lasts until one of the two is unconscious, dead or farther than 100 yards from the other. Someone with a permanent Essence higher than that of either character may open a lock by touching it and spending a mote. A torc's clasp cannot close on an entity with an Essence of 6 or higher; its power is too much for the artifact to contain.

This one's really a crapshoot. Blocking all Essence use is a tremendous power—but it's entirely self-inflicted, when two characters want to be sure neither one uses Charms. It provides a great advantage and abilities not otherwise available. On the other hand, your game may have little use for dueling torcs. If that's so, reduce them to Artifact 2 for the purposes of players buying them with points.

EVERYMAN ARMOR

Everyman armor looks like a plain steel suit of lamellar armor. It functions similarly, offering the same amount of protection, mobility penalty and fatigue. Before attunement, its only unique feature is near indestructibility. Attuning it requires six motes, at which point its mobility penalty and fatigue drop to zero. While wearing the armor, an attuned character may spend three motes to reflexively change her appearance. The character can look like any human she imagines, in any dress, and the armor can look like any sort of armor (but provides a constant amount of soak). Mundane attempts to see through the disguise fail, but people with inhuman sensory acuity may succeed. Their attempts are made at +2 difficulty on top of the character's additional efforts to conceal her identity. The only restriction is that the disguise *always* includes some form of evident armor.

In the event that a nonhuman wears everyman armor (such as a Fair Folk or beastman), that character can change his appearance but not his species. A wolfman, for instance, could look like any wolfman, but not a snakeman or human.

This is an effective power for any character who wishes to remain discreet or infiltrate an enemy's gang. It borrows mechanics from an Essence 2 Charm but costs less and has no limits (except species) on the identity a character can choose to display. That armor must always be part of the disguise is no more than a two-dot drawback, accounting for the reduced attunement cost.

GAUNTLETS OF DISTANT CLAWS

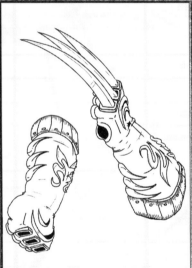

These fingerless gauntlets of a dark alloy do not restrict manual dexterity in the slightest. There are three depressions on the metal of the back of the hand. The gauntlets always come in pairs and require four motes each to attune. Although the gauntlets do not look like weapons, a character wearing them may reflexively extrude three sharp steel claws from the depressions in the back of one gauntlet or both. These make fearsome weapons, add two dice to climbing rolls and may be retracted reflexively.

Alternately, the character may fire the central claw of either gauntlet as a projectile, which remains connected to the gauntlet by a thin, nearly unbreakable chain. These claws can serve as weapons or grappling hooks, striking with enough force to pierce armor or embed themselves in walls and ceilings. Retracting a fired claw is a reflexive action and occurs with great force. The character can cause the claw to release its grip and return; otherwise, either the object attached to the claw flies to the character or the character flies to the claw as the chain winds up, depending on which is better secured. Using this method to move rapidly counts as the character's move action in a tick.

*This artifact resembles razor claws (Artifact 2, see **Exalted**, p. 388), but they have a number of advantages. The claws can retract, making the gauntlets available but nonthreatening. The ranged attack is based on the flame piece (see **Exalted**, p. 373) with one better accuracy and the bonus that the "ammunition" is free. It greatest advantage is the ability to pull objects to the character or pull the character to potential safety (or other places). None of these powers are amazing, but they are all quite useful individually. The collection of Artifact 1 and 2 powers add up to Artifact 3.*

Speed	Accuracy	Damage	Defense	Rate	Minimums	Attune	Tags
5	+4	+5L	+2	3	Str •, Dex •••	8*	M
5	+2	8L	1	15	—	8*	F**, P

* Attunement is for pair. ** Though not flame, the rules for flame type apply.

GHOST CESTUS

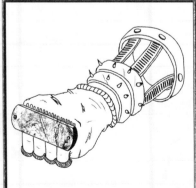

This fine, black-leather cestus has a solid smashing plate of mixed black and yellow jade, which gives it a mottled appearance. It may be worn and used by anyone without attunement. Whoever wears it can see and, in a way, touch immaterial creatures. A successful attack on an immaterial creature passes through it with meager resistance but devastates the victim's will. The player rolls (Strength + extra successes - target's highest Virtue). Each success drains a point of temporary Willpower from the target. This weapon is often found in the possession of the Immaculate Order, used to rob gods of their will and banish them or force penance upon them. Against physical targets, the weapon is simply a cestus.

*This artifact combines an Essence 2 power (Spirit-Detecting Glance, see **Exalted**, p. 221) with its own unique ability to drain immaterial creatures' temporary Willpower. The first marks it as a clear two-dot artifact, especially given the usefulness of seeing dematerialized entities, and the second nudges it toward Artifact 3 territory. The fact that mortals can use it and it requires no commitment sends it further upward. It provides no truly overwhelming advantage, so it is a high-end Artifact 3.*

Speed	Accuracy	Damage	Defense	Rate	Minimums	Attune	Tags
5	+0	+3B/special	+2	3	Str •	0	M

ILLUSION-SHATTERING MIRROR

These small hand-mirrors are backed by moonsilver instead of regular silver. When the mirror reflects a false image or appearance, from magical illusions to mundane disguises, the moonsilver alters the reflection to display the truth to anyone who looks in the mirror. Confronting a person suffering from an *illusion* effect with one of these mirrors shatters that effect. The mirror only performs its magic when attuned for eight motes.

This artifact definitely provides a great advantage. No illusions or disguises are safe against a character with the mirror, and it can even defeat some forms of mental influence. Some Charms may still confound the mirror if potent enough (see the sidebar "Powers Versus Powers or Charms" on p. 13). Still, this artifact is reactive, not active. It is a significant defense but no more; a character wielding it does not become able to accomplish amazing things. It can also be inconvenient to keep glancing in a mirror. Because it doesn't qualify for overwhelming advantage, it remains Artifact 3.

LAND SHIP

The keel of a land ship consists of white jade sandwiched between black jade; the rest of the ship is ordinary wood, forming whatever vessel the artificer desires (but no land ship has ever exceeded 60 feet in length). It must be attuned for 10 motes before it can sail on land. Then, the jade of the keel liquefies the earth and stone around the ship so that the ship can sail through them. Even large trees flow around the ship as it sails, though massive forests are very rough sailing. Once past the ship, the earth flows back together and resolidifies, leaving almost no trace. This can harm man-made foundations, but it's dangerous for the ship to do intentionally: sailing into a stone wall is like sailing into a waterfall, and a capsized land ship can sink into the ground, never to be seen again.

Even when the ship is destroyed, the keel can usually be recovered and used for a new ship. Using Sail Charms with an attuned land ship provides a 2m (minimum 1m) discount.

This ship provides rapid and relatively safe transport across huge swathes of Creation, land and sea, but the sand ships of the Southern deserts sail on land without magic; a land ship merely handles more diverse terrain. A land ship offers great advantages over people who must rely on horseback, though. The mote discount for Sail Charms pushes it from Artifact 2 to Artifact 3. Combining this with the folding ship (see p. 41) might make a decent Artifact 5.

SCABBARD OF THE LIVING WEAPON

This scabbard is made of a flexible but tough black leather of uncertain origin. When attuned for five motes, it changes to fit any daiklave the character also has attuned (a character with multiple attuned daiklaves chooses one). As long as that daiklave remains sheathed, the character cannot be harmed by mundane damage. Any attack backed by a Charm, made with a magical weapon or otherwise not mundane ignores this protection. Drawing the weapon ends the protection for the rest of the scene.

The scabbard of the living weapon offers a very useful power: the ability to completely ignore mortals. Not even artifact superheavy plate can do that. But its restrictions are hefty. The character must also have attuned a daiklave, and that daiklave must remain sheathed for the power to function. The defense also fails against Essence-empowered attacks. Since Essence-wielders make up the most effective opponents for Exalts, this defense is certainly not too powerful. It lands at three dots as something that cannot otherwise be done but is not always the answer.

SLING BOW OF ICE

These blue-jade-and-ice weapons were popular in the Low First Age when implosion bows and Essence cannon were unavailable—especially as crowd control weapons. They have a similar shape to composite bows, but the center of the high-tension cord is a thick leather cup with a good grip. Sling, or pellet, bows are slightly unusual weapons but occur in several areas of Creation.

This enchanted sling bow can fire any solid object that fits in the cup, though sling bullets work best and travel farthest. When used to fire a bullet made of black or blue jade (Resources 3 for 10) and reflexively primed with a mote of Essence, the bullet explodes into a 20-yard diameter cloud of freezing mist upon impact. The cloud hangs heavy; each success on the attack roll prevents the mist from dissipating for one minute. All living creatures within the cloud lose (6 - Stamina) dots of Dexterity, from shivering. These return at a rate of one per action once a victim is free of the cloud, whether because the cloud has faded or the person has fled it.

Enchanted black and blue jade bullets were once common. Artifact 1 for a packet of 20, these bullets did not require anyone to infuse them with Essence before firing. Even mortals could then use the sling bows effectively.

Statistically, the sling bow is a blend of the composite bow and sling—it does as much damage as a broadhead arrow with less range, but it can also fire capsules of acid or other creative ammunition. Its real power lies in its special bullets. The bursts are potent enough to pose a real threat on the battlefield. It has a strong drawback in the ammunition, though. Without those bullets, it's nothing much. This doesn't pull it down from being a three-dot artifact, but justifies zero attunement cost and the low price of one mote for a burst.

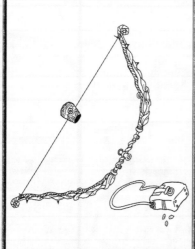

Speed	Accuracy	Damage	Rate	Range	Max Strength	Attune	Tags
6	+0	+2L	2	150	•••••	0	2

SORCERY-CAPTURING CORD (ARTIFACT ●●●-●●●●●)

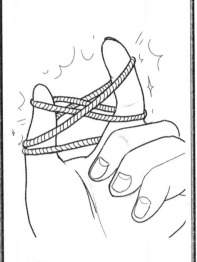

Sorcery-capturing cords come in three styles and three levels of power. One is made of threads woven from white, green, red, black, blue and yellow jade; it is Artifact 3. One is made of intertwining moonsilver and starmetal threads and is Artifact 4. The five-dot version consists of orichalcum alone.

The cord is about two feet long and immensely strong. It requires no commitment. When the character is the target or in the path of a spell, he may use a miscellaneous action to capture it in a knot tied in the cord. Essence channeled into the spell disappears into the knot in a dwindling display of power. Jade cords can capture Terrestrial Circle sorcery. Moonsilver and starmetal cords can capture that and Celestial Circle sorcery. Orichalcum cords can capture spells of all three circles. Capturing a spell requires that the character be able to take an action on the tick that the spell is released and spend temporary Willpower equal to the spell's circle: one for Terrestrial, two for Celestial and three for Solar. Cords can hold no more than three spells at one time, regardless of circle.

Releasing a spell is a miscellaneous action to untie the knot. The character must again spend Willpower equal to the spell's circle in order to channel the energies he is releasing. Spells with multiple versions take the shape intended when originally cast when released. Despite the names, these cords can also capture necromantic spells of the appropriate circles (see **The White and Black Treatises** for necromancy).

Capturing and redirecting Emerald Circle sorcery is very useful, but not overwhelming, and it costs a significant resource (Willpower). It is Artifact 3—about as useful as Emerald Circle Countermagic. Doing the same with the Sapphire Circle means that nearly every sorcerous opponent the characters might face can be subject to the cord. It enables the character to direct significantly more powerful sorceries, though it also costs more Willpower. It is very powerful, and qualifies for Artifact 4. Wielding this power over all circles of sorcery is unbelievable, not to mention the spells a character might traipse around with ready to set off. It should definitely be Artifact 5. Even with all this power flying around, the cords' enchantments are tempered somewhat by the fact that the character must time his action precisely.

THE ULTIMATE DOCUMENT

The ultimate document is a foot long sheet of blank pearlescent parchment. It's tough to damage, taking two health levels to damage and 4L/4B soak. It can be attuned for two motes. For six motes, the ultimate document becomes whatever document its owner imagines. It is flawless, written perfectly and in excellent calligraphy, with picture-perfect signatures in all the right places.

The artifact has two limits. It cannot duplicate official documents of Yu-Shan, and telling it to sets off warnings in the Celestial Bureaucracy: repeated offences may trigger censures. The falsified document also remains on the parchment for only one scene—it is excellent for showing people and fooling them, but letting someone walk off with it is *always* a mistake. People who do rarely see their ultimate document again.

Because it creates actually authentic documents (except that they're fake), the ultimate document presents a power unrivaled elsewhere. It's far from unbeatable, so it's not worth four dots, but it is impressive. It has a couple extra health levels and soak, which are worth a little, but its drawbacks are enough to counter both that and the minimal commitment. The scene-length effect is a good limit on the artifact's power.

ULTIMATELY USEFUL TUBE

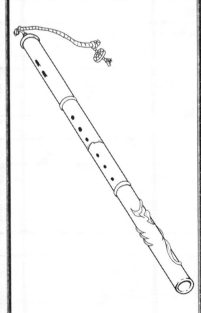

The ultimately useful tube is a foot-long bamboo tube. The lip of one end is faintly blue; the other lip is faintly red. It looks innocuous and requires five motes commitment.

An attuned character has a wide variety of options. He can twist the tube to reveal fingerholes and an embouchure to play it as a flute. Twisted back, no observer can find the holes. If used as a snorkel, the ultimately useful tube keeps out waves and water spray and maintains an ideal length up to two yards while the character changes depth. Used as a breathing tube in open air, the tube weakens airborne toxins, reducing their Damage ratings by half and their Toxicities by two. Twisting the tube the other way thins it to a half-inch diameter, allowing the character to use it as a straw and likewise weaken toxins imbibed through it.

The character can fight with the ultimately useful tube as a stick. By pulling on the ends, he can lengthen it to one yard in length and use it as a blowgun. The tube creates its own darts, costing one mote each. Blowing a dart out the blue end coats it with a sleeping poison; the red end creates a fatal poison. Darts are made of Essence and fade away at the end of the scene. Finally, the character can lengthen the tube to two yards in length, making it a fighting staff. Even to Essence sight, the ultimately useful tube always looks like a mundane implement, though the blowgun darts shine with Essence.

The first stat line describes the stick form, the second a staff, the third a blowgun. The sleeping poison is Damage special; Toxicity 3M; Tolerance —/—; Penalty -0; a target failing to resist falls asleep for 10 minutes or one hour, the character's choice on creation of the poison. The lethal poison is arrow frog venom (see **Exalted**, p. 131).

Appropriately, the ultimately useful tube is very useful. No power is very great, but it has a myriad of uses. Its stick, staff and blowgun traits are improved over the norm, but not by much. The poisons are effective but not mind-blowing. It could be a high-end Artifact 2, but the sheer range of its capabilities and its concealable nature make it a fair Artifact 3.

Type	Speed	Acc	Dmg	Def	Rate	Range	Min	Attune	Tags
Stick	4	+1	+4B	+2	3	—	Str ●●, Mrt ●	5	M
Staff	6	+3	+8B	+2	2	—	Str ●●	5	2, R
Blowgun	5	+2	1L	—	2	30		5	P

ARTIFACT ••••

ARMOR OF AQUATIC PUISSANCE

This heavy suit of articulated plate is composed entirely of black jade. Careful examination reveals spun black jade webbing inside the armor that makes it watertight once the helmet is locked into place. It requires eight motes commitment, after which the wearer can breathe underwater, perfectly control his buoyancy to rise or sink, and swim at twice his normal rate. The armor ignores water drag, eliminating penalties for fighting or moving underwater. The visor lets the character see through water as though it were air (though clouds of silt, ink and the like still obscure vision). Ranged weapons still suffer normal drag after leaving the character's hand. The armor has two hearthstone sockets, one on the forehead and one in the chestplate.

The armor of aquatic puissance provides clear superiority in underwater combat. Alone, the power might be a high three dots rather than four, but combined with a heavy suit of armor, there's no question.

Soak	Hardness	Mobility	Fatigue	Attune	Tags
+11L/13B	7L/7B	-2*	1	8	

* -0 mobility penalty underwater.

CLOAK OF VANISHING ESCAPE

The tough, white fabric of this cloak never seems to soil. It's thick enough to keep a traveler warm like a heavy mantle, but that isn't its purpose. The cloak's wearer can wrap the cloak around herself and disappear in a burst of white light, reappearing anyplace she can clearly see. It attunes for five motes, while activating the cloak requires five motes and several seconds of concentration. In combat, the character takes a miscellaneous action to activate the artifact's power before disappearing on her *next* action.

The character can take up to one additional living creature for an additional five motes, and she can travel no more than (owner's Essence) miles. Because the character must see her intended location, the cloak does not work well for the blind or in the dark.

Instantaneous teleportation is a great wonder in Creation, and this artifact makes a character almost impossible to corner or capture. It has the drawbacks of slow activation and limited targeting. It is possible to trap a character using this artifact (in a sealed cell or in total darkness) and to wound or kill her before she escapes—these justify the lower attunement and activation costs. Using it also means abandoning one's allies. This is a tremendous advantage, but not world-shaking enough to make it Artifact 5.

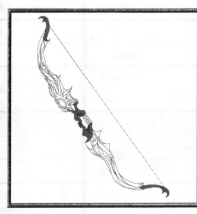

CRIMSON BOW

The crimson bow belonged to the First Age hero Ai, who helped end many Primordials with its arrows. It is king among powerbows, six feet in height and crafted from redwood and orichalcum. It is impossible to draw unless attuned, which costs eight motes. Arrows fired from this bow burn with the red light of the setting sun, transforming into bolts of pure Essence that defy attempts at evasion. These attacks always hit with a minimum of one success, regardless of the target's DVs; a target's only hope is to parry with a stunt or Charm, or to use a perfect defense. If the wielder chooses, he may reflexively spend four motes upon firing, allowing the arrow to strike immaterial targets and inflict aggravated damage.

Striking every target is a massive effect. It certainly qualifies as an overwhelming advantage, but not an unbeatable one. Perfect defense Charms can defeat the attack and the damage, and soak can reduce damage to minimum without any effort on the target's part. Even the additional power is impressive but not terrifying.

Speed	Accuracy	Damage	Rate	Range	Minimums	Attune	Tags
6	+1	+6L	3	400	Str ••••	8	2, B

FLYING SILVER DREAM

At its owner's command, this broad-bladed moonsilver daiklave flies from her hands to enter into battle itself. On her action, the character may choose to use it for offense or defense. In defensive posture, Flying Silver Dream circles its master and parries all attacks against her. This increases her DVs by 2 against all attacks that are not magically unblockable. Used for offense, the weapon attacks at its owner's direction with its owner's Attributes and Abilities; it may flurry as normal. The character may supplement these attacks with Charms as if the sword were in her hand, as long as the Charm use is legal.

Aloft, Flying Silver Dream has Dodge and Parry DVs of 8 and 10L/10B soak. Inflicting three or more levels of damage with a single attack knocks the blade down, grounding it until its master can pick it up and throw it into the air again. Flying Silver Dream has a setting for one hearthstone and costs eight motes to attune.

This weapon effectively doubles the number of attacks a character can make at once or increases the character's DVs significantly. That the blade's attacks can also be improved by Charms is impressive, effectively letting her act as the equivalent of two warriors.

Speed	Accuracy	Damage	Defense	Rate	Minimums	Attune	Tags
5	+3	+8L	+3	3	Str ••	8	—

FOLDING SHIP

This double-masted ocean-going merchant's vessel has a hull of strong, gold-tinged wood and steel-silk sails (see p. 158). It requires no crew: the ship handles its own sail, bilge and the like. It needs only a helmsman. From the helm, a pilot can verbally command the rest of the ship.

At its owner's command, the folding ship folds itself up in a visual spectacle, completing the one-minute process as a 1' x 6" x 6" box that weighs 20 pounds. It takes just as long for the boat to unfold. Twelve straight hours as a box repairs the ship of any damage it may take. If the owner wants, the folding ship can reassemble as a vessel with self-moving oars and a shallower draft for river travel. The attunement cost is 10 motes, and using Sail Charms with an attuned folding ship provides a 2m (minimum 1m) discount.

The folding ship offers complete mastery of water travel. Though it could certainly be more impressive (one of the First Age, hearthstone-powered ships, perhaps), it needs no crew but the character and is ideal for getting just about anywhere on the water. Plus, it's incredibly cool. This is a greater wonder.

KIND EDGE

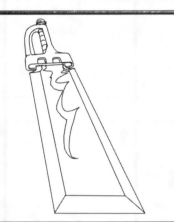

The kind edge is a reaver daiklave designed to capture opponents alive—or just hold them for execution. Its single great edge is slightly concave, but the rest of the weapon is precisely squared.

Kind edge costs eight motes to attune. When it inflicts damage, a human-shaped phantom leaps from the blade at the target. It body-slams the victim backward and pins him to the ground; the target immediately suffers a clinch attack using the wielder's (Strength + Martial Arts). The clinch roll benefits from any onslaught the weapon's wielder may have accrued and adds two automatic successes for every level of damage the attack inflicted. The projection remains, benefiting from its automatic successes on each roll to maintain the grapple, until the target breaks free. It then vanishes. Each phantom costs four motes; the wielder *must* spend these reflexively when she hits unless she does not have enough Essence to do so. Kind edge has space for two hearthstones.

Kind edge has slightly better statistics than a normal reaver daiklave. Its power occurs often but costs a medium amount of Essence, and the fact that activating isn't voluntary is at least a three-dot drawback. It doesn't reduce the artifact's rating by a level, but it helps balance the ability to leave struggling captives all over a battlefield.

Speed	Accuracy	Damage	Defense	Rate	Minimums	Attune	Tags
5	+3	+10L/3	+2	2	Str •••	8	O

MANACLES OF NIGHT

Manacles of night are a set of shackles with a fitting for two wrists and two ankles, designed to lock through a ring in the wall. They consist of orichalcum and soulsteel, twisted and folded together. Breaking free of these manacles requires a (Strength + Athletics) total of 20 for a feat of strength, and they have 20L/20B soak, 15 health levels to damage and 30 to destroy. A character bound by these manacles loses one mote of Essence each action (or five seconds) as the soulsteel drains them. He cannot use any Charms while bound, as the orichalcum forces his remaining Essence into impotent patterns. These were once the primary tools in imprisoning Exalted. An Artifact 3 version does not impede Charm activation.

As a tool that almost guarantees secure imprisonment of even powerful Essence users, this qualifies for Artifact 4.

PANACEA PIPE

Silver-engraved drawings of medicinal herbs cover the fine green glass of this hookah. Despite its fragile appearance, it's as strong as good bronze. Loaded with the proper combination of herbs depicted on the outside and lit with five motes, the hookah heals diseases. Each combination of herbs heals a different sickness, and many herbs are rare and expensive. Finding the proper combination and ingredients to heal a given disease requires research and exploration. With the right herbs lit, up to five people can smoke from the hookah and be healed of the specific disease. The pipe can cure even supernatural diseases, all the way up to the Great Contagion.

This is a very potent effect. The ability to cure the Great Contagion pushes it toward the five-dot level, but the limitation on how many people it can cure and the necessity to acquire the right ingredients and recipes triggers adventures—enough to push it down to Artifact 4.

PERFECTED KATA BRACERS

Perfected kata bracers are prayer strips crafted of a single magical material and curled into bracers. The strips' sutras are starmetal engravings, except in starmetal bracers—they use orichalcum. Attunement costs eight motes. When the character activates a Form-type Charm, the sutras inscribed on the bracers glow and lift from the artifact to engulf the character in light for a brief moment. For the rest of the scene, she gains several benefits.

She adds her Essence to the accuracy, damage and defense of her unarmed attacks and of attacks made with the active Form-type Charm's particular weapons. She may choose to inflict bashing or lethal damage at will and she may parry lethal attacks unarmed. In addition:

Orichalcum bracers let Solars inflict aggravated damage on creatures of darkness.

Moonsilver bracers provide Lunars additional flexibility, so they ignore cover and shields.

Jade bracers add Essence to Dragon-Blooded's soak and 2 to the Rate of their attacks.

Starmetal eases the flow of martial Essence for Siderials, reducing the cost of activating Charms of the same style by two motes (minimum 1).

Soulsteel makes an Abyssal's attack fatal if it inflicts more levels of damage than a mortal victim's Stamina.

Perfected kata bracers provide very significant effects. A skilled martial artist wielding them in battle has a significant advantage over her opponents, especially when wielding artifact martial-arts weapons. They suffer the small drawback of being incredibly obvious. If their benefits weren't limited to the battlefield, the bracers might be Artifact 5.

ARTIFACT •••••

CROWN OF THUNDERS

The beautiful crown of thunders is solid orichalcum with three hearthstone settings. Legend names its maker the Unconquered Sun, a gift for a hero of the Primordial War. Once attuned (10 motes), it increased each of her Physical Attributes by three dots, but it was a greater tool for rulership. Spending 10 motes give the wearer an aura of command that adds five dice to all social rolls for the rest of the scene. While that power functions, she may spend an additional 10 motes to appear glorious and mighty. Mortals may not attack her and treat all of her orders like compulsions. Other entities compare their Dodge MDVs to her player's social roll, which gains three bonus successes. Resisting this unnatural mental influence costs two points of Willpower, after which one becomes immune for a month and a day.

This is an incredibly powerful tool of command and could only be Artifact 5.

CRUCIBLE OF TARIM

The crucible is a huge brass basin with dragons worked in jade on the side. Its lid seals tightly for the crucible's use. This artifact captures a sorcerer's spells in liquid form for later use. The character must first place many occult ingredients worth Resources 5 into the crucible and render them down. After two days, the sorcerer casts her spell and lets the Essence follow the path of her attunement into the crucible, where it invests the liquid with its power. A small spigot in the basin drains the fluid into a special vial (included in the expenditure).

Later, using the spell is a simple matter of unstopping the vial and directing the reshaping Essence. Occult requirements make the vials fragile: should one break accidentally rather than be opened on purpose, the spell rips free and wreaks havoc, usually on the person holding it. The crucible of Tarim can capture any circle of spell in this way, though Solar Circle spells require the further sacrifice of a one-dot artifact. A sorcerer must be attuned, for 10 motes, for the entire distillation process.

The ability to have any number of any Circle of spells at one's fingertips is an incredible advantage. Hurling Death of Obsidian Butterflies is nothing when you see the Solar Circle's attack spells. The ingredient requirements are not small, but not large enough to bring it down a dot. The chance that the vials will break is also not large enough—but it certainly is fun.

DEATH AT THE ROOT

Death at the Root is a moonsilver grand grimcleaver, created as a planned byproduct of a Lunar's ritual suicide after the Usurpation. The great axe can fatally sever flows of Essence as well as blood. Its wielder may use it to target the Essence in a manse, demesne or persistent spell. The player rolls (Charisma + Essence) at a difficulty of the target's rating (for manses or demesnes). Success breaks all current attunements to the manse or demesne or reduces the demesne's rating by one. Attacking a spell has a difficulty of (spell's circle + 2) and cannot affect Solar Circle spells. If successful, the spell shatters as if struck with countermagic of an equal circle. Over week-long dramatic actions, the weapon can redirect dragon lines and shape the geomantic landscape, as if performing a year's worth of geomantic engineering. A single strike, directed at a demesne's geomantic stress-point, can trigger Essence buildup. (See Chapter Two for rules about creating and destroying demesnes.)

Striking a person inflicts damage as normal. It also allows the above roll to be made reflexively. Charms or other magical effects currently affecting the target end immediately if the minimum Essence score required to use them is equal to or less than the successes rolled; effects without minimum Essence requirements compare their creator's Essence score to the number of successes instead. Attuning to Death at the Root costs eight motes. The weapon uses the normal statistics for a moonsilver grand grimcleaver, and its wielder can always channel Conviction for any roll related to Death at the Root.

Death at the Root guarantees a character has vast control over the magical landscape in his life. He can destroy enemies' manses permanently and end most effects that protect them. This very clearly qualifies as Artifact 5, able to completely change the face of a game no matter who holds it.

EYE OF THE FIRE DRAGON

Ten Terrestrial master artificers forged this dire lance in secret just prior to the Great Uprising as a fearsome weapon against the tyrannical Chosen of the Sun. It is a thick-handled spear with two broad heads on one end. Its blades are a lightly textured matte black, the red jade showing through only at its highly-sharpened edges; a black cover of some leather-like material usually conceals the heads. It requires 10 motes to attune.

When the black cover sheaths the blades, the weapon appears completely mundane in Essence sight but inflicts only bashing damage; the head requires a miscellaneous action to cover or uncover. Exposed and used against a Solar, however, the weapon inflicts aggravated damage; the weapon's bearer gains +4 DV and MDV against all attacks backed by Solar magic; and successfully striking a Solar sometimes breaks their defenses. Roll one die for each beneficial Solar Charm affecting a struck Solar target: failure on the roll ends the Charm. Finally, the lance also enhances Fire Aspects' anima powers, empowering it to cause aggravated damage to Solars.

A Dragon-Blood wielding this weapon against a Solar will be a truly fearsome enemy. Compared to Death at the Root (above), its magic-ending power might seem a little weak, but the grimcleaver has average statistics for its weapon type; the dire lance is improved, inflicts aggravated (against Solars) and improves defense (against Solars). In its chosen arena, the Eye of the Fire Dragon is Artifact 5.

Speed	Accuracy	Damage	Defense	Rate	Minimums	Attune	Tags
5	+3	+10L/16L	+3	3	Str ●●	10	2, L, R

FORGOTTEN BLADE

Perhaps the Sidereals forged the Forgotten Blade in the High First Age, but records of the weapon are scant even in Heaven. The Forgotten Blade may or may not be beautiful—it is impossible to remember. This daiklave has average statistics, but as long as one does not look at it, one cannot remember its appearance. In fact, no one but the person attuned to it can remember it *at all* when not in its presence. This unnatural mental influence requires two Willpower to shake off for a scene.

The weapon does not hurt people physically. It inflicts 'phantom' damage (mark it with a circle in health boxes). Its damage rating is normal for a daiklave, but the character wielding it adds Intelligence rather than Strength to calculate base damage. Each level of damage the weapon inflicts causes the victim to forget how to use one Ability (determined at random) and the last five years of her life. Someone "killed" by the Forgotten Blade suffers complete amnesia. Victims suffer normal wound penalties due to disorientation. Ability use returns as the wounds heal (at the same rate as bashing), but lost memories are gone forever.

Compassionate warriors may prefer to cut away smaller chunks of memory or target specific memories with called shots. The difficulty of the attack increases by one ("forget only the last year," or limit the number of random Abilities) to four ("forget the last five minutes," or, "forget me completely").

As an amazing power without any real analog, the Forgotten Blade clearly represents a five-dot power. Its only drawback is that if its owner lets his attunement lapse, he forgets he owns it.

RING OF BEING

Forged in the secret manse at the heart of the Imperial Mountain, each ring of being is made only of a single magical material, purified a dozen times over. This complete purity, commingled with the Essence of their unique forge, affirms and protects its wearer's identity and nature. Only things of Creation proper can affect the character—the dead, Fair Folk, demons, gods and the Wyld cannot even target the character with their magic. They may use physical and social attacks, but everything else does not touch her. Elementals, however, are of Creation, and a weapon empowered as an artifact or by Charms still counts as physical force. A ring of being only functions for an Exalt natural to the magical material and costs 15 motes to attune.

This is very, very powerful. Its power names entire classes of entity that no longer threaten the character—at least not effectively. Mundane attacks could still take her down—don't expect to wrestle the Unconquered Sun and win—but it's not very likely.

SOUL MIRROR

This soulsteel grand daiklave is a flat black, the moaning spirits common to the magical material conspicuously absent. Four hearthstone sockets adorn the blade, which costs eight motes to attune. Tales say the Lover Clad in Raiment of Tears forged this weapon for her nemissary champion shortly after the Great Contagion. Two Dragon-Blooded martial artists managed to defeat the champion and hide it, but they disappeared mysteriously soon after.

Soul Mirror consumes souls. When it inflicts even a single level of damage, its victim loses one point of Willpower and (victim's Essence) motes as the blade tears away bits of soul. Soul Mirror absorbs the soul of anyone it kills, preventing it from going on to Lethe or the Underworld. It imprisons the soul in the blade, up to seven at a time. Reflexively, the character may command the blade to consume a captive soul for power. Sacrificing a captive soul increases the weapon's Accuracy, Damage, Defense *and* Rate by one for the next seven days, to a maximum bonus of +4 to each.

The blade also has a dreadful anima of its own. When it is first drawn or used in combat, the player makes a reflexive (Charisma + Presence + Essence) roll. Any characters whose MDVs are lower than the rolled successes suffer a -4 internal penalty to all actions out of fear; this unnatural mental influence costs two temporary Willpower to shuck off.

Soul Mirror has one final power. When its wielder suffers a blow that would reduce him to or past Incapacitated, he may reflexively sacrifice one soul and all his Peripheral Essence to Oblivion. He must have at least 10 motes in his Peripheral pool for this to work. The act completely negates the damage from that attack, heals all his bashing and lethal wounds and (Essence) aggravated wounds.

Yes, all its powers stem from killing people and using their souls as a mystic fuel. But horrific evil doesn't make this artifact any less of a massive advantage in battle and worthy of five dots.

CHAPTER TWO
DEMESNE, MANSE AND HEARTHSTONE

As Essence pours into Creation, the world shapes its meandering course. Most of Creation's citizens don't notice as vast flows of Essence stream past, rise, fall, are diverted, well up, or run off. In some places, though, so much Essence concentrates that even mortals feel it. Everything in such places, called demesnes, is steeped in Essence to the point that the whole area becomes more vivid, more intense—more *itself*.

The first geomancers practiced their art long before the human race existed. Modern savants know little about these races; but they know the reptilian Dragon Kings watched this flux and sought to control it. By looking around them, the Dragon Kings learned the Essence-shaping qualities of landscape. From their example, the first human geomancers gave the name of "dragon lines" to the world's great rivers of Essence, and said these currents showed the shapes of sleeping entities beneath. Accustomed to thinking of their craft as one that shifted the dragons themselves, the early geomancers coined a cautionary proverb: "Touch the dragon and it may turn over, but no one wishes the dragon to wake."

The pre-human geomancers did not wish to disturb the world too much (and perhaps anger its Primordial masters). They aimed for harmony. In time, they learned how to build in harmony with the unnerving wildness of demesnes and pacify their overflowing energies. Thus, they created the first manses, though their stone circles hardly resembled the polished edifices to come.

The discovery of the sheer power contained in each manse was swift. Soon, geomancers built manses as an end in itself. It didn't take long for ambitious geomancers to prod the dragon lines for power, but

they quickly discovered that ill-considered geomantic alteration could cause terrifying environmental catastrophes. For fear of awakening the dragons to wrath, strict laws regulated demesne creation and manse construction.

When the Exalted began building their own manses, they adopted the rules and safety precautions of the Dragon Kings. No matter how elaborate or eccentric the appearance chosen by the masters of the Old Realm, the deep structures of their manses adhered scrupulously to the ancient strictures—because their manses exploded if they didn't. The Shogunate eschewed even the superficial vagaries of design practiced by the Celestial Exalted, for the sturdiest and most reliable construction. The Dragon-Blooded also strove to build mundane buildings and communities according the principles of geomantic harmony, that the farmlands might stay fruitful and the populace contented.

In the Age of Sorrows, however, basic geomantic concerns and aesthetics are ignored more and more often, creating spiritless, inharmonious communities across Creation. Until recently, the Scarlet Empress kept a close watch on her nation's geomancy, and her edicts kept the Realm's practices in consonance with the land—but the commands of a vanished ruler matter little. Perhaps it's fortunate that modern geomancers lack the magical and material resources to try establishing new demesnes. Too many shortsighted or conflicting attempts to move and channel the dragon lines could lay waste to whole nations through famine, flood, storm or earthquake. Anyone who can shape demesnes would need to invest more effort than they wish, so Creation remains stable for now.

Geomancers in the Second Age usually satisfy themselves with building manses to cap existing demesnes—but should a geomancer find a greater demesne, it will do her little good. None of the geomancers in Creation know enough to fully command that power. Practically nobody in the world today could build a factory-cathedral—though this, along with everything else, could change with the Solars' return.

DETECTION

Essence-wielders can't help but notice manses and demesnes. Upon entry, an Essence-channeler feels the warmth of upwelling power as a tingling frisson across

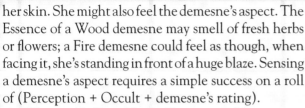

her skin. She might also feel the demesne's aspect. The Essence of a Wood demesne may smell of fresh herbs or flowers; a Fire demesne could feel as though, when facing it, she's standing in front of a huge blaze. Sensing a demesne's aspect requires a simple success on a roll of (Perception + Occult + demesne's rating).

The same roll enables an Essence-wielder to sense a demesne from a distance. The number of successes gives the number of miles away the character can sense the demesne; no successes means the character won't notice the demesne until she steps into it. Turning this about, a character's distance in miles from the demesne supplies the difficulty to sense it; add 1 to the difficulty if the character does not consciously try to locate it.

Mortals who are blind to Essence have a harder time noticing demesnes (assuming they don't realize on their own that a forest of living golden trees or a flaming lake is something special). A mortal's player needs a successful (Perception + Occult + demesne's rating) roll to feel a demesne's magic at all, and three successes to conclusively tell its aspect—again, assuming the mortal cannot tell at once from the manifestations of superabundant Essence. Mortals can only sense a demesne from at most a mile away, and being outside the demesne increases the difficulty of sensing it by 2.

Detecting manses uses the same rules as detecting demesnes, but because the Essence is harnessed and damped down, relevant rolls have their difficulties increased by 2.

Various rituals in the thaumaturgical Art of Geomancy increase the odds to detect demesnes and manses—especially from far away.

Demesnes

Demesnes are common in Creation. Few people live more than a week's ride on horseback from the nearest demesne, and a traveler can sometimes walk from one demesne to the next within a day. In some countries, such as the Realm, every local demesne is long since built into a manse. Still, not a person in the world hasn't heard stories of such beautiful, mystical places.

More than three-quarters of Creation's demesnes are rated three dots or lower. Of the rest, almost all are level 4. Level 5 demesnes are the stuff of legend. Physically, demesnes are rarely larger than a square mile, and weak demesnes may cover less than an acre.

Weak demesnes superficially resemble everyday Creation. Their superabundant Essence manifests in small ways such as trees whose leaves rustle despite the absence of wind, or brilliant sparks from any flame brought into the demesne. A demesne rated 3 or higher, though, produces blatantly uncanny effects such as music in the air or rocks that burn without being consumed. Ignorant folk may mistake powerful demesnes for pockets of the Wyld.

Each demesne has a predominating aspect. Most have lesser aspects as well, more lightly influencing their Essence. Prevailing theorists believe every dragon line has its own aspect, and their crossings create demesnes: hence, a dragon line of Hesiesh flowing over one of Danaa'd might birth a river demesne of cold, aquamarine fire. But this idea ignores the fact that—as geomancers tracing dragon lines have found—not only can dragon cross without generating demesnes, some demesnes aren't situated on dragon crossings. In fact, the most powerful demesnes in the world are usually nowhere near the dragon lines. And, of course, there are no Celestial dragon lines at all. At least, no one has found any: a few savants speculate that currents of Solar, Lunar and Sidereal Essence flow high in the sky, and occasionally touch down to form Celestial demesnes. Until someone finds a way to detect these hypothetical dragon lines, the theory remains nothing more than that.

Another, highly esoteric theory holds that demesnes are the lesser souls of Gaia. Just as the Yozis externalize their souls into hierarchies of demons, so does Gaia extend herself through creation in the form of demesnes. This theory has problems, too. In the great days of old, geomancers created demesnes. Did they create new souls for Gaia? Summon them? And again, what about Celestial demesnes, aspected to other Incarnae? Not to mention the horrible Abyssal demesnes…

In the end, most geomancers simply accept demesnes as a fact of Creation. In the Age of Sorrows, exploiting a demesne matters more than explaining it.

Power from Demesnes

The more Essence pours into a demesne, the more dramatically gorgeous and strange it becomes, but the power doesn't just run off in flickering sunlight and lakes of impossible depth. As noted on page 113 of **Exalted**, Essence-users can use a ritual to attune themselves to a demesne, and then can regain extra motes while there. They become a focal point for the demesne's wild Essence, but rather than being overwhelmed by the onslaught, most people feel charged with energy and sensitized to their environment. Striding through the demesne, they understand just how powerful they

ASSOCIATIONS

Aspects demonstrate themselves in a myriad of ways, and aren't always consistent. Essence is fluid, and many manifestations are possible: a gold forest seems obviously Wood-aspected, but could be a Solar or Earth demesne. The following associations are a mere sampling of potential appearances, influences, and products of aspects in both demesnes and manses.

Air: wind, lightning, storms, thought, music, silence, language, cold, fast, moving, precision, perfection, invisible, pervasive, travel, thrown, open, unlocked, academia, manual dexterity, sky, birds, memory for detail, pale colors, logic, philosophy, puzzles, independence, pride, Eclipse Caste, Maiden of Serenity, straight lines, mountain tops, sapphire, tin, dream-stone, blue jade

Earth: rock, sand, architecture, toughness, underground, ritual, tradition, internal, reliability, stillness, claustrophobia, humanity, civilization, tools, training, dedication, eternity, landmarks, white and brown, faith, mountains, goats, small furred animals, burrows, serpents, Zenith Caste, Maiden of Battles, right angles, caves, cities, farms, domestication, gems, white jade, lead

Fire: passion, heat, light, agility, animation, pain, danger, renewal, change, specialization, consumption, orange, quickness, immediate force, awe, conflict, sun, desert, volcano, phoenix, reptiles, lions, sacrifice, purification, instinct, great cats, desert snakes, Dawn Caste, Maiden of Journeys, acute angles, triangles, violence, ruby, red jade, steel

Water: intrigue, rain, subtlety, emotional memory, flexibility, acceptance, dark colors, manipulation, unpredictability, unexpected force, persistence, instinct, logic, philosophy, ice, storms, sailing, deception, grace, fish, versatility, depth, essential natures, purity, usefulness, mazes, complexity, calm, frogs, fog, Night Caste, Maiden of Secrets, waves, turquoise, pearl, coral, black jade, silver

Wood: plants, animals, seasons, growth, poison, birth, death, cycles, love, forests, green, brown, simple governance, joy, pleasure, spirit, gods, thorns, flowers, lust, reproduction, drugs, parties, predator-prey, Twilight Caste, Maiden of Endings, circles, spirals, rivers, emerald, amber, green jade

Abyssal: night, cold, sacrifice, pain, black, decay, blood, shadows, necromancy, battle, slaughter, seduction, war, ancestors, subservience, regret, depression, insanity, love, fear, disgust, beauty, funerals, introspection, aloneness, raitons, pomegranates, rulership, nocturnal creatures, swamps, cemeteries, battlefields, darkness, jet, iron, ebony, obsidian, slavery, soulsteel

Lunar: moon, night, silver, moonsilver, nature, animals, religion, purity, evolution, spirit, cycles, feminine, beauty, honor, motherhood, nurture, truth, defense, strength, battles, wisdom, awareness, internal, wit, responsibility, aloneness, water, love, sex, simplicity, destruction, equality, reflections, mysticism, the Wyld, insanity, rage, claws, heartbeats, bodies, crescents, fluidity, marriages, white and gray

Sidereal: stars, night, openness, wonder, Essence, potential, chance, reality, impossibility, age, history, academics, time, patience, pride, control, subtlety, planning, secrets, planets, occult, spirits, bureaucracy, foresight, writing, prayer, starmetal, quicksilver, five-pointed symbols, rituals, knowledge, wisdom, manipulation, stealth, spangled black or indigo

Solar: sun, faith, righteousness, charisma, dominance, civilization, yellow and white, gold, orichalcum, diamond, sorcery, skill, right, religion, bureaucracy, construction, leadership, invincibility, bursts, warmth, marble, open spaces, art, crowns, wars, blatancy, lions, simhata, light, olive, spear, shield, four arms, height, day, masculine, glory, fire, humanity

are, like gods walking the world. It feels good, but does lend itself to mania and megalomania.

HARVESTS: THE PEARL-COLLECTING RITE

Even with attuned characters claiming Essence, demesnes can't hold all their power. Each demesne has one major outlet, expressing its nature. Many are physical: Essence might imbue itself into fabulous tri-colored fruit growing from a Wood demesne's trees, or spill as molten iridescent metal into an Earth demesne's magma. Crystals are a common expression of a demesne's power, as if the Essence tried to form a hearthstone all by itself.

Once a month, a single person attuned to the demesne may use a Soul Sea Meditation, the Pearl-Collecting Rite, to gather the demesne's rich harvest—its

Essence token. The character follows the demesne's Essence flows to find where the Essence token has manifested, and coaxes it to him. This uses a roll of (Wits + Lore), difficulty 2. Botching causes them to hurt the character: harvested magma could burn his hands for three levels of lethal damage, while harvested songs could break his heart, rendering him unable to spend Willpower for the day. (See sample demesnes, starting on p. 55, for more examples.)

A character who carries the Essence token thereby regain (demesne's rating) extra motes per hour when away. Once the demesne no longer feeds it, however, the token starts denaturing—fruit rots, metal corrodes, crystals crack. Characters only gain Essence from a demesne's primary outlet for (rating) days after collecting it. The demesne does not produce another Essence token until another month passes.

Some demesnes grow metaphysical or immaterial harvests. One Southern demesne's main outlet is its feeling of caressing, comforting warmth; one Western demesne gives inhabitants heartbreaking melodies that fade from memory in a day. These mystical Essence tokens make wonderful exotic components for artificers across Creation, because their concentrated Essence can still be handled like physical entities—at least by Essence-wielders. The owner of the Western demesne's melody can sing it in the ear of another attuned person, who then remembers it and draws Essence from it, while the first person forgets the melody. The Southern demesne's token manifests as an immaterial veil of hot silk, visible to anyone with Essence perceptions, that can be passed among attuned people. Some demesnes are famous for a certain ingredient. (See the sample demesnes starting on p. 55 for examples of how to deal with different Essence-token harvests.)

If, through accident or design, a demesne's harvest is destroyed before it denatures, (demesne's rating x 4) motes of raw Essence explode through the surroundings. The motes are mostly harmless, invoking omens and minor geographical changes.

ATTUNEMENT

An Essence-wielder who attunes to a demesne can imbue herself with aspects of the demesne's power as well as drawing out motes of Essence. Because the geomancy of a demesne isn't intended for Essence-wielders, though, attunement also "enhances" a body with the demesne's geomantic flaws. Infused effects only apply as long as a person stays within the demesne.

Abilities granted to those attuned to a demesne should compare to those of a hearthstone one level

SOUL SEA MEDITATIONS: RITES OF DEMESNE AND MANSE

Attunement to a demesne is not just a way to access its power, but a new perception of Creation. Every Essence wielder can feel her inner nature, her unique core, the silent pool of her soul. When she resonates with a manse or demesne, she pours herself into the sea of Gaia. Though the word "attunement" is used to designate characters aligning themselves with a place's geomancy, attempts to sense the world's Essence are always a kind of attunement. Every Soul Sea Meditation might be thought of as attuning to a place.

Soul Sea Meditations are instinctive for Essence-channelers, though knowledge of the world grounds a character's execution of them: every aspect of Creation hides the keys to Gaia. Thus, they always use Lore as the relevant Ability. The basic rite of attunement to a demesne is called Bathing in the River Meditation. Some meditations can also be performed as rituals of thaumaturgy (see Chapter Four), and skill at the Art of Geomancy may assist in their performance.

Other Meditations follow later in the chapter, but do not include every possibility. Such rites take (place's rating) scenes to perform, unless otherwise noted. Distraction won't affect a roll, but anyone within the place's range can counter one ritual with another; successes are subtracted from each other. Failing a rite's roll inflicts a point of lethal damage as Essence slashes across the character's soul. Botches have variable, unfortunate effects.

lower than the demesne; some have drawbacks balancing their scale. As such, the river of azure flame (a demesne of rating 2) might render attuned characters immune to fire while there, even supernatural fire. However, it might then cause normal liquids to pain or poison them—making swimming deadly, drinking unbearable, and kissing awful.

DEMESNE-INDUCED MUTATION

The aspected Essence of a demesne streams over everything within the area, evolving it to suit itself. To a certain extent, of course, demesnes are defined by their environment; it's almost inconceivable that a Fire demesne form in the Western oceans. But things too

The N/A Demesne and Manse

A few demesnes are so powerful that geomancers cannot even measure their energy. In a sense, the Elemental Poles are themselves demesnes of limitless power. The Imperial Mountain, directly over the Pole of Earth, holds dozens of demesnes so powerful and unstable that even the Old Realm's Solars could not control them.

A few manses display similar power. Most importantly, the Imperial Manse channels enough power to attack any place in Creation. The Realm Defense Grid housed in the Imperial Manse not only draws energy from the powerful demesne beneath it, it also channels Essence from hundreds of linked war manses along the Blessed Isle's perimeter.

Characters cannot raise demesnes to N/A level, nor construct N/A manses. Like the fabled N/A Artifacts, these were the products of the Primordials themselves, or decades of work by millennia-old Exalts drawing on the resources of the entire Old Realm.

small to define a demesne will be eroded, influenced or entirely remade by it.

Passive, easily shaped people and animals (those with Willpower lower than the demesne's rating) will be attracted to a demesne when they encounter it. In a way, they fall in love with the place's vivid, expressive beauty. This is an Emotion effect. Others may share the opinion, but the demesne's energy has less supernatural sway over them.

Regardless of how they feel about a demesne, creatures that remain there for long feel its Essence soak through them. The effects are slow but unmistakable, as the Essence transforms their flesh and minds to match its own character. Although the resulting changes are fundamentally different from Wyld mutations, Storytellers may use mutations from **Exalted**, page 288, to emulate them. (See also **The Compass of Celestial Directions, Vol. II—The Wyld**, and **The Manual of Exalted Power—The Lunars** for more Wyld mutations.)

For every year a creature spends largely in a demesne, it gains one negative point and two positive points for mutations until (demesne's rating) years have passed—by then, it's reworked the creature's substance as much as it can. Poxes and deficiencies have a value of one point; afflictions/debilities, two points; blights/deformities, four points; abominations,

six positive points. Demesnes cannot mutate Essence-wielders, but mortals are forever remade.

Characters exposed to demesnes don't become addicted the way the Wyld-tainted do. Demesnes enthrall mortal creatures, but do not twist their souls in the manner of the Wyld. Creatures altered by demesnes also still survive in the rest of Creation, no matter how severely mutated they become. Whether they find the rest of Creation comfortable or wish to leave home is another matter. A woman of sunbeams, no longer requiring food or sleep, has little to discuss with the rest of humanity.

Objects left in demesnes are influenced, too. A God-Blooded hero of the Age of Splendor famously bore a hollow ebony daiklave carved with ever-burning runes. It was jade before he lost it for 20 years in a Southeastern demesne. The reshaped daiklave proved able to fill itself with fire that burned everything but living things—even marble, or clouds.

Essence Buildup

Cutting down fruit-bearing trees, blocking a lava flow, or other specific events might stop up a demesne's outlet. This is never good. The Essence builds up until it breaks loose in a tremendous explosion of mystical force. A powerful demesne's explosion can lay waste to a large area.

One scene after Essence buildup begins, a (Perception + Occult) roll, difficulty 3, will detect it; attuned characters notice automatically. Geomantic instruments can also warn of the coming eruption. The amount of time the place then has before it explodes in a vast rainbow of Essence is inversely proportional to its rating:

Demesne/Manse Rating	Time
1	Five months
2	Five weeks
3	Five days
4	Five hours
5	One scene
N/A	Five minutes
	Be somewhere else

At that point, everyone within (demesne's rating) miles takes (demesne's rating x 5) dice of aggravated damage from blazing Essence discharges. Players should make ([Dexterity or Wits] + Dodge) rolls for their characters to avoid splintering debris and Essence-lightning; each success reduces damage by one level. Armor soaks this damage normally, as well. Objects suffer double damage.

The demesne's power level then drops by one dot. The demesne is still damaged, though, and may erupt again five ticks later. The Storyteller rolls one die and adds the demesne's new rating: if the result is 6 or less, the explosion relieved the geomantic strain. If the result is 7 or more, the demesne sends out another blast, albeit at its new, reduced rating. This continues until the demesne stabilizes or destroys itself.

An exploding manse produces a partially contained explosion, but that makes the blast more intense. Add five dice to the damage, but reduce the area to (manse's rating x 100) yards. The remains of such a manse might be salvageable—it should be treated as a manse that has suffered Power Failure (see p. 62). Of course, the underlying demesne has lost power, too. In most cases, though, the whole place is destroyed.

On top of all this, everyone exposed to the explosion of Essence might be mutated. For each character, roll their (Willpower + Essence) at a difficulty of the demesne or manse's rating. On a success, the character resists the transform-ing Essence. On a failure, the character gains a pox. A botch inflicts a deficiency. Roll for each time the demesne explodes and bathes the character in Essence, and count up the total points of positive and negative mutation: two poxes might be replaced by one afflic-tion, or four deficiencies by a deformity.

DESTROYING A DEMESNE: THE OPEN-EYED DIVE MEDITATION

The Essence running through demesnes makes them hard to damage: natural events hardly ever trigger Essence buildup, for even the devastation of a flood or tornado tends to follow the existing Essence currents. Demesnes usually explode because of human action—accidentally or on purpose.

This Soul Sea Meditation reveals how to disrupt a demesne's heart. The character touches everything within, sensing the Essence patterns, until she finds the fracture points where she can inflict geomantic dam-age. The player rolls (Perception + Lore + Geomancy Degree), difficulty 3. The meditation does not grant the power to initiate that destruction, though—the character must do that herself. Botching inflicts a -1 internal penalty to mental rolls for the rest of the day,

as stray Essence bounces around distractingly inside the character's mind.

Once a character locates geomantic stress points, attacking each nexus involves an extended (Intelligence + Occult + character's Geomancy Degree) roll at difficulty 3. Each roll represents one man-week of work at sabotage. Essence buildup begins when the player accumulates (5 + [demesne rating x 5]) successes: it's *hard* to affect powerful demesnes, though they explode quickly thereafter. More than one person can engage in geomantic sabotage, working at a single character's direction.

A capped demesne becomes immune to simple geomantic sabotage. The flows of Essence are too tightly bound to the manse or stabilized by special artifacts called capstones (see p. 58). A manse, however, can suffer its own sort of geomantic sabotage. A capped demesne can also still be pushed to Essence buildup through the slower processes of large-scale geomantic engineering, described later in the chapter.

REPAIRING DEMESNES

Just as sabotaging a demesne takes a lot of work, so does repairing one. Once Essence buildup begins, there are two ways to stop it. The first is to cap the demesne, using the same capstones involved in manse construction. See page 58 for how to use capstones. Within a year, the demesne's Essence will stabilize into a new configuration… but the demesne's power drops by one dot anyway.

The other way is to repair the geomantic damage directly: replant trees, return a stream to its former course, and so on. This requires use of the Open-Eyed Dive Meditation to analyze the damage, then (Intelligence + Occult + character's Geomancy Degree) rolls at difficulty 3 for each man-week of work. The demesne is mended when the total successes exceed the number accumulated by the character who attacked the demesne.

CHANGING THE FACE OF CREATION: DEMESNE ENGINEERING

In the First Age, the Exalted knew how to create demesnes. That knowledge survives, but the geomantic processes demand a controlled environment, a huge amount of work, and a great deal of time—and aren't safe or reliable. Today, those who can do it don't bother, for even if they wanted demesnes badly enough to invest the years and labor, the chance of ruining swaths of the landscape restrain even Dynastic hubris. The Realm outright forbids very little… but the permit

processes for major geomantic engineering can take longer than the engineering itself. (See **The Compass of Celestial Directions, Vol. I—The Blessed Isle** and **The Manual of Exalted Power—The Dragon-Blooded** for insights into the Realm's bureaucracy.)

FINDING A LOCATION

To draw a new demesne from a plot of land, its geomantic potential must first be determined. Most places are of normal potential (0 potential rating)—they're aligned with several elements, their natural Essence isn't monopolized by anything nearby, and they aren't especially well-positioned. Some, however, are more likely spots: they might have mountains that could reflect and contain Essence, or rivers that could circulate it. These are aligned with one primary element, have a positive potential rating and can be forged into demesnes right away.

Geomantic surveying techniques can analyze the land's tendencies, finding demesnes or areas of high potential. A character needs some knowledge of geomancy to do this—at least an Initiate degree in the Art of Geomancy (see Chapter Three) or an Occult specialty in geomancy.

As the character surveys a region, her player makes an extended (Intelligence + Occult + character's Geomancy Degree) roll, difficulty 2. This roll takes an external penalty of at least -1 for every condition the character sets to her search. For example, "It must be Fire-aspected" might inflict a penalty of -1 in the desert but -5 in the Western islands. "It should be easily defensible" normally inflicts a -2 penalty, and the character needs at least War 2. The number of successes required equals (rating desired^2); each roll takes one month if searching for a demesne, two if only seeking an area of potential. With demesnes of rating 2+, the odds are high that something else has already claimed it. Modern geomancers, who don't wish to take the trouble to create new demesnes, often travel with troops.

A character who is very lucky might find a latent demesne. Dragon lines already cross there, or other features of the landscape concentrate Essence. In this case, the character only has to perform some special action to awaken the demesne. See "Activating Potential," page 53, for ways to do this. More likely, the character just finds a spot that has, so to speak, potential for potential. The local geomancy has aspects that could contribute to a demesne, but lacks other important elements.

CHANGING THE LANDSCAPE

An ambitious geomancer needs Lore and Occult scores equal to (demesne's desired rating + 3) to hope to create a new demesne. Thus, a savant with Occult 5 and Lore 5 might design a level 2 demesne, but not one of level 3. The Geomancy specialty counts toward these scores (hence, 3 Occult with a +2 in Geomancy is effectively 5). Fools who attempt large-scale geomantic manipulations beyond their competence may merely waste time, but could render the land sterile, reduce the lifespans of everyone living there, tear all joy from the air, or lay another local curse. Geomantic curses last indefinitely, so the Realm (and most other states) is very cautious about letting people try to create demesnes.

The geomancer raises the demesne's potential one level at a time—from 0 to 1, 1 to 2, and so on. If her survey succeeds, she not only finds a suitable location, she has a good idea what must be done to concentrate the flows of Essence. She'll need to undertake a number of specific, major local changes equal to the potential demesne's new rating. Calling these changes "major" is not an understatement: each one requires a year's effort. Examples of such undertakings include leveling a mountain, hollowing out a lake, committing genocide or spreading a new religion. Such labors involve a yearly Resources 5 expenditure for labor, materials and tools. Each alteration incorporates at least three associations with the demesne's aspect (see the Associations sidebar). The undertakings must also be precise: Every year, the character engages in another geomantic survey to make sure the land's Essence changes as intended.

For the player, creating a demesne calls for an extended (Intelligence + Occult + Geomancy Degree) roll against a difficulty of ([the level to which it'll be raised] + 2). The Storyteller makes this roll and keeps the results secret from the geomancer's player. A failure means a year of wasted effort. A botch means that the character thinks she's progressing—and is actually harming the world, inflicting some curse on the area that can only be repaired by spending a year unmaking previous work, then starting over from scratch. A character who tries to raise a demesne's power beyond her competence cannot do so… but the Storyteller rolls anyway, because botches and geomantic curses remain possible. The geomantic restructuring is complete when the extended roll accumulates ([demesne's next level] x 10) successes. After that, the character can activate the demesne, or begin another years-long effort to raise its potential still higher.

If the geomancer wants to bring out a demesne with an aspect other than the land's most obvious character, add 1 to the difficulty of her roll; if she seeks an aspect that currently hasn't any local influence, add 3. Thus, creating an Earth demesne from land dominated by Fire with Air and Earth overtones adds 1, but creating a Sidereal demesne from Fire land without a trace of star-Essence adds 3. Creating a Celestial demesne usually requires working from secondary aspects; locations that naturally concentrate Celestial Essence are incredibly rare.

ACTIVATING POTENTIAL: THE RITUAL OF IRRIGATION

Places with positive geomantic potential just need a sudden shock or burst of energy to become demesnes. Their Essence is like a river flowing behind a rock wall: punching through the wall releases a great rush. The Ritual of Irrigation sets the currents of Essence coiling in on themselves like dancing dragons, drawing in Creation's power, until they stabilize as a new demesne.

The ritual is a simple meditation at the latent demesne's geomantic heart. A character spends (demesne's rating) hours feeling the currents to Essence. When she knows and touches them all, she links them to herself by simultaneously flooding them with (rating x 20) motes of Essence. The Storyteller then rolls the character's (Intelligence + Lore + Geomancy Degree) at a difficulty of (demesne's new rating). Success means the demesne activates. A botch means Essence buildup begins.

If a single character lacks the Essence to activate the demesne, multiple characters can perform the Ritual of Irrigation and contribute Essence. However, the Storyteller must roll for each character, and every

roll must succeed for the demesne to activate. Any botch triggers Essence buildup.

ALTERING DEMESNES

Most geomancers never create demesnes. Indeed, some mystics call it a violent, unnatural tampering with Creation. Many geomancers, however, alter them, and not just with manse construction. The aspect of a demesne can be shifted, perhaps for a certain resource or to better serve a god, or an existing demesne can be strengthened.

Altering a demesne uses the same dice pool and time scale as creating a demesne from scratch. However, the difficulty of the extended roll and the accumulated number of successes are based on the demesne's current rating. Strengthening an existing demesne also uses the same dice system as strengthening a latent demesne, with the roll's difficulty and required number of successes based on the new rating. In this case, however, a botched roll causes Essence buildup and detonation instead of a geomantic curse.

Altering a demesne involves subtler processes than the massive labors involved in their creation. The geomantic engineer has her labor force perform chants and rituals, as well as small-scale works such as building large granite walls or moving trees.

A potent source of the desired type of Essence could also used to adjust the demesne's aspect. Examples include an artifact with a rating that equals or exceeds the demesne's level, or sorcery whose effects match the associations of the desired aspect. For instance, frequent casting of Stormwind Rider could help nudge a demesne's aspect toward Air. An Exalt with a permanent Essence at least equal to the demesne's rating could also speed the conversion through weekly deeds in line with the intended aspect. For instance, a deathknight could devour blood and souls to speed a demesne's conversion to Abyssal aspect; a Solar could hold court to arbitrate disputes and try criminals; or a Fire Aspect could burn every mote of his Essence through his anima at geomantically propitious places.

The Storyteller gives extra successes for each year of such Exalted activities. A simple, easily conducted action (such as the Solar's court, the Fire Aspect's anima burn-through or an Emerald Circle spell) conducted monthly contributes one success. An easy, weekly activity or a more difficult monthly activity (such as ritual sacrifice of a dozen people or casting a Sapphire Circle spell) is worth two successes. This could reach up to five successes, for an incredible activity repeated at least weekly, such as a Solar Circle spell, sprinkling the entire demesne with powdered jade, or dozens of Terrestrial Exalted burning through their Essence pools at once.

Spirits associated with the area and elementals of either the current or desired element automatically understand the alterations. They may work against the project: spirits, shaped by their domains, may not wish to become what the geomancer envisions, and elementals sometimes object to finding a new home. On the other hand, some could be pleased: a forest spirit rarely objects to more trees. Helpful spirits add one success per year, or two if at least one god or elemental has a higher Essence than the demesne's rating.

Bonus successes come *in addition to* the roll for each year of effort. They do not replace it, or render botching impossible.

Altering a demesne's aspect or strength ruins plans to cap it with a manse. The desired manse must be rebuilt too, to match the demesne's new aspect or strength.

REDUCING A DEMESNE

In a few occasions, geomancers have deliberately weakened a demesne. This involves the same geomantic engineering as creating or altering a demesne, but the difficulty and accumulated successes are based on the new, reduced rating of the demesne. Botching causes Essence buildup if the demesne isn't capped.

Why do such a thing? The annals of the Shogunate say the Dragon-Blooded used geomantic engineering to destroy a powerful Anathema who retreated to an invincible fortress-manse. They could not penetrate the manse, so they spent years wrecking the demesne, eventually forcing the cornered tyrant to emerge and fight for her life.

GEOMANTIC ARTIFACTS

Powerful, landscape-altering artifacts such as the singing staff (see **Exalted**, p. 392) and the grimcleaver called Death at the Root (see p. 42) can ease geomantic engineering. A character with a singing staff can perform geomantic engineering without the expense of a labor force (though it still takes years), and a week's worth of geomantic sabotage in a single day. Death at the Root affects Essence-currents directly. It achieves the same results as a year of geomantic engineering in a month, and a week's worth of geomantic sabotage in a single *scene*.

Yes, that's powerful. That's why they're rated Artifact 4 and 5.

PLACES OF POWER

A demesne might be nothing more than an oddly colored forest pool that local peasants avoid—or as drastic as an unbridgeable chasm blocking travel for miles. Parents could warn their children away from demesnes as deadly—or as holy ground. Travelers seek demesnes for healing vapors and magical commodities. Whole communities live in demesnes, with all the strangeness that entails, and stories spread to cities miles away. These are just ways mortals might see demesnes; for Essence-wielders, they're far more. A powerful demesne is a fight waiting to happen, and many an epic's been spun of the blazing battles fought by heroes for their land.

THE VALLEY OF BLUE MENHIRS

EARTH DEMESNE •

Perhaps the winds howling through this cold valley carry Essence of Air, for echoes refract unnaturally among its standing stones. A whisper from one end can be audible at the other, if the listener stood at a point with the proper acoustics. Those who know the place can easily find quiet corners, and often, in hushed tones, they'll point out to strangers that the menhirs are warm to the touch.

The few mortals who live among the menhirs grow taller, with a faint blue duskiness to their features. When they die, their bodies remain upright, loom larger and larger, and eventually calcify into gray-blue stone. Attuned characters also turn to rock if they die in the demesne, but in the meantime, their breath eases, centering their physical Essences.

Game Effects: After a year, mortals gain the poxes Skin Color (blue-gray) and Large, and the deficiency Atrophy (Wits) (see **Exalted,** p. 288). Attuned characters gain three dice to Resistance rolls while in the demesne, but become slow to act, losing a die on Wits rolls.

The Valley's Essence token consists of echoes, which attuned characters gather in their throats by calling low notes through the place; as they keep their mouths open, the echoes return and settle in their throats. For the following day, everything they say will echo. Botching the harvest renders them mute for a day.

RAGARA ANYA'S WHITE MULBERRY GROVE

WOOD DEMESNE •••

Warm and softly-scented, suffering the gentlest of rains and lightest of breezes, House Ragara's legendary mulberry grove was only claimed within the past two centuries. It's cared for by Ragara Anya, a plain, timid Dragon-Blood who seldom visits home. Middle-aged Anya found the grove herself on a long-ago retreat, and though she's happy to discharge her filial obligations by living there, she sometimes wishes the land weren't *quite* so valuable.

The grove's spare Essence grows into the mulberry leaves year-round, coloring them a disconcerting ivory. Tiny silkworms feed on them, and once a month, the resultant silk—also produced year-round—takes on an odd sheen. It's spun and sent on its way hastily, for the Essence bleeds out fast; but, arriving on time, infused Ragara silk commands an absurd price. Silken armor, style-changing clothing and other artifacts across Creation are sewn from the coveted textile.

Anya is required to oversee production on the looms outside the grove, a job she doesn't mind, and to meet with Ragara representatives to discuss policy, a duty she loathes. Once in a while, factions within House Ragara demand that the grove be surveyed for a manse. So far, economics and Anya have defeated them, but she loves her white mulberries, and grows more uneasy every time the idea's brought up. She suspects (correctly) that she's no match for the adept bureaucrats at home. Moreover, aside from internal House politics, Anya must be wary of local forces. The grove is far from its owners, and native governments eye it with increasing avarice—particularly in these troubled times, when Ragara needs troops elsewhere.

By strict order of the House, only Anya may live in the grove.

Game Effects: Mortals have never lived in the Grove, so its warping effects are unknown; the silkworms, its only fauna, show no physical changes. Ragara Anya's attunement whitens her skin and slows her aging (half normal rate; at three centuries, she looks only late middle-aged). She must take care with the silkworms, however, for they (and other herbivores) find her deliciously edible.

The Grove's Essence harvest takes the form of pale mulberry leaves, which can be plucked by hand if you can find the right ones. Over the next three days, they'll turn green, and then wither. Botching the harvest poisons the gatherer like a dose of coral snake venom (see **Exalted**, page 131).

The silk from the Grove is equal to that from Essence spiders (see Chapter Four). However, it loses its magic and becomes ordinary silk if it is not woven into an artifact and properly treated within one month.

XOLOTL, THE STAR GARDEN
SIDEREAL DEMESNE ••••

As the Maiden of Serenity spreads her constellations above, Xolotl lights the night. At high noon, Xolotl is dim—but at midnight, its neatly twining vines and perfect ranks of trees glow faintly blue against the blackness. Points of light fall slowly from the leaves, vanishing before they reach the ground, and nostalgia hangs in garlands from each branch. On the rare occasions that nostalgia has been harvested, the gatherers wept stars as they did it.

The Essence of Xolotl warps its residents into monsters who shun daylight. It strips the hair from animals and reverses their feet. Men become fleshless skeletons, or gain the heads of beasts. Still, those twisted by Xolotl are also lucky. When outsiders would die, these misbegotten things barely survive.

A man who attunes Xolotl won't physically change, but the nostalgia draped over the garden will flood him in a crippling wave. He forgets, for a time, whether he lives now or in episodes of his past; and can lose himself in his memories whenever he chooses.

Game Effects: Four years in Xolotl gives mortals the Ugly deficiency (see **Exalted**, p. 288) and three points of other negative physical mutations that the Storyteller chooses anew for each character. It gives them warped destiny as a blight: they are likely to meet misfortune, but their players can add four dice to any roll needed for the character to survive (if only just barely).

The Garden's Essence harvest is the nostalgia, and attuned characters gather it by considering lost people and joys. When they weep a star, they can catch it in a crystal phial. For four days afterward, they'll be heartsick for faces, feelings and places long forgotten. Botching the harvest loses them three cherished memories for a month.

THE BRIGHT PLATEAU
SOLAR DEMESNE •••••

High above a scrubby desert stretches a shining, empty plateau. Sunlight falls like a benediction on nothing but gold sand and the white and yellow jewels scattered thickly among the grains. Travelers who stumbled upon it and whooped with joy at their fortune have wept when, days later, the riches stuffed into their packs have melted away.

People who camp on the plateau soon feel lighter and stronger. Their passions remain intense as ever, but they find themselves gentler in expressing them. Once fascinated by the riches all around, they now feel merely aesthetic appreciation. If they have companions, they wonder how they could have missed their beauty: smiles seem whiter, eyes brighter, limbs straighter.

Eventually, they may need to leave for provisions or to continue on their journey. After all, the Bright Plateau is not a famous destination in itself. Still, most visitors come back again. The rest of the world dims in comparison, and they can't deny that the time there was good for them. Returning to the Plateau, they eat and speak less and less, contemplating the virtuous life as they bask in the sun's warmth.

Soon, their vision has become rarefied enough to see the golden silhouettes of animals, plants—even people. Not long after that, they join the others who have become sunlight.

Game Effects: Anything mortal that stays for five years gains an affliction that raises Appearance and Charisma by one, and another that raises Temperance by one. The creature also becomes an abomination of sunlight: it loses its voice, its body, and the need for food and sleep, and nothing but orichalcum and other sunlight-creatures can physically interact with it. Essence sight spots it, but otherwise it's invisible and dematerialized unless it enters shadow. The Mood Swings deficiency makes the creature unwilling to take initiative; the Atrophy deficiency, taken twice, reduces its Perception by two (minimum 1) when it tries to see anything but sunbeams or orichalcum; and the Diet debility gives it a dependence on sunlight (see **Exalted**, pp. 288-289).

Attunement to the Plateau grants +2 Appearance, +1 Strength, and +1 to every Virtue save Temperance, which gains +3. These bonuses can raise traits above 5. It also renders the attuned excessively philosophical and uninterested in action; they can no longer channel Willpower through any Virtue except Temperance.

The Plateau's Essence harvest is the gold and gems, which can be picked up by hand, but fade into nothing after five days. Botching the harvest makes them flare sun-bright, inflicting a terrible full-body sunburn for five levels of lethal damage (soaked naturally).

MANSES

Despite the name, manses are not always mansions and palaces. Any structure built to channel a demesne's Essence is a manse. Manses have included cathedrals, bridges, arenas, and in one famous case, a silk web woven among seven trees. Sometimes, a single room in a given building will be a manse; sometimes, many buildings complete one. Portions of the surrounding environment may also be an intrinsic part of a manse's geomancy.

Manse architects have wide choices in what they build, but certain demesnes demand certain treatment. Materials and design elements must harmonize with a demesne's aspect. A talented geomancer may insert opposing influences, but she'll need to know her craft well, taking care to balance the conflicting symbols. The "Associations" sidebar (p. 48) gives examples of design elements and influences for each aspect.

It's a rare manse that has no function save producing a hearthstone and restoring Essence. Most manses demonstrate at least a few other magical features. A manse's shape and the powers it exhibits usually have to do with its demesne's nature; still, such qualities are complicated, and can often be expressed in several potential ways. Many an inexperienced manse-builder has been surprised by both the final structure and abilities of her own architecture.

DESIGN

The basic skills necessary for manse design allow a character to write blueprints, but without greater expertise, she'll make little of the power at her command. The basic roll to design a manse (as described on p. 133 of **Exalted**) will suffice for a manse that caps a demesne and generates a hearthstone—but nothing else. The builder has no control over the hearthstone's powers and cannot give the manse any special abilities.

If a character wants to channel a manse's Essence into a specific power, she needs Lore and Occult scores of at least (power's point value + 2). For each power she intends to design into the manse (including the generation of a specific hearthstone), her player rolls (Intelligence + [lowest of Occult or Lore]), difficulty of (power's point value + 3). Even if a manse's "power" is completely passive (such as being defensible as a fortress), the character still needs to harmonize the structures needed for channeling Essence with this other architectural purpose.

Failure indicates the character may only include the power if she also includes another power of equal point value, chosen by the Storyteller. A botch on this roll renders the power damaged and unfixable (see "Damaged Powers," p. 62). Certain powers also need certain forms of expertise, depending on their effects.

Manse powers, point values, extra requirements and so on are outlined beginning on page 63.

CONSTRUCTION

Building a manse usually starts with a temporary cap on the demesne. Without an effective cap, the demesne's Essence warps the mortal laborers. Capping, however, carries risks of its own.

A demesne is temporarily capped using five cap-stones placed on suitable geomantic points. These occult devices may look like man-sized pillars cut with deep and glowing runes, spiky openwork globes or other forms. All weigh a thousand pounds, are constructed as level 3 jade-alloy artifacts, and must be alloyed with the proper magical material to establish Celestial or Abyssal manses. Each set costs Resources 5.

The five stones must be perfectly placed, represented by a difficulty 1 (Perception + Lore) roll. Botching this roll causes Essence buildup at the demesne's full rating.

PARTIAL CAPPING

Geomancers who lack confidence in their ability to create powerful manses—such as those from the Realm, who just can't design greater powers—may decide to build a manse at a lower level than its demesne's rating. This is a safe and economical choice, but the demesne's Essence won't be fully contained. Such a manse is statted out as a manse of the level it was built at—for instance, a level 3 manse on a level 5 demesne starts with 6 Creation Points (see "Manses Point-By-Point," p. 63) and a three-dot hearthstone—and *must* be constructed with the one-point power Essence Vents (page 67).

A partially capped manse also leaks Essence into its surroundings. Mortals who cannot channel Essence suffer one point of mutation for every level by which the demesne's power exceeds the manse, just as if they lived in a demesne. Fortunately, a person has to live in the manse 10 years before they suffer this effect. In the Realm, which has no choice but to partially cap a significant number of demesnes, servants and unExalted family members never spend more than seven or eight years at a time in such manses. A year spent free of excessive Essence exposure flushes out the mutagenic force.

ASSEMBLING A TEAM

A single person with the necessary Abilities can design a manse. However, a single person cannot usually *build* a manse. Constructing such an occult edifice requires a labor force. A prudent manse-builder also recruits a team of experts to deal with the various complications and difficulties that arise when a large construction project intersects with arcane forces.

The laborers themselves must be skilled stone-masons, carpenters or whatever other Craft specialty the manse requires. Everyone who works on a manse needs a Craft score of at least (underlying demesne's rating - 2), minimum 1, for their work to adequately channel the powerful Essence. Stonemasons need Craft (Earth); a topiary manse calls for Craft (Wood); and so on.

This assumes the manse's architect stays on hand throughout the construction to oversee the workers and check the geomancy as the manse is built. If the designer wants to spend more than a month at a time away from the construction site, she needs to hire a professional architect with an appropriate Craft rating of 4 or better, and foremen equal to 10 percent of the labor force, with Craft Abilities at least 1 dot higher than the laborers.

Building a manse may upset the local small gods and elementals, who may interfere with construction. A spirit negotiator skilled in Bureaucracy, Socialize or other social skills, as well as Occult, can appease the local spirit courts.

Cuts in the supply of construction materials can doom a construction project. A professional supply manager and comptroller can make sure everything and everyone reaches the building site on time and—just as important—everyone gets paid.

BUILDING MATERIALS

A manse should be made from materials that harmonize with its aspect. For instance, a Fire-aspected manse must be made principally from materials that owe their origin to fire, or are associated with fire, such as lava rock, glass or forged metal. A Wood-aspected demesne should be made, obviously, of wood or at least contain lots of wood. The "Associations" sidebar suggests possible materials for manse construction.

A few materials have no aspect. Marble is especially useful for manse construction, since it is both an excellent architectural material and is unusually receptive to all forms of Essence.

Or Just Hire a Contractor

A few very remarkable companies offer to handle every aspect of manse construction, from initial design to supplying the furniture. The Realm has three such companies: the Unworthy Disciples of Honored Pasiap, the Workers of Materials Mundane and Susanta's Men of Worthy Labor. The highly specialized academy, the House of Well-Favored Aspect (see p. 82), trains geomancers in manse design and can direct would-be manse builders to qualified graduates. Lookshy has a corps of geomancer-architects too, but they work for the Seventh Legion. They don't work for anyone else unless the Lookshy government approves it and sees advantage for itself. Large, wealthy states and cities such as Nexus and Chiaroscuro have manse contractors of their own.

Hiring contractors does not increase or reduce the cost of building a manse. It just changes how a character spends the money.

Building Styles

The style of a manse also reflects its aspect. There are no hard-and-fast rules or styles; a skilled manse designer intuits the forms that resonate with a demesne's Essence. These are merely suggestions of styles designers might find appropriate. See also the list of demesne associations, and associations with the Aspect Abilities of the Dragon-Blooded aspects. Celestial manses might also emphasize Abilities, activities and associations of a particular caste.

Air: High ceilings, large windows and hallways, courtyards, towers, clear glass, thin doors or curtained doorways, flags and pennants, music, curving forms, open layout, arcane symbols.

Earth: Rectilinear forms, black or white stone, low ceilings, heavy stone construction, few windows, packed dirt floors, brick or adobe walls, manses partly sunk into hillsides, actual caves, stone statues, compact layout.

Fire: Red, orange or yellow stone or terracotta, angular linear or recurving forms, pointed arches and domes, forged metal, glass, many fireplaces, candles or torches, multiple floors, sweeping stairways, weapons.

Water: Pools and fountains, excellent indoor plumbing, blue, green or purple stone or glass, smoothly curved layout and ornaments, few doors, nautical or oceanic ornaments, martial arts training facilities.

Wood: Wooden construction, trees and gardens, potted plants, multi-storied layout, organic forms, wide angle, artwork of everyday life, small, comfortable chambers, archery motifs, performance spaces.

Abyssal: Underground construction, tombs and graves, poor lighting, stagnant water, torture chambers, prisons, black stone or ironwork, bare chambers, secret passages, masks, bone and ivory ornament.

Lunar: Irregular, crescent or circular forms and layout, optical and architectural illusions, completely natural materials, mirrors, silver accents, shifting ornament, hunting trophies, animal forms.

Sidereal: Courtyards, skylights, rooftop observatories and amenities, shrines, secret passages and chambers, scientific instruments, macramé and netted ornament, star maps, complex geometric forms.

Solar: Tall buildings, towers, pyramids, large windows and skylights, domes with lanterns, white and yellow stone or tilework, golden ornaments, depictions of battle, rulership or worship, thrones, processional aisles.

Sorcerous Construction

Practitioners of Celestial Sorcery can learn a spell, Raise the Puissant Sanctum, that raises a manse from a demesne in a matter of days. (See **The White Treatise**, p. 79, for this spell.) The spell does not strictly require a design roll. Conjuring a manse that people can live in, however, calls for a normal design roll; so does giving the manse any preselected power or selecting its hearthstone. At the Storyteller's option, undesigned manses raised through this spell may have a full complement of points and powers, but the Storyteller selects them. The manse also gains extra design points for its lack of mundane amenities.

Shadow Manse

Last but not least, Essence-wielders involved in the process may take a month, Resources equal to the monthly cost of construction, and an (Intelligence + Craft [Earth]) roll to build a manse's occult shell, shaping Essence enough to produce a "shadow." The shell is built of enchanted paper specially made for the purpose, in a bamboo frame: both paper and bamboo are such neutral materials that they can't disturb the geomancy. The shadow manse fades into being over several days, and looks like a dark, translucent

version of the manse-to-be, its surfaces shimmering in key places, with sparks of color drifting through the immaterial walls.

An Essence-channeler can attune to the shadow manse. Attunement gives a character no Essence or hearthstone, but grants perception of its Essence flows: she'll automatically perceive Essence buildup as soon as it begins. Moreover, this shadow manse cancels a single 1 from any roll for redesigning or repairing a manse in the course of construction. On the other hand, the shadow manse itself is utterly fragile. If it takes even a single level of damage—treat the bamboo and paper as having 3L/6B soak thanks to the Essence running through it—the shadow manse collapses and Essence buildup begins. Prudent builders keep a duplicate frame handy, though they face a race against time to restore the shadow manse before the demesne erupts.

The Hearthroom

The most important part of the manse is its hearthroom, where Essence converges and crystallizes into a hearthstone. Despite its name, the hearthroom isn't always a room: for instance, the "hearthroom" of a manse that consists of stone pillars might consist of a large stone block with two intersecting shafts carved through it. In every case, however, the geometry of the hearthroom clearly converges on the spot where the hearthstone forms. That spot holds a plate, cup or container made of a magical material that performs the final concentration. The magical material usually resonates with the manse's aspect but the architect has some flexibility here: jade or starmetal usually work for any manse; moonsilver has an affinity for Air and Water, while orichalcum does not conflict with Fire. Soulsteel, however, can only be used in Abyssal manses.

Some architects rely exclusively on geometry and perspective to create the focus of a hearthroom. More often, though, architects use ornament to direct Essence and the eye. The simplest way is just to carve lines or chevrons pointing at the focus. Artwork can also define the focus; such as statues that all point toward the hearthstone plate, or murals whose composition draws the eye in that direction. Artwork also helps shape the powers of the resulting hearthstone. The structure and architectural ornament of the entire manse help tune the Essence to a particular goal, but the ornament in the hearthroom always gives a strong suggestion of the hearthstone's power—at least to a character whose player succeeds at an (Intelligence + [lowest of Lore or Occult]) roll. If the hearthroom lacks such ornament, either the designer didn't care what power the hearthstone had, or he was subtle and skilled enough to diffuse the Essence-tuning elements throughout the manse. In the latter case, the roll's difficulty rises to 3 and a character must complete a detailed study of the entire manse.

What Could Possibly Go Wrong?

If manse construction were simply a matter of time, money and materials, it would be pretty dull. Manse builders *pray* for dull. Their prayers are seldom answered… and thereby hang stories.

Geomantic Accidents

Any number of things could shift the local dragon lines. A flood or earthquake could change the landscape. Barbarian marauders could destroy another manse nearby. The builder has a choice. He can redesign the manse and every intended power (with a new set of dice rolls) to make allowances for the change. Or, he can try to produce some counterbalancing change in the landscape to restore the geomantic balance. Building a manse is slow enough that the character has a year to follow the latter course. The Storyteller makes the same roll for altering geomancy as used in demesne creation.

Changing the geomancy or the manse design in the middle of manse construction carries special risks, though. If a design roll fails, the associated power definitely comes out damaged. A botch triggers Essence buildup in the demesne. A failed geomantic engineering roll also causes Essence buildup.

Irate Locals

Do the people nearby want a new manse? If they don't, they can sabotage construction. Mortal locals can set fires, steal tools and building materials, topple capstones or threaten the workforce. If they have a geomancer of their own, they can attempt geomantic sabotage—attacking the Essence stress-points in the demesne, causing Essence buildup.

Fortunately, most remaining uncapped demesnes are usually in undeveloped wilderness, so powerful governments are then far enough away not to be an issue. Barbarians who try to interfere are dealt with by means of legends planted to make them fear and shun the area, small trinkets such as glass beads, or wholesale slaughter by mercenaries.

Local spirits can cause worse problems. They can shift Essence flows just by changing where they live. Any deity whose domain interacts with the emerging manse, or any local elemental of the same aspect as the manse, can anonymously interfere with its construction automatically as long as it has an Essence score of 3+.

Most geomancers bring in specialists: negotiators who've made a study of dealing with little gods. They spend their time visiting each spirit, making friends with some by offering favors, small sacrifices and magical gifts. Learning the politics of the local courts, they play factions against each other. A court's two viziers, for instance, might be solidly against human incursions into the demesne, but the majority of the courtiers might think it fun and interesting. In that case, the negotiator might arrange deals between the viziers and their lessers that cost the manse-builders nothing—or gain the ear of the court's leader and oust the viziers.

Spirit-negotiators who decide in the end that nothing will satisfy those interests can advise their clients of simple workarounds. The builder might distract the spirits from the demesne, such as by convincing local worshipers to follow different gods, thereby forcing them to manifest miracles and other efforts to bring them back into the fold. Perhaps the builder can use materials or wards that temporarily block elementals from the area. If a character doesn't hire a professional negotiator, he must do it himself. Powerful Exalts may be able to bully spirits into compliance, but even a Solar Circle might prefer to treat this as an exercise in diplomacy.

Supplies and Labor Issues

Other potential problems include supplies: teams in the wild require food and amenities from civilization. Materials also need shipping in. A designer may not be able to get around a necessity for obscure and valuable things: Chiaroscuro glass for special windows; rare flowers and spices to scent the air just so; furniture of platinum, or malachite, or upholstered in a brocade woven only in Tuchara.

Personnel problems can interfere with manse construction, too. Team members could quit, competing manse-builders could sabotage the project, or outside funding could suddenly be withdrawn. Many lonely sites bear the shattered ruin of a partially built manse, abandoned and allowed to blow to pieces.

Damage

A completed manse becomes exceptionally sturdy—sometimes uncannily so—thanks to the Essence running through it. A normal manse has an external soak of 12L/18B, and 6L/12B internally. A manse of living trees can be quite as sturdy as a manse of granite, too. Manses resist normal weathering and wear: wood doesn't rot, foundations don't settle, pipes

don't rust. The wild places of Creation hold many manses lost for centuries—even since the Usurpation—that remain intact, just waiting for someone to claim them. Other manses have easily held hundreds of residents for centuries at a time.

Nevertheless, manses can come to harm. Sufficient physical force, such as trees falling on them or Essence cannon fire, can still damage them. Other manses are physically fragile, or need constant maintenance to preserve their power. Worst of all, manses can come under geomantic attack: damaging select small portions of them can derange their energies, causing far greater physical damage or even sparking Essence buildup.

Vulnerabilities vary from manse to manse—vines twining around the doorframe could be necessary to a Wood-aspected manse carved into a tree, but irrelevant to an Earth-aspected copper palace. The Open-Eyed Dive Meditation (see pp. 51-52) reveals the geomantic stress-points in a manse. So will a careful geomantic survey. Once a character finds a geomantic stress point, she may attack it directly. This multiplies the damage done by the number of successes her player scored in the geomantic examination. The roll's difficulty does *not* reduce the number of successes for this purpose: if a person can find a weakness at all, any attack that penetrates the manse's soak will have terrible results. Thus, if an Exalt performed the Open-Eyed Dive Meditation and her player rolled five successes to recognize the importance of a Wood manse's vines, her attack that inflicts six levels of damage after soak would inflict 30 total levels on the manse. Any geomantic weak point can be the target of only one such attack, since the damage shifts the Essence flows to make that no longer a critical location.

The hearthroom is always a geomantic stress point. Any attack on the manse in this spot multiplies the levels of damage by five. For this reason, hearthrooms are usually strongly built and carefully guarded.

POWER FAILURE

Like any inanimate structure, a manse can endure a certain number of health levels before it counts as damaged (see **Exalted**, pp. 153-154). Once a manse suffers (rating x 20) points of harm, it counts as damaged and Power Failure occurs. For all Essence-related purposes, the manse loses one level. Its Essence-fueled powers weaken, attunement provides fewer motes per hour, and the hearthstone ceases functioning entirely. The hearthstone itself becomes brittle and vulnerable: simply dropping it can break it. Power Failure can happen more than once—until a manse reaches level 0.

At that point, its hearthstone shatters, all its Essence-fueled powers shut down, attunements are lost, and Essence buildup commences at its demesne's rating. The manse is utterly destroyed at that point.

While a manse is damaged to a certain rating, Essence-fueled powers that relied on its rating being one point higher become damaged (see below); those relying on its rating being 2+ points higher stop functioning completely. If a given Power Failure affects none of its powers, the Storyteller chooses one to become damaged. (Some powers are not Essence-fueled, but a quality of the manse's construction. The Storyteller is the final authority on which ones.)

On top of this, the manse's rating has dropped below the rating of its demesne (if it wasn't already). That makes it a partially capped manse. Superfluous Essence *must* go into Essence Vents (a 1-point power)—but the power is damaged, so the venting happens uncontrollably inside the manse, as an extra danger to anyone inside. The vents do not inflict further damage to the manse itself, though.

Every time Power Failure sets in, the Storyteller rolls one die. If it comes up lower than the number of levels lost to Power Failure, Essence buildup commences. Power Failure definitely happens when the manse's rating drops to 0.

DAMAGED POWERS

When powers are damaged, the geomantic architecture shaping them has become flawed and unreliable. They still fulfill their function, but not the way they should. For instance, Puzzle Manse (a 2-point power) rearranges its manse's rooms on a set schedule, but if it were damaged, it might randomly rearrange them. Sentient (a 5-point power) denotes a manse with its own mind and personality; if damaged, it could go mad and start killing its residents. Damaged manses with Password Activations (a 1-point power) might trade passwords among their functions, so a given password wouldn't do what the owner expected it to.

Specific powers can be targeted, if a character determines what components shape them. Rainbow Tabernacle (a 4-point power), for example, is constructed with gemstone insets to encourage sorcery. Characters whose players succeed on an Open-Eyed Dive Meditation roll could figure out that those decorations were important for a Rainbow Tabernacle and pry them from the walls, damaging the power. This is more difficult than just looking for a weak point, *any* weak point, to attack. The roll suffers an external penalty of 2 for characters who don't have a method of directly observing Essence, such as the Essence sight of certain armor or the Charm All-Encompassing Sorcerer's Sight (see **Exalted**, p. 222).

PATCH JOBS

If a manse's residents hurry, they can fix a damaged manse so failure does not become catastrophic. This requires a patch kit costing Resources 4. In addition to mundane implements such as mirrors, polyhedral blocks of rock crystal, lead foil and emblems of the five elements such as braziers, blocks of wood or bottles of water, the kit must include implements made from magical materials: bars and plates of jade-steel, wires of orichalcum or moonsilver, soulsteel spikes, and the like. To place these items so they redirect, stabilize and bleed off the manse's Essence, a character must meet the Ability requirements to design that manse. Her player then must succeed in a manse design roll at difficulty 3 for every level of power failure the manse has suffered: thus, if damage has reduced a four-dot manse to a two-dot manse, players must succeed at two rolls.

A patch job does not restore lost functions or reverse power failure. All it does is prevent Essence buildup and vents excess Essence harmlessly, buying time for complete repairs.

Fixing a damaged manse requires an extended Craft (Earth) roll to rebuild staircases, replace windows and tilework, and the like. The repair crew also needs a labor force with the same Craft (Earth) rating involved in building the manse. If the craftsman doesn't have access to the manse's blueprints or designer, he must have the Traits to design the manse in the first place. His player then attempts a normal design roll to fix it. Fortunately, the difficulty to fix a manse is one lower than the roll to design it, because most of the manse remains intact.

The expense also drops by one Resources dot, because most of the manse's structure still exists. For the same reason, repairs take half as long as building a manse from scratch, or 100 man-years of labor per level of power failure that must be reversed.

A manse reduced to 0 rating cannot be patched. At that point, only placing capstones on the geomantic centers of the underlying demesne can prevent Essence buildup and detonation.

MANSES POINT-BY-POINT

The number of Background dots a player pays for a manse is set by the power of the demesne it caps. The manse's power rating is also the most important measure of the manse's auxiliary powers. Some of

these abilities are magical; others are functions of the materials and design of the manse.

Apart from the Essence it supplies and its hearthstone, a manse's abilities are represented through Creation Points. These show how the manse's designer chose to allocate its mystical energies. Even if a manse's power has nothing to do with Essence, it still costs Creation Points: the designer sacrificed a degree of magical power to give the manse certain mundane qualities that were not geomantically optimum.

Creation Points are an out-of-game abstraction, like a character's Traits. They offer a framework for designing *player* manses, not all manses; a Storyteller who wishes to design a particularly powerful manse—perhaps the home of a Yozi, or the Imperial Manse itself—should feel free to give it as many points as she deems appropriate.

MANSES AND OTHER BACKGROUNDS

Other Backgrounds can prove useful when combined with Manse. Followers could staff a home. Familiars could guard it. Many options, such as guardians, are offered in this system, but players might not want to discount the flexibility offered by investing in separate Backgrounds.

SOURCES OF CREATION POINTS

A manse starts with (its rating x 2) Creation Points, which buy special qualities for the manse. The more Essence the designer has to play with, the greater and more diverse the powers its builder can design into it.

The usual geomantic architect designs a manse that people can live in, that's sturdy and doesn't require a lot of upkeep. Most builders also want the most powerful hearthstone they can manage. If a designer abandons these concerns and merely wants to control Essence as efficiently as possible, however, she can build a manse with greater power.

SACRIFICING HEARTHSTONE LEVELS

A manse will always produce a hearthstone in its geomantic center, the hearthroom. However, a talented geomancer can siphon off some of the Essence that would normally go to making a hearthstone, and channel it to other applications. A player who takes a hearthstone of a level lower than her manse's rating gains one Creation Point for every level she sacrifices; for instance, if she builds a four-dot manse

---

but only wants a two-dot hearthstone, she gains two Creation Points.

Reducing the hearthstone's power doesn't reduce the manse's rating. Thus, the aforementioned four-dot manse with a two-dot hearthstone is still a four-dot manse in every other way. People attuned to such a manse regain extra Essence, while inside, at the normal rate—in this case, 16 extra motes per hour. However, the hearthstone only grants its level of extra Essence, so a two-dot hearthstone—even for a four-dot manse—grants its bearer 4 extra motes per hour while away from the manse.

A hearthstone reduced to 0 still solidifies in the hearthroom. The manse will recognize whoever carries it as the hearthstone bearer. The stone can, if desired, be set into hearthstone sockets. However, the inert crystal grants no powers or extra Essence.

MAINTENANCE

This drawback represents how much upkeep a manse requires. Most manses are built solidly, by experts. They'll continue running perfectly to the end of time. Others were constructed by inexperienced geomancers who couldn't counterbalance their structural problems.

With still others, the builder did not consider maintenance a problem—she might have even considered it aesthetic. Because the occult design of a manse can have stranger flaws than those of mortal buildings, manse maintenance can take unexpected forms. One manse might require sacrifices at an altar, or that certain vows always be observed. Another might require that all the furniture be kept strictly in line with the walls, and lose power if anyone sloppily leaves a chair at the wrong angle.

The examples provided below give typical time intervals, time investments, and so on for each level of maintenance difficulty. They aren't automatically applied to every manse needing that scale of maintenance. Players should feel free to invent equally drastic forms of maintenance instead. Each dot of required Maintenance gives one Creation Point.

If a manse goes without upkeep, the processes keeping its Essence flows in line falter and eventually burst their channels. After the timespan (listed in parentheses) without maintenance, the manse suffers Power Failure (see p. 62). The manse *might* then stabilize… but the Storyteller subtracts the Maintenance rating from the result of the die roll to see if Essence buildup commences. Powerful manses with high Maintenance blow up *very* easily.

x   The manse requires no maintenance.

•   Every few months, the manse should be seen to, but the procedure can be accomplished in an hour by anyone with brief instructions on what to do. (One year)
Example: Altars to the Immaculate Dragons, where the hearthstone bearer performs a short rite at the start of the corresponding season.

••   The manse requires simple maintenance that can be accomplished by anyone with instructions, but takes a full day and must be performed once a month. (One season)
Example: Washing the manse in clean water on the night of the full moon.

•••   Complicated maintenance takes a full day and must be performed weekly either by an individual attuned to the manse, or by a technician with at least Occult 3, Lore 3, and Craft (Earth) 3. In sophisticated places such as a major city, it might be possible to hire such an expert for Resources 3. (One month)
Example: A temple requiring one silent and unwounded priest always dedicated to its service. Fresh flowers placed at five special locations in a palace.

••••   Every week, very complex maintenance must be performed for two days by the hearthstone bearer or a technician with at least Occult 3, Lore 3 and Craft (Earth) 4. Whoever does the work needs a team of assistants. In a very sophisticated locale such as Nexus, it might be possible to hire such an expert for Resources 3, or 4 if he has his own crew. Alternatively, less complicated maintenance is required daily, or incredibly demanding maintenance at a longer interval. (One week)
Examples: A factory-cathedral that devours an intelligent, Solar-aspected, live sacrifice every season. A living manse that requires frequent watering and pruning.

•••••   One scene of maintenance is essential every day, led by the hearthstone bearer or a technician with at least Occult 4, Lore 4, and Craft (Earth) 4; such experts are rare enough that they can name their price. The maintainer will need a 10-person team. (One day)
Examples: A palace where the servants tread out symbols of power as they go about their precisely timed, daily tasks. A tower that requires seven mortals singing at all times.

FRAGILITY

Most manses can suffer a fair amount of damage before they collapse, but some—made entirely of glass, for instance, or woven from living foliage—are more delicate. Each dot of Fragility gives two Creation Points.

Stronger manses may be purchased with the three-point Fortress power.

x   The manse has 12L/18B external soak, 6L/12B internal, and can take (rating x 20) points of damage before Power Failure.

•   The manse has 6L/9B external soak, 3L/6B internal, and can take (rating x 10) points of damage before Power Failure.
Examples: A web of silk steel strung between trees or spars. A glass palace.

••   The manse has no soak, and can take (rating x 5) points of damage before Power Failure.
Examples: A hedge maze. A multi-chambered tent of ordinary silk.

•••   The manse has no soak. Every successful attack causes Power Failure.
Examples: An array of mirrors, creating a manse of reflected light.

HABITABILITY

A design that people can live in, or at least move through without impediment, is not necessarily the design that channels Essence most efficiently. Sacrificing human concerns can net the builder extra Creation Points. Each dot of reduced Habitability gives one Creation Point.

Note that a manse's *location* does not affect its habitability. Just because a manse is inaccessible does not matter for purposes of Creation Points. Such locations offer advantages as well as drawbacks: a manse built atop a thousand-foot pillar, sunk in an ocean trench or buried beneath desert sands is bad because it's hard for the owner to reach, but good because it's hard for enemies to sabotage the manse.

x   The manse has all the zero-point amenities listed later in this chapter, or at least as many of them as the designer wants. It can become a comfortable home without much effort, or a temple, government office or other structure people use regularly.

•   Uncomfortable: The manse has no amenities, but at least it could provide shelter.
Examples: A mausoleum. A domed pavilion.

- •• Minimally Habitable: The manse makes no provision at all for people to live there. At best, you could camp in it.
  Examples: A circle of stone pillars. A grove of interwoven trees. A sculpted valley with shallow caves cut in the sides.
- ••• Uninhabitable: No one could possibly live in the manse, possibly because there's no inside to enter or its environment is utterly hostile.
  Examples: A giant statue. A network of incised and inlaid lines in a cliff face. A manse completely buried beneath desert sands.

Spending Points

Players spend manse Creation Points on the powers listed here, or on player-invented powers—but Storytellers should keep in mind that there are magics inferior manses just can't muster. Each power costs a certain number of points, and most powers can only be purchased for a manse whose rating equals or exceeds its point value.

Some listed powers are italicized; those are the exception. Such qualities aren't fed by the manse's Essence. Rather, they're a merit of the materials used in its construction, or were placed in the manse after it was built. Moonsilver wolves, for instance, could be created to guard any kind of manse. So, a player can't give a manse of rating 3 any powers costing 4 points or more unless they're italicized.

Different aspects of Essence work better for some powers than others. A power labeled "(Aspect) Favored" is considered to have a point value one lower when purchased for manses of that aspect. Thus, a player could give a Fire-aspected manse of rating 3 a 4-point power if the power were listed as Fire Favored, and it would cost 3 points, not 4. Other powers demand such specific kinds of Essence that it can *only* be purchased by the listed aspects. Such powers are labeled "Only (Aspect)" and cost the listed number of Creation Points, with no discount.

Finally, powers with listed Ability scores or other capabilities can only be built by an architect who meets those requirements. After all, no matter how skilled a geomancer is, she can't summon guardian demons if she never mastered sorcery. However, characters can always team up so one has the necessary manse design skills and the other has whatever other Abilities are needed. The aforementioned geomancer doesn't need to bind demons herself—she just needs to find someone who can. A player creating a manse to buy as a Background at character generation can ignore these requirements, unless her character built her own manse.

All powers only function within a manse's *range*: everything within its walls (or other bounds), as well as everything touching its walls, is considered in range, unless it's extended with a power.

Powers of a manse that partially caps a demesne function at the demesne's level rather than the manse's rating if their descriptions designate different effects for different manse or demesne ratings.

Zero-Point Powers

Every manse has these properties.

Attunement Recognition

Upon sensing them, the manse can tell who's attuned and who bears its hearthstone(s).

Basic Senses

If any other power's use requires the manse to target a creature, the manse has the senses to do so. Although it's possible to hide from a manse, it's not easy—even for magical beings. The difficulty to hide from a manse is (its rating), and dice pools to do so are reduced to 0 before Charm use. Immaterial beings disturb a manse's geomancy as much as material ones, so manses can sense them too. (Whether the manse can affect such creatures is another matter.)

Cosmetic Displays

Manses often manifest useless aesthetic effects, such as color-shifting walls or mirrors that reflect backward.

One-Point Powers

Comfort Zone

The manse moderates its internal environment for the comfort of residents, such as staying cool in the Far Southern desert, heating itself in the Far North, or maintaining breathable air despite being underwater. Alternatively, the manse adapts the inhabitants to suit its environment. The manse may be carved of ice or underwater, but everyone who enters finds it comfortable.

By taking this power twice, the manse maintains a Comfort Zone despite an environment that people would normally find swiftly lethal, such as very deep underwater or inside an active volcano. Everything within the manse's range is protected as if by Element-Resisting Prana.

This power is incompatible with a Habitability drawback.

ESSENCE VENTS

The manse was built on a demesne more powerful than it can contain, and must bleed off the spare Essence. A manse builder must assign one point of Essence Vents for every point by which the demesne's rating exceeds the manse's. One point of Essence Vents creates localized displays within or around the manse. Three points of Essence Vents creates a display that can be seen for miles, such as a jet of fire that erupts high into the air.

Essence Vents take many forms, from bowls of fire on the manse's roof to shimmering pools in each room's center. Though beautiful, Essence Vents are dangerous. Anyone touching one suffers (uncapped levels x 5)L/action (Trauma 5) environmental damage as long as she remains in contact.

MAGICAL CONVENIENCES

The manse has a few pleasant conveniences that go beyond the possibilities of mundane artifice. If a player wishes to make her Magical Conveniences accessible only to attuned characters or the hearthstone bearer, she can do so for free, but they can't easily be deactivated (or re-activated) by anyone without additional powers. Each purchase of this power grants (manse's rating) Magical Conveniences.

Examples:

• Scarlet candles light whenever anyone enters a room.

• Doors open when approached.

• Special sheaths in the armory keep stored weapons sharp.

• Azure canvases record spoken words in elegant calligraphy, erase on command, and print their contents onto normal paper.

• If the hearthstone bearer gives the kitchen raw food, it prepares a feast.

• An advanced training room has complicated training dummies, moving targets and variable difficulty settings.

• A self-updating moonsilver plaque in the library keeps a cross-referenced catalog of every book on its shelves.

MINOR TRICKS AND TRAPS
Craft (Various) 3, Larceny 3

To dissuade unwanted guests, the manse is installed with several relatively harmless means of keeping people out. Every purchase of this power grants (manse's rating) traps, each designed to be bypassed by anyone who knows the trick. Attunement to the manse grants

knowledge of those tricks. Characters can spot the trap with a successful (Perception + Larceny) roll, difficulty 2 if characters think to look for traps or difficulty 5 otherwise. A successful (Wits + [Athletics or other relevant Ability]) roll, difficulty 3, lets a character evade the sprung trap in some manner.

Examples:

• Trapdoors open when characters step on them. The unfortunates are conveyed through a chute into the freezing lake outside the manse. A catch in the hearthstone room deactivates the trap.

A successful evasion roll lets a character to catch the edge before falling.

• The manse is a complicated, Essence-blurred maze. Strange mirrors exhaust the eye, normal methods of navigation don't seem to work, and a lost wanderer always finds herself back at the beginning. Eventually, residents learn their way.

A successful (Intelligence + Investigation) roll, difficulty 3, lets a character navigate the maze. Every successful roll adds 1 success to this roll in the future; each attempt takes 10 minutes to one hour, depending on the size of the manse. Success with a threshold of three extra successes indicates the character has figured out the warped perspectives of the maze and can find her way through the manse without impediment.

• When a character enters the wrong room, the door slams shut and locks, leaving no way out.

If characters fail to spot the trap or leap out the door before it closes, they can pick the lock with a (Dexterity + Larceny) roll, difficulty 5. A (Strength + Athletics) total of 10 lets a character break the door with a feat of strength.

• One of the manse's hallways appears infinitely long, making intruders feel as though they're going nowhere. Only a leap of logic brings the characters to the realization that sometimes, forward is not always the way.

A successful evasion roll of (Intelligence + [Awareness or Investigation]) lets a character spot another route.

NETWORK NODE

The manse's geomancy harmonizes with other manses. They share information near-instantly—so, for example, a threat registered by one manse might trigger a self-destruct sequence in one across Creation. All manses in a network need this power. (The Imperial Manse, for instance, is the central node for the Realm's war manses.)

PASSWORD ACTIVATIONS

The manse resonates with something other than attuned characters. Though its senses aren't enhanced by this power, the manse can discern certain signals (words, gestures, knocking in a certain pattern, or whatever) and activate or deactivate certain powers when certain conditions are met.

SELF-DESTRUCT SEQUENCE

As a last resort, the manse can self-destruct. Only the hearthstone bearer can issue this order, using a means that the manse can recognize. Simple manses sometimes have ruby terminals to register the hearthstone bearer's touch for such a purpose. When activated, the bearer decides how much time—between 30 seconds and 30 minutes—to allow before the manse is lost. Until then, the self-destruct sequence can only be deactivated by her, or by damaging this power. The roiling Essence within and eventual explosion mirror the unfortunate conclusion of Essence buildup.

WELL-FLAVORED ASPECT

Manses designed for a certain person can resonate with the core aesthetics of that individual's Essence. Residing in such a manse is like dwelling in a universe tailored to one's preferences. If the hearthstone bearer shares the manse's aspect, everything about the manse subtly cooperates with her: she has dramatic lighting when she makes an important statement, nothing gets in her way when she's in a hurry, shadows conceal her when she hides. While the character is in the manse, her player receives a +1 bonus to every dice pool for her actions.

TWO-POINT POWERS

ARCHIVE

Occult black pools whose water grants knowledge, antique memory crystals or just a whole bunch of books record a vast amount of information within the manse. This archive contains information focused on (manse's level) broad topics, each the breadth of an Ability specialty. Thus, any roll that involves those topics gains the benefit of an extra specialty dot. This value cannot be used when determining Excellency dice pool limits. Archive examples include Fair Folk lore (Occult specialty) or siegecraft (War). This power could also represent other sorts of training facilities, such as a magical training room that helps improve gymnastic prowess (Athletics) or a spirit that teaches how to play the sanxian (Performance). Either way, the character effectively has a trainer if she wants to gain the specialty for herself, *or* to raise the base Ability—once.

Archives built in-game can only hold information the builder already possesses. The player or Storyteller can stock manses bought at character creation, since others built them, with specific powerful knowledge as chosen. At the Storyteller's option, one topic of the Archive may be replaced by one powerful and dangerous secret, or a selection of spells: five Terrestrial Circle spells, one Celestial Circle Spell, or one-third of the information needed to learn a Solar Circle spell.

This power may be taken multiple times.

BOUND SERVITOR

Craft (Magitech) 4, Craft (Genesis) 4, or other Abilities needed to create or permanently bind a servant.

The manse has a servant creature dedicated to protecting it and serving the hearthstone bearer. It could be just about anything: a clockwork automaton built using Craft (Magitech), a life form engineered using Craft (Genesis), an undead thing animated by necromancy, a bound demon of the First Circle, or some other enslaved unfortunate. Bound Servitor may be purchased multiple times.

A character who builds his own manse needs the Abilities or Charms to create or bind a servitor; a manse the character merely claimed could have anything. First Circle demons bound to the manse count as Bound Servitors, but Second Circle demons are Guardians (Power 3).

Other sorts of bound servitors can have game traits comparable to First Circle demons. A good way to design a bound servitor is to start with the Regular Troops/Rebels template (see **Exalted**, p. 279) and add a few Abilities, extra Attributes or supernatural powers. Since they are made to defend the manse (among other duties), servitors may have innate weaponry and natural bashing and lethal soak comparable to medium-weight armor.

A servitor may never change its Motivation to serve and protect, can't act against its Motivation of its own will, and treats any suggestion to knowingly act against its Motivation as an Unacceptable Order.

CENTRAL CONTROL

One vast room is filled with jeweled levers, crystal screens and rune-etched consoles that access every corner of the manse. Only attuned characters can use the room to take personal control of the manse (unless the Central Control comes with Password Activation). From the control room, characters can monitor sound and movement within range, set passwords, design illusions, aim and fire weapons, activate traps and so on. Without this power, all these functions are determined

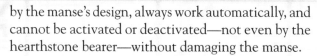

by the manse's design, always work automatically, and cannot be activated or deactivated—not even by the hearthstone bearer—without damaging the manse.

DANGEROUS TRAPS

Craft (various) 4, Larceny 4

The manse's secrets must be valuable, for serious traps await the unwary. They aren't designed to dissuade, but to cripple or kill. Each purchase of this power grants (manse's rating) Dangerous Traps. Usually, such traps don't reset themselves, but that would be an appropriate Basic Convenience (Power 1).

A trap can be spotted with a successful (Perception + Larceny) roll, difficulty 4 if characters think to look for traps or difficulty 6 otherwise. A successful (Wits + [Athletics or other relevant Ability]) roll, difficulty 4, lets a character evade the sprung trap in some manner.

Examples:

• When unattuned characters get halfway up a treacherous inclined hallway, flaming oil pours from the wall ahead of them and courses downhill.

In 3 ticks, the oil reaches the characters who slide, burning, downhill into a fiery pool unless the evasion roll succeeds. Treat the fire at a bonfire (see **Exalted**, p. 131).

• A main door has no handle and doesn't open when unattuned characters approach. In the center of the door, a face of jade and brass protrudes. His lips are pursed, with a small gap that appears to have a locking mechanism inside. If an unattuned character attempts to pick the lock, however, the mouth spits sticky, corrosive poison in her eyes and commences laughing maniacally at a volume that drowns out all natural sound for the remainder of the scene.

Anyone attempting to pick the "lock" with a conventional lockpick becomes the target for the toxic spray. Failing the (Wits + Dodge) evasion roll means the poison sprays in the character's face. Use coral snake venom for the poison (see **Exalted**, p. 131), but the corrosive spray also blinds victims. Succeeding at the Resistance roll means the blindness lasts only five minutes (only a few droplets entered the character's eyes); failing means the blindness lasts until an Exalted character heals all damage from the corrosive venom. Mortals are blinded forever. Creatures with natural hardness are immune to this effect, as are creatures wearing watertight eye protection.

• If the manse senses only unattuned characters in a certain room, a net of thin wires erupts from cracks in the tiled floor. At tremendous speed, it lifts all the characters in the room straight up into the sword-like spikes that emerge from the ceiling. When the manse detects no further resistance from the intruders, it drops them to the ground.

Bypassing the trap requires cutting the wires, firmly embedded in thin crevices between tiles, or disrupting the mechanisms in the corners of the walls. This requires a successful (Intelligence + Larceny) roll, difficulty 4. Once a character is caught, breaking the wires requires a feat of strength total of 10 to break, and doing so inflicts a level of lethal damage to characters who lack metal gauntlets or the like. The ceiling spikes inflict 10L piercing, and the subsequent fall at the end of the scene is 20 feet.

THE EYELESS SIGHT OF DAANA'D (WATER FAVORED)

The manse's delicate and sensitive Essence increases the difficulty of any roll to avoid its senses by 3. It also senses through mundane barriers up to an inch thick. Only Essence-created sensory barriers, such as Stealth Charms or certain spells, can block the manse's awareness. Treat the Eyeless Sight of Daana'd as Essence sight (see **Wonders of the Lost Age**, p. 85).

GEOMANTIC SUBTLETY

The manse's Essence structures are more complicated than usual, or a skilled architect disguised tell-tale architectural stereotypes. Unless an observer succeeds at a (Perception + Occult) roll, difficulty 3, she can't determine its aspect. Rolls to find the manse's hearthroom, damage its powers, or to otherwise figure out anything at all from its geomancy also suffer a -3 external penalty. This power has no effect within the hearthroom, where Geomantic Subtlety is impossible.

THE GLORIOUS HALO OF HESIESH (FIRE FAVORED)

Refracting crystals, focused elemental Essence, or other means can convey two- or three-dimensional visual illusions throughout the manse. This lacks the precision to create specific objects or people, but can create the suggestion of those things; for instance, Octavian, Demon of the Second Circle, couldn't be copied, but the manse could show a huge tusked monster riding a giant wasp.

Figuring out that an image is an illusion requires a successful (Perception + [Awareness or Investigation]) roll—normally a simple success, but many factors influence that difficulty, including visual conditions, distance, the brevity of a glimpse, a character's desire

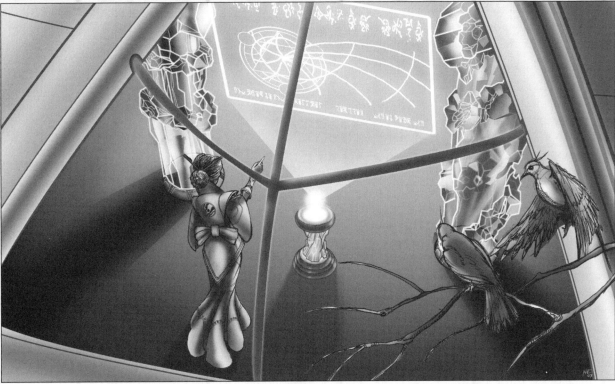

to be fooled, and so on. Like most powers, these illusions work on a set pattern unless the manse can adapt to outside influences or the whims of the hearthstone bearer.

The Glorious Halo of Hesiesh can broadcast a real-time image of the hearthstone bearer. Real-time conveyance is usually conducted to or from a specially prepared space, but with Central Control (Power 2), the hearthstone bearer can set up any area within the manse to convey any image.

HIDDEN PASSAGES
Larceny 3

For those who know its tricks, it's easy to get around the manse subtly; many of its doors are camouflaged. The secret passages open silently, and those who use them gain a +2 bonus to appropriate Stealth rolls. This power needn't always indicate actual passages—sometimes "one-sided doors" simply don't appear to have another side, for example. Noticing a secret door is a successful (Perception + [Awareness or Investigation]) roll, difficulty 2 if characters search deliberately or difficulty 4 if not. Hidden passages may include a secret escape route.

LIMITED MOBILITY

A manse must stay on the demesne it caps, but some manses can rise on pillars or sink into a pit, spin in place, or otherwise move in some limited manner.

This was more common in the Age of Splendor than in the Second Age, where architects find stationary manses quite challenging enough.

MELA'S SWEET WHISPER (AIR FAVORED)

Narrow flues, strategic bells or harmonic strings catching the wind enable the manse to produce and convey sounds. With no other powers, Mela's Sweet Whisper can welcome guests, berate intruders or facilitate communication between residents. With such additions as Invisible Theft (Power 4) or the Glorious Halo of Hesiesh (Power 2), other possibilities present themselves. With Central Control (Power 2), any auditory transmission can be accomplished.

Usually, such manses are designed to allow communication between certain locations, or from one spot to everywhere within. Manses don't naturally record such sounds, however, and reproduced noises are never entirely accurate. If someone tries to fool intruders with an auditory transmission, or unnerve them with sounds apparently from nowhere, the target can figure out what's going on if her player succeeds at a (Perception + [Awareness of Investigation]) roll.

PASIAP'S BURIED WHISKERS (EARTH FAVORED)

Buried jade channels or harmonic receivers extend the manse's sensory range beyond its walls. It can sense, but cannot use other powers, within a radius of (rating^2 x 100) yards.

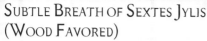

SUBTLE BREATH OF SEXTES JYLIS (WOOD FAVORED)

By mimicking the geomancy of a certain environment, the manse controls its indoor climate, manipulating temperature, humidity, light levels, scent, and similar factors, and eliminating small pests. This can keep the manse comfortable, such as Comfort Zone (Power 1)—or very unpleasant. Under no circumstances can the climate created by this power cause immediate damage. However, heat like a Southern desert at noon, or a moderate breeze at subzero temperatures, could both be dangerous.

This climate control is not *completely* effective. Lights uncontrolled by the manse still function in total darkness, a fire could be started on freezing indoor tundra, and the wind is never strong enough to knock anyone over. The Subtle Breath might be under the hearthstone bearer's control, directed from a Central Control, set by passwords, or be completely automatic—all approaches have their advantages and limitations.

SYMPATHETIC DREAM LINK

So well-harmonized is the manse with its hearthstone bearer that, when she dreams, they "communicate" symbolically. The hearthstone bearer always knows the condition of the manse and if anyone has intruded—but only while dreaming.

This power doesn't provide a manse with any special intelligence or cognitive functions, but manses with such a sympathetic link have reacted to their owners' unconscious wishes. If the hearthstone bearer's temporary Willpower falls below 3, her manse may act on her secret desires without explicit orders.

VEIL OF SHADOW

The manse is overlaid by a flowing, shadowed geomancy confusing enough to make eavesdropping difficult. When characters stand in certain areas—examples include corners, hallways, arches, et cetera—all attempts to perceive specifics about them from outside that area are subject to a -2 external penalty. This applies to scrying magic and other methods of distant perception.

THREE-POINT POWERS

ANALYTICAL SENSES (WATER, SIDEREAL FAVORED)

Whether the manse uses geomantically shaped jade lenses, delicate moonsilver and starmetal filaments or bound spirits of occult awareness, the manse can observe Essences within its range. It automatically detects and analyzes Obvious Charms, and can learn the capabilities of artifacts unprotected by wards or other such enchantments. Most importantly, it understands the invisible design of souls, noting each person's Essence rating, spiritual nature and occult alignments and anomalies—including taints from demonic powers or normally invisible Wyld mutations.

Without additional powers, however, the manse is fooled by Sidereal Fate-based concealment, and won't spot the effects of astrology. Powers specifically designed to fool Essence-bases senses can also confuse the manse. Occasionally, architects leave rare concealing magics out of the design, which then become a weakness of the manse—not necessarily by accident.

These senses may be linked to other powers through Password Activation. If the manse has Central Control or some way to communicate with attuned persons, it can be ordered to analyze visitors or objects, and report what it finds.

ARMORED

A manse with this power was built from exceptionally strong material, further reinforce by Essence, giving the manse more soak than usual. This power is not lost in Power Failure, and can be bought multiple times. However, no one in Creation has been able to give a manse more than two increments of Armor since the Old Realm.

Armor Taken	External Soak (L/B)	Internal Soak (L/B)	Example Material
Once	14/21	7/14	Thick granite
Twice	17/24	9/17	Thick metal
3 x	21/29	12/21	Super-heavy steel
4 x	26/35	15/26	Jade-alloy
5 x	32/42	19/32	Moonsilver, Orichalcum, Soulsteel

BOUND SERVANT FORCE

4 in appropriate Craft, or the ability to permanently bind Servitors

The manse is guarded by a unit of Bound Servitors with a Magnitude equal to its level. All such Bound Servitors use the same statistics unless the Storyteller chooses to differentiate between them. If used in Mass Combat, the Servant force has Drill of 3. The Servant Force can serve as a powerful tool in social combat, for it can't lose Magnitude due to loss of Loyalty.

This power may be purchased multiple times for additional Servant Forces. If all such forces are identical, their numbers may be combined to determine the total Magnitude of a single unit, as normal.

DIVINE OBSERVATORY (SIDEREAL FAVORED)
Mastery of Sidereal Astrology

Geomancy melds with astrology to track the movements of the Five Maidens, and altars give them worship. Quadrants, astrolabes and armillary spheres track every constellation, guided by starmetal ephemerides. These manses give their owners a nearly direct view of the Loom of Fate from Creation, and are coveted by Sidereals.

Most importantly, each Observatory's roof includes a downward-pointing lens, giving the pattern spiders a view of its residents. The spiders are less likely to ignore the immediate. For the purposes of Sidereal astrology rolls, a Divine Observatory reduces each difficulty by one. They also add (manse's rating) successes to astrological thaumaturgy performed by attuned characters inside.

DRAGON'S NEST ([ELEMENT] ONLY)

The manse's structure concentrates elemental Essence so strongly that every room is overwhelmed with its aspect. Light changes color as it enters, as do any objects left there for long. Moreover:

• Terrestrial anima banners of the corresponding element cannot damage the manse. The manse's energies absorb their physical power. People, however, are not immune.

• Appropriately aspected Charms and spells—including the abilities of elementals, Terrestrial Charms with the Elemental keyword, or spells directly affecting the element—have their final cost reduced by (manse's rating) motes, minimum 0.

• Children of Dragon-Bloods conceived within the manse gain a +1 bonus to their chances of Exaltation, as if a parent had high Breeding (see **The Manual of Exalted Power—The Dragon-Blooded**, p. 106). This increases to +2 if the child is brought to term within the manse. The Exaltation's aspect is hardly in doubt.

• The hearthroom of the manse is in a state of dangerous elemental upheaval. It's an environmental hazard with a Damage of 3L/action and Trauma of 5, ignoring armor. The hearthstone bearer is immune to this effect, but probably had trouble attuning in the first place.

EBON DRAGNET (ABYSSAL ONLY)

People who die in the manse don't escape its twisted Essence. Dying characters linger for one scene as the dragnet does its work. If the body's healed during that time, they can be saved. Failing powerful restorative Charms, however, the dead rise immediately as ghosts, and for the following scene, they're forced by the manse's dark geomancy to manifest on the premises. After that, they begin their "normal" ghostly existences.

(ELEMENT) DRAGON'S WILL ([ELEMENT] ONLY)

Structures of jade-magnetite alloy in the walls enable the manse to control elemental Essence outside itself. In one five-tick span, it can affect a volume of an element equal to its level in yards, cubed (for Fire, yards squared in surface area). Non-magical quantities of that element that fall within that size restriction cannot harm the manse, and against magical instances or amounts greater than it can control, all damage is reduced by (manse's rating x 2) dice. It can also move the element at three yards per tick; for instance, move enormous stone blocks, slosh water from fountains to put out fires, or animate the wooden furniture to attack intruders.

During any five-tick span, the manse can direct one instance of the element to make an attack, flip a switch, catch a falling vase, or perform some other complex or delicate action involving a target within (manse's rating) yards of that quantity. If necessary, this action uses a dice pool equal to (manse's rating x 2). Any damage inflicted equals the manse's rating, plus successes, and can be lethal or bashing, depending on what the manse aims to accomplish. Using this power, the manse can issue a feat of strength equal to (level x 2), or with a successful roll, it can impose a penalty equal to its rating on an intruder's player's roll (from distraction, pain, loss of balance or the like).

When manipulating an element, the manse can cause any number of diverse, imprecise effects so long as they do not create, destroy or fundamentally alter the element. Water could become ice or mist. Fire could turn green or flicker brightly. Earth could melt from sand to lava and solidify into obsidian (but cannot be pressured into diamond). A Wood-aspected manse could directly affect unintelligent life forms and mentally direct most untrained, Essence 1 animals. In an Air-aspected manse, air could refuse to enter an enemy's lungs or even spark with lightning. As always, manses that are more powerful can perform capable of feats that are more impressive.

EMERALD/IRON CIRCLE FEEDBACK
(SOLAR/ABYSSAL FAVORED)
Sapphire Circle Sorcery/Onyx Circle Necromancy

The manse's leaden pillars and runes of abalone suppress the forces of magic. Its hostile geomancy crushes any Emerald Circle spells or thaumaturgy used

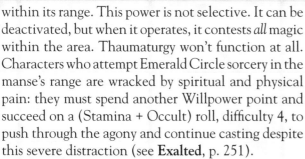

within its range. This power is not selective. It can be deactivated, but when it operates, it contests *all* magic within the area. Thaumaturgy won't function at all. Characters who attempt Emerald Circle sorcery in the manse's range are wracked by spiritual and physical pain: they must spend another Willpower point and succeed on a (Stamina + Occult) roll, difficulty 4, to push through the agony and continue casting despite this severe distraction (see **Exalted**, p. 251).

An alternate version of this power cripples necromancy of the Shadowlands Circle, as well as thaumaturgy.

FORTRESS (EARTH FAVORED)
War 4

Most manses are strongly built, but a manse with this power was specifically designed to resist attack. Windows are barred and crenellations fortify its walls, built of independently strong stuff and standing unfed by the manse's Essence. It may have a moat, drawbridge, boiling oil, and other protective measures against large-scale assault. Three of these hazards have danger ratings equal to the manse's level (see **Exalted**, p. 247). The fortifications are always defensive and short-range—artillery is covered by Integrated Essence Artillery (Power 4). What's more, the manse can sustain (rating x 25) levels of damage before suffering Power Failure.

This power cannot be lost during Power Failure. It is incompatible with Fragility. Each purchase of Fortress gives three additional defensive hazards and adds 5 levels to the damage threshold before Power Failure.

GUARDIAN
Craft (Magitech) 5, Craft (Genesis) 5, or other ability to bind a Guardian

As Bound Servitor (Power 2), save that a Guardian is considerably more powerful. Guardians are Second Circle demons or creatures of equivalent power.

PROVIDER (WOOD FAVORED)

Whether the manse is an underground cave system, habitation dome or multi-tiered tower city, it can care for a group of individuals whose Magnitude equals (its level + 1). Filters purify air and water, and jade-lined gardens grow and prepare food automatically. Animals that need more nourishment might count as two to five people, depending on appetite, but a group of the correct size can survive in a Provider manse indefinitely.

PUZZLE MANSE
Intelligence 5 or Larceny 5

Each room in the manse is individually aligned to a current of Essence that's been shifted, uprooted, and left to float. As a result, the manse's layout changes. Opening a particular door can lead to different rooms, staircases going up can open onto lower floors, and even such features as windows or fireplaces might lead to new places within the manse.

The designer has various options. The Puzzle Manse might rearrange the access between its rooms according to Passwords, or a set schedule. For a complicated system, the key to understanding the manse lies in a pattern or trick of the eye: a successful (Intelligence + Lore) roll deciphers the former, (Intelligence + Larceny) the latter, each at difficulty of (manse's rating). Before Charm use, players cannot roll a number of dice greater than the number of rooms they've spent at least one scene in.

Occasionally, Puzzle Manses are built to be solvable only by characters possessing specific Abilities, powers or even Virtues, but these are rare, and normal rolls might still apply. Some schemes, however, might not need a roll—it's something predetermined that observant players can figure out for themselves.

SHADOWLAND (ABYSSAL ONLY)
Ability to create a shadowland

Demesnes can exist in shadowlands; in this case, tendrils of iron and tokens of bone anchor a small shadowland to a manse. The manse might even envelop the shadowland; for instance, a bone-lined cellar with a door that merges with the Underworld at night. Fed by the manse's Essence, the shadowland becomes permanent, never growing or shrinking for any reason save Power Failure.

THE SILENT VOICE (AIR, SIDEREAL FAVORED)

Corners of the manse imitate corners of the mind and establish a rapport with sentient mental spaces. Those who address thoughts to the manse will be sensed—and receive responses. It could potentially "hear" mentally provided passwords, provide a mental directory of its cross-referenced library, or the like, but can't receive thoughts that aren't intended for it.

Mental communication happens as fast as speech or showing someone a series of pictures. Characters' abilities to remember enormous amounts of information aren't enhanced.

TEMPLE MANSE
Priesthood of the appropriate deity

The manse honors a god to the very roots of its design, celebrating the deity's greatness. Every inch of its architecture is a prayer. Servants or spawn of enemy powers—for example, Celestial Exalted, in

the case of Abyssal Temples, or raksha in Celestial Temples—can sense this and are anathema to it. They cannot naturally recover Essence or Willpower points while within range. If they foolishly attempt attunement, they'll suffer three unsoakable levels of aggravated damage from internal Essence burns.

Players receive one free bonus success on any roll for prayers issued to the deity from within the manse's consecrated walls. Furthermore, if a priest of the appropriate god makes a Resources 5 sacrifice—or sacrifices something otherwise priceless and powerful—the god receives a great boon: concentrated ambrosia in the shape of the sacrifice. This is often enough to provoke a response even from the Celestial Incarnae, who might provide a moment of wisdom or token blessing.

ULTRA-DEADLY TRAPS
Various Crafts at 5, Larceny 5

The manse has automatic defenses so powerful that escape, much less survival, seems in doubt. Ultra-Deadly Traps are intended to kill or capture, and are cunning and powerful enough to defeat the Exalted. Each purchase of this power grants one Ultra-Deadly trap.

Examples:

• When the characters enter a room, huge stone slabs fall onto every doorway, blocking any escape. Im-mediately after, the room begins detaching from the rest of the manse. After 10 ticks, the room and everyone within go Elsewhere—outside Creation itself. There they remain indefinitely; there will be no escape from the pocket realm unless the manse's hearthstone bearer chooses to release them, or the manse sustains damage.

A feat of strength of at least 15 is necessary to lift the slabs on the doors. Stone slabs have 25 lethal soak, 50 bashing, and 60 health levels.

• The manse contains a soul magnet that sucks living souls from living bodies. When people come near it, it activates with a dull gray light and a loud, low hum, and then swiftly drags them toward it. Nothing is within arm's reach for characters to catch, and once it touches them, the magnet wrenches their souls from their bodies.

The soul magnet activates when the first character approaches within 20 yards. It pulls characters five yards per tick with a Strength of 10, -1 for every five yards of distance. A successful (Wits + Athletics) roll, difficulty 2+, lets a character find some way to hold on; if characters who grabbed hold of something else have less Strength than the magnet does at their range, they must take a Miscellaneous Action each tick to roll (Stamina + [Resistance or Athletics]), difficulty (magnet's Strength - character's Strength), or be pulled

in. Characters hitting the magnet will be inactive unless they summon a feat of strength greater than the magnet's Strength. After that, they suffer three dice of armor-ignoring aggravated damage on every action until they die. The soul magnet has 9L/9B soak; every three health levels of damage done to it reduces the magnet's strength by 1.

• A glowing flambeau on the wall, that initially looks like a minor Essence vents, shoots serpent-headed bolts of deadly Essence lightning at anyone except the hearthstone bearer who comes within 10 yards of the flambeau and whatever it guards. The bolts have an attack pool of 12 dice, attack one target every tick, and deal eight dice of piercing aggravated damage when they hit.

WORKSHOP MANSE
Appropriate Craft at 5

Built for a long-ago craftsman of the Shogunate or before, the manse is one of the most well-equipped workshops in Creation today. The player chooses a Craft, whether mundane such as Water or esoteric such as Magitech or Genesis, to which her Workshop is dedicated. Those working there have the tools to repair virtually any wonder falling under that Craft's purview. It is a flawless workshop for artifact construction (see p. 28); if for Magitech or Genesis, it is a four-dot workshop for purpose of repairs on such items (see **Wonders of the Lost Age**, p. 9).

ZONE OF INFLUENCE

Sorcerously immaterial chains, perfectly calculated astrological effects or other technical wonders expand the manse's geomancy past the area it caps. Its range extends beyond its walls, to a radius equal to (rating^2 x 100) yards. It can sense normally within the zone and can use any powers there that the Storyteller approves—geomantic anomalies or spiritual interference sometimes interfere with certain powers.

FOUR-POINT POWERS

ABILITY ENLIGHTENMENT (AIR, SOLAR FAVORED)

The manse encodes knowledge in its structure, mystic arts have coaxed a hint of mind from its Essence, or perhaps a previous owner was so closely attuned to the manse that her knowledge passed to it. The manse "understands" orders beyond straightforward programming—but isn't sentient. Although it learns and remembers information, it can only grow so far, and has no consciousness or personality.

Effectively, the manse has four Abilities it can "think" about. Since the manse doesn't have At-

tributes, it receives an automatic four successes whenever a situation would call for a roll using those Abilities. The manse may need other powers to act on its Abilities, however.

Example: A manse is furnished in exact and courtly arrangements and lined with cultivated roses, whose colors are used to express a giver's intentions. Its geomancy expresses principles of empathy, etiquette and subterfuge. It effectively has Socialize 4. When the hearthstone bearer commands it to examine its residents' Motivations, it evaluates each person's facial movements, postures, words and reactions to the flowers and other cues. If one person displays her Motivation, the Storyteller applies an external penalty of that character's ([Manipulation + Socialize] ÷ 2) to the four-success reading Motivation roll for the manse. If any successes remain, the manse understands the character's Motivation and stores the information for future use.

Information a manse gains from its Ability Enlightenment can trigger other powers. Attunement can train characters in the manse's Abilities as if they had a teacher, up to the levels it possesses. Ability Enlightenment may be bought multiple times.

ATELIER-MANSE
Craft (Magitech) 5, other Craft at 5

The manse-machine is aligned with a certain elemental Craft and can quickly produce things chosen by the hearthstone bearer. It continues making whatever she designates until it runs out of raw materials, or she assigns it a new task. To set her manse for production, the hearthstone bearer must have the Abilities to design it. She must also feed it enough raw materials to make the product. It is a flawless workshop (see p. 28).

Unlike with Factory-Cathedral (Power 5), these manses can't make magitech. At most, it can duplicate the products of thaumaturgy. Atelier-manses always have Maintenance 3 (gaining Creation Points for that drawback) and Repair 4 (refer to **Wonders of the Lost Age**, p. 9). Artifacts are beyond them, but they aren't too limited: everything from swords (Craft [Fire]) to pieces of music (Craft [Air]) can be mass-produced in an appropriate atelier-manse. Use of a suitable atelier-manse also reduces the interval for Crafting rolls, whether for mundane items or non-magitech artifacts: from seasons to months, months to weeks, weeks to days, and days to scenes. Reduce the time one step for items of Resources value 3+, two steps for items of Resources 2 or 1.

CHASM OF THE MATERIAL

Material Essence within the manse is magnetized against its immaterial counterpart. The spiritual gap is

nearly impossible to cross, and makes unaccustomed residents feel uncomfortable, as if their flesh is too heavy and thick. No beings within range may dematerialize, and nothing immaterial may enter.

GREATER VEIL OF SHADOWS

As far as outsiders can tell, the manse isn't there. Its geomancy redirects the eye so subtly that one must literally stumble over it to notice it. It gives no non-tactile sensory impressions, and the land where it should be seems normal (though its Essence flows may be felt by sensitive characters or geomancers). Even battles fought within the manse won't be obvious. The only thing it can't mask is an anima banner bright enough to be seen to the distance of a spear's cast—for example, a Solar who's spent 11+ peripheral motes in a scene.

INTEGRATED ESSENCE ARTILLERY
Craft (Magitech) 5, War 3

The manse's Essence powers strategic heavy weaponry. This provides (manse's rating x 2) Artifact dots to spend on weaponry permanently tied to the manse's geomancy and secured in its structure. Because these artifacts are simplified versions with an enormous Essence source, they subtract 2 from their Repair Value and ignore requirements involving hearthstones with a value equal to or less than the manse's rating.

No weapon's Artifact rating can exceed the manse's own rating, and they must be aimed and fired with Central Control (Power 2) unless the manse has a power such as Ability Enlightenment (Power 4) it can use to fire them itself.

See **Wonders of the Lost Age** for large-scale Essence weaponry. Non-integrated Essence artillery is an artifact, and should be bought as a separate Background.

INVISIBLE THEFT

A mind is a space with its own mystical geomancy, each thought like a current of Essence. Odd, twisting structures in the manse emulate an empty mind, encouraging thoughts to circulate from their natural environment into its rooms. The manse can sense the thoughts of any mind within range. The hearthstone owner can command the manse to search thoughts right down to memories. The manse needs other powers, however, to understand or use the thoughts it reads, such as Silent Voice to pass thoughts to attuned residents, or Sentience to understand the thoughts itself.

Players must succeed on a (Perception + Occult) roll, difficulty 3, for their characters to realize that their minds aren't safe. This roll's difficulty drops to 1 if the manse rifles through memories, for the manse

then increases Essence circulation, and thoughts are dragged from their homes with unsubtle force. Though it may take characters a moment to comprehend the vague, headachy tingling behind their eyes, the sensation is instinctively understood.

A character with a lot of self-control might quell her thoughts so the manse cannot hear them—but it's not easy. Manses can still read the minds of actively guarding characters whose Dodge MDVs are lower than 8. On the other hand, characters whose players score four successes on a (Manipulation + Socialize) roll can actually fool a telepathic manse by imitating mental patterns different from their own.

OUTSIDE FATE
Craft (Fate) 5 or built by entities outside of Fate

The manse's designer exploited a gap in Fate's pattern. Though the shell of the manse's Essence seems normal, an unreal principle was built in through "outside channels"—demon craftsmen, perhaps, or Fair Folk—that disguise the place's existence from the Loom of Fate. Astrology cannot detect anything about the manse, and the eyes of Heaven do not see whatever happens within its range. Its residents are not removed from Fate, but their location is.

Aiding or abetting the construction—or existence—of such a manse is a dire Celestial offense against Yu-Shan's Bureau of Destiny.

RAINBOW/BLACK TABERNACLE (SOLAR/ABYSSAL FAVORED)
Adamant Circle Sorcery/Obsidian Circle Necromancy

Emerald, sapphire and diamond insets channel the manse's Essence into sorcerous power. Sorcerous spells cast within the manse's walls have their mote cost reduced by 10. If this would lower a spell's cost to less than half its original value, then it's instead reduced by half (round up). Furthermore, the manse adds one to the caster's effective Essence score when calculating the spell's effects. If the tabernacle is Black, ornamented with iron, onyx and obsidian, it affects necromancy instead.

SAPPHIRE/ONYX CIRCLE FEEDBACK (SOLAR/ABYSSAL FAVORED)
Adamant Circle Sorcery/Obsidian Circle Necromancy

As Emerald Circle Feedback (Power 3), save that this works against the Sapphire Circle as the earlier version does against Emerald, and automatically prevents the use of Emerald Circle Sorcery and thaumaturgy. An alternate version cripples necromancy of the Labyrinth Circle and below.

SOUL PRISON (ABYSSAL ONLY)
Iron Circle Necromancy

The manse pulls Essence from the Underworld as well as its demesne. It gains the effects of an Ebon Dragnet (Power 3) and binds anyone who dies within it. Such ghosts can't leave the manse's range and must forever obey the hearthstone bearer's commands to the letter, just as if they had been summoned and bound. (For more on ghost-summoning, see **The Black Treatise**, pp. 34-35.)

The manse can contain a unit of ghosts equal in Magnitude to its rating. When bought at character generation, Soul Prisons are stocked with weak ghosts, lacking equipment and Charms, but using the statistics of war ghosts (see **Exalted**, p. 318). The manse cannot trap ghosts whose Essence exceeds the manse's rating, but only very heroic ghosts will grow in power while under its awful influence.

The hearthstone bearer may release any ghosts at any time.

WYLD REVOCATION
(ABYSSAL, LUNAR, SIDEREAL FAVORED)

The manse's geomancy no longer shapes a real place at all; the architect has engineered a place where certain of Creation's principles don't apply, almost like the citadels of the Fair Folk. Things may no longer fall down, but simply float, or Obvious Charms might no longer have an Essence signature. In three-dot manses, only a single room may use this power, though it may be purchased multiple times; a four-dot manse (or one on a four-dot demesne) extends the effect every room; at rating 5, the power affects the entire range, even if extended with another power.

No one fully understands the principles of Creation, and they aren't what players might think of as the "laws of nature." Magnetism, gravity and so on are all Creation's laws, but so are the laws that say active Essence glows and the moon inspires awe. The Storyteller is the final arbiter of what natural laws exist and can be altered by this power. However, Abyssal manses tend to emulate aspects of the Underworld or Labyrinth; Lunar manses become fluid and shifting, like the Wyld; while Sidereal manses revoke principles of space or time, but also aspects of identity.

FIVE-POINT POWERS
ADAMANT/OBSIDIAN CIRCLE FEEDBACK
(SOLAR/ABYSSAL ONLY)
Adamant Circle Sorcery/Obsidian Circle Necromancy, plus Occult 6, Essence 6

As Emerald Circle Feedback (Power 3), save that this power works against the Adamant Circle as the earlier version does against Emerald, automatically preventing the use of Emerald and Sapphire Circle sorcery as well as thaumaturgy. An alternate version similarly affects necromancy of the Void Circle and below.

ALTERNATE LOCATIONS
Survival 6

The builder has given up to 5 other locations the same geomancy as the manse—and the manse may vanish from its current location and appear in one of them, while still drawing Essence from its demesne. This process takes one hour, cannot happen more than once a day, and transports everything within the manse's walls. Usually, manses are built to translocate on a set schedule. Buying this power twice enables the manse to shuttle between 25 locations.

FACTORY-CATHEDRAL
Craft (Magitech) 6

Faith, magic and technology come together in the factory-cathedral. Within its walls are produced glorious wonders reserved for the greatest gods and Chosen. Factory-cathedrals constructed indefatigable guards for the borders of Creation, the royal warstriders that once accompanied Dawn Caste generals into battle, and the components of the Realm Defense Grid. Almost no factory-cathedrals endure today, and those that remain are terribly damaged or lost to the impassable wilderness.

This power imparts all the benefits of Temple Manse (Power 3) and an ideal workshop (see p. 28) for Craft (Magitech), with the automated production of an Atelier-Manse (Power 4). A working factory-cathedral can make magitech artifacts rated 4 or lower, assuming the owner has the requisite Abilities and raw materials.

Factory-cathedrals all require Maintenance 4 and get Creation Points for this. The Maintenance has two aspects. Everyone who enters must undergo purification rituals, lest unclean Essence contaminate the delicate machinery. Every year, a factory-cathedral also consumes at least three exotic ingredients suitable for crafting artifacts rated 3 or higher: for instance, 10 talents of jade, a frozen lightning bolt and the blood of a Second Circle demon. They are also magitech artifacts with Repair ratings of 5. (See **Wonders of the Lost Age**, p. 9, for Repair ratings and more information on factory-cathedrals, as well as Chapter One of this book.)

Operating a factory-cathedral demands certain rituals and specialized knowledge that has largely been lost. Characters who want to use a factory-cathedral need to find the records or notes of the long-dead Exalted who built it.

INAUSPICIOUS CITADEL (ABYSSAL ONLY)
Obsidian Circle Necromancy

Looking down from the manse's lowest chamber is inadvisable, for a pit extends into Oblivion. The breath of the Neverborn fills the manse, and any action taken therein might impinge on their dreaming consciousness.

This power comes from a necromancer casting the spell Inauspicious Citadel (see **The Black Treatise**, p. 53). The spell creates a fortress with many properties of a manse. Casting the spell in a shadowland demesne can evoke a citadel that *is* a manse, though the character still needs all the skills to design the manse and any other powers.

This power gives the manse as many more Creation Points as the Neverborn feel like granting, plus Well-Flavored Aspect (Power 1) for free. However, the builder does not control how those extra points are spent: the Neverborn do (with the Storyteller as their stand-in). The Neverborn can also usurp control over any Essence-based powers of the manse, although they seldom rouse from their eternal death-dreams to do so.

An Inauspicious Citadel must always be in a shadowland. If its shadowland is destroyed, the manse suffers Power Failure straight down to rating 0.

INDESTRUCTIBLE
Every mortal Craft at 6

The manse's walls are impervious to damage. The hearthstone bearer may deactivate this power. Failing that, it suffers harm only from geomantic attacks.

ONE MIND WITHIN
Presence 6

Symbols of mastery fill the manse; its arches are high and spreading, and its halls intimidatingly wide. Like a manse built with Invisible Theft (Power 5), its architecture resonates with the mind, but its structure is unsubtly overpowering. It controls sentients within its walls, directing the activities of any thinking creature with a Dodge MDV less than 10. This is an Unnatural Mental Influence for Compulsion.

Resisting the manse's attempts to use oneself as a tool costs one point of Willpower, and grants freedom for one action. Beings with an Essence score at least equal to the manse's rating may shrug off this effect

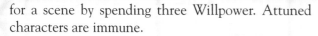

for a scene by spending three Willpower. Attuned characters are immune.

OTHERWORLD GATE
(ABYSSAL, SIDEREAL FAVORED)
Power to make a portal to another realm of reality

Somewhere within the manse—perhaps a soaring arch, a pit or an unpretentious door—stands a portal to a place beyond Creation. Any strange place the Storyteller accepts could lie beyond: Malfeas, Yu-Shan, the Labyrinth, the Wyld, Autochthon, who knows?

If the Otherworld Gate leads to Yu-Shan, this is a Sidereal power; if it leads to the Underworld, an Abyssal one.

OUTSIDE WORLDS WITHIN
Sapphire Circle Sorcery

The builder has used the spell Outside Worlds Within (see **The White Treatise**, pp. 77-78) to turn part of the manse into a bit of the outdoors, though the area actually remains bounded by the manse's walls. Tying the enchantment to the manse's geomancy makes it permanent. Other magic might create pocket environments such as paintings you can step into and they become real, or similar wonders. Unlike the Palace of Unreality (see below), everything in Outside Worlds Within is quite real—though it cannot leave the manse.

PALACE OF UNREALITY

The manse is dedicated to the unreal—and can support that unreality. Whether through sorcery, Fair Folk glamour or other magic, the manse can enmesh the people within it in powerful illusions. The illusions can affect all five senses, and will fool anyone whose MDV does not exceed 10. Each scene, the manse may create up to five illusions, which suspicious characters may resist by spending three Willpower points. (This cost drops to 1 if the illusion is shown to be false or it attempts to do something impossible.) Illusions may be people, attacks, traps, darkness, walls, or almost anything else, but they can't fool characters into thinking they're dead.

SENTIENT
Intelligence 6

The manse doesn't just imitate the processes of thought. Its Essence cycles have flowered into a new consciousness, complete with sense of self and personality. With tastes shaped by its architecture and the desires of its builder, the manse is creative: it extrapolates, guesses and invents. A manse painted with beautiful frescoes might have a strong artistic bent, while one built as a fortress would more likely be a brilliant tactician. It doesn't even have to like its hearthstone bearer—but it *must* obey her. If this power becomes damaged, however, the manse goes dangerously insane. Legend also says that the soul of an Exalt who is buried in a beloved manse can merge with its Essence to make it sentient, but the Immaculate Order condemns these stories as heresy.

The player distributes (manse's rating x 5) dots among the manse's Perception, Intelligence, Wits, Charisma and Manipulation. No Attribute values may exceed 5 without Storyteller permission. The manse's Motivation is probably to serve its hearthstone bearer, but some have been created with others. Moreover, though a sentient manse's Motivation is usually set in stone and sealed by its internal structure, in the past, at least one manse was designed to find its own way, as a person would.

The manse can have any Intimacies, Virtues to a maximum of 5, and as many Abilities as it can learn. Bought at character creation, the player distributes 25 dots among its Abilities, using the same caps as Attributes. Like any intelligent being, the manse feels, learns, forgets and grows over time; it gains and spends experience points as a mortal would.

HOMES AND HEARTHS

Harnessing orders of magnitude more Essence than the Charms of the Celestial Exalted, manses make their architects and owners famous for their taste—and power. Demesnes put their owners in touch with the raw wonder of Creation, but manses refine and perfect it. Manses have been command centers for Dragon-Blooded generals, dark havens for Abyssals against the rigorous Sun, and workshops for Solar artificers repairing the wonders of a lost age. A manse might yet decide the fate of Creation: the Imperial Manse, heart of the Realm Defense Grid, is key to the Scarlet Throne (not to mention the potential saving of the world).

THE NINE FILIGREED BRIDGES OF FELUBIC
EACH AIR MANSE •

Though crisscrossed and surrounded by chasms of dizzying depth, the town of Felubic is glad of it. Invading armies leave Felubic untouched, for the fine silver-blue lattices that bridge those fissures can narrow to impassability, and the chasms are so wide and sheer that other methods of crossing are more trouble than they're worth.

At her maturity, every citizen of Felubic learns the procedure to change those defensive bridges. She must

stand in the center of one delicately decorated structure and grip two specific struts. Then she need only look toward a given bridge and sing the note associated with the desired width. Although the bridge she addresses may be miles away, it instantly becomes wider or more slender. Receiving this important knowledge is a rite of passage for the people of Felubic, and rebellious or widely disliked young people are sometimes shamed by being taught last—or not at all.

The bridges, made of jointed metal struts less than an inch wide, are strong but light. They wind easily blows them into strange configurations. Sometimes one bridge gets so tangled that its Essence flows become confused and it stops working entirely. To prevent this problem, people tie lead weights to various points along each bridge; the weights' positions are exactly calculated and need adjustment once a season to accommodate the changing winds.

Students at the Academy of the Glorious Aspect (a respected local school of geomantic architecture) rotate the responsibility of monitoring the bridges' weights. In exchange for this service, the school's outcaste owner carries the nine hearthstones, which form in jade bowls at the center of each bridge.

The nine skystones of Felubic are cobalt orbs that balance perfectly without rolling away, no matter where they're placed. Each hearthstone grants +1 success to Athletics rolls, but only for keeping one's balance.

Game Effects: (Manse's rating of 1) x 2 + 1 Maintenance (weighting the bridges) = 3 Creation Points. Password Activations (1) allows characters who know the procedure to activate the Basic Convenience (1) of widening or narrowing a bridge, and Network Node (1) lets them change one bridge from another. Each bridge is its own manse with the same powers, not an interconnected piece of one large manse; in other words, the chasms contain nine very similar demesnes, not one.

THE SILVER-FLASH GROTTO
LUNAR MANSE ••

Shadows lie dark over a cave set in ice, above a sheer cliff slick with frost. Silver chains stretch across the entrance and through the interior caverns, hung with icicles and woven with evening-colored blossoms by the resident priest. Those silver-stemmed flowers take root in the ice itself, growing in profusion throughout the Grotto and opening beneath the light of the moon. Snowflake-fine panels of ice, shaped in circles and crescents, have been sculpted wherever it's open to the sky, reflecting Luna's light back at her in homage.

A lineage of silent priests dwelled in the Grotto for more than 1,000 years, but only one remains. Wrapped in tattered robes, she spends her time in contemplation, wandering through its secret places and receiving food by lowering a basket 3,000 feet to the ground below. The icewalkers keep up their tithes of reindeer-meat and summer greens, but nothing heavier can be exchanged—there are no materials with which to construct a better-engineered lifting system, and nothing strong and stable enough to support it if there were.

A bird-totemed Lunar has claimed the Grotto, but he spends little time there and barely acknowledges the priest. Silence and illiteracy impede her attempts to communicate that she must find new acolytes; she cannot seek them without his help, for a mortal couldn't possibly scale the cliff. Luna heeded her desperate prayers and sent him a dream, but he didn't understand it. The hearthstone bearer may only learn how necessary she is when she dies.

A Lunar version of the jewel of the celestial mandarin (see p. 105) crystallizes in a moonsilver cage, set in a ceiling crowded with icicles.

Game Effects: (Manse's rating of 2) x 2 + 3 Maintenance (silent priesthood) + 2 Fragility (thin ice, flowers and fine chains) = 9 Creation Points. The Grotto is a Temple Manse (3, available to manses of any level). A Veil of Shadow (2) protects many corners under icy overhangs; those formations often contain faux icicles of crystal that may be turned to open Hidden Passages (2), likewise Veiled. A Comfort Zone (1) makes the ice cave seem warm, while Well-Flavored Aspect (1) so far has not been enough to help the priestess to communicate through gestures. The Lunar just thinks she's lonely.

There must always be at least one silent priest or Power Failure will ensue, but she need not constantly stay in the Grotto as long as she continues to serve Luna. Each priest's initial dedication must occur there, though. Nor may priests be mute or otherwise crippled: the sacrifice comes from a whole self. Should the priesthood meet with misfortune, at least one must always be uninjured, or Power Failure will occur.

THE INFINITELY UNFOLDING MANSE

SIDEREAL MANSE ••• (BUILT ON DEMESNE ••••)

When her 400-year-old uncle died, Ledaal Ghirelle was annoyed to find she had inherited only a few rice paddies and a lot of wasteland. She became more interested when her new tenant farmers told her of a "place of floating folk and strange omens": a demesne. It wasn't, however, like any demesne she'd ever seen before. Ghirelle, a talented and ambitious sorcerer, decided to see whether she could cap it herself—in secret, for she didn't wish to give the demesne up to her House.

The local villagers informed her that the demesne hadn't been there 50 years before, but couldn't tell her how recently it had appeared. From her uncle's records, Ghirelle concluded that he hadn't noticed it before his death. She summarily slaughtered the mutated residents, made a few examples of other locals to keep the peasants quiet, and contacted an old architect friend. After swearing him to secrecy, she surveyed the land and got to work.

Ghirelle grew more and more intrigued as her peasant and demons laborers built from their blueprints; her friend, Peleps Jiro, grew more and more anxious. They'd designed an Air manse, for Air seemed most like the demesne's aspect, but the building didn't cooperate. Granite blocks would lift themselves and float to new locations. Departing one evening with three floors finished, the two returned to find the floors reversed. The top of the manse flatly refused to be roofed. Still, Ghirelle insisted that they push on, and when the manse was furnished, she immediately floated in to attune while Jiro looked anxiously on.

The manse was supposed to be tall and have a lot of rooms, but they were also supposed to go in order. Ghirelle noticed that the room at the end of the first floor's hallway has a window looking down from the seventh story. She doesn't mind those things, though—nor the fact that nothing has any weight in the manse, and she's had to learn to "swim" through air. She enjoys just exploring the building, and finds herself more pleasantly surprised by Jiro's unusual decorative choices every time she goes further in. The other day, she was thrilled to find a hall filled with bells that rang 10 seconds after she shook them, and she can't wait to perform some sorcerous experiments in the room with the self-lighting candles.

Jiro suspects that the underlying demesne is growing in power, but he can't figure out why. He thinks Ghirelle's memories are being rearranged, like the manse's rooms, but fears her temper too much to speak to her about it. Ghirelle vanishes within the manse for days, but Jiro lacks the courage to go past the first few rooms. Already, though, he can see how the rooms Ghirelle comes to differ from the rooms he visits—and from her increasingly incoherent descriptions, he's *sure* he didn't draw blueprints for the distant places she's reached. Worse, he can't imagine from where their

contents come. And worst of all, it sounds as if the geomantic influences reshaping the physical laws of the manse are actually changing in its faraway corners. That, Jiro knows, just shouldn't be possible.

Game Effects: (Manse's rating of 3) x 2 + 1 for seasonal Maintenance of an Exalt expending every last mote of her Essence pool = 7 Creation Points. Because it caps a level 4 demesne, the Infinitely Unfolding Manse has Essence Vents (1): small basins in every room gather translucence filled with sparks. The Puzzle Manse (3) power causing the manse's rooms to rearrange follows a different pattern for each person who enters—the room beyond a given door is set by the person who opens it. Each pattern is based on that person's star chart, and one must learn one's horoscope to solve it.

As for the Wyld Revocation (3, brought down from 4 by matching aspect), Jiro's right: It isn't possible for the power to inconsistently change Creation's laws throughout the manse. Jiro doesn't realize that in addition to removing gravity and an attuned resident's need to eat, the Wyld Revocation interacts with Puzzle Manse to send explorers into alternate versions of the manse: ways the manse *might* have been built, including different packages of changes to Creation's laws. There are no less than 25 alternate manses, one for each constellation of the Maidens; their study might provide insight into Sidereal arts, if anyone knew what to look for.

THE DROWNED MOSAICS OF SUMAN TZUNG

WATER MANSE ●● (DAMAGED; REPAIRABLE TO ●●●●)

Suman Tzung was considered the greatest student of Silur, a First Age sorcerer who founded a school of magic based on communication and symbolism. Tzung developed a mystically expressive runic language so well-constructed that Silurian sorcerers still use it today. In particular, the sorcerers of the Heptagram value the runes, and would like to learn them all. Sadly, Suman Tzung created only one key to his language—tiled in mosaics running through the 77 rooms of his home, a manse built to float over the undersea demesne it capped.

When the usurping Dragon-Blooded attacked Tzung, they chipped his house' curving porcelain walls and broke the main indoor stairway. The manse sank and historians believe it was destroyed—but it was built with all the care and knowledge of the First Age.

Tzung's 11 floors did not collapse, and none of his diamond windows broke. On a seamount a mile beneath the ocean's surface now lies a manse with pearl-studded walls, seashell carvings and rounded arches. Within, only three rooms have flooded; the rest are damp, but filled with air. Opening and closing an outside door quickly

enough will not even flood the rest of the manse. (Closing a door against the force of the ocean's depths does require a prodigious feat of strength, though.)

The new flaws in the manse's structure do make themselves obvious. Freezing rain and hail suddenly fall from the ceilings, while tsunamis rip through the great hall. Previously unflooded rooms become waist-deep in seawater, complete with fierce riptides and violent whirlpools, then drain several days later. Fortunately, Tzung's tasteful glass furniture wasn't necessary for the manse's geomancy: chairs and tables have shattered in every corner. A person who spent much time in the manse, even attuned, would suffer a similar fate, battered and slashed by currents loaded with shattered glass and dissolving Essence.

Tzung's mosaics were tiled in jade-alloy, however, and they remain perfectly preserved. Because the mosaics were constructed by means of rituals that drew on certain aspects of the medium, painted copies never fully conveyed their power. If the manse were rediscovered, the Heptagram would send emissaries (and navies) to view and claim the original runes.

Game Effects: (Manse's original rating of 4) x 2 = 8 Creation Points. Tzung's manse could move between its seamount demesne and the surface through Limited Mobility (2). Doubled Comfort Zone (2) kept it pleasantly warm and dry even under a mile of water. Aesthetic rivulets flowed neatly around residents' feet and unwanted visitors were buffeted away by waves, thanks to Water Dragon's Will (2, taken down from 3 by matching aspect). Now that it's lost two levels to Power Failure, those powers keep it mostly filled with breathable air, but their damage causes its internal storms as two levels of Essence Vents.

The manse's Archive (2) include the mosaics, which—to sorcerers of Silur's School only—offer a -5 difficulty reduction to rolls made to research new spells, a great secret replacing one specialty. The mosaics also provide specialties in Calligraphy, Cryptography and Arcane Symbolism.

For more on Suman Tzung's mosaics, Silur's School, and the Heptagram, see pages 33, 21 and 26-28 of **The White Treatise**.

THE HOUSE OF WELL-FAVORED ASPECT

FIRE MANSE ●●●●

The foremost geomantic academy in the world, the Realm's House of Well-Favored Aspect trains master sorcerers and inexperienced youths alike. Its outstanding curriculum and willingness to instruct from the ground up aren't just a factor of sagacious professors, though. The manse itself, an incredible inheritance from the Age of Splendor, also teaches.

Mere residence in the black-and-red halls of the House is an education. It may be the most beautiful manse in the world, for it hasn't just been built in resonance with its environment, but with the principles of architectural harmony themselves. Every measurement is faultlessly judged, every room an ode to the craft. The flames in each sconce leap to an ordained height, and the long triangular windows, though crimson-edged, filter light of utter clarity. Living there, even the slaves learn something of geomancy.

Beginning students learn where to stand before the manse's jade pedestals and how to phrase their questions ("House: Show me the 39 greater associations of Air"). At first they watch in awe, later with great attention as three-dimensional displays shimmer into existence above them and a crackling, asexual voice speaks their lesson. Often, they regret having to take their advanced classes from people.

Fire, observers agree, is not the best element for a teaching environment. While graduates of the House of Well-Favored Aspect are certainly knowledgeable, many feel a strange intensity for their work. When detachment might serve them better, these geomancers fall in love with what they build. Their initial lessons were of unparalleled completeness, but trained them to throw themselves into their designs without wisdom or emotional caution. Some weep when others live in their manses; others prefer to die than let one be damaged or restructured.

The House's hearthstone, a dark disc containing a red flicker, rotates among senior instructors. Its bearer's player gains +6 to geomancy rolls, but only in places the character loves.

Game Effects: (Manse's rating of 4) x 2 = 8 Creation Points. The manse's inherently instructive architecture is its Ability Enlightenment (4), dedicated to Occult, Lore, Craft (Earth) and Linguistics. This supersedes the centuries of accumulated lore about manse construction, which would otherwise form an Archive. Mela's Sweet Whisper (2), the Glorious Halo of Hesiesh (1, taken down from 2 by matching aspect), Password Activations (1) and the Linguistics 4 from Ability Enlightenment all combine to provide the curricula accessed by spoken questions.

LOOKSHY'S BURIED FACTORY-CATHEDRAL
SOLAR MANSE •• (DAMAGED; REPAIRABLE TO •••••)

Most folk of Lookshy know their city has two manses capping level 5 demesnes. Hardly anyone knows their city actually surrounds a third, sunk deep underground. Ancient Deheleshen was a jewel of the Old Realm, important enough that the Solars gave the city a supply of Essence rare even in those days.

Deep under the twisting halls of Lookshy's Academy of Sorcery at Valkhawsen lies a ruined labyrinth of tarnished metal. Advanced students learn they must don full-body suits of spun orichalcum-steel to survive walking under vents that shower them with glowing heat. Even this special garb, however, could not protect them from the tornadoes of golden-white fire that rage in certain immense shafts and chambers. They also learn they must never touch the huge spikes and shattered plates of pure orichalcum so carefully placed around these Essence-storms and at certain other locations. They see huge sunbursts of copper and gold set in the vaulted ceilings and between long-neglected altars, and know they tread in a wrecked palace of the Anathema.

Although this factory-cathedral's forges and altars are cold, it still needs Maintenance—for the city's safety. That maintenance takes the form of the seasonal sacrifice of sentient, sun-aspected Essence. Half-Caste children of Solar Exalted would suffice. An attuned Solar Exalt could also pay the price by bleeding herself upon the central altar; she wouldn't need to die, but the manse would drain her down to her -4 health level with aggravated damage.

Solars and their descendants being hard to come by, the General Staff addresses the problem by securing sunbeam people from the Bright Plateau (p. 56) and holding them in a greenhouse by means of orichalcum nets. Unfortunately, they don't breed as often as they could, and the General Staff must send occasional missions to the Plateau for more. Most of the General Staff have convinced themselves that the sunbeam people lack souls and were never human. It helps that they don't know their gestural language, and can't recognize their pleas for mercy.

Game Effects: (Manse's original rating of 5 x 2) + 4 Maintenance (sun-Essence sacrifices) = 14 Creation Points. Lookshy's factory-cathedral suffered three levels of Power Failure in the Usurpation. The Sidereals intended to destroy it, but not everything went their way in the Usurpation: brave Dragon-Blooded technicians patched it before it could explode from Essence buildup. The patches also reduce the Maintenance so keeping several sunbeam people captive suffices to keep the manse powered, if not functional. Visitors must also purify themselves by passing through burning vents of Solar Essence while wearing the orichalcum protective gear. It no longer deserves the title of Factory-Cathedral (5) anymore: buried, it cannot

send prayers to the Sun or receive the necessary blessing to construct artifacts. One Mind Within (5) once bent every thinking creature within its walls to the task of praying, defending it, and servicing its technologies, but now, its vast halls stand quiescent. It can no longer raise itself, in whole or in part, through Limited Mobility (2) to meet the Sun. Only its Password Activations (1) and Self-Destruct Sequence (1) still work—and only Sidereals know of the latter.

The broken orichalcum mirrors and shattered diamond lens-windows must be replaced, its metals polished, and its golden spires raised to greet the Sun (using Limited Mobility [2]) if a character wishes to repair this factory-cathedral. Unfortunately, the entire Lookshy Academy of Sorcery is in the way. Still, the sorcerer-engineers make use of the buried structure. The ferociously hot Essence Vents that bleed off excess power can smelt any metal and burn off physical and metaphysical impurities. Since the sorcerer-engineers consider this desirable, the Essence Vents [3] now constitute a power in their own right, replacing some of what existed before.

For more on Valkhawsen, see pages 24-26 of **The White Treatise**.

THE HIDDEN TABERNACLE

ABYSSAL MANSE •••••

At the heart of a gray tundra towers the most unfortunate shrine in Creation. Surrounded by bloody, tattered banners, under which ghosts and men fight side by side with black swords and undead war-beasts, a golden temple glows like a beacon. Banners, troops and citadel are devoted to the glory of the Shining One, the Deathlord known as the Bishop of the Chalcedony Thurible.

A muffled, discordant organ echoes through the citadel's doors. The single mortal guard warns visitors that worship is not today. Beneath the Great Hall, where the frozen organ moans unplayed and a basin of smoking yellow water swirls slowly, dozens of narrow tunnels split into hundreds—winding, intersecting and descending into a cold, black world. Ghosts trail through that echoing maze, seeking wisdom and truth. As their corpus wastes away, they find only emptiness.

The living are rarely foolish enough to venture into the tunnels. They prefer to worship the Shining One with violent piety. Thousands gather in the surrounding fields, in sects claiming the Tabernacle as their right and reward. They come thousands of miles through snow and war and know none are more ready to die in the act of killing than they are—and do.

Every seventh day, in makeshift shrines, survivors engage in sectarian rituals, consuming bloodied snow and scorched earth. Participants feel a transcendent closeness to the Shining One and redouble their battles the next day with eyes turned solid blue.

Eventually, one faction wins. Victorious, they venture to the Hidden Tabernacle as night falls at noon. The guard informs them that they're on time to worship, and the sect's head leads his followers in. He assumes a position at the organ, which draws out his blood and comes to life; as he drinks the yellow water, it brightens to blue. In the most violent battle of all, he consumes his cult before dying in agony. His body becomes an undead horror, and his soul joins those wandering the endless halls. The Tabernacle vanishes as daylight returns, beginning anew in a different field with a different flock.

Game Effects: (Manse's rating of 5) x 2 = 10 Creation Points—but as an Inauspicious Citadel (5), it defies normal Creation Point calculations. Its special connection to the Neverborn makes it a Soul Prison (4) for those who die within. The most potent ghosts become its guardians, but the others wander the underways in search of a truth they shall never find. Its hearthstone is a gem of the night sky (see p. 103). The Bishop lives there in contentment, surrounded by sweet incense, thanks to pleasant Basic Conveniences (1). The Neverborn grow impatient; if he doesn't expand his empire soon, he may lose his ghostly prisoners.

The Hidden Tabernacle is a universal truth. It could be in any of 25 Northern shadowlands by means of Alternate Locations (10). These regions are filled with religious battles; the bishop's agents could use wars as major undertakings to create new locations in shadowlands. Its mystery is the catacombs, empty and dark to the point where all are lost to Puzzle Manse (3).

As the Bishop sits in his library and reads, the books and the manse read him. As an Atelier-Manse (4) devoted to Craft (Water) and, to a limited degree, the Art of Alchemy, the Hidden Tabernacle brews the mutagenic yellow toxin of his thoughts and mixes it with the blood of his followers. The solution runs through underground channels to taint the surroundings, and his worshipers imbibe his absent will through its Zone of Influence (3)

Insane as they seem, the Bishop's followers are his center and self. His worshipers abandon their lives for their distant prophet, but even if they gain their reward, they die cold and alone. This reflects the Bishop's philosophy; wars between cults are his own introspection. His mind's spiritual poisons have spread through so many veins that his wisdom is unmatched, and forever bodiless.

Hearthstones

Hearthstones straddle the line between artifacts and natural wonders. Just as forging an artifact is ultimately similar to forging a sword or cutting and faceting a precious stone, altering the structure of a manse to create a hearthstone with specific properties emerges from other arts directly involving the natural world, like growing bonsai or designing an echo chamber. Any Essence-wielder can easily use a hearthstone if she possesses its associated manse, but creating a hearthstone is a complex task requiring both the correct sort of demesne and much skill and patience.

Some Exalts simply build whatever manse they can and accept whatever hearthstone forms. Building (or rebuilding) a manse so it produces a *specific* hearthstone uses the same process and dice pool as designing a specific power into a manse: the hearthstone's dot rating supplies the difficulty. Most of the work to reconfigure a manse's hearthstone takes place in its hearthroom, the chamber where the magical stone forms, but this does not reduce costs, difficulty or hazards in any way.

Few hearthstones are unique, especially the stones of lower power. Low-powered demesnes are both far more numerous and considerably easier to shape and control than powerful demesnes. As a result, many one- and two-dot hearthstones listed here are quite common.

Hearthstones of Air

Gem of Echoes (Manse •)

This oval black jewel glows softly with an inner light. It distorts and creates echoes of any sounds its bearer makes, such as footsteps or speech. This makes the bearer harder to locate by sound, imposing a -2 external penalty to all Perception rolls to detect or locate the bearer by sound.

Gem of Visitations (Manse •)

This multicolored, multifaceted gem is an example of an unusually specialized hearthstone. The possessor of this hearthstone can opt to receive an incoming Infallible Messenger mentally, without the visible and audible cherub effect, and can store and redisplay at will up to five Infallible Messenger missives. If the gem's owner casts Infallible Messenger herself, she can give the spell multiple targets at a cost of 5 motes per additional recipient, up to a maximum of five recipients. Finally, the bearer can personalize the cherubic display of the spell to a limited degree. However, the voice from the magical messenger remains the same as the character's own.

Hearthstone Duplication

The associations of elements and celestial aspects overlap to some degree. Therefore, manses of different aspects can sometimes produce functionally identical hearthstones. For instance, a hearthstone that augments Martial Arts prowess could come from a manse aspected to Water (the Terrestrial caste that favors that Ability) or the Sidereals (the most proficient martial artists in Creation). Storytellers can reassign hearthstones to different elemental or celestial aspects as they see fit, or create duplicate stones.

Hearthstones can also appear in versions of greater or lesser power. A more powerful stone might add successes instead of dice, augment a wider range of activities or otherwise offer greater benefits; a less powerful stone might offer smaller bonuses to dice pools, operate a limited number of times per day, require Essence expenditures or otherwise limit its power.

Sorcerer-architects have designed other hearthstones to modify single spells, but all such hearthstones are quite uncommon. Most sorcerers consider them a waste of geomantic resources.

Godspeaking Trillion (Air •)

This hearthstone resembles a square-cut piece of milky blue topaz. It gives the bearer's voice the timbre and intonation of one of members of the Council of Winds. Air elementals and gods of weather, wind and sky react more favorably to the character because he sounds like one of them. The character's player may apply either a +2 bonus to all Social rolls when dealing with such entities, or reduce their difficulties by 1 (to a minimum of 1). This includes Charms that must exceed a target's MDV to exert mental influence, but the player may not apply both advantages at once.

Jewel of the Flying Heart (Manse •)

This blood-red, triangular stone increases the bearer's Dodge DV by one. (This bonus applies to the final value, not the pool used to calculate it.) Setting this hearthstone in an edged weapon also grants a +1 bonus to all Melee attacks the bearer makes with that weapon.

Memory Stone (Manse •)

The character who carries this iridescent white, cubical hearthstone will never forget anything. Every image or incident, from a face seen in a crowd last week, to the contents of a treaty that he hurriedly read

before being chased off by guards, will be remembered in perfect and exact detail. The wearer's player can even make (Perception + Awareness) rolls after the fact for his character to notice further details about an event. Although this hearthstone does not allow the wearer to learn Abilities, Charms or spells any faster or easier, the wearer could read an ancient 1,000-page tome and perfectly remember every word and illustration 50 years later. These unnaturally sharp memories begin to fade to normal memories if the character ceases to be attuned to this stone for more than one day.

STONE OF QUICK THOUGHT (MANSE •)

This red-and-silver-banded oval allows the bearer to think faster and more clearly than usual. This stone provides the bearer with a +1 bonus to all Wits rolls.

STONE OF THE SPIDER'S EYE (MANSE •)

Thin lines of pale blue run through this square, white stone. This hearthstone grants the bearer the ability to see through magical concealments. The stone of the spider's eye can either cancel up to -2 worth of penalties to Perception rolls due to magical stealth or concealment, or grant the bearer two bonus dice to rolls to see through such enchantments. The bearer cannot apply both bonuses to the same roll.

CRYSTAL OF THE FROZEN NORTH (MANSE ••)

Snowflake patterns run through this translucent white, hexagonal crystal. The bearer becomes immune to all natural cold: he can comfortably swim in an ice-covered river or walk through a blizzard wearing nothing but this stone. In addition, the bearer can create cold by touch. Without spending any Essence, the bearer can chill a warm drink. Spending 1 mote allows her instantly to cool a red-hot sword without taking damage, or to freeze a square yard of water thick enough for a person to stand upon. Additional motes allow the bearer to freeze more water. Freezing a square yard of water well enough to allow a ridden or heavily laden horse to cross it requires 2 motes per square yard. This ice melts normally and in average temperatures lasts several hours. The cold generated by this stone cannot be used to put out fires—there's nothing solid enough to touch.

JEWEL OF SWIFT COMPREHENSION (MANSE ••)

This colorless ovoid of ice-clear crystal speeds the comprehension of visual information, from reading a text to searching a room. The bearer may accomplish such tasks a number of times faster than normal equal to her permanent Essence +1, without any loss of detail or understanding. A character with an Essence of 3 could thus read four times faster than normal. In addition, this jewel also reduces the difficulty of all Lore and Investigation rolls that involve reading or visual observation by 2 (to a minimum of 1).

PURIFYING MERCY STONE (MANSE ••)

This hexagonal crystal of clear rock quartz purifies the air around its wearer, keeping him safe from smoke, poisonous gases or even the stench of open sewers. This bubble of pure air extends for two yards around the bearer, so anyone who stays close to him is similarly protected. Smoke and visible vapors swirl around this sphere, clearly outlining its boundaries. The hearthstone does not allow the bearer to breathe underwater or in the absence of air, but it completely purifies the most poisonous air.

SAVANT'S ICY EYE (MANSE ••)

This cube of imperishable, clear-blue ice contains a myriad of shifting, crystalline patterns and shapes. The bearer instantly knows the exact number of objects that he can see and can estimate with almost perfect accuracy the total number of objects present if he can only see a portion of them. He knows the number of trees in a forest, soldiers on a battlefield or gemstones in a vault. This hearthstone also grants the bearer the ability to work with these figures with inhuman speed and accuracy. The savant's icy eye grants five bonus dice to any task that involves numbers and calculation.

STONE OF FIRST IMPRESSIONS (MANSE ••)

This opaque blue-and-white lens gives the bearer an instant sense of the intentions and immediate concerns of anyone she encounters for the first time. This sense occurs the moment the bearer begins to talk with or listen to the person. However, the stone only provides information about a single target per day. This stone also provides no information about someone's general personality or trustworthiness.

WIND JEWEL (MANSE ••)

This transparent, sky blue oval enables its wearer to control minor winds and light breezes within 10 yards. The bearer can easily perform simple feats such as clearing a room of smoke in a few moments, blowing out torches or stilling the wind enough to prevent uncovered candles from blowing out. Occasionally, tiny breezes play around the wearer when he feels some strong emotion.

The wearer can also precisely direct the wind so that it extinguishes only one candle in a candelabrum or riffles the pages of a single open tome, while not disturbing the other papers on a table. The character's player must succeed at a (Wits + Larceny) roll to perform such exacting feats. Failure mean that either the wind cannot achieve the desired task, or that it also affected nearby objects, while a botch means that the wind affected something quite different from what the character intended.

In addition, the bearer can summon a moderately strong breeze to help or hinder a ship. This wind adds or subtracts up to 10 miles per hour from the speed of any single craft up to the size of a yacht or small cargo vessel and up to 5 miles per hour for larger ships.

GEM OF ELEMENTAL TRAVEL (MANSE ●●●)

This hexagonal, brilliant-red hearthstone allows the bearer to walk safely over any generally horizontal or gradually inclined surface, including water, lava, mud, ice, quicksand, on top of a field of grain or on any similar terrain. The bearer can move over these surfaces without injury, slowed movement or an increased chance of slipping or falling. However, this stone does allow its bearer the ability to walk on air, walk up walls or on ceilings. The stone only allows horizontal movement over a liquid or an at least somewhat solid surface.

GEM OF FORGETTING (MANSE ●●●)

This smooth hearthstone is shaped like an arrowhead and covered in swirls of light and dark red. Anyone who meets the bearer cannot clearly remember her afterward. Even moments after seeing the bearer, no one can describe anything about her appearance, dress or mannerisms. Repeated and prolonged meetings gradually counter this effect, allowing the bearer's family and close companions to remember him clearly. Remembering the bearer after one encounter requires a successful (Intelligence + Awareness) roll at difficulty 3. Repeated or extended contact lowers this difficulty by 1 per full day spent largely in the wearer's presence, or by 1 for every three shorter encounters.

GEMSTONE OF SPOKEN LANGUAGE (MANSE ●●●)

This blue-green prism allows the bearer to understand and speak any language or dialect, no matter its origin. However, the stone's power does not extend to written language. The bearer can understand and speak any spoken language as if it were her native tongue, but cannot read or write any language she has not learned.

JEWEL OF WHISPERS (MANSE ●●●)

The owner of this dark blue cabochon can hear any sound occurring near the jewel as if she were actually present at that spot, regardless of her distance from

the stone. She can also speak and make her voice come from the jewel. To use this stone, the bearer need only leave it someplace she wishes to eavesdrop. She can then recall the stone to her over any distance. By merely willing it, she causes the stone to vanish and instantly reappear in its setting. If the owner wishes to recall this gem, no other hearthstones can be placed in the setting it last occupied.

KEY OF MASTERY (MANSE ●●●)

This flat, crystalline rectangle is normally clear but becomes cloudy when attuned to a spell. By attuning this stone to a specific sorcery spell, the bearer can reduce that spell's mote cost by (her own Essence x 2). However, this stone cannot reduce a spell's cost by more than half. Also, no combination of this stone with similar effects (such as the No Moon Caste ability) can reduce a spell's cost below 1 mote. While the user can possess more than one of these stones, only one can be attuned to a particular spell. Attuning this stone requires the bearer to meditate quietly with the stone for a number of hours equal to the normal Essence cost of this spell.

STONE OF EASY BREATH (MANSE ●●●)

The bearer of this cloudy, almond-shaped gem can breathe easily in any surroundings, such as at high altitudes, in smoke or toxic gases, or even underwater or buried alive.

LIGHTNING ROD GEMSTONE (MANSE ●●●●)

This short, faceted rod of deep purple renders the bearer completely immune to electricity. Any electrical discharge, whether natural or magical, that would strike within 10 yards of the bearer is instead drawn into the stone and harmlessly absorbed.

STONE OF AIRWALKING (MANSE ●●●●)

This spherical white stone looks like a tiny, solidified cloud. Whenever the bearer of this stone desires, she can walk upon the air instead of the ground. Although she still moves at her normal movement rate, the character can walk safely across water or quicksand by walking on a layer of air lying above the surface. In addition, the character can walk up or down the air as easily as others walk up or down a staircase. With sufficient climbing, the character can walk along miles above the ground. If the character trips or is knocked down, however, she can still fall to her death unless she can get her feet under her; her player must successfully roll (Dexterity + Athletics) at difficulty 3. Also, the stone only allows the character herself to move in this fashion. Any steed she rides must still travel along the ground.

TWICE-STRIKING LIGHTNING PRISM (MANSE ●●●●)

This prism-shaped crystal appears at once metallic and transparent. By spending one Willpower point, the bearer can reflexively add 2 to her Essence rating for calculating the effects of a single Charm or spell. As long as the bearer has sufficient Willpower to spend, she can use this stone as often as desired—but the stone does not enable a character to learn Charms above her normal Essence.

GEM OF THE WIND'S SECRETS (MANSE ●●●●●)

This hearthstone, a flawless diamond the size of a man's fist, was never meant to be worn. The only known example of this stone comes from the Aviary in Lookshy, where it tracks the various flying vessels and creatures in and around the city.

When anyone attuned to the Aviary touches this stone, it projects an image of every thing that flies within 100 miles around itself. This projection clearly differentiates all flying vessels by their size, airspeed and direction (in relation to the Aviary). The user can then sort this projection to eliminate small objects such as birds or bats. He can also magnify any individual image so that it appears as it would if the user was within 500 yards away on a clear sunlit day, regardless of the actual light levels. This stone even reveals dematerialized spirits: only Celestial or Solar Circle sorcery or Charms that require an Essence of 4 or more can hide a flying object or individual from this stone.

THIRD HAND ORB (MANSE ●●●●●)

This smooth silver oval can store any sorcery spell within it, so that its bearer can later release it. To use this stone, the bearer must ritually attune it to a spell she knows. This takes as many hours as the base Essence cost of the spell, without interruptions. At the end of this ritual, she casts the spell into the hearthstone. She may then release this spell as a reflexive action at any time, as if cast by the wearer. The spell stored inside the Third Hand Orb is lost if the stone is ever caught within the radius of a Countermagic spell sufficient to dispel the spell inside. Essence committed to casting the spell is committed until the spell is released.

HEARTHSTONES OF EARTH

GEM OF DIGNITY (MANSE ●)

This transparent, egg-shaped stone glows with a soft light. It enhances the bearer's dignity and poise, so that any social attacks to make him look foolish or stupid are at +2 difficulty.

GEMSTONES OF SYNCHRONICITY (MANSE •)

A few manses are designed to divide their power among multiple hearthstones. These octagonal, bright green crystals always form in groups of two or more—one for each dot of the manse's power. Multiple characters attuned to the manse can each bear a Gemstone of Synchronicity and regain Essence as they normally would from a one-dot hearthstone.

Each bearer can faintly sense the pains and emotions of the others. Although this can be unpleasant at times, only the most extreme pain can cause serious distraction. In such cases, the other bearers suffer no more than a one die penalty to all actions. If one of the bearers dies, the others feel her death as a searing pain of the heart that lasts for a full minute before easing. Each bearer also knows the distance and direction of all the other stone bearers. Most importantly, however, when bearers of these hearthstones fight side by side, they gain a +1 bonus to attempts to coordinate their attacks.

HARDENED SPIRIT GEMSTONE (MANSE •)

This octagon of dark, perfectly clear amethyst grants its bearer one additional die to all Conviction rolls, including rolls to regain Willpower. The bearer must have a permanent Willpower of 6+ or a Conviction rating of 3+ to gain this benefit.

STONE OF BREATH (MANSE •)

This circular hearthstone is pale green, flat and opaque. It allows the bearer to breathe with maximum ease and efficiency in all circumstances. This improved breath provides an additional three dice to all Resistance rolls.

STONE OF COMFORT (MANSE •)

Although this hearthstone looks like a simple oval of white jade, it can impart the calm stability of elemental Earth to a troubled and damaged mind. Once per day, its bearer may touch the stone to someone who suffers from a derangement and ease that person's insanity for a scene.

STONE OF EARTH'S BLOOD (MANSE •)

This oval stone is marbled with russet and maroon. This stone can temporarily save the bearer's life if he is poisoned, or grant him a short period of sobriety during an evening of debauchery. By spending 1 mote of Essence per minute, the user can completely defer the effects of any poison or intoxicant in his system. If the character stops spending or runs out of Essence, the full effects of the poison or intoxicant instantly return. The stone does not eliminate or shorten the effects of alcohol, drugs or poisons; it merely puts them off until later.

STONE OF HUMBLE GLORY (MANSE •)

This faceted pentagonal jewel shines like a silvery mirror. The bearer's player gains a bonus equal to the average of her character's Conviction and Temperance (round up) to any Social roll where the character tells the truth without exaggeration or deliberate deception.

COLD IRON BAUBLE (MANSE ••)

These small spherical hearthstones of black iron are relatively common on the Blessed Isle, especially in Earth manses near the Imperial Mountain. However, they are most treasured in those portions of the Threshold that adjoin the Wyld. Any weapon fitted with a cold iron bauble inflicts aggravated damage to Fair Folk, just as if the weapon itself was made of cold iron. This hearthstone also inflicts a -1 external penalty on any Fair Folk powers used against its bearer.

EYE OF THE FIRST GOAT (MANSE ••)

This stone looks like a pale orange eye with a slitted, dark red pupil. Its bearer's player gains a bonus to all Athletics rolls equal to one-half of his character's Temperance, rounded up. In addition, the bearer gains a +1 bonus to any Melee attacks made with a blunt weapon set with this hearthstone.

GEM OF PERFECTION (MANSE ••)

This smooth, moss-green oval enables its bearer to ignore the effects of any long-term injuries, scars or birth defects. Congenital conditions, paralysis and chronic pain all instantly vanish. It can even restore missing limbs or organs, although an entire limb requires two months to regenerate. The bearer cannot ignore penalties from recently suffered wounds, but after a week of healing all remaining wound penalties vanish. After carrying this stone for two months, all of the Crippling effects of injuries and defects are permanently restored. Such benefits do not reverse themselves if the character later loses the hearthstone.

The Exalted seldom suffer long-term crippling, but the Gem of Perfection trumps any enduring damage induced by Charms. It also heals damage from wounds suffered *before* Exaltation. Enlightened mortals, who learned to Channel Essence without Exaltation, value the Gem of Perfection even more highly.

KILL-HAND GEM (MANSE ••)

This greenish-black stone is shaped like a jagged-edged triangle. When desired, it hardens the bearer's hands and feet, allowing him to deal lethal damage with all unarmed attacks.

SPHERE OF BALANCE (MANSE ••)

The bearer of this white-veined, dark-green orb gains superb balance and stability on her feet. Whether walking along a tightrope or dashing along wet ice, her Athletics is treated as 4 greater than it really is for purposes of keeping her balance on unstable footing (see **Exalted**, p. 155). If that isn't enough for the character to keep her balance automatically, the (Dexterity + Athletics) roll for her to avoid falling still receives a +2 bonus. So do rolls to resist knockdown.

A similar, three-dot hearthstone gives its bearer *perfect* balance and renders him completely unable to be knocked off his feet, so long as he keeps at least one foot on the ground.

SPIDER'S EYE STONE (MANSE ••)

The sparkling blue veins in this smooth gray stone resemble a spider web. This hearthstone's bearer can see through the eyes of any spider within a 10-yard radius. This effect also works on all spider-like creatures, including anuhles (spider-demons), spider beastmen, Lunar Exalted in spider form and other spider-like creatures.

STONE OF THE EARTHWEB (MANSE ••)

Black veins crawl across this rough, light-gray octagon. An Exalt bearing this hearthstone never need fear sneak attacks or stumbling around in the dark. While wearing it, the Exalt can feel the earth around her just as a spider can feel the strands of its web. Within a radius of 10 yards, the Exalt feels everything resting upon the ground or on the same floor that she stands upon. She can feel size, approximate weight and any movement of all such objects and individuals. A large chest would be a heavy rectangular weight, while even the most carefully hidden assassin would feel like a live person standing very still.

So long as the bearer stands upon the ground or a floor that is built directly upon the ground, she can feel everything upon the ground that is within her range. However, if she stands on the upper story of a building, then these perceptions only apply to objects and people resting upon that upper floor. Also, the mystical perception granted by the hearthstone does not extend to anything that is not on the floor. Hanging lamps or assassins crouching on desks cannot be felt with this item (although the desk might seem oddly heavy). In addition, the character will not trip over obstacles in the dark or suffer other penalties to movement based on poor visibility.

GEM OF SAFE HARVEST (MANSE •••)

This hearthstone looks like an irregular lump of unpolished, dark-yellow amber. It transmutes anything eaten or drunk by the bearer into safe and nourishing food. Nothing the bearer ingests can cause her any harm, even if it is poisoned with the deadliest alchemical venom. The bearer finds a diet of seawater, Yozi venom and fragments of driftwood to be as safe and nourishing as the finest meals served to princes and kings.

GEMSTONE OF THE BROTHER'S BOND (MANSE •••)

These stones seem like smooth, water-worn pebbles made from a mixture of the five colors of jade. The bearer can attune herself to all other individuals attuned to the manse simply by spending a point of Willpower. This link precisely duplicates the effects of the spell Sworn Brothers' Oath (see **The Manual of Exalted Power—The Dragon-Blooded**, pp. 122-123), except that the Oathbond has a fixed rating of 5.

GEMSTONE OF THE WHITE JADE TREE (MANSE •••)

This blue-violet cabochon glows with a pale inner light. This stone hardens the bearer's skin; any damage the character suffers after soak is cut in half (rounding all fractions upward). This same hardness reduces the possessor's movement speed by half, rounding all fractions down. This penalty applies to all forms of movement, but can be cancelled by removing the stone from its setting. Doing this also instantly cancels the stone's beneficial effects.

JEWEL OF THE MASTER'S HAND (MANSE •••)

Intricate copper filigree covers this rich brown orb. Its bearer gains extra deftness and insight into artifice. The hearthstone gives a +4 bonus to Craft (Earth) rolls, a +2 bonus to Craft rolls aspected to other elements, and a +1 bonus to esoteric Crafts such as Magitech, Moliation or Glamour.

STONE OF TEMPERANCE (MANSE •••)

This oval, sea-blue stone gives its bearer three additional dice to all Temperance rolls (allowing the character's Temperance dice pool to exceed five dice). This includes channeling Willpower through the Virtue (see **Exalted**, p. 129). However, the bearer's player *must* roll the character's Temperance whenever the character wishes to act contrary to this Virtue, and the stone's bonus dice also count toward these rolls. The bearer of this hearthstone becomes exceptionally resistant to temptation, bribery or corruption. However, he also becomes virtually incapable of bias, deception, betrayal or impulsive action. There are similar hearthstones aligned with the other three Virtues.

Earth-Commanding Stone (Manse ••••)

This rough-textured stone looks like a sphere of fired red clay. It allows the bearer to shape and command unworked earth and stone. Without spending any Essence, she can shape unworked stone by hand as if it were soft clay. This stone resumes its normal hardness as soon as the character ceases to touch it. Sculpting anything complicated or precise certainly requires some sort of Craft (Earth) roll, set by the Storyteller.

The stone's bearer can also command dirt, mud, gravel and unworked stone at a distance by spending 2 motes of Essence per action. If she does this, she can cause the land within (Essence x 5) yards of her to shape itself into any form it could naturally assume, including rounded walls, deep pits and similar forms. The area shaped in a single action, however, is limited to (Essence) yards in any direction. These changes require one minute to complete, because earth moves slowly, and the character must concentrate on directing the ground during this entire time. As a result, this stone cannot be used to attack anyone who can move. If the bearer spends 7 motes of Essence, she can control the earth in this fashion for one full scene.

Stone of Refuge (Manse ••••)

This dark green gem looks like a rough, uncut crystal. Its bearer can sink into and become a part of the ground. She can only enter surfaces made from dirt, gravel, mud, or stone that is part of the earth. Paving stones or a tiled floor cannot be entered, but the wearer can fade into floors made by pounding and grading the local dirt or smoothing and polishing the native stone. Once inside the ground, no trance of the bearer's presence can be seen, heard or smelled. However, Charms for magical perceptions, such as All-Encompassing Sorcerer's Sight, instantly reveal her presence.

Minor damage to the ground, such as removing a handful of dirt or heavy things falling, does not disturb the character. However, digging into the ground above her inflicts one level of bashing damage on the bearer and immediately forces her out of the ground. The character cannot see anything while merged with the ground, but she can hear events on the surface as well as if she were in a nearby room. She can also feel the vibration of heavy footfalls or other movement above. The bearer will starve as normal, but cannot suffocate. The character may emerge whenever she wishes; entering or leaving the ground is a standard miscellaneous action.

Willstone of the Strategos (Manse ••••)

This bright-red, spindle-shaped hearthstone has a dark-purple center. This stone provides the commander of any battle with profound insights into the likely course of events and how he can use his troops to best effect. When in mass combat, the player can roll the character's (Wits + War) as a Speed 3, -0 DV action: Every two successes scored (round up) adds 1 to her unit's Valor, and every four successes (round up) adds 1 to all of the unit's other dice pools involving mass combat. If this stone raises the combat unit's Valor above 5, the soldiers become temporarily immune to fear and will not fail any Valor checks until their Valor falls to 5 or lower.

The commander must be able to communicate with her troops to grant them these benefits. Also, all bonuses are reduced by one every 6 mass combat ticks. Bonuses gained from successive rolls do not stack, but higher rolls can supplant earlier rolls at the bearer's option. Charms (including Excellencies) cannot be used to improve the (Wits + War) pool, but the character can channel Virtues to do so—Valor is always appropriate, and Conviction normally is.

Iron Soul Stone (Manse •••••)

This smooth, rounded gray stone looks like an ordinary rock with no special properties. However, it protects its bearer and everything he wears or carries from all effects of the Wyld. It also inflicts one level of aggravated damage every 5 ticks to any Wyld-touched creature (including the Fair Folk and mortals assimilated by the Wyld) who comes within five yards of the bearer. Wyld creatures killed by this deadly power vanish in a puff of fine dust.

All creatures associated with the Wyld can sense the stone's deadly cold from 15 yards away. Also, all Fair Folk within a mile instantly sense if the bearer brings this stone into any portion of the Wyld deeper than the Bordermarches. Nearby Fair Folk may attempt to destroy the stone and its bearer, drive the bearer out of the Wyld, or simply flee, as they judge their strength compared to the stone's bearer's.

Hearthstones of Fire

Gem of Night Vision (Manse •)

As fire gives light in darkness, so the bearer of this clear, crystal cabochon can see in any non-magical darkness as if he had a bonfire… without the need for a light source that might give him away to an enemy. Even in complete absence of light, the bearer sees clearly out to 10 yards and murkily out to 20 yards. (See **Exalted**, p. 135, for rules about poor visibility.)

IGNITION GEM (MANSE •)

This clear, reddish-orange teardrop enables its bearer to ignite any flammable material simply by touching it with the stone and breathing on it gently. The stone produces a brief magical spark. All fires lit by an ignition gem are completely ordinary from then on and can be extinguished normally.

JEWEL OF FIRE SENSE (MANSE •)

The bearer of this translucent red sphere can sense all sources of fire within one mile. The player rolls (Perception + Awareness) at difficulty 2. Each success lets the character know the direction, distance and approximate size of every fire within range, starting with the largest and working down in size. This hearthstone provides no other information about the local terrain. In the Far North, however, it gives invaluable aid to finding nearby settlements.

MEMORIAL IRON (MANSE •)

This hearthstone looks like a smooth nugget of polished iron. Its bearer can vividly recall (and mentally relive) any particularly positive and will-reinforcing memory. This recollection fires her resolve, enabling her to recover one point of temporary Willpower each day. This is in addition to any Willpower recovered through the normal, daily Conviction roll.

STONE OF CIRCULATION (MANSE •)

This translucent green oval improves the bearer's blood circulation, aiding her survival in harsh climates. Although it cannot prevent environmental damage from extreme heat or cold, it does grant a +1 bonus to any Stamina or Resistance rolls concerned with enduring heat, cold or dehydration.

STONE OF PASSION (MANSE •)

This dark-purple teardrop improves the sound and quality of its bearer's voice whenever the bearer speaks about a topic about which he cares deeply. The bearer's player gains one additional die on all Charisma and Manipulation-based rolls that have to do with such topics.

STONE OF THE LIGHT SLEEPER (MANSE •)

A glowing sunburst marks this fiery red disk. It enables the bearer to awaken instantly and with no clumsiness or confusion. Also, the bearer awakens at the slightest touch or unusual noise, which can make it difficult for her to sleep in a noisy location such as the common room of an inn.

BATTLE FIRE RUBY (MANSE ••)

This hearthstone is a fine ruby with 10 identical, kite-shaped facets. This stone continually fills the bearer with aggression and certainty. When rolling the character's Conviction or Valor, add two dice to the roll. Likewise, when rolling Compassion or Temperance, subtract two dice from the roll (to a minimum of one die).

GEM OF SEDUCTION (MANSE ••)

This deep purple hexagon changes to dark blue in bright sunlight. It makes the bearer seem more attractive, especially to anyone to whom he is attracted. The gem gives a +1 bonus to all Appearance rolls or +3 to any rolls involving seduction.

GEMSTONE OF LAST RESORT (MANSE ••)

This smooth, dull-brown stone is speckled with black. Its bearer can ignore all wound penalties during a combat. When the character reaches Incapacitated, this effect ends immediately, and he can still die. The bearer can choose to invoke or cancel the stone's power at will. Wounds sustained while the bearer used this power take twice as long to heal, and the Essence cost of any Charms or other magics used to heal these wounds is doubled.

HEARTH'S FIRE (MANSE ••)

This orange-and-red crystal looks like a frozen tongue of flame. It bursts into flames the instant the bearer places it on any solid surface. Regardless of the weather, the stone creates a fire two meters in diameter, which burns without fuel and is hot enough to keep a dozen people warm and dry even in heavy rain or extreme cold. The stone will ignite a flammable surface. The bearer may safely snuff the fire with a thought. Otherwise, it burns until sunlight strikes it on the following dawn.

PRISM OF FOCUSED PASSION (MANSE ••)

This prism-shaped carnelian allows the bearer to inflame passions in others. The bearer can amplify any emotion, turning vague resentment into raging jealousy, slight nervousness into unbridled terror or mild attraction into panting lust. The bearer of a prism of focused passion gains three additional dice on all Presence or Performance rolls designed to inflame emotions. Also, for purposes of resisting these inflamed passions a target's Temperance is treated as if it were two points less than it is (to a minimum of 1). The latter effect works only on a single target at a time.

THE SENTINEL'S STONE (MANSE ••)

Narrow black streaks run through this spherical, smoky-white stone. At night, the streaks seem to move in a slow circle. The stone grants a +1 bonus to all Awareness rolls, increasing to +3 if the bearer specifically stands watch.

DISCORD STONE (MANSE •••)

The bearer of this dark-blue disc can make people around her argue and disagree. The character can affect (Essence x 2) people, and this power can only be used once per day. To affect a target, the bearer must be within 10 feet and her player must win a resisted (Essence + Willpower) roll. If the target succeeds, his moment of truculence passes. Otherwise, his player must succeed at a Temperance roll or spend a Willpower point for the character to resist any opportunity to argue with another person. The effect lasts for half a day, or until the character spends three Willpower points. After the effect ends, targets whose players successfully roll (Intelligence + Occult), difficulty 3, realize that these pugnacious urges were some form of unnatural mental influence.

FIRE DRAGON'S SCALE (MANSE •••)

This wedge-shaped piece of cat's eye protects its bearer with heat drawn from the Elemental Pole of Fire. The stone channels this heat into any melee weapon that strikes the bearer. Metal weapons instantly become red hot and wooden weapons catch fire. The player of the weapon's wielder must succeed at a Willpower roll, difficulty 3, or the wielder drops the weapon. Even if this roll succeeds, however, the attacker suffers environmental damage from holding onto the burning or heated weapon (1L/action damage, trauma 1). Fire-aspected Terrestrial Exalted who have ignited their animas are immune to the effects of this hearthstone.

GEM OF DESIRE (MANSE •••)

This transparent yellow hearthstone is shaped like a faceted heart. Once per day, the bearer can inflame

someone with desire for some specific object or person. Such desires can range from a sudden thirst for any strong alcohol to a passion for a specific person. To inflict this desire on someone, the bearer's player must succeed in a reflexive, resisted (Willpower + Essence) roll while the character is no more than 10 yards from the target. If the target succeeds, she is unaffected by this desire. If she fails, she feels this until the sun next rises. If she botches this roll, she feels this desire for the next week. For this duration, the target must make a Willpower roll with a difficulty equal to half the bearer's Essence (round up) to avoid any opportunity to satisfy her desire.

GEM OF THE BURNING HOUSE (MANSE ●●●)

This two-inch cube of polished crimson stone makes the bearer and everything he wears or carries immune to all harm from normal heat and fires, including any damage caused by smoke inhalation. The bearer could enter a burning building or wade in lava without harm, but would still take damage from an attack with magical fire or Charms such as Fiery Arrow Attack. However, even if the bearer is attacked by magical fire, neither her nor anything she wears or carries will ever catch fire.

GEM OF WHITE HEAT (MANSE ●●●)

This translucent, red-orange dodecahedron grants another Essence user the ability to surround herself with an aura of fire identical to a Fire-aspected Terrestrial Exalt's anima power. Fire-aspected Dragon-Blooded who use this stone add this damage to the normal damage done by their anima power.

Producing this imitation anima banner costs Essence. Double the number of motes the character spends, however, to find the intensity of the flaming aura conferred by the hearthstone. (Of course, the Essence expenditure may well trigger the character's own anima as well.)

BLOODY-EYED BURNING JEWEL (MANSE ●●●●)

This hearthstone is transparent, four-sided jacinth with a deep red sphere at its center. Its bearer can shoot bolts of brilliant fire from her eyes. The attack uses a (Wits + Awareness) attack roll and has the following stats below.

A target may dodge the attack as normal, and may parry it using stunts or Charms that defend against non-material ranged attacks. Armor only soaks this damage if it is composed of one of the magical materials.

BRIGHT EYE OF THE FIRE DRAGON (MANSE ●●●●)

This octahedral ruby holds a fleck of iridescent black in its heart. Its bearer can see through any fire within (Essence) miles as if he were standing at the fire's location. The bearer also automatically knows the approximate distance and location of any fire within range. The bearer's player rolls (Perception + Awareness) to find how clearly the character can see through the fire through which he wishes to look. The bearer can watch his enemies through their campfire or look down upon a battlefield by firing a burning arrow into the sky. The hearthstone's owner can look through both magical and supernatural fires or even the bodies of fire elementals.

CANDENT CARBUNCLE (MANSE ●●●●)

This irregularly rounded stone looks exactly like a glowing coal and is always warm to the touch. As a reflexive action, the bearer can make any weapon he wields burst into flame. Not only does the weapon's damage increase by +4L, but it ignites any flammable objects as if it were a lit torch. A character who fights without weapons can envelop her hands and feet in fire. A character who uses a bow or other missile weapon can also coat them in flame; indeed, he can use the Candent Carbuncle on all missile weapons thrown or fired in a flurry or using extra action Charms. Flaming weapons continue to burn for 5 ticks after they leave the wielder's hands.

Both the bearer and the weapons become immune to these flames. The hearthstone's owner also gains +5 soak against all damage caused by fire—bashing, lethal or aggravated.

FIREBIRD GEM (MANSE ●●●●●)

This palm-sized, egg-shaped ruby glows with a flickering golden light. Its owner can transform herself into a human-sized bird made of living fire. This transformation requires 5 ticks and has no defensive penalty. Everything the character wears, including all weapons and armor, are also transformed. This firebird can fly 300 miles per hour, but the character must return to her natural form at either midday and midnight, whichever comes first, and rest for at least an hour before continuing. At the end of a flight, the

| BLOODY-EYED BURNING JEWEL | | | | | | | |
Speed	Accuracy	Damage	Rate	Range	Minimums	Cost	Tags
4	+0	(Essence x 2)L	3	20	—	—	F

character is as hungry and exhausted as if she had spent the same period running.

While in the form of a firebird, the bearer can ignite flammable objects with a touch. All attacks are made as if she wielded any melee weapons she carries, but with an additional +2 bonus to damage because of the heat of her flames. She is also protected normally by whatever armor she is wearing. She cannot use any missile weapons in this form. Also, the touch of any liquid more substantial than fog or mist instantly returns the character to her normal form.

FIRE-EATING ROCK (MANSE •••••)

This hearthstone looks like a globe of gray rock flecked with red sparks. The hearthstone can consume any natural fire, from candles to conflagrations, leaving any material that was burning cool to the touch (although it doesn't heal or repair any damage the fire has already caused). At its bearer's will, the rock can consume all fire in (Essence) yards. The hearthstone's wearer can cut a swath through a vast inferno simply by holding the rock in front of him and walking into the fire. This stone also absorbs the heat from lava and similarly hot substances, leaving them cool to the touch and hardening them if they were molten.

The fire-eating rock has no affect on magical flames such as the anima power of a Fire-aspected Dragon Blood. However, it can extinguish ordinary fires ignited by a magical flame. Also, this stone can douse a fire elemental. If the stone attempts to absorb a fire elemental, the players of the bearer and the elemental enter a resisted Willpower roll. If one party has a higher permanent Essence, his player adds the difference to his dice pool. If the hearthstone's bearer wins, the elemental is drawn into the hearthstone and the bearer regains a number of motes of Essence equal to the elemental's permanent Essence. If the elemental wins, the stone shatters, but reforms normally in its manse.

GEM OF BONES TO FIRE (MANSE •••••)

This palm-sized slab ranges from blue-purple at one end to green at the other, with a jagged layer of gold at the purple end is a jagged layer of gold. The bearer concentrates. If his player succeeds at a (Manipulation + Socialize) roll at a difficulty of the target's Essence, the hearthstone's bearer has managed to catch his target's eye. The target's player then attempts a Willpower roll at a difficulty of the number of successes the bearer's player received. If the target fails, her bones ignite, inflicting two levels of unsoakable lethal damage every five ticks until death or until the bearer loses sight of her. If the target can escape the bearer's line of sight, the burning stops, and she may heal as normal.

HEARTHSTONES OF WATER

CRYSTAL OF SEAWALKING (MANSE •)

This faceted oval stone is a shimmering opalescent blue. The bearer can walk on water, quicksand, wine, or other liquids as if they were dry land. The bearer cannot ride a horse or other creature, but he can walk or run normally and can carry any load he can normally carry. Also, by merely willing it to be so, he can temporarily cancel the stone's affects and can dive safely into water. When using the stone, the bearer will not sink into lava or boiling oil, but this will not prevent his feet from being burned.

GEM OF THE NOBLE BROOK (MANSE •)

This perfectly smooth, pale pink sphere prevents the bearer from having any Social Trait that is below average. If the carrier has an Appearance, Manipulation, or Charisma of 1, this Trait is raised to 2 for as long as the character wears the hearthstone and remains attuned to its manse.

JEWEL OF THE CLEVER MERCHANT (MANSE •)

This silvery-white, many-faceted oval grants a +3 bonus to all Mental or Social rolls involving trade, bargaining, contract negotiations and other business dealing.

THE LABYRINTHINE EYE (MANSE •)

Alternating bands of gold and brown cover this spherical stone. Its owner can always find a path to the exit or the center (her choice) when navigating any building, maze or similar structure. The paths that lead to either destination become immediately obvious to the bearer. The labyrinthine eye conveys no knowledge of whether or not a particular route is safe—only which routes lead to the exit or the center and, if there are several options, the relative lengths of the available paths.

LULLABY STONE (MANSE •)

This pale-blue, translucent oval enables its bearer to enjoy a peaceful, restful sleep free of nightmares or insomnia. It trumps any external circumstances, including climate, deprivation or noise. In addition, any attempts to invade the bearer's dreams (such as using the stone of dream entrance; see p. 103) suffer a -2 external penalty. Any Charm, magic or drug that induces nightmares or turns the bearer's dreams against her automatically fails.

FOUNTAIN-SUMMONING STONE (MANSE ••)

This flawless, oval emerald always feels cool and slightly moist. It can call water from the earth to create a spring of pure, fresh water in any location, from the hottest desert of the Southlands to a filthy alley in Nexus. The bearer need only stamp his foot against soil, rock or worked stone in contact with the earth, and the spring instantly appears. The duration of the spring depends upon the location: In a desert, the flow of water continues for a few hours, while in a moister climate it might run for an entire season.

A fountain-summoning stone cannot call a spring from a floor that is enchanted, made of metal or one of the magical materials, or above a basement, tunnels or other worked openings in the earth. No more than one fountain can be summoned in any area 50 feet on a side, and the stone cannot be used more than once a scene.

GEM OF TEARS TO POISON (MANSE ••)

This smooth, azure teardrop transforms the bearer's tears into a mild poison (2B/1 day, 3M, —/—, -3). These tears have no effect on skin contact, but they induce pain and vomiting if ingested or introduced into a wound. Tears do not become poisonous until they are shed. Tears not ingested within one day of being shed revert to normal tears.

GEM OF YOUTH (MANSE ••)

This smooth black lens contains a fossil shell in its center. Anyone bearing this stone never grows visibly older: His skin remains unwrinkled and his appearance is frozen at the moment he attuned himself to it. However, the gem of youth does nothing to lengthen the bearer's lifespan; he only *looks* younger than he is. A bearer who loses or ceases carrying this stone resumes his visible aging at the normal rate; his appearance never catches up with his true age.

KATA-SCULPTING GEM (MANSE ••)

This pearly white disk glows with a faint white light that brightens and dims in time with its bearer's heartbeat. The gem allows a Dragon-Blooded martial artist to focus her Essence so that she can activate any known Celestial-level Form-type Charms without her player having to succeed at a (Dexterity + Martial Arts) roll. Only Terrestrial Exalts with Martial Arts of 3 or more possess the precision needed to use the instinctive knowledge of fighting katas provided by this hearthstone. This stone also reduces the Essence cost to activate all Martial Arts Form-type Charms by 2 motes (minimum of 1); all Exalted can gain this benefit.

MIND-CLEANSING GEM (MANSE ••)

This sea-blue topaz dodecahedron helps its bearer to resist all attempts to dominate or influence his mind. Bearers gain +1 to both their Dodge and Parry MDVs. In addition, if touched to someone who is under any form of unnatural mental influence, the stone gives the target a chance to break free. If the target's player wins or ties an opposed Willpower roll against the controller, the stone instantly frees her from this mental influence.

PEARL OF WISDOM (MANSE ••)

This iridescent-blue pearl continually fills its bearer with calm serenity and self-control. It brings peace to the violent and restraint to the impulsive. When rolling the character's Compassion or Temperance, add two dice to the roll. On the other hand, when rolling Conviction or Valor, subtract two dice from the roll (to a minimum of one die).

STONE OF RECOGNITION (MANSE ••)

The bearer of this irregular, blue-white orb can make other people believe they have met or heard of her before, which may help in many deceits or attempts at persuasion. Whenever the bearer wishes, her player and the player of a designated target make a reflexive and resisted (Willpower + Essence) roll. If the target's player fails, that character assumes he has either met or heard of the bearer before and thinks well of her. On a botch, the target has positive memories of spending time with or hearing many stories about the bearer and considers her a good and honorable person whom he likes. The stone's bearer gains two dice on any Social roll against the target that involves trust or convincing the target to believe something. If the target's player wins or ties the roll, however, the target feels only a vague sense that the bearer seems somewhat familiar.

BLOODSTONE (MANSE •••)

This faceted, rectangular stone is a deep sea green flecked with blood red. It purifies and controls the blood of anyone who carries it. While carrying such a stone, the bearer becomes immune to all non-magical diseases and poisons, from arsenic to plague. The Exalt also gains no effect from alcohol or other intoxicants, other than enjoying their taste. In addition, the bearer automatically resists all magical poisons, such as Yozi venom or poisons produced through Charms or thaumaturgy, though he still suffers some effect (see **Exalted**, pp. 130-131). Finally, the bearer also never bleeds, even if a limb is severed. Although all wounds produce normal damage, the character never loses blood from her body and so never need worry about bleeding to death.

JEWEL OF DAANA'D (MANSE •••)

The bearer of this watery, dark-blue sphere gains a special rapport with water elementals. When she summons water elementals, her spell or thaumaturgical ritual takes her only half as long and costs half as many motes of Essence (count every mote spent as two). The bearer also gains three dice for all rolls to influence water elementals, including binding or banishing them. These benefits do not apply to *gods* of water.

Manses aspected to other elements may produce analogous jewels.

STONE OF AQUATIC PROWESS (MANSE •••)

This hearthstone looks like a smooth ovoid of pure water bound into a solid shape. It becomes completely invisible if placed in water. Most examples of this hearthstone come from manses that are partially or completely submerged.

Anyone attuned to this hearthstone becomes fully amphibious. Not only can the user breathe water and survive swimming in near freezing seas without harm, he can also swim as fast as he can run. The character's swimming Move and Dash distances are not cut in half, and no Athletics roll is needed (see **Exalted**, p. 145). All fatigue and mobility penalties for armor

are reduced by one while the character is in water. Characters wearing light or medium armor can swim normally. Those wearing heavy or superheavy armor cannot swim, but can comfortably walk along the bottom of a river, lake or ocean. The user can also fight normally in the water and suffers no penalties when fighting aquatic creatures.

STONE OF GENDER TRANSFORMATION (MANSE •••)

This peach-colored, almond-shaped crystal enables its bearer to change gender at will. This transformation is instantaneous and can be made as a reflexive action.

The transformation leaves the character moderately recognizable. The stone does not significantly alter the character's size or features: A tall, muscular man, for instance, becomes a tall, muscular woman. Any character who knows the bearer can recognize her with a successful (Perception + Awareness) roll. Factors that may increase the roll's difficulty include radically different clothing, a hidden face or not having seen the transgendered character in a long time.

STONE OF JUDGMENT (MANSE •••)

The bearer of this smooth cabochon of the finest lapis lazuli gains an uncanny sense for when people lie. If she asks someone whether he committed a

crime or other harmful act, the bearer's player reduces the difficulty of the (Perception + [Investigation or Socialize]) roll to determine the truth of any answer is reduced by -4 (to a minimum of 1).

GEM OF MASKS (MANSE ••••)

This rainbow-colored crystal sphere has cloudy, rough spots on its surface. While possessing it, the bearer may change the details of her head and face. She cannot use it to change anything about the rest of her body beyond changing the color of her skin and body hair to match that of her head. However, any feature on her head (eye or skin color, nose, lips, the shape of her face, hair color, texture and length) may all change to resemble any human, beastman or other roughly human-like creature. The gem of masks cannot alter or hide caste marks, though. The bearer can use this stone to duplicate the appearance of someone she knows well, but cannot duplicate the subject's height or build. The ability to change one's appearance this way gives a +4 bonus to Larceny rolls involving disguise.

GEMSTONE OF SOLID WATER (MANSE ••••)

The bearer of this teardrop-shaped, deep blue hearthstone can solidify—not freeze—an area of water or other liquids, such as oil or wine. For 2 motes, the bearer can solidify (character's Essence x 4) cubic yards of liquid. The effect lasts for one scene. This solid water must be at least one yard wide, but can be in any shape the character desires.

Solidified liquid becomes strong enough to support a caravan of loaded yeddim or to stop a speeding ship in its tracks, but remains sufficiently flexible that a ship that runs into it at full speed takes no damage. Any fish or other beings that swim in this water are not harmed—but a swimmer who needs to breathe and who is trapped in this solid water can suffocate.

The bearer can use this stone as often as he wants. The bearer cannot use this stone to solidify living blood, but he can use it quite selectively. For example, at a banquet where both his friends and his enemies were present, he could solidify the wine in the goblets of his enemies, while allowing his friends to drink freely… or the reverse, so his friends can pretend to drink while only his enemies consume poisoned wine.

GEM OF SLEEP (MANSE •••••)

This translucent, cobalt-blue sphere allows the bearer to force other creatures to fall asleep. The bearer must catch the target's eye, which requires a successful (Manipulation + Socialize) roll at a difficulty f the target's Essence. Then, the target must resist by her player making a Willpower roll at a difficulty equal to the number of successes on the previous roll. If the target fails this roll, she instantly falls deeply asleep and remains asleep for five minutes. If the target botches, she falls asleep for six hours. Success means that the target feels briefly tired but remains awake. Targets who fall asleep may be woken normally in any fashion that would awaken someone from a deep sleep, but awaken no more swiftly than normal. If used in combat, this stone requires five ticks to use and imposes a -2 penalty to the bearer's DV.

HEARTHSTONE OF WOOD

DRAGON WILLOW AGATE (MANSE •)

The bearer of this hemisphere of green and dark umber agate adds +2 to his DV pool against all Archery attacks and all attacks made with wooden weapons. The bonuses from this stone add to the bonuses gained when Wood-aspected Dragon-Blooded activate their anima power.

THE FARMER'S STONE (MANSE •)

Any crops tended by the owner of this angular, pale-blue spindle grow and bear unusually well. If these crops receive at least minimal water and care, they yield an unusually abundant and early harvest despite poor soil or weather. This hearthstone affects any size of farm, so long as the bearer regularly helps to tend it.

The bearer may also aid a farm that he does not normally work by spending one full day tending it shortly after planting has taken place. When used in this fashion, the stone aids up to (bearer's Essence) square miles. In either case, the stone only protects the crops from natural problems such as droughts, flooding, insects or blights. It provides no protection against armies burning or trampling the fields, although the stone would help the fields recover more rapidly than normal.

GEM OF INJURY SENSE (MANSE •)

Fine, iridescent cracks run through this transparent, blue-green teardrop. The hearthstone's bearer can sense injuries or illnesses as glowing patterns overlaying the bodies of any person or animal she can see clearly. The information revealed by this stone does not provide an exact diagnosis but does tell her both the location and severity of any problem. In addition to reducing the difficulty of Medicine rolls to treat patients she examines by -1 (to a minimum of 1), the stone also allows the bearer to see at once if living allies or foes are near death. She can also tell the living from the undead in even the dimmest lighting.

JEWEL OF YOUTHFUL SUPPLENESS (MANSE •)

This faceted, scalloped-edged garnet makes the bearer exceptionally limber and flexible. Her player gains two dice to all Athletics rolls. In addition, she can both dislocate and relocate all of her joints at will, without discomfort or harm. This ability grants her two dice to any Larceny rolls to escape bondage.

STONE OF SHELTER (MANSE •)

This green-flecked, dark-blue spindle guides its bearer to locations sheltered from the elements. This shelter can range from a welcoming caravanserai to a hollow tree, but it is always dry and protected from both wind and rain. However, the shelter need not come with food or drink and may have other occupants.

STONE OF THE EMERALD ROOSTER (MANSE •)

This polished green cylinder has a rainbow sheen. The bearer gains a bonus on all Survival and Resistance rolls equal to one-half his Valor, rounded-up.

STONE OF THE HUNT (MANSE •)

Swirls of light and dark green cover this polished sphere. Its bearer gains an instinctive understanding of the drives and emotions of wild animals. This ability grants two dice to all rolls involved in hunting, taming, tracking or otherwise understanding wild animals.

GEMSTONE OF DEEP DRINK (MANSE ••)

This sharp-edged chunk of grass-green stone grants its bearer the ability to drink as many and as much intoxicants as she likes without incurring any penalty. The stone protects a character from all the affects of alcohol and more exotic drugs and renders her immune to all natural ingested poisons. Other than their taste, everything from alcohol to the juice of the deadliest poisonous berries becomes as harmless as pure water.

OPAL OF THE HUNTED (MANSE ••)

This polished sphere is a green-and-violet opal flecked with gold. It gives a +2 bonus to Wits or Perception rolls to detect ambushes. If the bearer is ever successfully ambushed, the stone also increases her DV by 1 (see **Exalted**, p. 155) against unexpected attacks; this bonus affects the final value, not the pool used to calculate it. Finally, the stone gives three dice to all rolls to evade tracking and pursuit (see **Exalted**, p. 140).

SCINTILLATING GEM OF ALLY'S EMBRACE (MANSE ••)

This pentagonal gem is banded with the five colors of magical jade. The gem's bearer can perform Charms that require him to touch the target at a range equal to his Essence in yards, but only for Charms that empower his allies, such as the Solar Charm Essence-Lending Method or the Dragon-Blooded Charm Strength of Stones Technique.

STONE OF MENDING FLAWS (MANSE ••)

This spherical, green-and-blue-striped hearthstone has a porous appearance. Its bearer can mend small tears, cracks, flaws or blemishes on any non-living material at a touch. Each use of the stone repairs an area up to five feet in diameter. This stone will not repair anything made of the magical materials, nor any other magical or enchanted items, including both artifacts and manses.

The hearthstone can restore age-ruined cloth, rusted swords or old books so that they look newly made, but it cannot replace missing pieces larger than a lentil. To repair an item, the bearer must touch the stone to it for at least a minute. This stone can be used no more than once per scene, but its owner can use it repeatedly to repair even the largest non-magical objects that are still relatively intact.

SURVIVAL STONE (MANSE ••)

Brown striations mark this leaf-shaped, green hearthstone. Although the bearer can still feel thirst and hunger, she cannot die of either. Also, she suffers no impairment from either condition for her first four days of deprivation. Past this point, her intense pangs of hunger or thirst inflict a -1 internal penalty to all die rolls.

ADDER'S EYE (MANSE •••)

This polished wedge banded with gold and black is much prized by assassins and other people who hunt large and dangerous prey. Any artifact weapon set with this hearthstone becomes coated with a deadly venom. If set in a powerbow, the adder's eye envenoms any arrows fired from this bow. This poison acts as coral snake venom (see **Exalted**, p. 131).

The Adder's Eye is only effective when set into weapons that draw blood (though if you could hold a person down and wipe an envenomed goremaul on an open wound, that would work). Its use is always obvious because the weapon visibly drips venom and traces remain in the wound.

GEMSTONE OF ENTRANCE (MANSE •••)

The owner of this faceted, shimmering blue hexagon can unlock all locked doors and windows at a touch. However, this stone only opens locks on points of entrance and egress and has no affect on locked strongboxes or shackles.

GEMSTONE OF MENTAL HEALTH (MANSE •••)

This cloudy orange ovoid instantly and permanently cures its bearer of any derangements or other

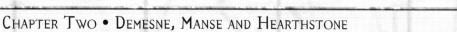

forms of madness. Any new types of insanity inflicted on the bearer are cured as quickly as they are gained. What's more, the wearer automatically overcomes unnatural mental influences, such as the obsession induced by a gem of desire, within one scene.

GLADESTALKER'S STONE (MANSE •••)

If set in a powerbow, this deep-red cabochon adds three dice to its Accuracy and another three dice to its Damage.

STONE OF RESILIENT BAMBOO (MANSE •••)

This cylindrical stone gleams with the bright, opaque green of living bamboo. Its bearer's intrinsic lethal soak equals her Stamina. She can also parry lethal attacks unarmed without a stunt. In addition, the bearer regenerates one level of lethal or bashing damage every hour. This stone does not speed the healing of aggravated damage.

STONE OF THE SURE PATH (MANSE •••)

Yellow striations run through this red prism. Its bearer can find her way to any destination. The more she knows about this destination, the shorter and more direct her path becomes. If the bearer has ever visited this location, the stone leads her there by the shortest and most direct route. If she knows only rumors or suppositions about her destination, the path will be longer and is more likely to hold danger. Regardless of her knowledge, though, the path always eventually leads to the intended destination. In the most extreme cases, this path may take years to walk. Also, the hearthstone will lead the bearer in circles if the destination is hidden by sorcery.

SONG OF LIFE STONE (MANSE ••••)

At will, this sphere banded with brown and white forces plants to grow with unnatural speed and vigor anywhere within the sound of the bearer's voice. Trees put out leaves, flower and bear fruit out of season in the span of an afternoon, while vines and other plants undergo a year's growth in a single scene. This unnatural growth ceases at the end of the scene, but the affects remain. The stone's power also brings wilted or dying plants instantly back to full health. It can even restore dead plants to life as long as they are still rooted

in the ground. The bearer can fill a barren or ruined field with ripe grain in a single scene and could bless several dozen square miles of land in a day.

STONE OF HEALER'S FLOWER (MANSE ••••)

Merely by touching this unpolished, bright blue disk to a living creature's flesh, the bearer can instantly heal the target of all her injuries, regardless of their severity. However, this stone will never heal anyone who has used it to heal anyone else. Also, immediately after using this stone to heal, the bearer suffers half the damage he just healed (rounded up). This damage must heal normally, without the aid of Charms, artifacts or drugs short of the celestial wine of Yu-Shan, or the stone shall never work for that character again.

JEWEL OF THE FOREST WARRIORS (MANSE •••••)

Opaque brown veins run through this translucent, emerald-green triangle. The bearer can animate trees as warriors by touching the hearthstone to a tree and committing 2 motes. The tree then uproots itself and gains both mobility and limited intelligence for the next scene. If the bearer also spends a point of Willpower, the tree remains active for the next full day. Animate trees can be verbally commanded and possess a basic knowledge of strategy and tactics. Tree-minds are too alien to affect by either mundane or magical persuasion, however, and the stone insures their absolute loyalty; treat them as automatons. If the hearthstone is broken or unattuned before the trees' animation expires, however, all animate trees are no longer controlled and defend themselves from whatever they perceive as threats—which may extend to attacking anyone who carries fire or chops wood.

A forest warrior has the following combat stats, as seen below.

STONE OF LOYALTY (MANSE •••••)

This brown, opaque lens inspires fanatical loyalty in everyone the bearer knows. For anyone under the bearer's command or who has sworn an oath of loyalty to her, even thinking of betrayal requires a difficulty 5 Conviction roll. For friends and allies of the bearer, the difficulty of this roll drops to 3. Players of even casual

FOREST WARRIOR				
Str/Dex/Sta	Per/Int/Wits/Will	Health Lvls	Atk S/A/D/R	Dodge DV/S
7/3/6	2/2/2/5	-0x3/-1x3/-2x3/-4/I	Branches: 6/6/7L/2	2/5L/8B
Abilities: Awareness 2, Dodge 2, Martial Arts 3, Resistance 3, War 1				

acquaintances must succeed at a simple Conviction roll to betray or consider betraying or opposing the character. If the individual honestly considers the betrayal to be trivial, or done in the bearer's best interests ("I must save my friend from herself!") the difficulty of this roll drops by 1 (to a minimum of 1).

> ## PECULIAR HEARTHSTONES
>
> Most hearthstones grant simple, straightforward powers to their owners, and manse designers try to produce such hearthstones. A few hearthstones, however, confer *odd* powers.
>
> Student architects at the House of Well-Favored Aspect learn, for instance, of the liquid fire cabochon, a hearthstone of Fire. It imbues the body fluids of its bearer with fierce combustive power and ignites them the moment they lose contact with the bearer's body. While this makes the owner hazardous to attack, sweaty clothing bursts into flames and going to the bathroom becomes an exercise in pyrotechnics. The hazards of certain other body fluids do not bear thinking about. Worst of all, the Cabochon does not give its owner any special resistance to fire.
>
> Various hearthstones of Wood protect their owners from poisons and intoxication. The crystal venom jewel does so by concentrating all drugs and poisons in its bearer's system into a nugget the owner then vomits forth. The one small compensation for the unpleasantness of this purgation is that the toxins can be dissolved and re-used. Its owner, a member of House Cynis, uses the jewel to concoct unusual drug mixtures in his own body, for later distribution to friends and enemies.
>
> Some unusual hearthstones come about because the manse's builder didn't aim for a particular power. Others happen because the architect bungled the manse's design (or redesign) or because a manse suffered damage. On rare occasions, a hearthstone produced by mischance proves useful enough that geomancers try to duplicate it.

CELESTIAL HEARTHSTONES
ABYSSAL HEARTHSTONES
LIFE-DRAIN STONE (MANSE •)

This polished, deep-purple teardrop becomes blood red in direct sunlight. If his player wins a resisted (Willpower + Essence roll), the bearer can inflict weariness on others. Any target whose player fails this resisted roll feels listless and tired until she next sleeps, temporarily losing one from her Wits score. Characters whose players botch this roll also temporarily reduce their Permanent Willpower by one until they next sleep. The stone's effects do not stack, so repeated attacks on a target serve little purpose.

ROAD OF HATRED STONE (MANSE •)

This gray-and-black, lens-shaped hearthstone reinforces Intimacies based on hatred of someone or something. That Intimacy effectively becomes a second Motivation for the hearthstone's owner, as far as social combat, mental influence and recovering Willpower are concerned.

> ## ALTERNATE INTIMACIES
>
> Although **Exalted** describes Intimacies as something a character loves, hatred and other strong emotions can also supply a basis. They work just the same for social combat: "I hate the Guild and you *cannot* talk me into helping them." Basing Intimacies on different emotions does not affect a character's starting or maximum number of Intimacies—and as with any Intimacy, the Storyteller can declare a driving hatred, phobia or the like has fallen off the character's list of Intimacies if the player repeatedly passes up chances for the character to act on this supposedly strong commitment.

FALSE DEATH STONE (MANSE ••)

This pale-yellow amber sphere is marked by a dark crack through its center. It allows the bearer to instantly place herself in a death-like trance. The bearer appears dead to anyone who examines her, but remains conscious and all of her senses continue to function normally. She wakes instantly whenever she chooses or if the stone is removed from her body. In this trance, the bearer does not require food, water or air and is immune to the extremes of climate. However, she is still susceptible to injury.

FLAWED GEM (MANSE ••)

This transparent, violet-blue hemisphere enables the bearer to make non-living substances decay at great speed. When the bearer touches an object for one minute and wills it to decay, cracks radiate from this point of contact and encompass are area up to two

yards in radius. Over the next 24 hours, the object ages and crumbles. These flaws gradually reduce the soak of any item and reduce its health levels. After 24 hours, the object counts as damaged (see **Exalted**, p. 154) and its soak has been halved (round down).

A 3-dot version of this stone also exists. It makes objects decay in 10 minutes instead of 24 hours. Neither stone affects any of the magical materials, hearthstones or any other magical or enchanted items.

GHOSTWALKER CRYSTAL (MANSE ••)

The bearer of this dark-blue octahedron becomes very difficult to follow. Increase the difficulty of any rolls to follow her or to hear or see signs of her passage by 2. However, this stone does nothing to conceal her scent and so hounds or other creatures that rely primarily upon smell can track the bearer normally.

DEATH-SENSE STONE (MANSE •••)

This disc of opaque white enables the bearer to sense any deaths that occur within a one mile radius. He knows their precise location and can easily find the location. He can also sense and locate any deaths in this radius that have occurred within the last month and can tell the exact moment of each death. The

bearer gains no information about a death other than its location and time.

STONE OF DUST (MANSE •••)

This spherical gray stone's surface seems covered in powdery dust. If the character spends 1 mote of Essence and touches any single item made of dead organic tissue, such as leather, bone, wood or ivory, he can instantly turn the object to dust. The character must touch the item directly, and the item can weigh no more than (character's Essence x 10) pounds. This stone does not affect artifacts, enchanted items or undead of any sort.

ICE GEM (MANSE ••••)

This translucent, slightly bluish cube looks like a chunk of ice and stays perpetually cold. Whenever the bearer desires, she can reflexively cover herself and all of her melee weapons with a brutally frigid aura of cold. As long as the target is not immune to cold all melee or unarmed attacks by the bearer inflict an additional +4L damage. Also, anyone who is not immune to cold suffers five dice of lethal damage if they strike the bearer with an unarmed attack.

GEM OF THE NIGHT SKY (MANSE •••••)

This transparent black hemisphere is filled with tiny, starlike sparks of light. If the bearer concentrates for a minute, he can plunge an area up to a half mile radius around himself into night. The bearer determines the size of this area. The darkness produced by this stone is identical to normal night in all ways and lasts as long as the bearer desires. This unnatural nightfall frightens most ordinary mortals, though: Extras may suffer a -1 internal penalty to Wits or Willpower rolls due to panic, or may require Valor rolls to face anything else that seems the least bit threatening.

WITHERING GEM (MANSE •••••)

This translucent, faceted black rectangle enables its bearer to inflict deadly ailments on others. To use the stone, the bearer spends 1 mote of Essence, and his player attempts a resisted, reflexive (Willpower + Essence) roll against the target. If the target's player fails this roll, her character automatically contracts a magical illness with a Morbidity equal to the bearer's permanent Essence, and a Difficulty to Treat and Treated Morbidity equal to half the bearer's permanent Essence (round up). The symptoms resemble consumption (see **Exalted**, p. 351). While the character is ill, she suffers a -3 internal penalty to all actions. This disease can be treated normally with charms and alchemical cures, but cannot be treated with normal medicine. The character can use this stone as often as desired, but the disease is not contagious.

LUNAR HEARTHSTONES

GEMSTONE OF SHADOWS (MANSE •)

This faceted rod is made of silvery crystal. It allows the bearer to summon deep shadows around himself. At the bearer's command, these shadows can have a diameter of up to two yards, but can also be made smaller. Only magical light can pierce these shadows, but they are not completely opaque. The bearer can see out of them and anyone looking in can see vague shapes. This shadow increases the difficult to spot or recognize anyone inside by 2, higher if the surroundings are also relatively dark. In any well-lit area, however, the shadow itself becomes exceedingly obvious. Regardless of location, this shadow also increases the bearer's Dodge and Parry DVs against all ranged attacks by 1. Anyone else who enters the shadow-zone does not gain this advantage against the bearer, though: the hearthstone's owner can see perfectly well in the zone of darkness (though the hearthstone grants no benefit in seeing through darkness beyond that area).

CHAMELEON STONE (MANSE ••)

This triangular prism, colorless in itself, takes on the color of whatever surface it lies against. Similarly, its bearer can change his skin, hair and eye color, as well as general features such as eye and nose shape, to match the natives of the local area, wherever and whatever that may be.

JEWEL OF THE GRACEFUL COURTIER (MANSE ••)

This oval, opalescent jewel seems to shift color with every change of light and background. The jewel's bearer blends easily into any social situation with the protean ease of the Changing Moon Caste, and never makes an unintentional faux pas: The stone adds one success to all Socialize rolls, making botches impossible and failures less likely in even the most demanding social venues.

JEWEL OF THE RABBIT'S SWORD (MANSE ••)

This yellow-green stone periodically changes its shape and the number of its facets. Its owner's player can reroll all 1s in a single roll by spending one point of Willpower. This power can only be used once for any single roll.

ORB OF THE UNNOTICED PREDATOR (MANSE •••)

This flattened sphere is patterned like the skin of a leopard. The stone prevents its bearer from leaving tracks, even in thick mud or fine dust, and eliminates all traces of her scent and the scent of anything she wears or carries. These benefits also extend to any animal she rides and to anyone she carries, but do not extend to any companions moving on their own. If the bearer moves in a slow and stealthy fashion, the stone also mutes any noises she makes and bends shadows to her advantage, increasing the difficulty of all Awareness rolls to notice her presence by 1.

SNAKESKIN STONE (MANSE •••)

This smooth, irregular stone appears covered in black, red and white snake scales. The next time an injured owner sleeps, she sheds her skin. This process closes wounds and heals scrapes and burns, but does not repair the damage of deep wounds or damaged internal organs. As a result, the bearer heals all bashing damage and half of all lethal damage (round up). The hearthstone does nothing for aggravated damage. It also does not affect Lunars' moonsilver tattoos or other magical markings, but after shedding her skin, the bearer looks uninjured unless examined by a physician. A single set of wounds can benefit from this stone only once.

STONE OF DREAM ENTRANCE (MANSE ••••)

The owner of this smooth, oval moonstone can enter the dreams of others. To do so, the bearer must either

be able to see or touch the target, or must have spoken to the target for at least a minute within the previous 24 hours and know her name. The bearer may observe the subject's dreams, speak with the dreamer or alter those dreams as he pleases, turning them into marvelous fantasies or horrific nightmares. A dream of suffering death or serious harm costs the dreamer one point of temporary Willpower unless her player succeeds at a difficulty 2 Willpower roll to wake up from the nightmare. No matter how horrific the dream, dreamers cannot lose more than three points of Willpower per night.

Other people can wake up the dreamer by all normal means. The dreamer also awakens at her normal rising time. The dreamer's player must succeed at an (Intelligence + Awareness) roll to remember these dreams; additional successes provide greater detail.

WILDERNESS GEM (MANSE ••••)

This rough, pale-purple triangle gives its bearer an unparalleled understanding of the wilderness. The bearer can easily find food and shelter, instinctively understands the habits of animals, can easily track prey and can accurately predict the weather. This stone adds two successes to all Survival rolls and enables its bearer to perform supernatural tracking.

GEM OF MADNESS (MANSE •••••)

This hearthstone looks like a jagged, irregular fragment of jet-black rock. Anyone who physically attacks the bearer goes insane. This insanity takes the form of an extreme expression of the character's dominant Virtue (or one of her highest Virtues, if her two highest Virtues have the same value). The Virtue Flaws of Solar Exalted (see **Exalted**, pp. 103-105) are typical examples of this type of madness. Mortals cannot control or mitigate their reactions to this insanity and always suffer the full manifestation. However, the madness may differ from an Exalt's actual Virtue Flaw; the episode of madness also has no affect on an Exalt's current accumulation of Limit.

Exalts and other Essence users can attempt to gain partial control of the insanity (use the rules for partial control listed under the Virtue Flaws). However, gaining partial control is more difficult than with an ordinary Limit Break. Such a victim must spend two points of Willpower, and her player must succeed at a (Willpower + Essence) roll with a difficulty equal to the hearthstone bearer's Essence. If this roll fails, the victim cannot control the insanity unless she repeats the Willpower expenditure and her player rolls again. This roll may be repeated as often as desired, but at least one long tick (one minute) must pass between attempts at partial control. This insanity lasts between one scene and one day, as listed in the description. Until the madness ends, repeated attacks on the hearthstone's bearer do not cause additional insanities.

SIDEREAL HEARTHSTONES

EVER-OPEN EYE (MANSE •)

The bearer of this dull-gray disk of smooth stone can remain awake without fatigue or impairment. However, after he has been awake for two full days, his player must roll (Stamina + Resistance) at difficulty 1. For every additional full day the bearer refrains from sleeping, the difficulty of this roll increases by +1. If the player ever fails this roll, the bearer starts hallucinating. These waking nightmares impose a two-die penalty from all rolls and cause the character to behave erratically. Regardless of how long the bearer has remained awake, though, he requires only eight hours of sleep to be fully rested and remove all penalties or necessity for further rolls.

GEM OF HOLINESS (MANSE •)

This hemisphere of silver-flecked blue stone imbues its bearer with a general aura of holiness. If the character avoids words or actions that obviously contradict this aura, anyone meeting her instinctively regards her as trustworthy and devout. If they don't know better, they may assume she is a priest. The bearer receives one additional die to any Manipulation or Charisma rolls to gain trust or convince someone of her honesty.

GEM OF STARLIGHT (MANSE •)

This rod of silver crystal is lit from within by faint sparkles that look like starlight. The bearer can cause it to glow with a cool light that is never painful or blinding. The stone's glow can do everything from dimly illuminating a small room to lighting a large hall with brilliantly glittering starlight.

GEM OF OMENS (MANSE ••)

This transparent blue-gray, faceted oval stone gives its bearer glimpses of the future in the patterns around her, such as the flight of birds, the glinting of sunlight on a lake or the ridges of sand on a beach. These omens are sometimes baffling and always incomplete, but they offer information about the future gleaned from the Loom of Fate itself. The character concentrates on some pattern or event (usually one found in nature), and the player rolls (Intelligence + Occult). Excellencies can be applied normally to this roll. Success provides some small knowledge of the near future. This predicted future is not fixed and can be changed based on the information in the omen.

The specific events predicted by the omen cannot be chosen by the bearer but always directly relate to her or her companions—they might involve the future of a proposed commercial venture, a coming betrayal by a loved one, or simply the quality of her coming meal. This stone can be used no more than once a scene, and using it more often than a few times a day usually results in the omens revealing increasingly trivial predictions.

One or two successes reveal nothing more than a basic gauge of success or desirability. A proposed commercial venture involving a trading ship will fail, the bearer's upcoming meal will be fraught with danger… Three or four successes reveals some information about the causes of this prediction—the commercial venture will fail because the ship is lost in a storm or the bearer's next meal will be fraught with danger because someone will make an attempt on the bearer's life during the meal. Five or more successes reveals a few details about this information such as the approximate location and type of the storm that sinks the vessel or that fact that the attempt on the bearer's life involves an ambush when she gets up from her meal.

JEWEL OF THE CELESTIAL MANDARIN (MANSE ••)

This transparent, faceted square stone glows with a faint violet light. The stone surrounds the bearer with a subtle aura of Essence that causes gods, demons and elementals to regard him as unusually dignified and well-spoken. This stone reduces the difficulty of all Social rolls the bearer's player uses on such beings by 2 (to a minimum difficulty of 1). This aura is imperceptible to all other beings except gods, elementals and demons and so has no affect on any other creatures.

GUARDIAN GEM (MANSE •••)

This shimmering silver sphere allows the bearer to influence both her own fate and the fate's of others. Twice per story, the bearer's player can reroll any of the character's own rolls. Twice per story, the player can also force someone else to reroll one of his character's actions. Once the bearer's player sees the result of the reroll, she decides whether to keep the original or to use the reroll. The bearer can also sacrifice one of these reroll opportunities to subtract two health levels of damage (after soak has been taken into account) from any attack upon herself or another being.

PRECISION OF FORM GEMSTONE (MANSE •••)

This brilliantly iridescent, egg-shaped opal reduces the Essence cost to use all Martial Arts Charms of a particular style by 2 motes after the character activates that style's Form-type Charm. This effect cannot reduce the mote cost of a Charm to less than half its original value. The bearer also cannot activate any Charms of another martial arts style until she abandons the Form she has already chosen. A character could abandon one Form, however, and then activate the Form-type Charm of another martial arts style, gaining the mote discount for all Charms of that style.

GEM OF WISE DISCERNMENT (MANSE ••••)

This hexagonal hearthstone is as clear as pure water. A person can easily look through the largest central facet. Looking through this window allows the bearer to see anyone who is invisible and to pierce all disguises and illusions, from mundane disguises to dematerialized spirits and the transformative glamours of the Fair Folk. This stone cannot detect lies or other non-visual deceptions; nor will it reveal anything about someone's character. However, the bearer can see a Lunar Exalt's Tell.

HOME'S HEARTH (MANSE •••••)

Each side of this irregular, six-sided gemstone is a different color. Once per day, it allows the bearer to teleport himself and up to five other people to or from the stone's manse. The stone can transport the bearer and his companions from anyplace in Creation to the manse in the blink of an eye. However, teleportation from the manse is limited to 100 miles' range. Also, while the stone can transport characters both to and from the Wyld, this carries some danger. To do so, the bearer's player must roll (Wits + Occult). Failure results in the characters all landing somewhere random in the Wyld. A botch additionally renders the stone useless for 48 hours, neither permitting another teleportation attempt nor granting Essence.

SCRYING STONE (MANSE •••••)

The bearer of this black stone can see visions of other times and places in its flat, highly polished surface—visions of the past, the present or the potential future. They either illuminate some aspect of what will happen or lend some understanding of the situation that the Exalt does not yet have. While every vision is a literal view of some real or potential event, the visions come without context or explanation: The bearer's player must roll (Intelligence + Investigation) to decipher the visions; Excellencies can apply. As with the gem of omens, more successes indicate more extensive and precise knowledge—but the scrying stone can also provide information such as a view of an enemy's

face or a chance to watch a long-dead sorcerer cast a spell. (Such potent and precise information would require at least five successes, though.)

SOLAR HEARTHSTONES

BEACON OF THE UNCONQUERED SUN (MANSE •)

Despite its name, this gold-spangled crystal cabochon works for any Exalt. When its bearer places the beacon to her forehead and expends a mote of Essence, her caste mark blazes and projects a beam of light for the rest of the scene. In conditions of less than perfect lighting, this beam provides clear vision to a range of 15 yards, and (if necessary) murky vision out to 30 yards. However, the narrow beam illuminates an area only 5 yards wide at the end of clear vision, or 10 yards wide at the end of murky vision.

OATHSTONE (MANSE •)

This spherical, blood-red hearthstone is unusual in that using it involves giving it away. When the owner makes a bargain, treaty or other agreement with another person, he can give that person the oathstone as a token of the deal. The stone enforces the bargain exactly like the Eclipse Caste anima power (see **Exalted**, p. 127), except that neither party needs

to pay any Essence to seal the oath. If either party breaks the agreement, he horribly botches one of her next vitally important rolls. In addition, both parties instantly know that the agreement has been broken. If the agreement is broken, mutually dissolved or simply concludes naturally, the stone instantly reappears in its rightful owner's possession. Also, even after giving the stone away, the giver regains Essence from it as if she still carried it.

JEWEL OF THE LAWGIVER'S AUTHORITY (MANSE ••)

This brilliant-yellow, hexagonal crystal reduces the difficulty of all attempts to sway the opinions or beliefs of others by 2 (to a minimum of 1). It applies to both speech and writing.

SPHERE OF COURTESANS' CONSTELLATION (MANSE ••)

This gold-flecked, orange globe raises its possessors Appearance to 3, if it does not equal or exceed that value already. The bearer's Appearance drops to its original level the moment the Sphere leaves his person. In addition, the bearer's player gains a +2 bonus to all Performance and Presence rolls.

CRYSTAL OF LEGENDARY LEADERSHIP (MANSE •••)

This rounded, many-faced green triangle enhances the bearer's ability to lead others. The bearer's player gains one bonus success to any Presence, Performance or Bureaucracy rolls involving leadership or governance, as well as to any War rolls involving rallying troops.

GEM OF SORCERY (MANSE •••)

Though transparent, this many-pointed crystal has an oily golden sheen and glows with inner light. Once per day, its bearer can reduce the cost of casting a spell by 10 motes.

STONE OF FINAL REST (MANSE ••••)

This polished onyx sphere recalls the anima power of the Zenith Caste in its power to sanctify tombs and lay the dead to rest. By a touch, the bearer can return zombies, skeletons and other mindless necromantic creations to true, inanimate death. Ghosts suffer one level of aggravated damage for every 5 ticks they spend within five yards of the bearer. Normally, they attempt to avoid the bearer if he comes within 10 yards. All undead see this stone as a painfully blazing light, and although it does no harm to them, Deathlords and deathknights find this light as unpleasant as would any other denizen of the Underworld.

Ghosts can sense the presence of this stone from 100 yards away, and both Abyssals and Deathlords instinctively know the distance and direction of any such stone within (Essence) miles. Deathlords also know if such a hearthstone crosses the border of one of the shadowlands they control. The Stone of Final Rest does not function in the Underworld. In shadowlands, it has no affect on ghosts and only inflicts one level of aggravated damage per action when touched against physical undead. However, all residents of the shadowland within a mile instantly feel its presence.

STONE OF INHUMAN BEAUTY (MANSE ••••)

This iridescent white oval adds four dots to the wearer's Appearance, raising it to a maximum of 7. In addition, the bearer cannot be made to look anything other than beautiful: nothing short of Solar Circle Sorcery can even temporarily reduce his Appearance. If dressed in rags and covered in mud, he appears handsomely disheveled; if disguised to look horribly scarred, he seems to bear noble wounds that must obviously have come from performing some grand feat of heroism. Other people always notice the bearer unless he uses stealth, Charms or the cover of darkness to conceal himself. This is good when giving a speech… not so good for a discreet meeting with an informant.

GEM OF PERFECT MOBILITY (MANSE •••••)

This brilliant-red, faceted square glows as brightly as a candle. Any Exalted bearing it is as swift as a beam of sunlight. A character attuned to the hearthstone halves (round up) the number of ticks all actions require, without causing any penalties and may divide her dice pools normally to gain additional actions. In addition, these increased speed also applies out of combat, allowing the character to walk, run or sprint twice as fast as normal. The only limitations on using this hearthstone are that sorcery still takes the normal time to cast, and that using these additional actions makes the character appear inhumanly fast. Anyone seeing the character move or react this rapidly will know she is not human. The additional action gained from using this hearthstone is incompatible with all Extra Actions Charms. The character can use one or the other, never both.

CHAPTER THREE
THAUMATURGY

The Exalted absorb prodigious reservoirs of mystic energy and channel them to perform legendary miracles. Thaumaturgy lacks the raw power of the Charms and spells of the Exalted, but it is embedded in the natural laws and principles of Creation. Mortals who understand how to coax the existing Essence patterns of the world can perform minor miracles without the control of Essence that comes with Exaltation. With the right technique, the thaumaturge can call upon dead ancestors, invoke the perfect form of a mundane weapon or tool, or brew an alchemical mixture that slows his aging. Rare is the community without a local wise woman or savant whose rituals smooth relations with the gods, heal the sick and ward off danger.

THE ANNALS OF THAUMATURGY

When Gaia and her brethren built Creation, and every time they modified it, their actions embedded the principles of thaumaturgy into the world. Whether the Primordials intended for mortals to discover rituals with which to manipulate Creation, we cannot say; although it is clear that the gods were meant to do so. Rather, they set independent processes in motion that continue to shape and reinforce Creation in an infinitely recursive manner. Perhaps the clearest example of this lies in elementals, where each exists as an ever-smaller entity that embodies the same Essence as its greater, even though they were originally designed as five unique beings of vast power and singular purpose. Only a system of infinite complexity could provide a fortress against the Wyld's infinite adverse possibility. Fortunately for mortals, the thaumaturge doesn't have to understand the whole of Creation to manipulate one part of it, any more than a tree needs to understand the stars in order to grow a new leaf. It is enough for mortal thaumaturges to learn the occult connections within Creation and coax them to appropriate purposes.

—Excerpt from Oadenol's Commentary on the Procedures of Creation

Mystic lore among mortals developed over thousands of years. As relative latecomers to the intelligent species of Creation, human beings can scarcely claim to have first discovered the Arts of thaumaturgy. Nonetheless, they have become its most prolific practitioners. The black-feathered but earthbound alaun perished during the Primordial War, and the triangular-headed race of magi-scientists who worshipped Autochthon fatally angered their patron long before that. Innumerable gods perform rituals to maintain of Creation, but usually they know only a handful of Procedures inherent to their nature. Exalted can practice the Arts, yet commonly shirk their study in favor of the greater power of Charms and sorcery.

Students of thaumaturgy seek out magical lore, and fortunately, the millennia have left them much to find. From the halls of Yu-Shan to the ruins of the alaun and Dragon Kings, ancient secrets await rediscovery. Instructional texts range from the temple scrolls of Great Forks or the Immaculate Order to the magitech manuals of the First Age and the Shogunate. Storytellers and players can find examples of such sources throughout this section.

IN THE BEGINNING

The first and most numerous practitioners of thaumaturgical Procedures are the gods themselves. While powerful gods often spend much of their time on the Games of Divinity or the politics of Yu-Shan, the lesser gods spend most of their time preserving Creation. The Charms of gods are merely incidental to their function, used to correct extraordinary disruptions to their activity. Most of the time, a god simply performs a simple ritual behavior and an act of will. Virtually all gods know and practice inherent thaumaturgical Procedures.

Mortals see the effects but seldom think about the divine activities behind them. When a brickmaker places his wares in the kiln, the least god of that block of clay meets with the least god of the fire. The fire-god sings the Song of Ardent Unity, infusing its heat through all it touches. The clay-god responds with the Mudra of Isolate Stability, asserting its intent not to be consumed. Together, these divine procedures harden the clay and its least god changes nature to match. Clay becomes bricks.

Only gods can use the fundamental procedures of thaumaturgy in their pure form. No one else really needs to. Mortals, however, can approximate the songs, words, gestures and symbols used by the gods, and combine them in novel ways. They can also recombine the physical substances of Creation and coax their least gods to interact in unnatural ways. This is mortal thaumaturgy.

THE PROCEDURES OF CREATION

For every concept of importance, Yu-Shan has a god. Long ago, Ryzala, the director of the Bureau of Heaven,

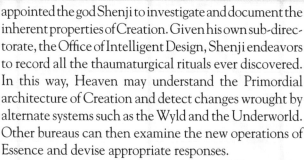

appointed the god Shenji to investigate and document the inherent properties of Creation. Given his own sub-directorate, the Office of Intelligent Design, Shenji endeavors to record all the thaumaturgical rituals ever discovered. In this way, Heaven may understand the Primordial architecture of Creation and detect changes wrought by alternate systems such as the Wyld and the Underworld. Other bureaus can then examine the new operations of Essence and devise appropriate responses.

During the First Age, Solars recognized Shenji as the god of thaumaturgy, and early temples honored him for this. Later, the Solar Deliberative forbade his worship to anyone who wasn't approved to study the Arts.

The Procedures of Creation is the massive collection of scrolls held by the Office of Intelligent Design. The documents consist of exquisitely fine silk-paper scrolls written in silver and golden inks with full-color illustrations. Unfortunately, scribes of the sub-directorate continue to add footnotes and comments to pages without regard for mortal vision. Much of the collection is so thoroughly documented that the individual pages are unreadable to anyone without Charms that can pierce thousands of years of layered ink.

Game Effects: *The Procedures of Creation* library contains almost every thaumaturgical Procedure ever discovered. Most of them, of course, are not usable by humans—they are divine thaumaturgy. As mortals recombine the elements of Creation, however, they devise new procedures for Shenji's staff to record. Rites that have only been performed outside of Creation proper (i.e., in the Underworld, Wyld or Malfeas) are unlikely to be in the *Procedures*, but the scrolls contain every ritual used in Creation.

The scrolls are written in Old Realm (Yu-Shan dialect), although some reference diagrams or sources in other tongues. Unfortunately, many pages are literally unreadable without supernatural senses. Also, the collection is organized in such a single-minded manner that finding and studying a single specific ritual is relatively easy, but trying to master a Degree extends the training interval to years (although only requiring the regular number of Occult dots). With time and effort, however, a student might learn nearly any ritual ever devised, one at a time.

The *Procedures* contain, quite literally, all the natural science of Creation. The potential benefit to sorcerous and thaumaturgical research, manse and artifact design and other arcane pursuits is limited only by a scholar's intelligence and persistence. If a savant has access to the *Procedures*, her player can add one bonus success to any Craft, Lore, Medicine or Occult roll per week of study, to a maximum of the character's Intelligence.

Availability and Cost: One can study *The Procedures of Creation* only in the Office of Intelligent Design in Yu-Shan. Gaining permission usually requires a supplicant to prove she has legitimate business on behalf of the Celestial Bureaucracy. With a stunt and a compelling argument (Manipulation + Bureaucracy, difficulty 5) a thaumaturge might convince Shenji or his officers of the importance of a ritual to the proper function of Creation. Stealing or copying a few of the scrolls might be possible, but Shenji is an Essence 7 celestial god with a staff of lesser gods in attendance. Thieves invite the wrath of a powerful Celestial god, and the divine allies he can bring to bear against them.

Artifact Level: The entire collection of scrolls is Artifact N/A, but also takes up an area larger than the Imperial City. Any individual scroll (or copy) would be worth Resources 3 at least.

OBELISKS OF THE ALAUN

The black-feathered alaun were so favored by the Primordials that they lived on the southwestern plains of the Isle of the Gods. This simple species worshiped their creators without question, and for this, the Exalted slew them during the Primordial War. Few of their works remain, but there are remnants of their black stone obelisks, carved from the mountains of the Dragon's Nest Range near Lord's Crossing and diligently transported onto the plains. Each obelisk is a tall slender black stone with faintly birdlike features, carved with prayers to the Primordial creators. Most have been destroyed, deemed heretical monuments by the First Age Solars and, later, by the Immaculate faith.

Game Effects: Designed to offer eternal prayer, these rough monuments contain secrets that aid in the study of the Art of Spirit Beckoning. If one can understand the Old Realm script (alaun dialect), then the monuments might act as an instruction manual. A single obelisk contains only a single Procedure, but a would-be student with access to at least seven of the monoliths could learn the Initiate Degree. Studying 20 of the stones might suffice to learn the Adept Degree. It is doubtful, however, that more than a few dozen obelisks yet survive.

Although the Art did not yet exist, the *Obelisks* inadvertently contain prayers that now behave as rituals for the Art of Demon Summoning. Dangerously, none of these rites offer any protection against demons—only rites such as *Summon*, *Beckon* and *Demonsight*. Additionally, reading the prayers within a certain area

of the mountains near Lord's Crossing might attract the unwanted attention of the ghosts of dead alaun, surprised to hear their ancient orisons profaned by usurpers' tongues.

Availability and Cost: Found in ruins in the southwestern reaches of the Blessed Isle, although fragments of a few have been incorporated into later structures, particularly in small, out of the way villages or the illicit shrines of infernal cults. A perfectly intact *Obelisk* is worth Resources 4, but owning it invites negative attention from the Immaculate Order. Reputedly, House Tepet donated a few to the Heptagram rather than destroy them.

Artifact Level: Not an artifact.

THE DRAGON KINGS

Organized thaumaturgical study among humans began during the time when the Dragon Kings dominated humanity. Before the gods gave the Exaltation to mortals, humanity held no importance in Creation. Mortals were brighter than the alaun, but not as favored by the Primordials. The mighty Dragon Kings ruled the four corners of the world, while the gods resided upon the Blessed Isle. Given dominion over humans, the Dragon Kings weren't sure what to do with them. Humans seemed too weak to serve as soldiers and too short-lived to master the advanced crystal and vegetative technology of the Dragon Kings. Mortals were also deemed rebellious and proud, and thus considered poor slaves.

A few Dragon King savants nevertheless spent centuries trying to teach human servants their reptilian paths of magic. Occasionally, a mortal absorbed some tiny aspect of a particular effect and copied it. Such successes seemed promising at first, yet human students could not develop the Dragon King's mystic paths. Most Dragon King researchers gave up and sought simpler tasks for the "lesser" race. Humans who committed violent crimes were even turned into ritual sacrifices, their hearts offered up to the Unconquered Sun.

Some humans escaped and fled the cities of the Dragon Kings, living in the wild or settling small villages. Humans who had tried to master the Dragon King paths put the lesser tricks they had gained to use, helping their compatriots in a myriad of little ways. Away from the watchful eyes of their reptilian masters, they exchanged secrets and experimented with the world around them. A body of shared thaumaturgy rituals slowly grew, pieced together by mortal savants and bolstered by rites learned from sympathetic gods who saw mankind as a new source of worship. The fundamental practices of thaumaturgy as the "Arts" developed during this period.

Inevitably, the Dragon Kings captured practitioners of the Arts and discovered their new aptitude. The minor talents of these human thaumaturges did not impress Dragon King savants, but the savants recognized the potential for the study to grow. Finally, a field of interest gave the Dragon Kings hope that they could develop a proper purpose for human beings.

Under Dragon King tutelage, the study of thaumaturgy flourished. Some Dragon Kings even spent time learning the Arts as a curiosity, though the power of their own magical paths overshadowed human thaumaturgy. Generally the Dragon Kings preferred to act as patrons to skilled thaumaturges, who became valued servants and aides. These practitioners were called *amiliki*, or "adepts," and received authority over their fellow mortals.

When the gods Exalted human beings to serve in the war against the Primordials, the role of the Dragon Kings changed forever. The reptiles suffered tremendously during the war, with whole nations exterminated; yet, they might have recovered if they had kept the gods' favor. Instead, the Incarnae gave Creation's rule to the Exalted, as reward for their glorious victory over the Primordials. The roles of mankind and the Dragon Kings suddenly reversed. The Exalted raised mortals to primacy while their reptilian allies struggled to retain their culture. Within a few centuries, humanity eclipsed their scaled predecessors.

For more information about the rise and fall of the ancient Dragon Kings, see **The Scroll of Lesser Races**.

THE CRYSTAL OF KUAN

The Arts evolved most rapidly among those practitioners with Dragon King patrons, who could already manipulate Essence and organize schools. With access to growing libraries of lore and well-stocked laboratories, the *amiliki* and their First Age counterparts (with Exalted patrons) produced many of the greatest discoveries in the field of thaumaturgy. Perhaps the most accomplished Dragon King patron of thaumaturgy was the Pterok known as Kuan of the Plain.

The Dragon Kings learned to store information in special reading-crystals. *The Crystal of Kuan* is a clear, flat, rectangular plate eight inches on a side and an eighth of an inch thick. Its surface bears the faint blue marking of the Kuan's name. It contains thousands of pages of research on thaumaturgy.

During the Shogunate period, soldiers loyal to the Daimyo of Deheleshen took *The Crystal of Kuan* from the

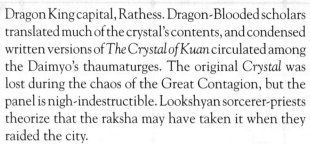

Dragon King capital, Rathess. Dragon-Blooded scholars translated much of the crystal's contents, and condensed written versions of *The Crystal of Kuan* circulated among the Daimyo's thaumaturges. The original *Crystal* was lost during the chaos of the Great Contagion, but the panel is nigh-indestructible. Lookshyan sorcerer-priests theorize that the raksha may have taken it when they raided the city.

Game Effects: To view the contents of the original *Crystal*, the user must spend 1 mote of Essence per scene. The text is written in the Dragon King tongue. For someone who can understand that tongue, the *Crystal* counts as an instruction manual for the Art of Geomancy up to the Master Degree and the Art of Enchantment up to the Adept Degree. The Arts of Astrology, Husbandry, Spirit Beckoning and Weather Working are described to the Initiate Degree. Much of the text was written by human thaumaturges, and their glowing tributes to their patron Kuan provide enough information about Dragon King society that the *Crystal* may also act as a tutor for a Lore Specialty (Dragon Kings +1).

Printed Shogunate-era translations, written in Old Realm, are condensed and offer instruction up to the Adept Degree in the Arts of Enchantment and Geomancy, and the Initiate Degree for Spirit Beckoning. Post-Contagion renditions, written in Riverspeak, lose much more of the original language, and offer only the Initiate Degrees in Enchantment and Geomancy. A new translation of the original could offer its full benefit, but this would require the painstaking attention of someone who could faithfully reproduce all of the mystic diagrams and subtleties of the work.

Availability and Cost: Unique, though other Dragon King scholars and their staffs may have scribed similar crystals. Shogunate-era translations cost Resources 4 and Riverspeak editions cost Resources 3.

Artifact Level: • for the original. The written translations are not artifacts.

THE FOLK TRADITION

The *amiliki* were not the only mortals to practice the Arts. Escaped students sometimes encountered other people who possessed various minor magical rites—yet had no known ties to the Dragon Kings. They found witches and shamans who dealt with local spirits and brewed magic from animal parts, herbs and minerals. These folk thaumaturges handed down their skills through generations of oral tradition, their source lost in myth. Most *amiliki* guessed that the arcane customs

of the hinterland adepts must have come from the gods of the wild reaches.

Reactions varied when these disparate thaumaturges came together. Sometimes, they took the opportunity to study each other's techniques, both sides gaining greater understanding. Unfortunately, many meetings instead resulted in conflict as indigenous magicians felt threatened by outsiders or escaped *amiliki* scorned and sought to dominate the thaumaturges they considered inferior. Any attempts by *amiliki* to re-create the colleges of the Dragon Kings or create a thaumaturgical aristocracy failed, though. In the wilds of Creation, the tradition of trusted student and wise mentor flourished while mystic societies quickly fell to infighting.

After the Primordial War, the Solar Deliberative brought all of Creation under its sway. The Old Realm assimilated many folk cultures, but not all. The Solar Deliberative crushed anyone who openly defied its rule. Some barbarian tribes and rejectionist refugees, however, fled into the Wyld-tainted borders of the world. Other cultures found the Exalted god-kings would ignore them if they stayed quiet and hidden in deep forests, swamps, deserts or wastelands. These small, marginal cultures kept their own folk thaumaturgies throughout the Old Realm.

They could not hide completely or forever. As the Solars consolidated their rule, however, they saw no threat from a few scruffy tribes and backwater villages. A few of the Exalted paid enough attention to notice the folk thaumaturgy traditions, and felt enough curiosity to learn and record their rituals.

THE GENESIS OF HEATHEN RITUAL

The Solar known as the Radiant Dowager became fascinated with the thaumaturges whose lore had nothing to do with Dragon King patrons. Sensing that the march of civilization would eradicate their culture, she bent her impressive resources to studying and recording their mystic knowledge.

In her monograph, *The Genesis of Heathen Ritual*, the Radiant Dowager concluded that some folk traditions of thaumaturgy descended from mortals studying under terrestrial gods, others from prehuman races and fragments of Dragon King lore. A few mortal visionaries seemed to discover rituals through unexplained inspiration, but she could not definitively prove that point.

Copies of the Radiant Dowager's work circulated among Exalted scholars during the First Age, but many Solars disapproved of her assertions that the Arts were not given to mortal races by the Unconquered Sun via the Dragon Kings. Lunars sometimes disliked her arrogant views toward "barbarian" tribes, while Lawgivers

disliked her respect for prehuman species. Nonetheless, the Radiant Dowager became the reigning expert in the field of parallel thaumaturgic origin theory.

Shogunate censors found much of the Radiant Dowager's work inconsistent with the Immaculate philosophy and destroyed it. However, records of Radiant Dowager's scholarly lectures on the subject survived in a number of recorders of everlasting glories kept by various secret societies.

Game Effects: All of Radiant Dowager's works are written in Old Realm. A recorder with one of her lectures might contain enough information to teach the Initiate Degree in Alchemy, Enchantment, Geomancy, Husbandry, Spirit Beckoning, Warding and Exorcism, or Weather Working—or it might contain only a few Procedures (at the Storyteller's discretion). The forgotten Stalwart Temple in the Radamant Prefecture on the Blessed Isle (see **The Compass of Celestial Directions, Vol. I—The Blessed Isle**, p.123) also contains complete records of the Radiant Dowager's researches.

Availability and Cost: Recorders of everlasting glories with collections of the Radiant Dowager's works may hide in the archives of the Heptagram, the Lookshy Academy of Sorcery or other arcane academies. Paper transcriptions from such devices might turn up in any arcane collection, but provide only a few Procedures each.

Artifact Level: •• (recorder of everlasting glories, **Wonders of the Lost Age**, p.61)

THE FIRST AGE

The ascendancy of the Exalted, and by association the human race, freed the *amiliki* from Dragon King dominance. Although this liberated mortals from reptilian governance, their Essence-wielding superiors once again overshadowed thaumaturges who did not Exalt, this time in the form of the Exalted. Initially, however, the Exalted sported several *amiliki* within their number, and therefore shared an interest in the continued practice of thaumaturgy. In its early days, the Solar Deliberative encouraged Exalts to learn thaumaturgy: the same schools that taught mathematics and history offered courses in the Arts. The academy of Sperimin even taught thaumaturgy alongside sorcery. In the Old Realm's height, most First Age farmers could call for rain when their crops needed it and skilled savants competed for positions in the workshops of the Exalted. Much of the thaumaturgy devised in the Old Realm, however, was meant to assist Exalted sorcerers in constructing manses and artifacts.

As the Old Realm decayed into madness and tyranny, Exalted views changed, and the Deliberative restricted the practice of thaumaturgy. Some of their growing distrust of mortal magicians stemmed from a vague uneasiness that somehow those beneath them might try to replace them… as they had overthrown the Primordials. Unknown to the Exalted, the Great Curse fed upon these suspicions.

Legitimate concerns arose, too, when the occasional thaumaturge would perform terrible deeds. Some savants became corrupt, seduced by the very demons they summoned on their Exalted masters' behalf. Other practitioners abused their powers for petty spite or ambition, with offended thaumaturges calling down storms on those who insulted them and jilted lovers brewing philters to enthrall the objects of their obsession. A few thaumaturges became so envious of the power of the Exalted that they pushed their abuses beyond the limits of reason, trying to claim similar power for themselves.

The restrictions upon thaumaturgy escalated from licensing requirements to harsh punishments for anyone who defied the Exalted. At first, the Deliberative limited those Arts that interfered with the spirit courts or gave access to demons. Solar leaders argued that the gods needed respite from mortal interference and that demons were too cunning and treacherous for mere mortals to handle. (As power and arrogance grew, they stopped wondering if demons were too cunning and treacherous for the *Exalted* to handle.) Later, any thaumaturgy that could potentially inflict harm was deemed hazardous and heavily restricted. Eventually, the Solars declared the entire field too dangerous for those who were too weak-willed to use them responsibly. Only those mortals deemed trustworthy by their Exalted lords were allowed to study the Arts at all, and even then, they were constrained to whatever knowledge their patrons felt was necessary to their duties. Savants no longer competed simply to see who would work with the Exalted. They competed to see who could gratify the Exalted enough to practice thaumaturgy at all.

In the final centuries of the Old Realm, thaumaturges fell into three categories: Exalted, servant or malcontent. The Exalted were above mortal reproach, so those who wanted to study thaumaturgy could do so without restriction. If the Solars ever wondered if thaumaturgy might somehow enable rivals to overcome them, then such worries were dismissed. How could these petty rituals compare to the power of Exalted Charms and sorcery? Unruly Exalts were eliminated, when necessary, and the particulars of whether or not they happened to exercise the Arts never entered consideration.

Mortal thaumaturges acted as skilled assistants to the Exalted. These magicians carried out innumerable tasks too delicate for enslaved demons and too petty for the Exalted themselves. From carefully tending the forges of factory-cathedrals to maintaining the First Age's vast arsenal of magitech, these savants became the unacknowledged bedrock of the era's omnipotent industry of artifacts. The Deliberative even sanctioned special units, called gunzosha, whose mortal soldiers wore magitech armor that vastly magnified their might in combat… if the wearer would sacrifice years of his life. Under Dragon-Blooded lieutenants, these thaumaturge-warriors served with distinction in countless skirmishes against the Fair Folk and rebellious outlying provinces.

The third category of High First Age thaumaturges consisted of malcontents who studied in secret. Some of these groups emerged from the efforts of Terrestrial Exalted, or even the occasional Celestial (usually a Lunar), who saw little point in restricting such minor magic. Others were the result of persistent efforts by dedicated mortal masters of the Arts who felt they should know whatever they could learn. Some groups used complex codes and elaborate misdirection in hopes of avoiding the attention of the Deliberative's magistrates. Other societies hid their works in plain sight. Ordinary books, ranging from guides to regional cuisine to syrupy court poetry, hid occult secrets behind a veil of mundanity. Many of these secret societies moved to the hinterlands of the Old Realm, while others chose to hide within the plebeian class in gatherings as diverse as communal farms, craft guilds and monastic orders. Occasionally, grandiose or blatant works of illicit thaumaturgy occurred during this period, but time and censorship by the authorities destroyed most knowledge of their existence. Nonetheless, if suppressing the study of the Arts made them less prevalent, it rendered a few practitioners more dangerous. Forced to hide their Arts, they grew less scrupulous about what they hid.

A Lover Clad in Blue

This text is an example of the secret manuals of the Old Realm. On the surface, it is a luridly illustrated story of the torrid sexual escapades of Balablara, the Half-Blood daughter of a sorcerer and his demonic neomah slave. Drawn to her own kind, she seduces the neomah who tries to convince her to poison her father with a hairpin. Overhearing the exchange, her father misunderstands and orders the demon to kill his daughter. Its aim is untrue, and strikes the sorcerer by accident. As she clutches

the stiffening body of her father, Balablara banishes the neomah for a night and a day. She knows the demon will return for her the next night, but cannot afford more materials to ward it off. She prostitutes herself for the money to do so. The rest of the book details the year and a day she spends sleeping with various partners so that she can resist the demon, until ultimately the demon is forced back to the Yozi realm.

More than one demon-tainted thaumaturge cult owed its origins to the secret Procedures contained within the book. Solar agents destroyed such cults but never figured out that this tawdry sex tale was the source—no doubt because no Solar Exalt paid attention to such minor cults. Numerous copies of *A Lover Clad in Blue* survived the Usurpation, and the Shogunate did nothing to eliminate the text as they felt it painted Solars as the Anathema they meant them to be. Two centuries ago, an obscure bookmaker in Chiaroscuro translated the work into Flametongue, with faithful renditions of the illustrations.

Game Effects: Hidden within the illustrations and the text are encoded rites related to demons. If she successfully cracks the codes (Intelligence + Linguistics, varying difficulty), a thaumaturge could gain the Initiate (difficulty 3) or Adept (difficulty 4) Degree in the Art of Demon Summoning. Two Procedures from the Master Degree are contained as well (difficulty 5): *The Year and the Day* and *Beckon Sondok*.

Availability and Cost: *A Lover Clad in Blue* is illegal in Lookshy, as its depiction of demonic sex offends the sohei priests. In the Realm, the Immaculate Order also objects to the text, but the book is easily available to patricians and Dynasts. Copies in Old Realm cost Resources 3, while the Southern translation can be purchased for Resources 2. Should someone ever reveal the book's secret, it would surely be banned in most civilized states.

Artifact Level: Not an artifact.

THE USURPATION

Thaumaturgy played a surprising role during the Usurpation, considering its relative puny might when compared to Exalted Charms and sorcery. The Dragon-Blooded commanders of the gunzosha turned these artifact-encased soldiers against the Solars and their servant creatures. The gunzosha were often effective at delaying Solar forces until the Terrestrials could unleash surprise attacks or battlefield-grade weapons. Secretive groups of thaumaturges provided innumerable talismans and enchantments to the cause, albeit often unwittingly, long before the rebellion was even set in motion. Once

the initial ambush of the Solar Exalted at the Calibration feast occurred, and widespread fighting began, hundreds of underground cabals across Creation threw their support behind the revolt. Harboring long-held resentment against the Deliberative for its oppression of the Arts, these cloistered savants hoped to cast down the old regime and gain power and respect in the new. As the end of Solar dominance became evident to all, exiles at the edges of Creation invaded the very lands they once called home.

While the gunzosha and invading outcasts were directly involved in deadly combat, most thaumaturges chose less straightforward approaches. Rituals designed to beckon living creatures lured the mortal progeny of the Solars into mind-numbing emotional traps for their parents. Wards designed to protect against the Solars granted their enemies precious moments in numerous conflicts. Demons called by thaumaturgy kept their free will, but many nursed bitter millennia-old dreams of revenge and gladly attacked the nemeses of their Primordial creators. The products of Alchemy and Enchantment armed the gunzosha and Dragon-Blooded alike, while even the most cowardly astrologer or geomancer could provide useful predictions to the warriors of the Usurpation.

GUNZOSHA TACTICAL MANUALS

These specialized devices were revised numerous times during the High First Age and the Shogunate. At any time, the complete manuals contained more information than a single soldier could normally learn… at least in the shortened lifespan of a gunzosha warrior. Manuals were usually divided into 25 different modules designed for sharing within a scale of gunzosha. Each soldier studied one module, usually the one most suited to his job within the unit. Whenever necessary, and commonly during downtime, gunzosha would trade modules. This helped relieve boredom and honed their skills.

Each of the *Gunzosha Tactical Manual* modules consists of a blue-jade-alloy polyhedron about an inch across. It plugs into the armor's helmet through its sensory augmentation crystal-visor. The visor displays the information as quickly as the wearer wants.

Unfortunate accidents have occurred when Second Age savants have mistaken these devices for lightning boxes (see **Wonders of the Lost Age**, p. 60). An (Intelligence + Lore) roll, plus some familiarity with at least one of the two devices, is required to notice the difference. This roll is difficulty 2 if the would-be user is familiar with only one of the two, or difficult 1 if she has used them both. Determining the correct purpose

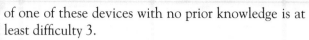

of one of these devices with no prior knowledge is at least difficulty 3.

Game Effects: Activating one of these modules requires the user to wear an active suit of gunzosha commando armor (see **Wonders of the Lost Age,** p. 81). Additionally, the user must pay one temporary Willpower point to access the module for an entire day. A complete set of 25 manual nodes operates as a tutor for all of the following: Lore 4, Occult 3, Craft (Magitech) 3, Craft (Air) 2, Craft (Fire) 2, Craft (Water) 1, Art of Enchantment (Adept Degree), Art of Alchemy (Adept Degree), Art of Warding and Exorcism (Adept Degree), War 3 (Coordinated Attacks +1), and the *Aegis-Inset Amulet* Procedure. Additionally, the text gives the user's player a -1 difficulty (to a minimum of 1) to repair rolls for gunzosha armor, aegis-inset amulets and gunzosha tactical manual modules. If a student has access to less than a full set of the modules, the Storyteller should divide the 25 points of skill or specialty tutor options offered and determine which are available to the user.

Availability and Cost: The Realm possesses only a single complete set of the modules at the House of Bells, plus an assortment of incomplete modules scattered among the Great Houses and military bases. Since the Realm does not field significant units of gunzosha, these devices are mostly kept for their military history applications. Lookshy keeps one full set in their Academy of Sorcery, one full set in the fortified caves beneath the city, and circulates three sets among their active gunzosha units. Lookshy sorcerer-engineers currently attempt to restore three other incomplete sets and hopefully create some new ones. Occasionally, scavengers discover lone modules lost to the diaspora of the Great Contagion. Usually, they sell them to Lookshy or the Realm, but a determined buyer might outbid the military powers of the Second Age.

Artifact Level: • for each *Gunzosha Tactical Manual* module. A module is a magitech device with a Repair Rating of 1.

THE SHOGUNATE

The battles of the Usurpation raged for a generation before the Solars were finally defeated. Having found the Arts remarkably useful to their cause, the newly formed Dragon-Blooded Shogunate eliminated or relaxed many of the restrictions on thaumaturgy. Unfortunately, the war destroyed most of the field's greatest masters and best libraries.

Since they could not produce the self-repairing Solar wonders of the High First Age, the Shogunate Dragon-Blooded needed a well-educated class of thaumaturgical engineers to maintain their magitech. Particularly in the early years of the Shogunate, the state supported numerous academies dedicated to the Arts, and Dragon-Blooded artificers directly sponsored the most promising students in return for their later service.

At first, the Shogunate's master may have truly intended to spread thaumaturgy throughout society. As the Dragon-Blooded discovered how much of the Old Realm's civilization depended on the Celestial Exalted, however, they became more interested in controlling the Arts than advancing them. Thaumaturges had to work for the State, protecting crops, dealing with spirits who rejected Dragon-Blooded authority and—most of all—building and servicing magitech weapons.

The Terrestrials (and their Sidereal silent partners) also acquired the same suspicions that had afflicted the Solars. If thaumaturgy was potent enough to hinder centuries-old Solar god-kings, it was too potent for the safety of the Dragon-Blooded. The Shogunate needed the labor of demons, but demons continued to trick, delude and destroy mortals. Thaumaturgy must be licensed, its teaching controlled—for the good of the State, the people and their Dragon-Blooded rulers.

Despite the nascent Immaculate faith extolling the Terrestrials' right to rule, the Dragon-Blooded could not inspire awe and devotion as the Solars once did. Bolder thaumaturge cabals rebelled against the limitations, and their suppression encouraged others to take a stand as well. After a few disasters and revolts fueled by thaumaturgy, the Shogunate ruthlessly cracked down on the Arts. Anyone who didn't work for the Dragon-Blooded was forbidden to study thaumaturgy, and violators received death. Just as the liberators from Solar tyranny ended up relying on slave labor, they ended up restricting the Arts as much as the Solars ever had.

As before, this merely drove the private study of thaumaturgy underground and forced people who wanted to learn the Arts to bargain with demons or practice illicitly. A few benevolent practitioners studied in secret. Outside of the approved practices of dedicated gunzosha warriors and sponsored thaumaturgical engineers, however, the exercise of thaumaturgy largely became the province of intellectual criminals and occultist radicals. Many of the greatest secret societies of the era were merely demonic cults, their mastery of the Arts descending from their dark patrons. In the wild places and fringes of Creation, however, folk magicians continued to practice their own ancient arts.

THE COMING OF THE SECOND AGE

While some savants argue that the Second Age properly began with the Usurpation, it is more commonly held that the Great Contagion marked its start. The Contagion crushed human civilization, including the agencies that held thaumaturgical wisdom in reserve. Masters of the Arts fell to the supernatural plague as surely as anyone else, and the Wyld consumed many of their greatest libraries when the borders of Creation collapsed. Nonetheless, many useful elements of mystic lore spread among the survivors. Numerous thaumaturges delayed death for a time by warding themselves from all contact, thereby keeping the plague away. Forlorn thaumaturges often devoted their last hours to recording their secret rites, and a few desperate Dragon-Blooded commanders distributed vast libraries of classified material to survivors to prevent them from being lost forever. As the Wyld flooded into Creation, gunzosha were spread to every corner of the world. When the Contagion finished its course and the Scarlet Empress drove back the Fair Folk invasion, surviving gunzosha were often left alone and cut off from any command structure. Many of these survivors settled down with whomever remained alive nearby and taught their thaumaturgical lore to anyone who demonstrated talent.

With nine-tenths of Creation's population dead, the barriers of authority dissolved, and remnants of the Arts spread widely amongst those who outlasted the supernatural plague. Arguably, the practice of thaumaturgy has become nearly as common in some parts of Creation as it was during the early centuries of the First Age. Inarguably, however, it is less advanced. As the Shogunate-era Dragon-Blooded struggled to maintain civilization, people valued practical results more than occult fundamentals. Many rites were handed down from master to apprentice without anyone understanding the principles behind them. Now, with the Shogunate in ruins and its survivors picking over its corpse like raitons, immediate effects were even more important than mastering the theories behind them.

As the people of Creation rebuilt civilization, their approaches to the Arts varied. In small villages or the wilderness, shamans and witches practice in accordance with tribal customs or solitary desires. In the growing cities, the study of the Arts has been shaped by the relationships between its students and those who governed them. Some rulers, including the Scarlet Empress, saw thaumaturgy as a potential weapon, too useful to ignore and too dangerous to allow in the hands of their enemies. Nations such as Lookshy and

Thorns saw the Arts as vitally necessary to the reestablishment of society. Pragmatic states such as Nexus and Sijan simply thought of thaumaturges as mortals whose personal motives were at least as important as the fact they knew a few magical tricks. Will the Time of Tumult bring a rebirth of thaumaturgical wisdom in the wake of the return of Creation's greatest sorcerers? Or will the spiraling chaos lead to another dark era of oppression and ignorance?

MYSTICAL GROUPS

The ordeals of sorcerous initiation are so demanding that only a fraction of Exalted become sorcerers. This fact, combined with the high cost of esoteric texts and exotic materials required for spell research, makes schools and societies of sorcery quite rare. The Exalted have a far easier time learning thaumaturgy. Not only do the few schools of sorcery also teach the Arts, but many lesser academies in Creation offer a thaumaturgical curriculum. Exalts can also arrange for informal tutoring, usually by serving as an apprentice to a master of the Arts.

In tribes or small villages, an apprentice probably has her mentor all to herself, but mystics in more populous areas often join organized groups. The success of an occult association depends upon factors such as the members' personalities, the approval (or disapproval) of the local powers that be, and the ravages of time. A few organizations have existed since the First Age, though the passage of at least 15 centuries has muddled their traditions or even caused their origins to be forgotten. However, most mystic societies survive only a generation or two before withering away or splitting into smaller, often hostile, factions.

Thaumaturgy is easily learned by the Exalted, however, for the same reason that swordplay is easily learned: because lots of mortals do it. The Dragon-Blooded, Lunars and Sidereal Exalted have their own arcane societies, but an Exalt does not have to rely on them. A reborn Solar probably *cannot* rely on them. For this reason, therefore, a Lawgiver who wants to learn thaumaturgy may need to find a mortal teacher and address him as "Master"… perhaps a disconcerting experience for someone who just got used to the idea she is potentially one of the most powerful people in the world.

THE ARCHITECTURE OF A MYSTIC ORGANIZATION

Groups dedicated to the practice of thaumaturgy vary greatly in size and purpose. They range from intimate pairings of mentor and student to massive state-sponsored industrial magitech facilities. Large organizations obviously are more likely to have greater impact on Creation, though the vagaries of fate are not always so predictable. The reason for a group's existence shapes its character, image and relation to the rest of the world. The sorcerer-assistants of Lookshy are widely respected by the city-state's citizens, yet common targets for enemy spies. Infernal cults, on the other hand, usually stay small and secret in all but the most corrupt lands, for their presence attracts violent opposition from virtually everyone else.

GROUP SIZE

The Apprentice: The time-honored tradition of mentor and student still forms the most common "group" of thaumaturges. Apprentices usually trade physical chores, such as cleaning the teacher's house and laboratory, for training in the Arts. Less fortunate students become veritable slaves to domineering, abusive masters, enduring backbreaking manual labor—or even nastier "service"—for the (sometimes false) promise of tutelage.

This model has endured naturally for thousands of years. In larger communities, masters often take on more than one apprentice or join with other thaumaturges with similar purpose.

Small groups: Mystic organizations consisting of 2 to 10 thaumaturges, plus any students currently in training, easily evolve when a master's former students stay in close contact. Unfortunately, these little lodges often fall apart upon the eventual death of their central figure, when students squabble for leadership. Other small groups form around a common purpose: a political goal, fraternity within a school of magic or even simple friendship. Organizations of this size may be wealthy or locally influential, but their fortunes often depend on their leadership. The master's death, or the loss of the group's patronage by the local king or guild, can leave the members struggling for direction or even doubtful about their next meal.

Medium groups: Smaller groups that survive long enough can outgrow their roots. Sometimes, one or more of the master's students demonstrates her own talents for leadership and works to build the organization rather than setting out on her own. Alternatively, if the group serves another party, its sponsor may decide to expand the scope of the mystical group. Mystic societies with 10 to 30 thaumaturges, with dozens of apprentices or servants, may become local powers in their own right. While their influence is generally limited to a single locale, they can usually obtain some degree of protection, sometimes even in the form of private soldiers.

Large groups: Few mystic groups grow larger than a few dozen members. Those that do exceed that mark usually enjoy the support of a powerful ruler, or take that role for their own leader. Dozens of thaumaturges work together to recruit talented apprentices and direct hundreds of lackeys toward their goals. Groups of this size virtually demand a degree of wealth merely to operate. Sometimes, large organizations manage to remain secret, but most of them are publicly known, if not feared.

Massive groups: Creation holds no more than a handful of truly massive mystic organizations, each boasting hundreds of thaumaturges supported by a huge body of servants and students. Only groups with greater purposes, beyond their magical practice, ever gain such momentous power. Organizations of this size are nearly impossible to keep secret, and most of them benefit from widespread respect. State-sponsored mystic groups with this kind of clout include the monks of the Immaculate Order and the sorcerer-assistants of Lookshy. Although never officially endorsed by its focus, the Cult of the Scarlet Empress is widely recognized throughout the Realm. In contrast, the furtive Cult of the Darkness' Unseeing Eye is spread throughout the South, but it is divided into small cells, which are largely blind to each other's existence.

GROUP PURPOSE

Every mystic organization originally gathers for some specific reason, even if it is just to share a cup of rice wine with friends at the local teahouse. Over time, its purpose may change or expand to encompass more than one goal. A band of drinking buddies may boldly swear to challenge the king's corrupt rule, while a team of mystics initially gathered to defend their city against Fair Folk raiders might start demanding regular payoffs for their protection.

Camaraderie: These thaumaturges congregate primarily to talk shop and enjoy each other's company. The group may share other goals, too, but companionship comes first. New associates are sometimes frustrated that parties and other social activities matter at least as much as magical studies. The bonds of friendship don't instantly extend to recruits, either. Groups based on camaraderie rarely survive beyond the initial membership unless they find a greater purpose. Nevertheless, most people crave contact with people who share their interests, so this remains one of the most common type of mystic society.

Defense: Few places in Creation ban thaumaturgy outright, but many locales restrict its use to some degree. A few rebellious souls always defy such restrictions,

THAUMATURGICAL GROUPS AND BACKGROUNDS

Exalted uses Backgrounds (or the lack thereof) to reflect the place a character occupies in the world, from enjoying a wide network of well-informed associates to being the god-figure of a powerful cult. A naïve young apprentice probably doesn't have much in the way of support, as represented by Backing or Influence, but she may nonetheless attract the attention of a powerful teacher (a Mentor). Charismatic magicians often attract hangers-on or hire bodyguards (Followers), and the Exalted sometimes even become the object of outright worship (Cult). On the path to mystic power, many thaumaturges collect powerful friends (Allies), tap into alternate supplies of knowledge (Contacts) and garner significant wealth (Resources).

If your character belongs to a mystic group, think about what she gets out of it. Try to reflect this in the way you spend your initial Background and bonus points during character creation. Don't sweat it too much, as you can always raise these Traits during play. If your Storyteller requires experience points to pay for increased Backgrounds, then discuss the growth of your character's ties with the world and use your experience to reflect this. If your Storyteller prefers a fluid system, then she is likely to tell you when your Backgrounds should be raised or lowered to reflect the events of your **Exalted** series instead of counting points of experience.

whether for purely selfish reasons or legitimate dissent against an oppressive regime. Often, they seek out fellow activists with whom they can share the risks inherent in the pursuit of forbidden knowledge.

Other mystics gather for mutual protection against a hostile environment, using their magic to defend themselves and their community. Regions threatened by Fair Folk or shadowland incursions often depend on the wards of powerful thaumaturges.

Groups formed to oppose governmental forces suffer violent ends more often than they overthrow the current establishment. Those who serve as guardians for their communities usually benefit from popular support, so long as the threat remains and they survive to defend against it.

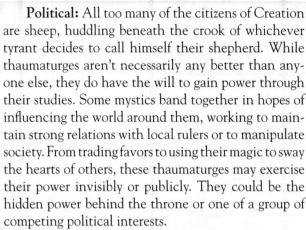

Political: All too many of the citizens of Creation are sheep, huddling beneath the crook of whichever tyrant decides to call himself their shepherd. While thaumaturges aren't necessarily any better than anyone else, they do have the will to gain power through their studies. Some mystics band together in hopes of influencing the world around them, working to maintain strong relations with local rulers or to manipulate society. From trading favors to using their magic to sway the hearts of others, these thaumaturges may exercise their power invisibly or publicly. They could be the hidden power behind the throne or one of a group of competing political interests.

The purposes of such societies vary widely. While the thaumaturges of Paragon ruthlessly support their monarch, the monks of the Immaculate Order are not afraid to pressure the mightiest Dynasts to follow the philosophies of the Perfected Hierarchy.

Economic: Skill in the Arts is a valuable talent. Many cities have mystic guilds that trade in talismans and potions. On the other hand, every ruler wants higher tax revenues, and it is a rare organization that doesn't seek special treatment or fall prey to targeted tariffs. Unless an economic group of thaumaturges gains powerful allies, it eventually attracts the special attention of the Guild. Very few groups can withstand the machinations of the Guild, and sooner or later, most of them fold or seek refuge with some other influential partner.

Power: When a young student dreams about learning the Arts, he usually imagines that he will become a powerful magician who dominates the forces of nature, the spirits and the people around him. For some thaumaturges, this desire for power becomes paramount. Groups with this kind of leadership won't settle for less than complete control over the world around them. Predictably, groups with this outlook often destroy themselves. Power-hungry thaumaturges eventually realize they don't want to share control, and infighting then tears the group apart. Even if a leader emerges who can keep the other thaumaturges in line, Creation holds entities and organizations that can swat down the mightiest thaumaturge—such as greater gods, Lunar elders, the Immaculate Order and Solar Circles with a taste for justice.

Cult: This type of organization centers around a single powerful entity or a small group of such beings. Sometimes, the cult focuses on a charismatic thaumaturge, but most honor one or more Exalted, gods, elementals or other supernatural entities. Despite the disapproval of some within the Immaculate Order, untold thousands worship the Scarlet Empress. The divine

trios of Great Forks and Whitewall rule their respective cities and enjoy large followings. The fortunes of a cult may rise and fall over the years, but even a group that fades into obscurity can return to power provided the cult's central figure survives.

A cult's activities don't always involve thaumaturgy, but its magical origin generally ensures some exposure to mystical knowledge. Many cults enjoy popular support, but others face strong opposition. Yozis and Deathlords appeal mostly to the decadent, the dispossessed and the insane. Their cults operate in secret, faced with the constant threat of extermination by the Wyld Hunt or outraged local militias.

MYSTICS OF THE SECOND AGE

The threads of the future have yet to weave their way through Loom of Fate, but the mystic organizations found here will be an important part of its unfolding pattern. The Maidens do not so easily reveal all of their secrets, though, and groups yet unseen may play greater roles than anyone imagines. Use these organizations to enrich your series and provide deeper background for your character, or take them as sources of inspiration and create your own thaumaturgical associations.

THAUMATURGY IN THE REALM

The Arts are legal in the Realm, but their practice is restricted according to Immaculate principles, bureaucratic protocol and the whim of the Scarlet Empress. The Immaculate Order wants individuals to fill their proper place in the Perfected Hierarchy without hindrance from unnecessary distraction. The Thousand Scales are protective of the position of authority the Empress has afforded them. The Empress simply regarded anyone with power as a potential threat to monitor and counterbalance. The Imminent Registrar of Mortal Occultists and Savants attempts to satisfy these competing demands.

See **The Compass of Celestial Directions, Vol. I—The Blessed Isle** for the whole complicated, expensive system. In brief, the Realm demands that would-be thaumaturges pay for a license and study from state-approved teachers and texts. The program of instruction takes five years and is not cheap, but it turns out competent magicians and savants (minimum Occult 3, Lore 2, and an Initiate Degree in at least one Art is required to pass).

Even with a thaumaturge's license, mortals are not normally allowed to summon elementals or demons. Except for monks, mortals are not supposed to be interacting with spirits in any way apart from honoring them

on Immaculate holidays. Mortal monks are expected to have limited contact with spirits, including driving off those who defy the ways of the Perfected Hierarchy. Nevertheless, they are mortal and are not generally supposed to summon demons or elementals.

The Dragon-Blooded of the Realm face fewer restrictions. The Scarlet Empress recognized that the innate powers of the Exalted generally exceed those of thaumaturgy, and that attempting to keep her Exalted subjects from learning the Arts was not worth the effort. By restricting thaumaturgical lore for the general populace, she encouraged Dragon-Blooded to see it as a special privilege rather than an incentive to thwart her authority.

Nevertheless, demons and elementals present a serious danger when treated without care, whether the summoner is mortal or Exalt. Anyone, mortal or Exalt, who wants to legally summon spirits within the Realm must gain a special demonologist or elementalist license—and a mortal thaumaturge needs a Dynast or Immaculate to vouch for her. If a Dragon-Blood is actually a sorcerer, and not merely a thaumaturge, she must also submit an entry to the Office of the White Registry in the Imperial City (see **The White Treatise**, p 14, and **The Manual of Exalted Power—The Dragon-Blooded**, p. 25). The Realm does not tolerate mortal sorcerers.

The Realm holds summoners responsible for anything their spirit minions do. A license insures a demonologist or elementalist against mischief that result in less than one obol of damage. Beyond this, however, any crime committed by a demon or elemental incurs severe punishment. The demon or elemental may also be banished or slain. A summoner may not simultaneously keep more than three summoned beings in Creation without special dispensation from powerful authorities.

Imperial officials limit the practice of other Arts wherever they feel that the Immaculate Philosophy or the security of the Dynasty is threatened:

• The Immaculate Order believes that ghosts have turned aside from the cycle of reincarnation that leads to enlightenment. The Art of the Dead is permitted only to perform appropriate death rites or to help lay the dead to permanent rest.

• Only legionnaires, House soldiers, magistrates and Black Helms may use thaumaturgy with military application.

• Duplicating or interfering with the blessings of the Exalted is restricted, as well.

• Alchemical solutions may not increase the lifespan of mortals by more than 25 percent.

• Drugs such as bright morning are illegal because they allow mortals to interact with spirits.

• Using astrology to read the future of a Dragon-Blood is prohibited.

• Because of its wide-ranging effects, another Imperial body, the Bureau of Climatic Deliberations, must approve the operations of thaumaturges who practice the Art of Weather Working. Although weather-workers are held to strict rules, even if they are Dragon-Blooded, they also have opportunities to work with well-connected Exalts and powerful magitech artifacts. See **The Compass of Celestial Directions, Vol. I—The Blessed Isle**, pp. 34-35, for details of Realm weather control.

THE IMMACULATE ORDER

Monks of the Immaculate Order are excused from many of the Realm's regulations, but the rules of the Order are quite as stringent in their way. Terrestrial Exalted lead the Order (with secret Sidereal backing), but mortal monks outnumber Exalted members by dozens to one. As spiritual caretakers of the Realm, monks must protect the community from rogue spirits, arrange the worship of important gods at the appointed times, bless births and weddings, officiate over death rites and care for the mind, body and soul of the citizenry. Mortal and Exalted members both learn thaumaturgy to help achieve these goals.

The Immaculate Order particularly favors the Arts of Spirit Beckoning and Warding and Exorcism. The latter enables a monk to drive off rogue gods or hungry ghosts and protect the community from other harmful influences. Spirit Beckoning smoothes relations with the Celestial Hierarchy, though many gods wish the Order would pray to them more often than the Immaculate calendar decrees.

The Order doesn't ignore the other Arts, however. Astrology helps determine when the Anathema will appear so that the Wyld Hunt may destroy them. Celestially guided itinerants, who are always Dragon-Blooded, also use the Art to predict unrest within the Realm, bolstering their reputation for rooting out corruption within the government and sedition by rebels, bandits or rogue deities. Alchemy and Husbandry are recognized for their value in healing. The Art of Enchantment combined with Warding and Exorcism creates protective talismans.

The Order discourages its monks from learning the Arts of Demon or Elemental Summoning—a monk does need a demonologist or elementalist license to study these Arts and accepts regular scrutiny by his superiors. Immaculates usually leave Weather Working to the Bureau of Climatic Deliberations. Degrees in the Art of the Dead are unknown within the Order, although a handful of Procedures related to death rites are taught.

Special: The Immaculate Order values the Art of Geomancy because Immaculate doctrine associates control of Essence with spiritual and moral enlightenment. Some mortal monks learn to manipulate Essence through thaumaturgical rituals and rigorous asceticism. Once they achieve this goal, they can learn the Five Dragon Style (see **The Manual of Exalted Power—The Dragon-Blooded**, pp. 189-191) and perhaps other supernatural martial arts. Indeed, Immaculate monks are the *only* mortals in the Realm whose use of Charms is tolerated, and even they are only allowed Charms from an approved martial arts style. If other mortals try to imitate the powers of the Exalted, they commit heresy—but monks who use the Charms of an orthodox martial art *prove* the Immaculate path leads to enlightenment.

THE CULT OF THE SCARLET EMPRESS

The Cult of the Scarlet Empress has never enjoyed official sanction. The Immaculate Order calls the Empress the most enlightened of all Dragon-Blooded, but that doesn't make her a god. The adherents of the Cult

---

THE LAW AND THE REALITY

More than 100 million mortals inhabit the Blessed Isle. Searching through ever-growing records of licensed thaumaturges is a time consuming effort, and most enforcement authorities cannot easily detect the use of the Arts. Nearly every village boasts a wise old mystic who could never afford a thaumaturgy license. Even in the Imperial City, the poor scrape together what they can manage to beg the blessing of the neighborhood wise woman. Various craft guilds may even purchase one or two thaumaturgy licenses yet house dozens of unlicensed practitioners, passing off their work as that of a single licensed master. Heretical secret cults, inspired by sly Yozi demons or rebellious gods of the Blessed Isle, offer magical power to their most devoted adherents.

The Dynasty bends its own rules, too. Dragon-Blooded commanders sometimes teach legionnaires how to enchant their blade or pray to the war gods. House sorcerers don't always file the paperwork for their laboratory assistants. The mortal staff of the Heptagram absorbs rituals like a sponge soaking up water, and the Sidereals entrenched in the school never submit its daily routines to the scrutiny of clerks. Individuals who know at least one thaumaturgical Procedure aren't necessarily less common than elsewhere in Creation, they are simply more circumspect about it.

go beyond appropriate reverence, but no one's ready to denounce any form of esteem for the Empress. The Empress never publicly addressed the propriety of her cult, and her stance has varied from periods of unspoken approval to covert crackdowns. The Immaculate Order sometimes issues muted, indirect approval or muted, indirect criticism, but most of the time tries to pretend the cult doesn't exist.

With no real cohesion except a shared reverence for the same central figure, the Cult of the Scarlet Empress stays unorganized and informal. Repeated cycles of suppression have crushed would-be leaders within the Cult, while the shifts from indifference to quiet favor have left members unsure how they might best serve their holy matron. Nevertheless, membership in the Cult is often a useful way for young Dragon-Bloods and patricians to meet potential patrons. Citizens of lower classes sometimes form cult groups of their own.

Without a central direction, members of the Cult develop their own informal traditions, from celebrating days they think are important to the Empress to sacrificing things they think she would value. Cult rites often take place on the anniversaries of their matron's wedding days, revelations of Imperial consorts or birthdates of her direct children.

The Cult of the Empress would be nothing but an eccentric social club, except that people often ask their gods to protect them. Every citizen of the Realm knows the Empress saved Creation and protects the Realm. Long ago, her devotees started calling on her to banish ghosts, bring them luck and protect them from life's other common hazards. Not long after, some cultists learned enough thaumaturgy to give some force to those desires.

High-ranking members of the cult strive to learn the Arts of Enchantment or Warding and Exorcism. Mortal members sometimes use geomantic procedures to attune to artifacts, demesnes or hearthstones—they can't *use* them, but they value the experience as a way to be more like the Exalted and, therefore, closer to the Empress.

Cultists believe that their rituals call on the Empress' power. And they work. Whether their working has anything to do with their faith doesn't really matter. The cult ties every ritual or talisman to some tale about the Empress. For instance, one story says that the scarlet crane, a bird that lives in the Juche Prefecture and the Scarlet Prefecture, received its crimson hue by the Scarlet Empress's blessings. The cult thus uses scarlet crane feathers in a luck charm. Whether the story or the charm came first, no one now can say; such is the nature of folk thaumaturgy—even when the folk are Princes of the Earth.

The Cult of the Empress currently undergoes rapid changes sparked by their matron's disappearance. Since she vanished, the Cult has drawn together in unprecedented unity. Larger congregations than ever found before gather in hopes of summoning the Scarlet Empress to restore order and put Creation right again. Some members study other thaumaturgical Arts in search of clues to the Empress' whereabouts, such as Astrology… and Demon Summoning. Disturbing reports from magistrates and Black Helm authorities suggest that some of these rites include human sacrifice, and that Cult cells have tried to obtain samples of hair or blood from Dragon-Blooded who are of close lineage with the Empress. Savants in the Realm fear that the Cult's ignorant, fumbling efforts may threaten the Realm as much as any Dynastic infighting.

SORCERER-ASSISTANTS OF LOOKSHY

The power of Lookshy depends on its arsenal of magitech and other artifacts. To maintain this arsenal and craft new weapons, the General Staff instituted an Academy of Sorcery that eventually claimed the entire Valkhawsen District of the city. The Academy strives to train as many Exalted sorcerer-engineers as possible… but the city-state doesn't *have* enough Exalted to do all the work. Of necessity, dozens of mortal thaumaturges—sorcerer-assistants—graduate with every Dragon-Blooded sorcerer.

The Academy concentrates on the Arts of Enchantment and Alchemy. The other Arts are largely left to the members of the Academy's brother institute, the sorcerer-priests of the Chaplainry. Citizens of Lookshy are expected to serve in the Seventh Legion, and thaumaturges are no exception. However, a skilled practitioner can generally count on serving with little to no combat duty: she is more valuable servicing the city-state's magitech arsenal. Of course, the military needs technicians in the field, too. Thaumaturges who fanatically desire to serve in battle are encouraged to join the elite gunzosha commando units.

The sorcerer-assistants of Lookshy benefit from the city's strong dependence upon magitech and military prowess. They fall into several groups.

Sorcerer-priests, also called sohei, work with the Chaplainry to exorcise hostile spirits and summon such beings when it is necessary—often in the midst of battle. Since true control only comes with sorcery, thaumaturgical assistants to sorcerer-priests practice only minor summonings of elementals and beckonings of small gods, and then only under sorcerous supervision. They are usually limited to investigation, exorcism and warding duties.

Sorcerer-engineers, or wai tan-junai, create and maintain magitech. They must know at least four spells of the Terrestrial Circle, as well as thaumaturgy. Senior sorcerer-engineers rarely leave the city and spend much of their time in the Academy of Lookshy, the district around it or the caverns beneath.

Sorcerer-technicians, or shugan-junai, assist the wai tan-junai in caring for artifacts and crafting new ones. They also provide magical support for the Legion in combat. Most of them are mortals and only know thaumaturgy. The General Staff wants one sorcerer-technician for every fang of the Seventh Legion. This goal may not be completely realistic, but the General Staff seems set upon achieving it.

Armigers are special troops trained to protect the city's valuable sorcerer-engineers. Though some armigers are powerful God-Bloods or other strange creatures, most are thaumaturges. These trusted assistants may carry weapons in every situation (even during reports to the General Staff) and serve as personal bodyguards tasked to prevent the loss of Lookshy's most precious personnel. It is also tacitly understood that an armiger has the duty to kill a sorcerer-engineer who tries to defect or faces capture by enemies who might extract strategic information.

Gunzosha are elite soldiers who sacrifice years of their lives to bear the powerful gunzosha commando armor in the service of Lookshy. These individuals need extensive ritual and surgical preparations to use their special armor. They also help maintain their own equipment. Only the most fanatical patriots receive gunzosha duty, for Lookshy closely guards the secret of the armor's production and the implantation procedures needed to create these super soldiers. Gunzosha can achieve nearly any military rank, though their careers are generally shorter than those of their compatriots.

For more information on Lookshy, its military and its magitech, see **The Compass of Terrestrial Directions—The Scavenger Lands**. Information about the Lookshy Academy of Sorcery can be found in **The White Treatise**.

THE CULT OF THE DARKNESS' UNSEEING EYE

Banished from Creation and trapped within a hell composed of their own forms, the defeated Primordials hunger for revenge upon the rebellious gods and their Exalted warriors. Their prison is not perfect, and the Yozis whisper dark promises to those mortals who will listen. Many wicked or deluded cults of mortals serve the secret purposes of the Yozis, and one of the largest of them is the Cult of the Darkness' Unseeing Eye.

Small cabals of this cult are spread throughout the South. Each cell has little contact with the others; most members do not know they belong to a larger organization. In fact, some cultists think they belong to some other secret society. The demon-worshipping Salmalin (once served by the Solar Exalted Harmonious Jade) is really part of the Unseeing Eye, though only the highest leaders of the Salmalin know this.

The cult owes its spread, if not its origin, to the venerable Literary Resurrectionist Society in Chiaroscuro. This handful of bookmakers transcribes and sells ancient works. Two centuries ago, this scholarly guild translated A *Lover Clad in Blue* into Flametongue and distributed it for sale throughout the South. Whether they did this unprompted, no one can say—but since then, the Cult of the Darkness' Unseeing Eye has hired these scholarly artisans to translate several other books whose obscurity matches their antiquity.

Sondok, She-Who-Stands-In-Doorways, a Demon of the Second Circle, directs the Cult of the Darkness' Unseeing Eye when she is able. While she lacks the supernatural genius of greater demons, she plans cleverly and patiently. Her cult's cell structure makes it impossible to root out and destroy, though this also renders it unable to mount any strong, unified action. The cult achieves its goals through subversion, secrecy and stealth, though it does not shirk from violence when it seems expedient. Demon-hunters and state authorities that capture Sondok's cultists cannot figure out her grand strategy. According to the records of First Age sorcerers, Sondok is angry, cold and totally devoted to her tasks… whatever they are. She is also a consummate fighter with blood eternally encrusted beneath her black talons.

The Cult of the Darkness' Unseeing Eye uses symbols associated with Sondok, even if its members don't always know their source. They often dress in dark red leather and black or red silk, and frequently dye their hair black. For jewelry they favor gold and garnets, with wolves' ears and the dead roots of trees forming an odd ornamental theme. Those who enjoy the company of a pet often prefer a bedraggled brown dog. For weapons, they prefer swords, axes or tiger claws. Sondok's devotees cultivate a peculiar breed of poisonous red mushrooms, reputedly left by Sondok's footsteps, and employ it in their assassinations. Stories say that the constellations are faintly visible in Sondok's blood-filled eyes, and this

leads some of cultists to practice an inauspicious form of astrology. The most knowledgeable of her servants sometimes have a black tattoo upon their left breasts in the form of intricate bird-claw marks. The most fanatical file their teeth to sharp points. All of these trappings are common in the thaumaturgical rites of the cult.

The Cult of the Darkness' Unseeing Eye focuses, of course, upon the Art of Demon Summoning. Few members develop actual Degrees in the Art beyond the Initiate level, but priests often learn a few Procedures from the Adept and Master Degrees, particularly *The Year and the Day* and *Beckon Sondok*. Beyond demonic lore, the Art of Astrology interests a few fervent cult members. The cult's astrologers strive to discover the most inauspicious moments of their enemies to guide their clandestine operations. Some of the cult's most influential members are disaffected astrologers who left the Varang City-States to escape their assigned lots in life. Otherwise, the cult's thaumaturgical knowledge is largely focused on individual Procedures that aid in stealth or combat. Cult members often possess appropriate Backgrounds, particularly Contacts or Backing (Unseeing Eye).

SONDOK'S MUSHROOMS

The cult slips Sondok's mushrooms into spicy food or coats weapons with a concentrated blood-red paste made from them. The mushrooms are equally lethal in either form, with these traits: Damage 9L/action, Toxicity 5, Tolerance —/—, Penalty -5. Resources 5 (3 for cult members).

THE SALINAN SOCIETY

The Salinan Society draws its inspiration from one of the greatest sorcerers of the Old Realm. The society claims it began with Kazenbi, a mortal thaumaturge who served the great Salina and shared her belief that Creation itself was the greatest guide to enlightenment. After centuries of chaos and suppression, no one can prove Kazenbi existed. Nevertheless, the Society's study of magical theory and its relations to thaumaturgy remain valuable after more than 1,000 years.

The Salinan Society is a loose fraternal organization dedicated to sharing thaumaturgical techniques. Though individual members have entertained ambitions for power, the organization as a whole survives by avoiding politics. The Society has no central leadership; each group forms around one or more senior members, who teach students interested in the Arts. While groups

may exchange letters, they know their Arts derive from Creation and no master could possibly keep them for himself. Functionally, the Salinan Society consists of scores of separate thaumaturgical cabals spread across Creation, operating independently and sharing information when they feel like it.

The Realm and the Immaculate Order condemn the Salinan Society because it acknowledges Salina as a Solar Exalted. Members who lie within areas influenced by the Immaculate faith often dislike thinking that their founder had ties with an Anathema, but they don't want to change established texts, either. (Occasional revisionists argue that Kazenbi was the truly enlightened one and Salina the Anathema stole his insights.) In regions of the Threshold where the Immaculates have little presence, the Salinan Society operates more openly. Of course, every locale presents its own challenges, including the potential for oppressive or magic-hungry regimes.

Salinan thaumaturges are true savants who see thaumaturgy as a way to understand Creation. While they maintain many ancient texts, they engage in a great deal of research, too. Many cabals own transcripts of the Radiant Dowager's *The Genesis of Heathen Ritual*. These sometimes lead Salinan savants into less civilized areas in search of shamans or witches, hoping to discover folk magic never recorded in the scrolls of the scholarly. Other groups organize expeditions into the edges of the Wyld, hoping to recover lore lost to the Great Contagion. Still other members experiment and observe Creation in hopes of discovering its secrets directly.

The loose dispersal of the Society means that a student is usually limited to texts held by his local cabal. Provided he doesn't bring trouble to the group, however, they aren't likely to judge him for his studies. If a rite is embedded in Creation, it must have some legitimate purpose. Unfortunately, different cabals may not trust each other despite their shared ideals. Since the Society

THE FOUNDER'S RETURN?

Every Society member has the same thought if they learn that the new Solar Exalted carry memories from First Age incarnations: *Where's Salina?* The current host of her Exaltation could answer a lot of their questions, historical and otherwise, and gain the allegiance of thaumaturges scattered throughout Creation. It would be most unfortunate for Creation if her Exaltation turned out to be held by an Abyssal.

doesn't even try to enforce orthodoxy, cabals frequently drift off into their own doctrines and obsessions that clash with the parent group's traditions. Enough true Salinan groups and texts always survive, however, to keep the Society going.

THE THAUMATURGE

Given that mortals outnumber Exalted by at least 10,000 to 1, the wonders of thaumaturgy are vastly more common than sorcery. Practitioners of the Arts come from cultures that range from Wyld barbarians to the Realm. Such diversity makes generalization difficult, but a handful of common archetypes exist. Five such archetypes are briefly described below, along with notes about Traits they most commonly share. The Occult Ability isn't repetitively listed, as it is important to all thaumaturges.

Even though sorcery and Charms greatly overmatch thaumaturgy, a prudent Exalt does not dismiss a skilled practitioner of the Arts. Minor magics can still prove deadly if applied with care and cunning, when a foe is at his weakest—or when several thaumaturges work together. What's more, any of these five types of thaumaturge may have wider social connections that could cause further trouble for an arrogant Exalt.

CULTIST

Some thaumaturges align themselves with powers greater than themselves. This might happen through an honest religious conviction or a desire for access to godly might. Some want to control the actions of others as a god's deputy, while others merely seek a sense of belonging. The nature of a cult matters at least as much as the thaumaturge's own desires. A well-intentioned individual duped by the Cult of the Darkness's Unseeing Eye probably becomes corrupt and dangerous, while the most power-hungry priest of the three gods of Great Forks is constantly pressured to serve the community. Most cults center upon a being of great supernatural power, and thaumaturges tap into the mystic secrets these entities offer to the faithful.

Traits: The Performance Ability matters a great deal for its use in religious ceremonies, and tricking people in the case of less savory cults. Other Abilities vary according to cult's nature: combat Abilities for war gods, Craft for a smith god, Larceny and Stealth for secretive groups. Cultists who aspire to leadership develop Presence. Backgrounds such as Allies, Backing, Contacts and Influence represent the thaumaturge's ties to the cult. If the thaumaturge is high in the cult's ranks, she might enjoy the aid of numerous Followers and access to cult Resources.

Cultist thaumaturges usually favor Spirit Beckoning, though cultists dedicated to the Yozis or the Underworld prefer Demon Summoning or the Art of the Dead. Any cult might use Enchantment to craft talismans that assist the faithful in secular life as well as cult activities.

MONK

Monks and other holy men and women express religious devotion through lives of spiritual discipline. The Immaculate Order is certainly the largest such religious body, but other groups in Creation practice

similar lifestyles. The rigid practices of the Brides of Ahlat, the Southern God of War, are a good example, for these fierce warriors rival mortal Immaculate monks with their fanatic devotion and martial skills. Other holy men and women express their devotion by helping the poor, traveling as mendicant preachers, or ascetically renouncing the world, the flesh and temptation. The self-discipline inherent to these groups lends itself to thaumaturgical study, and most monks enjoy public support that makes it easy to maintain collections of suitable training material.

Traits: The discipline of the monastic lifestyle usually demands the Resistance and Integrity Abilities. Not all groups practice them, but the Immaculate Order in particular stresses mastery of Martial Arts. Itinerant monks learn Survival, and Linguistics if they travel widely. A smattering of Presence, Performance and Bureaucracy are often gained while serving the needs of the organization and its adherents. The Resources Background is rare, since monks often take vows of poverty, while the Mentor Background is especially appropriate.

Immaculate monks favor the Art of Warding and Exorcism, while Geomancy provides a potential path to practicing the supernatural martial arts. Other holy folk may prefer Arts that help them in their lives of service, such as Alchemy for monks who run a charity hospital.

SAVANT

Many thaumaturges learn the Arts through formal training, at one of the schools that teach it or apprenticed to a talented master. These mystics approach the Arts in a scholarly fashion and generally gain employment with respected groups within society. The sorcerer-assistants of Lookshy are a fine example of this archetype, as they pursue vigorous curricula of magical lore and use them to maintain the city's magitech arsenal. The Salinan Society, on the other hand, avoids worldly entanglement but members pursue systematic programs of experiment and exploration. Savants aren't limited to civilized societies, though: the tribal witch who knows the properties of a thousand healing and harming herbs is a savant, too. Savants are defined not by their setting, but by their hunger for knowledge.

Traits: Savants favor Intelligence, Lore and Linguistics. Those who train as enchanters typically learn Crafts. Other savants study Medicine and become accomplished doctors. Long interaction within scholarly communities may lead to Socialize or Bureaucracy. A savant trained by a master usually has a Mentor, while demand for her skills permits Resources. Savants tend

to favor the Arts of Enchantment, Alchemy and Geomancy, but anything is possible.

SCAVENGER LORD

The wonders of the First Age, virtually ubiquitous in their time, become dangerous weapons or valuable luxuries in the Time of Tumult. Extracting these wonders from ruins and tombs is a hazardous task that demands a rare combination of quick wits, physical prowess and attention to details of ancient lore. Although scavenger lords are best known in the East, these explorers can operate anywhere in Creation where First Age structures beg to be explored. Successful scavenger lords often semi-retire and sponsor the expeditions of younger scavengers: they know that sooner or later they could die through a single mistake in trying to circumvent a First Age building's defenses. Since most ancient defenses rely in part upon magic, wise scavenger lords try to learn some thaumaturgy.

Traits: Scavenger lords need Awareness and Investigation to survive their expeditions and find the loot they seek. Linguistics (particularly Old Realm) and Lore provide valuable understanding of First Age threats. Larceny and Dodge prove remarkably useful in defeating troublesome barriers or ducking deadly traps. Artifact and Resources are appropriate Backgrounds for scavenger lords who enjoy any success. Most scavengers employ a small expeditionary team, which is easily represented by Followers or Allies. Scavenger lords are eclectic in their studies of thaumaturgy, tending to gather a body of useful Procedures rather than mastery of any particular Art.

SHAMAN

A witch or shaman learns from tradition, the small gods she strives to exploit and appease, and the world around her. Unlike the cultist or monk, she treats the gods as a threat or resource as much as figures to be worshipped. Unlike the savant, the shaman cares more about results and serving her community than about systematic acquisition of knowledge. Whether she lives in an isolated village or with a nomadic tribe, the shaman becomes an important figure to her people through her Abilities and Arts. She might arrange for better weather, call wild beasts to the hunt, and ward off dangerous foes. Of course, some shamans are feared and tolerated only because they are necessary.

Traits: The Medicine Ability is important since most shamans serve as healers in their communities. Lore is virtually required, usually specialized in local spirits. Tribal shamans tend to master Survival, while Performance and Presence help them negotiate with spirits.

Shamans usually enjoy Influence in their community. Friendly spirits or ancestral ghosts become Mentors or Allies, and some shamans will attract a Familiar. Powerful shamans might enjoy access to Resources, Followers or even their own Cult. Almost every Art has its uses for a shaman, from Alchemy to brew magical medicines to Weather Working to aid the village croplands.

THE ARTS OF THAUMATURGY

Savants classify thaumaturgical rituals into 11 *Arts*, each of which constitutes its own Occult specialty: Alchemy, Astrology, the Dead, Demon Summoning, Elemental Summoning, Enchantment, Geomancy, Husbandry, Spirit Beckoning, Warding and Exorcism, and Weather Working. Most of the Arts have existed in one form or another since before humanity existed. Three were created after the Primordial War: the Art of the Dead, the Art of Demon Summoning and the Art of Elemental Summoning.

Rituals within an Art share common elements. If one knows several rituals within an Art, others become easier to learn. A thaumaturge who learns a single Procedure, and stops there, may never make these connections. Once she learns multiple related Procedures, she can piece together the principles of an Art. The Degrees of the Arts express how well a thaumaturge understands those principles.

Rituals in this chapter are divided according to their Arts and are presented in the same format as the sample rituals from **Exalted**, pages 137-139. To recap:

Name (Minimum Degree, Attribute, Difficulty, Casting Time): Effect.

Any special considerations, such as unique tools, expenditures or non-standard dice rolls, are described along with the Effect.

Some rituals' names use "Wild Card" forms such as *Summon (Species)* or *Ward Against (Creature)*. These entries represent groups of rituals with similar effects and game mechanics, such as *Ward Against Elementals*, *Summon Demons*, and so on. The standard classes for thaumaturgy are Beasts, the Dead, Demons, Elementals, Exalted, Fair Folk, Gods and Humans. The (Species) term means that a ritual affects a particular sub-class within these broader classes, such as *Summon Erymanthos* or *Beckon Solar Exalted*. Characters with an appropriate Degree can learn rituals that affect all members of a single class; isolated Procedures can only affect a single subclass. Many of these rituals, however, can be learned as part of at least two Arts. A *Ward Against Demons*, for instance, could be learned either as part of the Art of Demon Summoning or the Art of Warding and Exorcism.

HOW MANY RITUALS?

The rules of **Exalted** aim to make thaumaturgy as multipurpose as possible, but weaker than Charms, sorcery or necromancy. An experienced magician might know scores of rituals, each designed for a specific limited purpose. Technically, a thaumaturge can use any ritual for which she possesses the proper Degree in the appropriate Art, but things aren't really that simple. Even the greatest thaumaturge cannot automatically produce an alchemical mixture he has never seen simply because he is a Master of Alchemy. Knowing the underlying theories of an Art to a particular Degree does *not* mean that a character instantly knows every ritual within that Degree.

Players should work with their Storyteller to decide which rituals their characters reasonably know already, and keep track of new ones learned during play. A thaumaturge character from the West would need a good reason to justify knowing the secret ritual that Eastern shamans use to harden ironwood. By the same token, why would an Eastern shaman know rituals to call storms at sea?

Common sense and character concept may be enough for players and Storytellers to decide what rituals a character may know. The need to buy separate Arts and Degrees goes a long way to keeping thaumaturgy broad-based yet limited in scope. If you want a stricter guideline (as an option), you might limit starting characters to a maximum number of rituals per Degree based on Intelligence, Lore or Occult rating. The thaumaturge then can learn more rituals as game events allow.

THE ART OF ALCHEMY

The greatest of all First Age alchemists was almost certainly the Twilight Caste Tarim, who surpassed thaumaturgical mastery of the Art and devised a means to condense the shaped Essence of sorcery into physical formulas. Thaumaturges cannot match the might of Tarim's creations, but the Art nonetheless produces miraculous feats.

Alchemy combines aspects of pharmacy, metallurgy and other Crafts that combine and transform different ingredients. The "rituals" of the Art—which alchemists often call formulas—take place in a laboratory stocked with equipment as mundane as a mortar and pestle or as exotic as the occult mirrors used to smelt orichalcum.

As well as commonplace techniques such as boiling and crystallizing, alchemists employ strange operations such as calcination, rubification and insufflation. An alchemist may combine herbs, minerals and animal parts into magical medicines transform lead into gold, or even grant mortals some of the inherent qualities of the Exalted.

In addition to the Occult Ability, alchemy requires knowledge of diverse living and unliving substances, so an alchemist needs at least Lore 2 to gain a Degree, and Lore 4 to become an Adept. For most formulas, the practitioner must have at least one dot in Craft (Water) for each Degree, unless that procedure is a healing one, in which case it requires at least one dot of Medicine per Degree. Some formulas might require dots in other Crafts, instead. Unless otherwise indicated, assume that a formula requires Craft (Water).

Alchemical formulas that add to Attributes or Abilities count as dice added by Charms. Most alchemy cannot affect spirits or the dead. Some formulas do not affect the Exalted, especially those designed to temporarily give mortals Exalted characteristics. Unless otherwise specified, the effects of an alchemical formula typically last for one scene. Drinking or applying an already prepared alchemical mixture is generally a miscellaneous action.

MAGICAL MATERIAL REFINEMENTS

The Procedures that smelt moonsilver, orichalcum, starmetal and soulsteel are all part of the Art of Alchemy. See page 23 for these rituals of the forge.

Alchemical Touchstone (0, Perception, 1, one action): When expertise at Lore isn't enough to identify a substance, an alchemist can rub it against a specially treated ceramic plate—a touchstone—and glean clues from the streak left behind. Other "touchstones" are fluids dripped on an unknown substance. Each alchemical touchstone detects the presence or absence of a single substance or property, such as jade alloys, Wyld-taint or snake venoms. Compounding a touchstone may take days, but once made it can be used quickly. A touchstone stays usable for a season.

Life's Little Luxury Blends (0, Intelligence, 1, one hour): Numerous minor formulas lie within the alchemist's grasp. She might concoct such things as deodorant, superior cleaning agents, dyes that resist fading or trick powders that foam when introduced to alcohol or vinegar. Storytellers should consider other similarly innocuous formulas. Each formula is a separate Procedure.

Blood-Staunching Compress (1, Intelligence, 3, one hour): Bandages steeped in this compound automatically cause a wound to stop bleeding, and wounds wrapped in these bandages do not re-open unless the character's player botches a combat or Athletics roll. The compound retains its potency for one year, unless used. Requires Medicine.

Draught of Blessed Respite (1, Intelligence, 2, one hour): This potion lets its user get a full night's sleep under nearly any circumstance. A half dose, mixed with wine, puts the imbiber into a half-sleep for four hours. During this time, the user can function if necessary, though all of her dice pools involving Perception, Wits and Dexterity are halved (and that's *after* Excellencies and other Charms). Every full hour of this state counts as two hours of sleep.

Each use of this formula creates five doses, which retain their potency for three years. Blessed Respite addicts people who use it more than (Stamina) times in a week. Use the Wyld Addiction rules from **Exalted**, page 288, substituting references to the influence of the drug for that of the Wyld, and using a difficulty equal to (half the doses taken during the week). Requires Medicine.

Eagle's Eye Potion (1, Wits, 3, one hour): This preparation grants preternaturally clear sight, giving one extra die to all vision-related Perception rolls. The effects last for five hours. Other potions exist for other senses: Fox's Ear, Bloodhound's Nose, Exquisite Chef's Palate and Blind Courtesan's Caress Potions for hearing, smell, taste and touch respectively.

Hero's Recovery (1, Intelligence, 3, one hour): This potion's effects last for half a day per dot of Stamina the recipient has. During this time, a mortal recovers from injuries as an Exalt does. Serious injuries may require more than one dose over the course of recovery, but mortals cannot stand more than (Stamina) consecutive doses without doubling their healing times instead. Requires Medicine.

(Type) Venom-Allaying Draught (1, Intelligence, 2, one hour): Each of these draughts is a different formula, specific to a particular poison or venom. Once applied, it allows a mortal's player to make a (Stamina + Resistance) roll to resist a toxin at the same difficulty as though the character were Exalted. These antitoxins retain their potency for five years. Requires Medicine.

Wound-Cleansing Unguent (1, Intelligence, 1, two hours): If a patient is treated with this unguent after

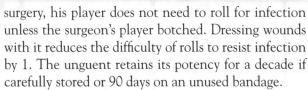

surgery, his player does not need to roll for infection unless the surgeon's player botched. Dressing wounds with it reduces the difficulty of rolls to resist infection by 1. The unguent retains its potency for a decade if carefully stored or 90 days on an unused bandage.

Age-Staving Cordial (2, Intelligence, 3, one hour): The alchemist brews a dose of age-staving cordial (see **Exalted**, p. 378).

Ardent Embrace Resin (2, Intelligence, 2, one hour): Despite its romantic name, this formula is a lethal weapon. The recipe creates a goo that bursts into flame on contact with air or water, and sticks to whatever it touches. It is typically used by packing it into fragile vials or capsules and throwing it at an enemy. If it hits, the enemy suffers environmental damage equal to a bonfire (see **Exalted**, p. 131) for the next minute.

Final Vengeance (2, Wits, 3, one hour): Final Vengeance is a powerful painkiller and euphoric. Used mostly by fanatics and assassin cults, this mixture causes the user to ignore all wound penalties and receive automatic success on all Valor checks (whether he wants to succeed or not) for one scene. When its effects end, the user's Stamina drops to 1; he regains one dot per day of complete rest. While his Stamina is reduced, all healing takes place at half normal rate and non-magical methods cannot increase this.

Munificent Antivenin (2, Intelligence, 3, one hour): This powerful elixir can negate even the deadliest poisons, though it does not repair damage already done. Once ingested, the antivenin purges all poison from the user's system. The poison sweats from his skin and is vomited forth violently, painfully rendering the user Inactive for 5 ticks per dose of poison in his system. Afterward, the subject is fatigued, suffering a -2 internal penalty until he can rest for at least four hours.

Philtre of Desire (2, Intelligence, 2, one hour): These potions inspire emotional reactions in the desired target. One version gives the imbiber a two-die bonus to Performance, Presence and Socialize rolls made against the victim. Another version reduces the imbiber's Mental DV by 2, making Social attacks easier. Creating a philtre of this type normally requires an arcane link to the victim as part of the formula, although this can be ignored at the price of a +1 difficulty. For +2 difficulty, a philtre can be brewed that gives bonus dice to the imbiber's Social attack rolls against any target. Botches while using a philtre increase in severity, leading to decades-long hatred or all-consuming jealous obsession. Once created, these philtres retain potency for only a month.

Tiger's Heart Elixir (2, Wits, 3, one hour): This elixir emboldens the spirit and drives away fear and doubt, giving the user +1 Valor for all purposes for the rest of the scene. Other formulas boost Compassion, Temperance and Conviction.

Valiant Warrior Formula (2, Wits, 2, one hour): This formula appeals to mortal soldiers who wish to compete with great heroes. For one day after its use, the user is no longer treated as an extra. She has the full complement of seven health levels, can spend Willpower for bonus successes or through Virtues, counts 10s as two successes, requires damage to be rolled and is capable of stunts.

Deathlord's Breath (3, Intelligence, 4, 20 hours): The alchemist brews a dose of Deathlord's Breath. A ghost cannot cross a line of this magical dust unless its player succeeds at a Valor roll at difficulty 3; hungry ghosts cannot even try unless some entity of greater power compels them. The barrier of dust retains its potency for one month, after which the difficulty on the Valor roll falls by one per week until the powder is spent.

When it touches the living, however, Deathlord's Breath acts as a slow but deadly toxin (Damage 7L/day, Toxicity 4L, Tolerance —/—, Penalty -3). Worst of all, a person slain by Deathlord's Breath doesn't stop moving: his body becomes a zombie (see **Exalted**, pp. 314-315), while his lower soul becomes a hungry ghost (see **Exalted**, pp. 317-318). Deathlord's Breath is illegal in the Realm and most civilized countries. The toxin remains potent for decades.

8-Scream Devil Powder (3, Intelligence, 4, one hour): The alchemist brews a dose of 8-scream devil powder (see **Wonders of the Lost Age**, p. 74).

Heavenly Transmutation Processes (3, Perception, 7, one hour per Resources 4 quantity of final material): The alchemist masters the secrets of turning base materials into more noble ones. He can turn lead into gold, pig iron into finest steel and pale, flawed corundum into rubies. Each process is a different Procedure. Transmutation takes about one hour per unit of material (one hour minimum) and results in half as much total material, with a final value of Resources 4. An alchemist cannot make more than one unit of final material at a time.

Internal Alchemy (3, Stamina, 3, two miscellaneous actions): Mastering this technique enables the character to create another alchemical thaumaturgy formula he has mastered using his own body. Casting this ritual requires one miscellaneous action spent consuming the requisite materials and one miscellaneous action spent processing them inside the thaumaturge's body. If the alchemist is successful, he is affected by the formula

he created. Botches result in the caster being poisoned (default to coral snake venom if the Storyteller doesn't feel some other poison is more fitting). Using Internal Alchemy costs 1 Willpower in addition to that required by the other formula. Requires Medicine.

Seven Bounties Paste (3, Intelligence, 4, one hour): The alchemist brews a dose of seven bounties paste (see **Exalted**, p. 378).

Sweet Cordial (3, Intelligence, 4, one hour): The alchemist brews a dose of sweet cordial (see **Exalted**, p. 378).

Wind-Fire Potion (3, Wits, 4, one hour): Soldiers who have used it say this potion makes them as quick as the wind and ferocious as fire. Commanders are careful with its use, though, because it makes people harder to control and can have serious side effects. For one scene, the mortal user gains +1 die to all actions involving her Physical Attributes, Wits and Valor, but loses one dot of Compassion, Temperance and Intelligence. Furthermore, the imbiber no longer counts as an extra (see Valiant Warrior Formula). Heroic mortals gain two additional -4 health levels.

Once the potion wears off, the positive effects go away, but the negative effects remain for an equal number of scenes. Wind-fire potion can addict someone who uses it more than once in a month. Use the Wyld Addiction rules from **Exalted**, page 288, substituting references to the influence of the drug for that of the Wyld, and using a difficulty equal to (doses taken during the month + 2).

THE ART OF ASTROLOGY

Every god in Creation has a star in the heavens, and their endless dance across the sky writes the destiny of the world large for all to see—or at least those who know what these signs mean. The heavenly Bureau of Destiny and its Sidereal Exalted agents can manipulate these signs to powerful effect. Mortal thaumaturges know nothing of this, but they understand that the stars have much to reveal to the wise.

The Art of Astrology relies upon gaining important details about its target and translating that information into complex charts that map out the influences of the stars upon the target's fate. Though the Exalted control their own destiny to various degrees, even they do not entirely escape the tapestry of the Loom of Fate. Whatever the stars may currently show, powerful Essence-wielding beings such as the Incarnae, beings outside of fate and the Bureau of Destiny can change events to render such predictions obsolete. The stars reveal likely futures and predominant influences, but free will remains ineluctably woven into Creation.

Astrology requires a quadrant or astrolabe, theodolite and other instruments to measure the positions and brightness of celestial objects, as well as lorebooks that record centuries of past observations and their inferred effects within Creation. Astrological rituals usually require little in the way of disposable components, but reusable components cost at least Resources 3. A master's observatory costs Resources 5.

See **Exalted**, page 138, for more Astrology rituals. The Lesser Divination, Divination and Greater Divination rituals require an astrological profile generated by the Compile Chart ritual.

Varangian Casting (0, Intelligence, 3, one hour): Within the star-obsessed Varang City-States, every child receives her place in society according to the signs of her birth. Their system is not perfect, but Varangian attentiveness to the workings of fate is a large part of their successful bid to maintain an orderly society. With success, the astrologer learns a single important future Ability of the child (barring relevant interference). Such knowledge suggests where in the social order a person might find contentment. For adults, the Varangian Casting reveals one Favored Ability or one Ability rated 3 or higher. This ritual requires an astrological profile generated by the Compile Chart ritual.

No Varangian astrologer would ever admit failure with this ritual, for fear of ostracism or even death. Even if a seer wanted to admit failure, botches render convincing false results. Different seers may even achieve different results, successful or not. Some claim that the Varangian Admiral Lallimes naturally favors the art of the sword, although his official casting predetermined his current role as master of his nation's navy.

Predetermined Attributes (1, Intelligence, 4, one hour): Certain aspects of a being's life are predominant, and these are often reflected by her Attributes. This ritual enables the astrologer to determine whether Physical, Social or Mental Attributes will be primary for a child, barring future interferences. This ritual requires an astrological profile generated by the Compile Chart ritual.

Reactive Planning (1, Wits, 5, one hour): If the astrologist successfully predicts a Lesser Divination, Divination or Greater Divination, she may then compile a list of factors and omens that can increase the client's chances of future success. One time in the near future, the player of the astrologer's client can reduce the difficulty of a single roll by 1. This bonus remains available until the Storyteller deems that circumstances have changed too much to gain its effect; the bonus definitely ends with the current story.

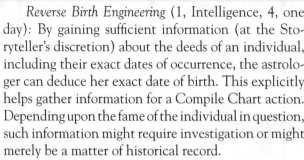

Reverse Birth Engineering (1, Intelligence, 4, one day): By gaining sufficient information (at the Storyteller's discretion) about the deeds of an individual, including their exact dates of occurrence, the astrologer can deduce her exact date of birth. This explicitly helps gather information for a Compile Chart action. Depending upon the fame of the individual in question, such information might require investigation or might merely be a matter of historical record.

Brighter Star (2, Perception, 5, one hour): Astrologers notice that the stars seem to favor certain people. This rite shows a person as "favored" if she is an Exalt or possesses the Destiny Background (see **Scroll of the Monk**, pp. 151-152), though the astrologer has no indication which of these it might be. This ritual requires an astrological profile generated by the Compile Chart ritual.

Natural Virtues (2, Intelligence, 4, one hour): With careful study of the target's compiled chart, the astrologer can determine her primary Virtue due to its endless influence upon her life. This ritual requires an astrological profile generated by the Compile Chart ritual.

The Fallen Star (3, Perception, 5, one minute): This rite depends upon one of Yu-Shan's great secrets: starmetal is made from soul-forged gods cast to the earth. When successfully performed, this ritual allows the caster to sense whether anything that he can see clearly with unaided eyes is partly or wholly composed of starmetal.

Excellent Orrery Design (3, Intelligence, 5, one year): Through observations of the sky over the course of a year, the astrologer plans the design for an incredibly accurate orrery—a device that mimics the motion of the sun, moon, stars and planets. If she then builds it, her player may use it to gain bonus dice on rolls to perform other astrological rituals. The device is constructed using normal item creation rules (see **Exalted**, pp. 133-134). A Resources 4 orrery grants +1 die, while a Resources 5 orrery grants +2 dice on Art of Astrology rolls that involve its use. First Age orrery artifacts, such as that hidden in the fallen city of Rathess, can have greater effects.

The Art of the Dead

During the early First Age, this Art was largely restricted to laying ghosts to rest, and some thaumaturges called it the Art of Lethe. Over time, the practice took on darker connotations, becoming more feared respectively with the discovery of necromancy, the Great Contagion and the rise of the Deathlords.

In the Time of Tumult, only a few places in Creation permit open dealings with the dead and the Underworld. The Morticians' Order in Sijan uses the Art of the Dead to facilitate their covenants with the deceased; inhabit-

ants of the Skullstone Archipelago also use its rituals for similar purposes. The Raiton Academy on Nightfall Island teaches the Art alongside true necromancy. Beyond those three bastions of the Art, merchants who travel near established shadowlands sometimes hire savants who can deal with the dead.

Both the reusable tools and consumed ingredients of this Art's rituals frequently are made from parts of corpses: bone amulets, crowns and rods, cups and braziers fashioned from skulls, cords of mummy-hair, candles of human fat and the like. Rituals also employ substances used in embalming, such as pitch, bitumen, natron and myrrh. Only the rituals of warding and banishing, which rely more on salt, incense, bells and other emblems of purity and the sacred, are likely to eschew materials and operations that would not offend most community standards.

In addition to the rituals here, see **Exalted**, pages 315-317, for information about the exorcism and summoning of ghosts.

There are Art of the Dead versions of the following Art of Warding and Exorcism rites: *Alarm Ward Against (Creature)*, *Lesser Ward Against (Creature)*, *Ward Against (Creature)*, *Greater Ward Against (Creature)*, and the relevant *Ward Maintenance* and *Keyed Ward* rituals. These wards only work against ghosts, zombies, necromantic beasts and the like. The Art of the Dead's versions of *Dishonest (Creature)'s Rebuke*, *Expulsion* and *Banish (Creature)* only work against ghosts. See the relevant Art of Warding and Exorcism rules, pages 141-144.

Pierce Shadowland (0, Wits, 2, one minute): This quick ritual involves intense concentration and perfect timing while dripping a bit of blood on a shadowland's border. The ritual enables the thaumaturge to pass through the shadowland's border into either Creation or the Underworld at any time of the day or night. Each additional entity brought through the border adds one minute to the ritual.

Summon Ghost (0, Charisma, 2, 15 minutes): Ghosts are frightfully easy to summon, as virtually any apprentice of the occult can tell you. At a location important to the deceased, a thaumaturge may call a ghost through offerings of grave goods and fresh blood. The roll's difficulty decreases by 1 if performed in a shadowland or the Underworld; increase it by 1 for each 100 years the person has been dead and if summoning a ghost by its qualities rather than its name. When performing this ritual in a shadowland, failure means that five (usually unwelcome) ghosts show up for each success by which the attempt falls short. Ghost summoned by this ritual manifest visibly and audibly but remain immaterial

unless the ghost can materialize on its own or the summoning takes place in a shadowland.

Blood Magic (1, Stamina, 3, five minutes): Blood is a powerful conduit for living Essence. Thaumaturges who are willing to sacrifice themselves or others can tap into a powerful source of magical energy. For each level of lethal damage the thaumaturge suffers, or that she ritually inflicts upon a helpless sacrificial victim, she generates one mote of Essence that she must channel immediately. This might allow her to do such things as: activate (but not attune) an artifact, cast another ritual using reduced resources, or replenish her Essence pool (if she is enlightened or Exalted).

Body Preservation Technique (1, Intelligence + Medicine, 1, one hour): Through various occult and medical methods, the thaumaturge preserves a cadaver so that it does not suffer any decay for one day per success rolled. The ritual may be repeated sequentially and indefinitely, but the effects do not stack. Some thaumaturges perform this ritual for legitimate purposes related to burial rituals, while others merely preserve the corpse for use in making zombies or necromantic war machines.

Deathsight (1, Perception, 3, five minutes): After anointing her closed eyes with blood and certain rare herbal juices, the thaumaturge opens them to perceive immaterial ghosts with all senses for the rest of the scene.

Speak with Corpse (1, Perception, 2, one minute): This ritual requires the whole skull of a corpse; if there isn't enough meat on the bones to hold the jawbone, the thaumaturge must wire the jaw using human sinew and iron pins. The ritual itself involves a period of osculation that most would consider abhorrent. Afterward, the thaumaturge may ask and receive an answer to two questions, plus one question per threshold success. Corpses entreated with this ritual only know what their bones have seen since the day before their deaths; to learn what it saw while alive, the necromancer must seek the extant spirit.

Raise Corpse (2, Intelligence, 3, one hour): To reanimate the dead, a thaumaturge must whisper several things the deceased once held secret. The corpse rises as a zombie (see **Exalted**, pp. 314-315). The zombie follows the thaumaturge's instructions as a simple person would. After one week per threshold success, the enchantment falters—though the ritual can be performed again.

Three Days of Hun and Po (2, Charisma, 5, one hour): When a vengeful soul dies, the higher soul or hun remains with the lower soul—the po—until the end of the third night, granting it increased intellect. (See **Exalted**, pp.

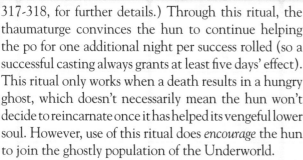

317-318, for further details.) Through this ritual, the thaumaturge convinces the hun to continue helping the po for one additional night per success rolled (so a successful casting always grants at least five days' effect). This ritual only works when a death results in a hungry ghost, which doesn't necessarily mean the hun won't decide to reincarnate once it has helped its vengeful lower soul. However, use of this ritual does *encourage* the hun to join the ghostly population of the Underworld.

Summon Nephwrack (3, Wits, 4, one hour): Only the most skilled mortal thaumaturge dares trying to summon the Neverborn's loyal spectres all the way from the Labyrinth. The ritual uses a dust from the Underworld and blood from several rare creatures, dried in a jade crucible, and then mixed in a mortar fashioned from a skull. The thaumaturge prays over this abhorrent mixture, and then eats it. The ritual projects a call to the Labyrinth's depths. If the ritual succeeds, the nephwrack comes within the next three nights. When a thaumaturge's player botches, that thaumaturge is rarely seen again.

THE ART OF DEMON SUMMONING

The Art of Demon Summoning came into being shortly after the Primordial War. This dangerous Art taps into the inescapable oaths laid upon those Primordials who chose surrender. When called to service according to the ancient compacts, a creature of Malfeas must attend the summons. Sadly for Creation, every summoning releases demonic influences upon the world, and Creation's citizens must remain ever vigilant against the potential sinister affects thereof. Worse yet, the terms of these oaths merely bind demons to serve Exalts and gods who are powerful enough to enforce their will. Mortals may invite demons into Creation, but the provisions of those oaths do little to protect them and do not allow them to extract slavish servitude.

Demon summoning involves elaborate ceremonies with numerous components, both reused and consumed. Many ceremonies require drawing a magic circle or other diagram. Tools include braziers burning stinking incense; weapons; knotted cords, keys and other symbols of bondage (and its removal); talismans scribed with the symbol of a demon or demonic species; and discordant musical instruments suitable for the spawn of the maimed and twisted Primordials.

See **Exalted**, pages 138-139, for more Demon Summoning rituals.

There are Art of Demon Summoning versions of the following Art of Warding and Exorcism rites: *Alarm Ward Against (Creature)*, *Lesser Ward Against (Creature)*, *Dishon-* *est (Creature)'s Rebuke*, *Expulsion*, *Ward Against (Creature)*, *Banish (Creature)*, *Greater Ward Against (Creature)*, and the relevant *Ward Maintenance* and *Keyed Ward* rituals. These wards only work against demons. See the relevant Art of Warding and Exorcism rules, pages 141-144.

Banish the Faithless Servant (2, Essence + Willpower, 2, miscellaneous action): With this ritual, a thaumaturge may attempt to banish a demon of the First Circle *only if* he was the summoner (usually via *Summon [Species]*). With a miscellaneous action, the magician enters a contest of wills against the demon. Each participant's player rolls (Essence + Willpower) until one side achieves a net number of successes equal to the other contestant's Essence. Each roll requires another miscellaneous action for each participant, and neither can take any non-reflexive actions during the contest without automatically forfeiting. Unfortunately for the thaumaturge, his rolls are difficulty 2, and he needs to show the demon its special sigil. If the thaumaturge wins, the demon disappears back to Malfeas in a flash of green fire; if the demon wins, the thaumaturge may not attempt to banish it again for five days.

Summon (Species) (2, Intelligence, 5, six hours): This ritual works as noted in **Exalted**, pages 138-139. It is mentioned here to clarify that the summoning must begin at sundown, as with its superior, sorcery equivalent, Demon of the First Circle.

Each ritual summons one and only one kind of First Circle demon. Each type of demon has its own sigil and array of plants, animals, stones, color combinations and other symbolic elements that must be used in its summoning. Erymanthoi, for instance, loathe cats above all other creatures, and so, their summoning must involve killing a cat and offering its blood.

Beckon (Unique Demon) (3, Intelligence, demon's Essence, six hours): With greater mastery of the Art of Demon Summoning, the thaumaturge may beckon one of the demons of the Second Circle and open a way for it to enter Creation. This ritual must begin at sunset on the night of a new moon or one of the nights of Calibration, although some demons have alternative times and conditions under which they might be called instead. Unlike their inferiors, demons of the Second Circle are not bound to answer: they may choose to ignore the call altogether if they wish. As with the Summon (Species) ritual, the thaumaturge cannot control the demon and must bargain or plead for whatever aid it renders.

Each of these greater demons requires a different ritual, unique to its nature, that incorporates distinctive symbolic elements. Beckon Sondok, for instance, involves use of a battleaxe, the lethal red mushrooms

her cult holds sacred, an image of a wolf and offerings of garnets and the decaying corpse of a dog.

Five Days Foresight (3, Manipulation, 5, six hours): Few sages know that a summoned demon departs Malfeas across the endless desert of Cecelyne five days before the summoning actually takes place. The twisted and fractured connections between Creation and Malfeas give the Yozis and their servants strange insight into Creation's future. A thaumaturge who knows this ritual can open a mystic connection to a demon currently in Malfeas and ask it a question about the future. Unfortunately for the magician, she does not know which demon she contacts, nor can she compel it to tell the truth (or speak for that matter). The thaumaturge can only issue whatever appeal she thinks most likely to bring her a response. Storytellers might have the demon honestly reveal some relevant information or admit its lack of knowledge… or the demon might lie. Many demons take delight in giving honest answers that corrupt or doom the querist.

The Year and the Day (3, Manipulation, 5, miscellaneous action): A persistent thaumaturge can rid Creation of a First Circle demon. This ritual only works for a banisher who has successfully repelled a demon from her presence repeatedly for a period of a year and a day. Finally, she uses this ritual, and if successful, the demon returns to Malfeas in a burst of green flame, not to return until someone summons it again.

THE ART OF ELEMENTAL SUMMONING

The original elementals were gargantuan spiritual embodiments of the five elements, created by Gaia and bound to the will of the gods. When the gods rebelled, the Primordials struck against the elementals first, shattering their bodies and scattering their Essence across Creation. This scattered Essence birthed the elemental breeds known today, but the strictures the gods laid upon the originals persist. As the presence of elementals became evident to the Exalted, the Chosen discovered methods to call upon elemental aid. In the Ages since then, thaumaturges have devised or discovered many rites related to the elementals.

Rituals in this Art always involve some literal or symbolic form of the desired element: the burning of rare woods and oils for Fire, crystals and implements of stone for Earth, sprayed perfumes for Air, and so on.

There are Art of Elemental Summoning versions of the following Art of Warding and Exorcism rites: *Alarm Ward Against (Creature)*, *Lesser Ward Against (Creature)*, *Dishonest (Creature)'s Rebuke*, *Ward Against (Creature)*, *Banish (Creature)*, *Greater Ward Against (Creature)*, and the relevant *Ward Maintenance* and *Keyed Ward* rituals. These wards only work against elementals. See the relevant Art of Warding and Exorcism rules, pages 141-144.

Elemental Sight (1, Perception, 3, five minutes): Spreading a handful of carefully blended ash, fine sand, powdered incense, wood shavings and colored dye throughout the target area and speaking the Mantra of Gaia's Eye, the caster can perceive the shape of immaterial elementals in the area for one scene.

Jade Extraction Method (1, Intelligence, 3, five minutes): The magical materials naturally possess greater than normal amounts of Essence. The elementalist can sublimate a bit of jade and thereby extract Essence from it. With success in this ritual she destroys an obol's worth of jade and gains four motes of Essence. The thaumaturge must channel this Essence immediately. She might activate (but not attune) an artifact, cast another ritual using far less resources, or replenish her Essence pool (if she is enlightened or Exalted). The ritual may only target small bits of jade, and they cannot be part of an artifact or enchanted object.

Summon (Species) (2, Charisma, 5, four hours): An elemental of the desired type is drawn along the dragon lines of Creation to the caster's location. Each ritual summons a different kind of elemental that has Essence of 3 or less. Thaumaturges have no power to command summoned elementals, but they may bargain with them. Some breeds of elementals perform specific services in return for specific offerings. Others form private pacts in return for favors from the thaumaturge. For instance, a wood spider might tell forest secrets in return for offerings of blood and a plot of cultivated land allowed to grow wild once more.

Beckon([Species) [3, Charisma, 5, four hours): A master of the Art can call elementals with Essence 4 to 5 and appeal for their help. These powerful elementals often have lesser elemental servants that they may send in their stead to answer a summons. Conversely, a thaumaturge might be able to contact mighty elementals such as the dragon Fakharu by working through elemental messengers—but that is probably a work of years.

Invoke the Elemental Benediction (3, Intelligence, 5, six hours): Beginning this ritual at dawn and continuing until noon, the thaumaturge invests a single object weighing five pounds or less with one of the five elements, at the cost of 1 Willpower. In the future, someone holding the object can spend 1 Willpower to activate the appropriate Elemental Benediction (see **The White Treatise**, p. 57) upon the object for a single scene. Once the scene has passed, the effect is gone, and the object can no longer invoke the benediction unless this ritual is performed again.

THE ART OF ENCHANTMENT

Some ancient texts say the Primordial Autochthon invented this Art, and some practitioners still honor the Great Maker. Thaumaturges in the Old Realm and Shogunate made many discoveries of their own, though. In the fallen glory of the Second Age, people throughout Creation value the ability to enchant discrete items and to help maintain the magitech of previous times.

Objects to be enchanted must generally be of an appropriate Resource value (as listed in the **Exalted**, p.138), although they may be someone else's craftwork. Efforts to enchant an object personally crafted by the thaumaturge gain one extra die. Enchantment tools and processes vary incredibly, from the intricate and specialized instruments of Lookshy's sorcerer-assistants to the talismans of wood, bone, shell, feathers and animal sinew crafted by barbarian shamans.

See **Exalted**, page 139, for more Enchantment rituals, and **The Compass of Celestial Directions, Vol. II—The Wyld**, page 142, for talismans to protect against the Wyld.

Analyze Talisman (0, Perception, 1, five minutes): These simple tests reveal whether an object is enchanted. With at least three successes, the caster gets some basic idea about the enchanted object's nature, while five successes pinpoint its purpose.

Fading Color Treatment (0, Intelligence, 2, five minutes): Lookshy security personnel use this Procedure to craft their district transit passes, while clever enchanters find other applications. The thaumaturge alters an object's surface to give it a particular color in a desired pattern. At the time of the ritual, the thaumaturge specifies the duration of this treatment. When that period expires, the altered portion changes to a dull gray hue.

Strengthen Ironwood (1, Intelligence, 2, three hours): The thaumaturge uses secret Eastern techniques to enhance this wood's qualities. See page 157.

Enchant Lucky Rock (2, Intelligence, 3, 25 hours): The thaumaturge enhances the power of a normal "lucky rock" and transfers its properties to a weapon. See page 157.

Process Steelsilk (2, Intelligence, 3, 25 hours): The thaumaturge understands the techniques required to manipulate steelsilk. See pages 158 and 159.

Aegis-Inset Amulets (3, Intelligence, 5, 200 hours): This specially designed process creates a single set of aegis-inset amulets. These magitech amulets require occasional maintenance (Intelligence + Lore, difficulty 2, one hour), but otherwise last a lifetime. See aegis-inset amulets, **Wonders of the Lost Age**, page 71.

Warding Talisman (3, Intelligence, 3, 50/100/150 hours): This ritual is used to create one of the talismans described on page 379 of **Exalted**. The thaumaturge must determine the desired effect before beginning work, and falling short means her efforts are wasted. One net success is required for each point of the talisman's rating, and 50 hours of work per rating point are required. If the ritual is successful, the talisman lasts until damaged or destroyed. Charms against disease require the thaumaturge to possess one dot of Medicine per rating point. Good luck charms and walkaways require one Degree of the Art of Geomancy per rating point. Warding charms require one Degree of the Art of Warding per rating point. A thaumaturge may substitute appropriate Procedures for the requisite Degrees, but doing so limits the type and rating of the talisman created.

THE ART OF GEOMANCY

Geomancy is the art of detecting and manipulating Essence flows. At its basic levels, this allows thaumaturges to perceive Essence. Eventually, a master might even become enlightened and gain access to her own Essence pool. More surprisingly to those who do not understand the Art, the thaumaturge may tamper with the Essence flows of others or sense them from afar. This might allow her to smooth or frustrate the interaction of the target with Creation or even grant a limited ability to scry upon distant locations.

The most distinctive tool of the geomancer's trade is the compass plate, a bronze plate engraved with concentric circles and marked with the elemental poles, the constellations and other symbols. Detection rites often involve spinning a spoonlike instrument of jade-infused magnetite on the plate. Geomancers also use pendulums, weights and globes of various metals and minerals, as well as theodolites and other surveying equipment. The geomancer's greatest instrument, however, is the land itself. Rituals with long-term effects usually involve constructing special buildings or reshaping the local landscape with small hills and valleys, creeks and ponds, trees, boulders and other features.

See **Exalted**, page 139, for more Geomancy rituals, and Chapter One of this book for the massive geomantic operations that affect demesnes and manses.

Dragon Line Compass (0, Perception, 1, five minutes): The motions of a compass plate or a jade-and-crystal pendulum reveal when the thaumaturge stands within (successes x 10) yards of a dragon line. Once the character locates a dragon line, he can follow it for one hour before needing to perform this ritual again.

Alloyed Essence Indicator (0, Intelligence, 5, five minutes): This simple ritual identifies an object as an artifact, a hearthstone or otherwise imbued with magical powers. It tells nothing about the nature of those powers.

Magical Attunement (0, Wits, 3, 20 minutes): By handling and practicing with an item, an enlightened mortal may duplicate an Exalt's innate ability to attune to an artifact by committing the requisite amount of Essence. Mortals never gain the magical material bonus of the item. Enlightened mortals do not require this ritual to use their Essence pool to activate artifacts with an Essence cost but no commitment required.

Bathing in the River Meditation (1, Intelligence, 1, place's rating hours): This rite duplicates an Exalt's instinctive ability to attune to a demesne or manse. A character who cannot channel Essence gains no benefit from this (unless the character wants to live in a demesne without suffering mutation), but it feels incredible. Such a character can also attune to a hearthstone and gain its benefits, including Essence recovery if the character can channel Essence.

Dragon Nest Compass (1, Perception, 2, five minutes): Mortals cannot easily sense a demesne from far away, and even the Exalted have trouble locating a manse. This ritual provides mystic detection of greater sensitivity. For each success, the thaumaturge can de-tect the presence of a manse from one mile away, or an uncapped demesne from two miles away. Put another way, the distance in miles sets the difficulty to detect a manse or demesne. The ritual only gives the direction to the manse or demesne, but spending 1 Willpower suffices to continue taking readings (each taking five minutes) for the rest of the scene.

Pearl-Collecting Rite (1, Wits, 3, [demesne's rating] hours): This rite enables a mortal to find and collect a demesne's natural Essence tokens the way an Exalt would, as described on pages 48-49. Unlike an Exalt, however, a thaumaturge does not need to attune to the demesne. Even if the thaumaturge cannot personally channel Essence, she may still use the Essence token in other rituals.

Ritual of Dedicated Purification (1, Perception, 2, one hour): Preparing ahead of another ritual, the thaumaturge (and any assistants) cleanse themselves and the ritual area, using pure elements such as rainwater, unscented soap and sanctified candles. If successful, the thaumaturge's player can reroll a single botch during the procedure that follows, as the sanctification of the site and participants aids in preventing backlash and mishaps.

Open-Eyed Dive Meditation (2, Perception, 3, [place's rating] hours): This rite enables a mortal to find the geomantic stress-points in a manse or demesne, as described on pages 51-52.

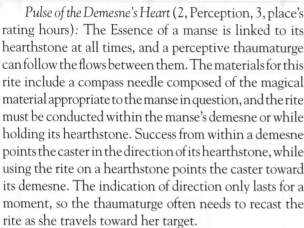

Pulse of the Demesne's Heart (2, Perception, 3, place's rating hours): The Essence of a manse is linked to its hearthstone at all times, and a perceptive thaumaturge can follow the flows between them. The materials for this rite include a compass needle composed of the magical material appropriate to the manse in question, and the rite must be conducted within the manse's demesne or while holding its hearthstone. Success from within a demesne points the caster in the direction of its hearthstone, while using the rite on a hearthstone points the caster toward its demesne. The indication of direction only lasts for a moment, so the thaumaturge often needs to recast the rite as she travels toward her target.

Rattle the Sanctum's Gate (2, Manipulation, 5, one hour): This rite can only be performed at the entrance to a spirit's sanctum. By tampering with the Essence flows through discordant techniques, the thaumaturge slows the flow into the sanctum. During the hour-long ritual, the amount of Essence regained by the sanctum's owner drops by one mote per success, to a minimum of one, so long as the spirit remains in the sanctum. Most spirits will not tolerate this, and are likely to come out to deal with the thaumaturge. Yu-Shan is not a valid target for the rite.

Essence Enlightening Sutra (3, Intelligence, 5, five years): This long ascetic regimen can awaken a mortal's Essence. With success, a mortal becomes an enlightened mortal with an Essence pool. It is much safer than the *Essential River Channeling* ritual that achieves the same effect (see **Scroll of the Monk**, p. 19), at the cost of taking five years instead of 24 hours.

A little-known Old Realm version of this rite, called the *Yoga of Celestial Refinement*, requires Lore 4 and Martial Arts 4 to use. For a Dragon-Blood, 10 years of ascetic study and successful use of this modified Procedure enables the Exalt to learn Celestial martial arts (though she must still find an appropriate tutor).

House of Good/Ill Fortune (3, Perception, 5, one hour): Examining the local Essence flows, the geomancer may create a design that benefits or harms a structure's or landscape's occupants. The rite doesn't actually enact these changes; they must be put into place by building or landscaping according to the geomancer's design. Once the structure or area meets the requirements, those within benefit or suffer from the rite's effect. This might be a Blessing or Curse (as per **Exalted**, p. 139) affecting one occupant per month. A blessing might reduce the virulence of a disease striking the household, the inhabitants might experience a good crop that year, or the like. The effect lasts at least one month per success.

Geomantic Countermagic (3, Intelligence, 5, one hour): Sometimes called Marble Countermagic by those with pretensions to sorcerous power, this rite enables the caster to disrupt existing thaumaturgical works. The magician must first use Essence Sense to spot the target effect. Each success gained removes one success from the targeted thaumaturgical effect.

Scrying (3, Perception, 5, one or more hours): Items exhibit an arcane link with their own substance, and a skilled magician can use this fact to sense a target from afar. The thaumaturge must possess a sample of the person or object he wants to observe, which could be the hair or blood of a person or horse, or wood shaved from a ship's prow. Each hour, until the caster chooses to stop, his player makes an extended (Perception + Occult) roll, gathering successes. A botch ends the ritual with all accumulated successes lost. When the thaumaturge chooses to complete the rite, she may observe the target for a single scene provided it lies within a number of miles equal to her successes.

THE ART OF HUSBANDRY

From calling wild beasts to the hunt to protecting fruit trees from pests to manipulating mortals, the Art of Husbandry has existed as long as humanity itself… maybe as long as the gods themselves, for many of its feats hew closely to the divine procedures that maintain Creation. Mortal practitioners have discovered innumerable secrets from those gods who hold purview over living things.

There are Art of Husbandry versions of the following Art of Warding rites: *Alarm Ward Against (Creature)*, *Lesser Ward Against (Creature)*, *Ward Against (Creature)*, *Greater Ward Against (Creature)*, and the relevant *Ward Maintenance* and *Keyed Ward* rituals. These wards only work against living mortals, animals or plants. See the relevant Art of Warding and Exorcism rules, pages 141-144.

Judge the Pure Beast (0, Perception + Survival, 1, one minute): Observing an animal carefully, and whispering a prayer to the god most appropriate to the beast, the thaumaturge analyzes its behavior. With a success, the thaumaturge can determine whether an animal is a normal specimen, without magical properties, Wyld taint or the like. If the beast is not normal, the thaumaturge learns this, but the rite does not reveal what precisely makes the animal unnatural. This ritual has no Resources cost.

Warding the Crops (0, Intelligence, 1, five minutes): The thaumaturge forbids one kind of pest from attacking selected plants, plus one additional pest per Degree in the Art. The ritual protects one acre of grain, vegetables or other small plants, or five trees, grapevines or other large plants. The protection lasts one week per success.

Summon (Species) (1, Charisma + Survival, control rating - 2, two hours): Whistling up prey to be slaughtered or calling in the herds of Marukan, the thaumaturge may summon the nearest specimens of a particular breed of non-magical animal. The difficulty of this rite equals the creature's (control rating - 2), with a minimum of 1. Extra successes may reduce the ritual's casting time by 15 minutes each, to a minimum of 15 minutes, or increase the number of animals called. Calling a specific animal known to the thaumaturge is possible at +1 difficulty, unless the character owns the animal; in that case, the difficulty drops by -1 (minimum 0). The summoned animal must exist within one mile per dot of the magician's Essence, or the ritual fails. The rite does not transport the animal to the caster's side. The beast must travel there on its own.

Control (Species) (1, Manipulation + Survival, control rating - 1, miscellaneous action): From calming an unruly horse to convincing a bird of prey to bring the character a rabbit, this ritual allows a thaumaturge to give a single animal simple instructions and expect them to be obeyed. The desired action must be within the beast's capacity to understand. This ritual has no Resources cost.

Summon Human (2, Manipulation, Mental Dodge DV of target, one hour): The ritual compels a selected human to come to the thaumaturge; a victim travels according to her own abilities. This compulsion is an unnatural mental influence, which may be overcome as normal by spending a point of Willpower. For this ritual, Exalted count as humans. So do beastmen, Wyld mutants and people altered by demesnes or other supernatural forces, but the difficulty increases by 2. The thaumaturge needs two ways to specify an individual person, such as a personal name, a genealogy back three generations, or samples of the person's hair or blood.

Improved (Species) Breeding (3, Intelligence, 5, one hour): Performing this ritual enables the magician to breed animal stock unnaturally well, quickly magnifying desired traits. The exact effects of this are up to the Storyteller, but they might result in such things as breeding a faster hose, a larger bird or a more venomous snake. The Marukani horse breeders and the hawkriders of Metagalapa have used this ritual for centuries; so have the Haltans in breeding animal companions for greater sentience (though in this case, a pair of old and cunning Lunar Exalted must also receive some of the credit). Other thaumaturges might use it to produce equally wondrous beasts. Although the ritual itself takes only an hour (and is performed right before breeding the animals), the thaumaturge must select the best

stock available and care for the female throughout the gestation to ensure its success.

THE ART OF SPIRIT BECKONING

The coin of the gods is prayer, and the Art of Spirit Beckoning perfects those prayers in order to gain special favor. The gods are not subject to summoning, but they can be beckoned and may answer those who please them. Little gods are more likely to pay attention to prayers, but are less capable of granting boons. Greater gods can perform great miracles, but are less likely to respond.

The following section also includes some rites specific to individual gods, though Storytellers can readily adapt them to other deities as necessary.

Spirit Beckoning rituals generally include some physical record of a plea, such as a prayer strip, and some form of offering. Beckoning a god becomes far more difficult if the thaumaturge does not know what the god likes; in that case, a ritual's difficulty increases by 2.

There are Art of Spirit Beckoning versions of the following Art of Warding and Exorcism rites: *Alarm Ward Against (Creature), Lesser Ward Against (Creature), Dishonest (Creature)'s Rebuke, Expulsion, Ward Against (Creature), Banish (Creature), Greater Ward Against (Creature)*, and the relevant *Ward Maintenance* and *Keyed Ward* rituals. These wards only work against gods. See the relevant Art of Warding rules, pages 141-144.

Spirit Sight (1, Perception, 3, five minutes): Filling the air with prayers, the thaumaturge makes the gods nearby manifest to her senses for the remainder of the scene.

Beckon [Little God] (2, Charisma + Performance, 6 - Resources value of offering, one hour): The thaumaturge prays to one of the lesser gods, those with less than Essence 5, and seeks its favor. Prayers may be conducted without this ritual, as detailed in **Exalted**, pages 378-379. Using this ritual means the supplicant is treated as a priest of the god in question or, if she is already a priest, then the prayer roll's difficulty is reduced by 1. The ritual also can only call little gods who keep their sanctum within (god's Essence x 10) miles of the thaumaturge.

The Hecatomb (2, Charisma + Performance, 2, special): This ritual practiced by the followers of the Southern war god Ahlat involves the ritual slaughter of 100 cows. The ritual ensures the fertility of the tribe's cattle and women for one month per success, up to a year maximum.

Beckon (Greater God) (2, Charisma + Performance, 6 - Resources value of offering, one hour): This ritual works like *Beckon (Little God)*, except that it applies to deities of 5 or greater Essence. Such deities may well send subordinates to answer the thaumaturge's call.

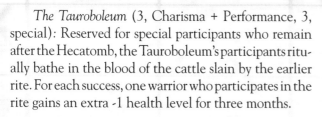

The Tauroboleum (3, Charisma + Performance, 3, special): Reserved for special participants who remain after the Hecatomb, the Tauroboleum's participants ritually bathe in the blood of the cattle slain by the earlier rite. For each success, one warrior who participates in the rite gains an extra -1 health level for three months.

The Art of Warding and Exorcism

Warding rituals create mystic barriers against intrusion or contamination—and Creation holds many entities that people want to keep out. Warding techniques range from unbroken lines of salt that hold back the dead to glyphs carved in door lintels and windowsills that keep out Fair Folk in the East.

Wards can be stacked. When two different wards might affect the same creature, both of them operate. If a thaumaturge places multiple identical wards, only the strongest remains. Thus, a house warded against Fair Folk with an Alarm Ward, Lesser Ward and Adept-level Ward against Fair Folk might trigger an alarm, force the invader to spend a Willpower point and physically prevent its progress. If the first Lesser Ward against Fair Folk was cast with two successes, then a five success Lesser Ward against Fair Folk would supplant it.

Exorcism takes a more dangerous course. The exorcist directly confronts a malign entity and tries to force its departure. Over the millennia, thaumaturges have devised wards against just about every sort of creature, but exorcism affects only spirits: ghosts, demons, elementals and gods.

Rituals of exorcism always involve some sort of religious paraphernalia. It also employs substances that symbolize purity, such as salt, or that target creatures find specifically baneful, such as iron against the Fair Folk.

The art of Warding and Exorcism also includes techniques to sense the sometime-unseen targets of its other rituals.

Sensing the Barrier (0, Perception, 3, one minute): This simple ritual reveals the presence of every mystic barrier within sight, even if it would not affect the thaumaturge. This ritual merely reveals the existence of a ward; it does not reveal what the ward protects against, its strength or any other details.

Thrice-Warded Gateway (0, Dexterity, 2, one minute): Repeating a short prayer to a god of locks and wards seven times, and wrapping the handle with a bit of twine, the magician causes a door to act as if it were stoutly barred for the next hour. This rite does not strengthen the door's structure, so it might still be forced.

Alarm Ward Against (Creature) (1, Perception, 1, one hour): The thaumaturge sets up an invisible magical line that alerts the character whenever a particular type of creature crosses the ward. The alert only reaches the thaumaturge if she is within one mile per success she gained during its casting. The alert can manifest as anything from an enchanted bell that rings to a pricking sensation in the thaumaturge's thumbs.

Once placed, this ward endures for one day. Magical methods of avoiding detection, including Charms, must exceed the ward's threshold, although sorcery and necromancy that prevent detection automatically succeed. The ward protects an area at most (character's Degree in Warding x 20) feet in any direction.

Deathsight (1, Perception, 3, five minutes): See this rite's entry under the Art of the Dead, page 134.

Demonsight (1, Perception, 3, five minutes): See this rite's entry under the Art of Demon Summoning, in **Exalted**, page 138.

Elemental Sight (1, Perception, 3, five minutes): See this ritual's entry under the Art of Elemental Summoning, page 136.

Lesser Ward Against (Creature) (1, Manipulation, 1, one hour): Employing components antithetical to the particular type of creature, the thaumaturge evokes an invisible magical barrier that discourages its approach. A Lesser Ward acts as a deterrent rather than a physical barrier. A creature needs Dodge MDV at least equal to the number of successes achieved on the thaumaturgy roll in order to ignore its unnatural mental influence. A creature affected by the ward may spend 1 Willpower *per scene* to ignore its effects, though doing so may incur Limit when applicable. Once cast, the ward lasts for one day. The ward protects an area at most (character's Degree in Warding x 20) feet in any direction.

If the thaumaturge limits the ward to blocking only a specific subtype of a particular class, such as hungry ghosts or Solar Exalted, then he gains an extra die to roll for each Degree he possesses in the Art of Warding. Procedures taken for this ritual are always limited to a specific subtype and do not gain this bonus.

Spirit Sight (1, Perception, 3, five minutes): See this rite's entry under the Art of Spirit Beckoning, page 140.

Alarm Ward Maintenance (2, Perception, 3, five minutes): The more effort put into a ward, the greater its effect. A careful sprinkling of salt might last for only a day, while stone grooves carved and filled with hardened cakes of salt might last indefinitely (if they are kept dry and nobody steals the salt). Likewise, glyphs carved in a wooden plaque last longer than symbols scratched in the dirt. If a thaumaturge succeeds with this ritual, she enables a ward to last longer: another day with a single success; two successes adds a week, three adds a month, four adds a season, five adds a year, and every additional

success adds another year. Wards that truly last indefinitely require binding the ward to some sort of talisman using the Art of Enchantment: the talisman requires the same Degree of mastery in the Art of Enchantment as the basic barrier does in the Art of Warding.

Dishonest (Creature)'s Rebuke (2, Intelligence, Difficulty, 10 hours + miscellaneous action): The four versions of this ritual deal with gods, demons, elementals and ghosts, respectively (with individual Procedures covering specific subtypes). In the first part of the ritual, the thaumaturge spends 10 hours inscribing special prayer strips. In the second part, the thaumaturge casts the strips into the air and mutters a quick prayer while expending the Willpower needed for the ritual. The caster may then perform a single attack against a dematerialized spirit using a weapon or barehanded. For the rest of the scene, he may attempt additional attacks at the cost of another Willpower point for each attack. This rite doesn't grant the ability to detect the spirit. That must be gained in some other fashion.

Expulsion (2, Manipulation, spirit's lowest Virtue, 10 minutes): Some spirits and ghosts can enter mortal creatures and take control of their bodies. A skilled thaumaturge can drive out an entity that has used a Charm or Arcanos to possess another being. The effort to do so is an extended roll, with a difficulty equal to the spirit's lowest Virtue, requiring an accumulation of successes equal to twice the spirit's highest Virtue. Each roll requires 10 minutes and costs the thaumaturge 1 Willpower.

Note that this ritual can expel any possessing entity *only* if a character learns it as part of a Degree in the Art of Warding and Exorcism. The versions learned in the Arts of the Dead, Demon Summoning, Elemental Summoning and Spirit Beckoning only affect the single class of entities that form the special concerns of those Arts. The same goes for learning Expulsion as a Procedure.

Lesser Ward Maintenance (2, Perception, 3, one day): As Alarm Ward Maintenance, but extending the duration of any Lesser Ward.

Ward Against (Creature) (2, Intelligence, 1, one hour): This ritual works like a Lesser Ward, except that it creates a physical barrier against the warded creatures rather than a mental deterrent. The strength of the ward equals the number of successes the thaumaturge's player gains during its creation. A warded creature cannot pass through the barrier unless its Essence exceeds the strength of the ward, in which case it may tear a hole in the ward through which other creatures may pass. A creature that is blocked may also spend 1 Willpower to assault the ward, rolling its Essence in dice, with each success reducing the ward's strength by one. The assaulting creature suffers a number of dice of bashing damage equal to the current strength of the ward, soakable only by Stamina and other natural soak. If the ward remains strong enough to block the creature, it may choose to attack it again for another Willpower point. The ward protects an area at most (character's Degree in Warding x 20) feet in any direction.

Warding of Undue Influence (2, Wits, 3, miscellaneous action): The thaumaturge tries to protect those around him from supernatural deceptions. This rite costs 3 Willpower. While invoked, all beings within (caster's Essence x 5) feet are treated as being two points higher in Essence for the purposes of resisting Fair Folk glamours, Charms that deal with manipulating emotions or perceptions, and supernatural effects with similar effects. Charms that are rolled against a fixed difficulty to affect emotions or perceptions have their difficulty raised by 1. This ritual's effects last for 10 minutes and move with the caster.

Banish (Creature) (3, Manipulation, special, one minute per roll): A thaumaturge forces a spirit to vacate her presence, at least for a time. Each version of this ritual works similarly against a god, demon, ghost or elemental.

The players of the exorcist and her target engage in a contested roll, the thaumaturge's (Manipulation + Occult + Degree) against the spirit's (Willpower + Essence), with each roll costing the exorcist 1 Willpower and a minute of work. The target must reflexively expend 3 motes of Essence for each roll or forfeit the contest. If the exorcist achieves a number of net successes equal to (the spirit's Essence + highest Virtue), then the spirit must leave the area immediately and stay away for a time. Gods are banished for an hour, demons for a night and a day, and elementals for a week. Extra successes double the banishment period (one hour, two hours, four hours, etc.). Ghosts must return to the Underworld, but if the exorcist gains twice the number of requisite successes, then the ghost is usually laid to rest permanently.

Unfortunately for the thaumaturge, the target entity may perform whatever actions it might normally—albeit as part of a flurry, with resisting the exorcist as its first action—while she must devote her entire concentration to the ritual. Wise exorcists perform this rite behind powerful wards or a screen of defenders. Celestial Incarnae, powerful elementals (such as lesser elemental dragons or better), demons of the Second and Third circles, and Deathlords may only be banished by a thaumaturge who has a permanent Essence at least equal to their own, with the banishment lasting for only one scene, and the prospect of success in these situations is dim indeed.

Breaking the Ward (3, Perception, 3, one hour): This ritual lets the caster weaken or even destroy an existing ward. Every success removes one success from the ward it is used against, beginning with duration-granting successes created by ward maintenance rituals, and only proceeding to reduce the base ward once the maintenance successes are gone. If the character is subject to the targeted ward, any failed attempt with this ritual subjects the thaumaturge to any negative effects or backlash from the ward (such as the bashing damage from attacking a Lesser Ward).

Greater Ward Against (Creature) (3, Intelligence, 1, two hours): This ritual works like a Lesser Ward, except that it creates a mystic shield rather than a mental deterrent. The strength of the ward equals the number of successes the thaumaturge's player gains during its creation. A warded creatures cannot enter the warded area, launch physical attacks of any type into it, or make any type of magical attack (including mind influencing Charms and spells) into it, unless its Essence exceeds the strength of the ward, in which case it may tear a hole in the ward through which other attacks may pass. A creature that is blocked may spend 1 Willpower to assault the ward, as per Ward Against (Creature) rituals. By itself, a Greater Ward

is *not* damaging, but if it is cast in conjunction with a Ward Against (Creature), then the damage caused by that ward becomes lethal and equals the strength of both wards added together. An assault against a target protected by both wards damages both wards equally and only requires 1 Willpower point.

Keyed Ward (3, Wits, ward difficulty +2, one hour): Sometimes, it is inconvenient to have a ward affect every member of the group it is designed to restrict. This ritual is always cast in conjunction with another warding ritual and limits the scope of the other rite. The casting time adds to that of the other ritual, and the thaumaturge must succeed in a roll at (the other ritual's difficulty + 2). With success, the thaumaturge specifies a condition where the other ward lets creatures through.

The condition described must be something objectively definable that could be deduced through mundane means. "Those who have my sigil tattooed on their back," "my honored ancestor ghosts," "those who say the word 'hallelujah' while passing through the door," or "the Dragon-Blood named Sesus Nagezzer" are all valid conditions. "The person who is telling the truth" or "followers of the Bull of the North" are not—the ward cannot read minds or otherwise probe a creature to determine truthfulness or loyalty.

Failure on the Keyed Ward ritual roll means the other ward operates in its normal fashion, while a botch engenders some unexpected condition instead.

Ward Maintenance (3, Perception, 3, one day): Works as Lesser Ward Maintenance except it applies to an Adept-level ward. Alternately, the thaumaturge can use this ritual to restore a damaged Adept-level ward to full strength.

THE ART OF WEATHER WORKING

The Council of Winds is a powerful elemental court that influences virtually all of the weather in Creation. Most often, they obey the plans of the Bureau of Seasons, but clever magicians can beseech them to arrange for particular conditions in a region. Effects might be as small as a simple breeze to snuff out a candle or as large as a powerful storm, depending upon the thaumaturge's skill and the plans of the elementals involved.

Whenever a thaumaturge makes more than one request during the same two day period, she must spend twice as long enacting these rituals, and her player suffers a +1 difficulty per subsequent request made before leaving the Council alone for at least a week. Most elementals capable of directing large weather patterns have servants to answer for them and are thus generally immune to summons. Botches or particularly egregious uses of this Art can lead to dangerous retribution on the part of the Council of Winds or the Bureau of Seasons.

Different cultures may use different tools for weather working. Some brew strange potions in cauldrons; others tie elaborate knots in cords. Every ritual, however, includes some form of offering to the elementals.

Foretell Weather (0, Perception, 2, one minute): Whispering to the winds, offering incense and listening for its answers, a thaumaturge uses this ritual to predict the weather, with each success representing one day in the future. Subsequent events of which the Council of Winds was unaware at the time of the ritual may change the Council's course and render this rite's results irrelevant.

Minor Changes (1, Charisma, 3, 10 minutes): The thaumaturge may convince local elementals to enact minor alterations to the weather. Each specific ritual evokes one minor change, such as raising a fog or a breeze, reducing rainfall or snowfall, changing the direction of an existing wind, or the like. No change is itself improbable; it merely happens when the thaumaturge would like it to. Changes never extend over more than a square mile or last more than an hour.

Transform Weather (2, Charisma, 4, one hour): True manipulation of weather becomes possible. Each ritual seeks to persuade the Court to change a storm to a gentle rain, a blinding heat to a pleasant summer day, and other significant, distinctly improbable alterations. Changes never extend over more than two miles' radius and last four hours.

Major Changes (3, Charisma, 5, one day): The thaumaturge can convince the Court to make huge changes such as summoning up gales or giving rain during a drought. Each ritual can affect an area up to five miles' radius for an entire day.

INVENTING NEW RITUALS

The rituals in this chapter are only a sample of the thaumaturgical rites practiced in Creation, and thaumaturges invent more as time goes by. A character who wants to invent a brand new ritual needs at least 10 dots divided among Lore, Occult and one other Ability that is relevant to the ritual's intended purpose. For instance, a ritual to confer some special property on weapons would call for Craft (Fire), while a new alchemical drug or poison would require Medicine. At least one Ability must be rated two dots higher than the Degree of the new ritual.

The character spends months in a suitable research facility, trying out different ingredients and ceremonial processes. Of course, the "research facility" depends on the Art: an alchemist works in a laboratory, while a spirit beckoner works with offerings, altars, hymns, dances and other religious paraphernalia.

Each month of research is a Resources (ritual's Degree + 1) expenditure. For each month, the thaumaturge's player rolls (Intelligence + Lore), at a difficulty of (ritual's Degree + 1). The thaumaturge succeeds when the accumulated successes equal (5 + [ritual's Degree x 5]). Any botch in this extended roll, however, indicates a fundamental flaw in the research program. The character cannot try again until at least one of her relevant Abilities has risen by one dot.

Just because a thaumaturge has the relevant Abilities and can define a feat, however, does not mean that a suitable ritual can be invented, though. Some feats just aren't possible. For instance, alchemists have devised dozens of recipes for yellow jade... and every one of them has failed when they tried to demonstrate it to someone else.

CHAPTER FOUR

MAGICAL FLORA, FAUNA AND PHENOMENA

This chapter describes the various naturally occurring magical plants, animals, minerals and environmental oddities of Creation and the products made from them. None of these natural wonders were intentionally created (although the Exalted sometimes duplicate them). Instead, they are the result of exposure to the Wyld or demesnes, natural evolution, curses, magical mutation, lab accidents, and other similarly unique and unusual events. The inhabitants of Creation have learned to make use of some of these wonders and to fear and avoid others.

PARASITIC POSSESSORS

Two threats to humanity move out from the Eastern Wyld. They already afflict the Eastern states and parts of the Scavenger Lands and actively seek to spread to other parts of Creation. Each menace uses human victims to propagate itself.

CHAKRA ORCHID

This animate and deadly plant comes from the deepest forests of the Far East. Chakra orchids are parasitic plants that require living creatures to gestate to an adult state. As the plants grow in their victims' flesh, they infiltrate a victim's brain and take control of his body. Any reptile, mammal or human can become a host for the chakra orchids' insidious seeds. Only birds and water creatures are immune, and so, chakra orchids attempt to slay or drive off such creatures.

Some savants speculate that the five types of chakra orchid are five life stages of the plant. Each type bears flowers of a different color, but each color is merely a specialized variety of a diverse species.

The best thing one can say about chakra orchids is that they attack shadowlands: The sickly mortals who dwell in shadowlands make easy prey for the deadly flowers, and the flowers infest zombies as easily as they do mortals. Shadowland territory covered by the ruling golden blossoms returns to Creation. The chakra orchids have reclaimed several villages and a few small shadowlands for Creation, though no humans were left to appreciate the change.

Chakra Orchid Seed Infestation

Two types of chakra orchid, the scarlet bloom and auric blossom, can infest victims with their seeds. This infestation is treated as a disease (see **Exalted**, p. 350).

Virulence: 6   **Difficulty to Treat:** 5
Morbidity: 7   **Treated Morbidity:** 5

Symptoms: Victims of these seeds start with a cough, and as the day proceeds, they develop a fever, sore throat, and eventually severe pain throughout the body as the seed roots in the spine. Within several hours, victims are bedridden and incapacitated, delirious and most often screaming incessantly. They turn silent a few hours later, their fever vanishes, and they become drones possessed by one of the various chakra orchid types. The victim seems recovered… but actually, he has died, and the first buds of the orchid's flowers emerge from the back of the neck.

Duration: Infestation manifests almost immediately, and it only takes a day before the victim succumbs to the chakra orchid. A flower always blooms within 24 hours unless treated.

Vector: Seeds can be ingested accidentally or on purpose. Auric blossoms (see below) produce a number of different seeds that can be carried by victims, the wind or deluded cultists. The seeds produced by the scarlet bloom are always tiny and airborne.

Treatment: There is no known mundane cure for chakra orchid infestation, only treatments that may aid the patient's struggle against it. However, Charms, sorcery and mortal alchemy can all provide cures. No matter how lucid a victim may seem, however, nothing can be done to save her once a flower blossoms on the back of her neck—except to kill her body so she can rest in peace. The ghosts of people who were still walking around have exposed some orchid infestations.

Cobalt Bloom (Worker)

Worker drones produce blue flowers at the base of their victim's neck. These infested creatures possess only rudimentary intelligence and cannot communicate. They often spend their time clearing undergrowth or chopping down trees near the central bloom.

Victims become stronger than in life, but move slowly. Other signs of the infestation include enlarged extremities and a greenish tinge to the sufferer's veins. Cobalt blooms only live a month or two before the victim

finally succumbs to the infection, and then, other blooms gather the corpse and take it to the central stem, where golden flowers soon sprout from the body.

Cobalt blooms principally infect humans, though any large animal can fall victim. Use the write-ups of Farmers/Townsfolk/Citizens/Slaves (see **Exalted** pp. 278-279), but add 2 to both Strength and Stamina, and reduce Dexterity, Intelligence and Wits all to 1. Cobalt blooms are extras when they fight at all. They prefer to attack by mobbing single targets.

Alabaster Bloom (Warrior)

Warriors sprout white flowers. These parasites possess sufficient cunning to follow orders, attack in groups and use tactics. Some infected creatures utter discernable battle cries. Victims of the warrior blooms are agile and covered in a natural bark-like armor. They grow wooden claws and fangs. Alabaster blooms can live up

to a year before the body succumbs to infestation. See page 150 for stats.

Argent Blossom (Emissary)

Silver flowers crown the green, half-plant heads of emissaries, and their extremities resemble plant stems. These rare flowers only infect intelligent prey. Their intelligence, however, comes solely from the plant within the infested creature: Emissaries retain

no memories of their previous lives. Unlike the cobalt and alabaster blooms, creatures infected with the argent blossom do not have their Physical Attributes modified. All argent blossoms replace the creatures' Attributes with their own.

Emissary blossoms negotiate with human settlements near orchid habitations. They offer boons to humans who help the chakra orchids, but the chakra orchids keep these promises only until they feel strong enough to mount an attack against the settlement. Nevertheless, the argent emissaries are so insidious that they sometimes organize small cults of orchid worshippers. Cultists give their lives willingly to infestation and fanatically protect the central stems. Argent blossoms do not seem to succumb to the same life cycle as the other chakra orchid infections, though they do die from violence or misfortune. See page 150 for stats.

Other Notes: Argent blossoms always flee when confronted with violence. They emit a high-pitched wail that calls all alabaster or cobalt blooms within half a mile to come to their defense.

SCARLET BLOOM (INVADER)

The white blossom warriors usually defend the central blossom while red-flowering invaders attack nearby human settlements. The infestation follows a slightly different course than usual. Infested creatures retain most of their memories and intelligence, though the infection drives them increasingly insane. Many villages in the East fall to chakra orchids after a single villager returns, feverish, raving and with no memory of her infection. Eventually such victims turn violent, attacking their friends and families, until they begin to foam at the mouth and gibber. Their bodies bulge in odd places as they have seizures and soon die.

After death, the body must be burned within an hour, or red flowers erupt violently from the corpse, bud, bloom and go to seed within the span of a night. Once the seed pods form, they explode, sending tiny spores into the air. These seeds seek the breath of the living, planting themselves within the throat of the orchids' new victims. Most commonly, victims become cobalt bloom workers or alabaster warriors. Rarely will the budding plant climb up the neck to form the argent wreath of the emissary.

Other Notes: Scarlet blooms do not augment the infested creature's traits. The infested (but not yet dead)

creature has an inexplicable urge to get to the nearest settlement, however, and often is driven by this compulsion for many miles, well past its fatigue point.

AURIC BLOSSOM (CENTRAL STEM)

The vines that produce the fist-sized, golden-hued auric blossoms grow to cover most of the ground around the initial infestation site and climb up any available structures. Auric blossoms feed on the corpses brought to it by cobalt blooms. The auric blooms have a shared intelligence that grows as the whole plant grows. They communicate their wishes telepathically to all other types of blooms and blossoms. Other chakra orchids can also share their knowledge with the central stem when they are within 20 yards of it.

Auric blossoms may produce seeds at will, generating the spores necessary to infest a victim with whatever subservient flower type that the central stem chooses. Cultists are given a fruit to eat that will infest them more easily and less painfully than unwilling hosts, who have seeds forcibly implanted down their throats. See page 150 for stats.

Other Notes: The stats on page 150 are for an average specimen about the size of a small village. For larger central stems, double the number of -0 health levels.

Auric blossoms make up to five attacks in a flurry without splitting their dice pools. Auric blossoms always summon aid from all blooms nearby. This usually means 20-30 cobalt blooms and 15-25 alabaster blooms. Ordinary humans and Exalts may notice the telepathic summons if their players succeed at (Perception + Awareness) rolls, difficulty 5.

If an auric blossom reduces a character in a clinch to incapacitation, it uses its seed infestation attack on that character.

If the plant itself is incapacitated, it must still have its entire root system dug up and destroyed, or it will grow back in a week. Auric blossoms heal three health levels per day.

HEART WASPS

Swarms of heart wasps move through the Eastern woods, leaving destroyed villages in their wake. Like ichneumon hunters, these parasites use humans as

living incubators for their young. However, they also use humans as shelter and food by colonizing a victim's body and using it as a living puppet. A single wasp cannot dominate an adult human, so the insects invade the body in droves, forcing their way into any of the Nine Gates of the Flesh—or making new orifices of their own. Multiple round scars and sores signal a heart wasp infestation to the experienced observer, as does the subtle rippling of the skin caused by wasps moving about inside the body.

Once the heart wasps take control of a human, they send it about its regular business. The bugs are mildly empathic: worker wasps seek out farmers, artisans, and laborers; warrior wasps, the biggest and strongest members of the community; drones, the shiftless and good-for-nothing; and queens seek out the most prominent females. Queens then transfer larvae to child hosts via hideous parodies of kisses.

The wasps' pretense at ordinary rural life is designed to keep visitors at ease long enough to infest them. Urban society is too complex for the wasps' limited intelligence, so wasp swarms that infiltrate large towns and cities are usually detected and burned out in short order. If the swarm isn't caught in time, however, it can completely infest a village within a day. A given community can sustain a swarm for many weeks: Wasp-infected humans continue to eat, and sustain the wasps along with themselves.

The wasps do not care to farm or trade, so eventually, they exhaust a village's resources. The wasps then leave their hosts by chewing an exit out through the chest. This wound over the heart kills the host and gives these hideous beasts their name. Only the queens maintain their host bodies until the bitter end, often making their way afoot to their new community, leaving behind a corpse-littered village.

Eastern villagers have developed a number of defenses against heart wasp infestation. Travelers with visible sores are turned (or sometimes beaten) away at a town's edge. Fire can burn a host clean (this drastic measure requires inflicting at least three lethal levels of burns). Smoke affects heart wasps much as it does regular insects, slowing them down or driving them

from a host. These insects also avoid water, and many Easterners survive a swarm attack by seeking refuge in a pond or stream. Certain rare herbs repel heart wasps and are much sought after by villages. Essence users attacked by heart wasps have successfully warded off wasp attacks through magic of air and cold, and a Terrestrial Exalt's anima banner destroys any wasp it touches. Also, the Zenith anima flare burns the wasps out of a host, disintegrating them and leaving the host in relatively good condition, if the infestation is caught early.

The traits on page 150 are for a warrior-infested human (i.e., the local blacksmith or town bully). Queens, drones, workers and larvae have slightly different abilities and attack forms, often as per the original human host. However, no matter which form of heart wasp infests it, every infested human gains an extra -0 and -1 health level.

Other Notes: Wasps who infest Essence users can use simple abilities such as anima powers and reflexive Charms, but their use of such powers should reflect the wasps' rather dim consciousness. Sorcery is beyond their ken.

HEARTWASP INFESTATION

Heartwasp infestation is treated as a disease. "Death" from a heart wasp infestation means that a host is completely under the swarm's control. Her mind has been subsumed by the hive consciousness of the swarm, and nothing short of magical intervention (such as the aforementioned Zenith anima flare) can restore her to herself.

Virulence: 5   **Difficulty of Treatment:** 4
Untreated Morbidity: 5 **Treated Morbidity:** 4
Symptoms: An infestation's symptoms include a humming originating deep within the body, an eerie rippling effect located just beneath the skin and sores or pox marks generally located on or near the cheek bones (wasp hosts use clothing to conceal most other entry wounds).
Duration: An infestation can last for several months, depending on the host's health and size. Hosts with the ability to use and channel Essence can sustain an infestation of wasps for much longer than ordinary humans.
Vector: The wasps are their own vector. Unlike normal diseases, however, a group of wasps can choose whether to infect a host (so a dull-witted farmer attacked by warrior-hosts will likely be restrained until a worker-host can be found to infest him).
Treatment: Mundane treatments include moxibustion (burning particular herbs against the victim's skin), fumigation and injecting tinctures of wasp-repelling

Name	Str/Dex/Sta	Per/Int/Wit/Will	Health Lvls	Atk (S/A/D/R)	Dodge DV/S
Alabaster Bloom	3/4/5/	3/2/3/3	-0x2/-1x3/ -2x4/-4/I	Claw: 5/5/4L/3, Bite: 6/8/6L/2	4/5L/11B

Abilities: Awareness 2, Dodge 4, Presence 2, Martial Arts 4, Resistance 3, Stealth 3, Survival 3, War 4

Argent Blossom	2/2/3/	3/3/2/7	-0x2/-1x3/ -2x3/-4/I	Claw: 5/3/3L/3	2/2L/5B

Abilities: Awareness 3, Bureaucracy 3, Dodge 3, Linguistics 2 (Native: Riverspeak; Low Realm, Woodtongue) Martial Arts 1, Performance 2, Presence 3, Resistance 1, Socialize 2, War 1

Auric Blossom	3/1/1/	5/3/2/9	-0x21/I	Clinch: 4/6/5B/5	0/1L/1B

Abilities: Awareness 3, Bureaucracy 2, Lore 3, Martial Arts 2 (Grappling +3), Resistance 3, Stealth 5, War 2

Heart Wasp Victim	3/2/3	2/1/3/6	-0x3/-1x3/ -2x2/-4/I	Punch: 5/5/3B/3, Kick: 5/4/6B/2, Axe: 4/5/8L/2, Knife: 5/5/4L/3	2/0L/2B

Abilities: Athletics 1, Awareness 1, Dodge 2, Martial Arts 2, Melee 2, Presence 1, Resistance 1, Socialize 1, Stealth 1, Survival 1, War 2

herbs under the victim's skin. Less adept healers simply burn their victims and hope the wasps leave before they kill their patient. Healers treating infested individuals must take precautions to avoid a swarm attack. Heart wasps driven from a host body are often desperate and ready to seek out the nearest available shelter. Eastern physicians dose themselves with wasp-repelling herbs prior to using these same herbs on their patients. Zenith Caste Solars may use their animas to cleanse one victim per mote spent (they must touch victims barehanded). Other Exalted may use magic to heal the infestation as if it were a normal illness.

OTHER CREATURES

Many other creatures with magical powers dwell in Creation. Some of them are dangerous… but also potentially useful.

BEE OF ZARLATH

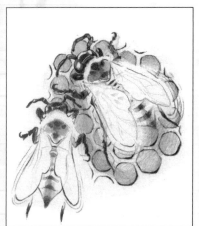

Although they are now known only to a few savants and scavenger lords, the bees of Zarlath were one of the most exquisite natural wonders of the First Age. The plum-sized bees glow with golden light, and their wings are ephemeral creations of glowing Essence. A few savants of First Age lore also know that those bees take the nectar from roses that only bloom by sunlight and oleanders that only bloom by moonlight and work it into a magical honey with a multitude of useful properties. The bee's Essence-enhanced beauty is so great that characters who wish to attack or otherwise attempt to harm one must first succeed at a Willpower roll with a difficulty of two. However, very few have the opportunity even to see these rare bees.

Today, Zarlath lies hidden deep in the Southeastern Middlemarches of the Wyld, protected by the automated defenses of a long-dead Solar's citadel. Once a year, the bees journey beyond its walls and through the Wyld to stable Creation, gathering nectar from sane flowers before they return. Following the bees through the Southeastern jungles and Wyld would be extremely difficult. Few have attempted to find their hives and steal their honey; even fewer have returned.

See page 154 for bee stats.

EARTH-SHATTERING WORM

These creatures look like earthworms magnified to a yard or so long, and made of solid ruby or sapphire. They can burrow through any earth or stone, leaving distinctive tunnels in the rock. Enough of them can undermine an area to collapse buildings or cause local earthquakes. Earth-shattering worms hate captivity and can dig through any substance other than the magical materials or the ruby and sapphire of which they are made.

The worms need no food or rest, and do not age. New earth-shattering worm eggs generate deep underground where the influence of the Elemental Pole of Earth is strongest, amid veins of sapphires and rubies, and hatch when they have grown large enough.

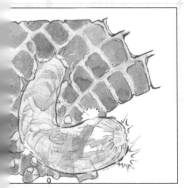

The Mountain Folk of the Realm sometimes persuade the worms to dig in particular areas or directions by setting mercury lures. The worms enjoy the taste of quicksilver: a few ounces intoxicates a worm for several hours.

Earth-shattering worms cannot attack humans or other living beings but are difficult to destroy. They react to attacks by burrowing away from their attackers.

One in every thousand earth-shattering worms has unusually high mental capabilities (Intelligence 4, Wits 4). Such worms can lead dozens or hundreds of their ordinary kindred in swarms that can topple castles or collapse mines. These highly intelligent worms often seek human worship and sacrifices of quicksilver. Since they have no real way of communicating this, they choose a town and start undermining buildings—especially temples—until the humans living there begin offering sacrifices and prayers to stop the destruction.

See page 154 for worm stats.

Essence Spider

Essence spiders are the offspring of ill-tempered wood spiders (see **Exalted** p. 306) and giant burrowing spiders (see **Exalted** p. 347), creating a new species that breeds true. The magical spiders are both intelligent and capable of speech, but remain inhuman, predatory arachnids the size of tigers. During the First Age, the Solar Exalted enslaved them to produce their beautiful and exceptionally strong silk. The Usurpation liberated the spiders. Small communities of Essence spiders now live throughout the Far East and on a few isolated islands in the West.

Essence spider silk can be woven into both steelsilk sails and silken armor, and so, their silk is much in demand. They trade their silk to outsiders, but value their privacy, taking a dim view of those who attempt to cheat them, and resist to the death any attempt to enslave them. More than one ambitious Guildsman has sought to trick

Essence spiders into a particularly unadvantageous deal, and instead become their prey. Spider colonies leave the drained, silk-wrapped husks of their enemies outside the groves or caverns where they live.

See page 154 for spider stats.

Fire Ants

These rare creatures resemble ants four inches long, glowing the color of a banked fire. They live in colonies of several hundred and always build their nests in the magma of volcanoes. Lava infuses their bodies, and neither heat nor flame can harm them.

Each fire ant warren has a single queen. These foot-long insects live at the bottom of the nest, where temperatures are highest. The queen commands the workers and directs the hive, but never leaves her chamber unless the entire nest is in danger. All other fire ants will fight to the death to protect the queen.

Fire ants like to eat meat. The colony sends out hunting parties of 10 to 30 that swarm over their prey, cooking the victim with their heat. The raiders eat their fill and carry leftovers back up the volcano to their nest. Fire ants can carry almost 10 times their own body weight. The creatures have a rudimentary hive mind: Individuals aid one another against more dangerous prey, and the entire party retreats together if a target proves too dangerous.

However, cold makes fire ants sluggish and clumsy. They steam when hit with water. A cup or more of water thrown on a fire ant inflicts 1L unsoakable lethal damage. They also lose their footing on wet surfaces, and become disoriented. The stats below are for an average hunting party of 20 fire ants. For a larger group, add four additional health levels and increase the Martial Arts rating by 2.

See page 154 for stats.

Other Notes: Fire ant shells can be made into clothing or footwear that grants the wearer 3L soak against heat or flame. Also, weapons that pierce their skin may melt or burn. Weapons made of the Five Magical Materials and metal weapons of exceptional workmanship are not affected, but roll a die each time a normal metal weapon strikes an ant. Each success subtracts 1 from one of the weapon's values (attacker's choice). Wooden weapons of any quality burst into

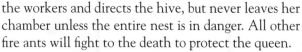

flame upon contact with a fire ant, losing one point per strike, and unarmed characters suffer 2L fire damage per strike against a group of fire ants.

These small, tailless monkeys have long, silky, dark-red fur and are barely a foot tall. Although they can live off the fruits of the forest and small prey such as mice, squirrels or snakes, they crave to eat the bones of sorcerers. Swarms of these creatures often haunt ancient ruins or the tombs of long-dead sorcerers, in hopes of finding more bones to devour.

Ink monkeys were created in the First Age at pets. After a surreptitious diet of magic ink, some of them gained a malicious intelligence, a skill for crafting intangible illusions that look and sound real, and a taste for the bones of sorcerers. Ink monkeys will not attack a person who is clearly more powerful than they are (such as an Exalt displaying an anima banner). They prefer to attack petty magicians, shamans or similarly low-powered wielders of enchantment. The monkeys separate targets from the rest of their group by creating the illusion of an elephant, dragon or some other large and dangerous creature, in order to scatter the party. Alternatively, they may attempt to lure a victim away from the group by acting like innocent but tame creatures. When the target is alone, they attack.

These creatures can be tamed if they are separated from their family while only a few days old, but they tend to grow malicious as they age. Their brains, when ground up with certain herbs, can be used to create salves that prevent inflammation of wounds and halt infection.

A solitary ink monkey's illusions cover no more than a three-yard cube, but a group of monkeys can act together flawlessly to evoke larger illusions. The illusions affect sight and hearing, but no other senses. Charms of Essence perception reveal the illusion; so does a successful (Perception + Awareness) roll at difficulty 3.

See page 154 for monkey stats.

Niljake

The Wyld has warped these large, lizard-like creatures so that nature abhors a niljake. These creatures can simply run through a forest while tree trunks, shrubs and other natural obstacles silently bend out of their way. The plants twist themselves back to their original forms when the creatures have passed. The effect doesn't work on rocks, buildings or other non-plant obstacles, but

a niljake can move quickly and soundlessly through the thickest forests and ambush its prey.

A niljake is about the size of a large dog, with small, clawed forelimbs and extremely powerful and disproportionately large back legs that propel it through the woods at tremendous speeds. Niljakes crouch low when they run, allowing them to stay out of sight until they attack.

Niljakes are difficult to fight in a forest. Putting your back against a tree won't help much, since a niljake can come at you right through the tree, which completely silently bends out of the way—not a single leaf rustles when this happens. A niljake's favored tactic is to make a single swift attack, vanish into the forest and return a few minutes later, repeating this process until its victim bleeds to death. The reptiles can also claw or swat with their long, heavy tails.

Niljakes are very fast. Their Dash and Move are both twice as fast as normal, and they can run as fast as a simple horse relay.

See page 154 for niljake stats.

Serpent of Colorless Fire (Firesnake)

Serpents of colorless fire, or firesnakes, are well known to the firedust prospectors of the Far Southern deserts. These four-to-five-feet-long transparent vipers carry fiery venom that literally burns victims to death from the inside.

Heat and flame cannot harm firesnakes at all, and they feed upon firedust. Thus, caravans and military caches of the powder attract the firesnakes. Their feeding may cause fiery explosions.

Certain disreputable merchants in the cities of the South offer a bounty for living firesnakes, as they breed and sell these deadly creatures to assassins and collectors of exotic beasts. Others are more interested in the glassy skins the creatures leave behind when they molt. Some of the finest and costliest crystal in the South is crafted by melting firesnake molts; they also find use in artifacts related to flame or fireproofing.

Because of their transparency, attempts to locate a firesnake by sight are at +3 difficulty. The serpents are never automatically visible: even spotting a firesnake resting in open sight requires a (Perception + Awareness) check. Anyone attempting to defend against a striking firesnake also suffers a -2 penalty to her Dodge or Parry DV because the snakes are so difficult to see.

Firesnakes generate enough venom for five successful strikes per day. Although rolled like any other poison, this venom inflicts fire damage. The damage also ceases once the victim's player succeeds on three (Stamina + Resistance) rolls, which can include the initial roll to resist the poison. The victim suffers -4 to all actions until this damage ceases.

Southern assassins sometimes use firesnake venom. It bursts into flame upon exposure to air, so most uses result in only 3L/1L damage, with no further rolls. However, skilled assassins use special darts or arrows to keep the poison airtight until it is delivered to their victim's bloodstream, whereupon it functions normally.

See page 154 for firesnake stats.

SNAKEBUD TREE

This plant/animal hybrid came from the Wyld but has spread into the Scavenger Lands. From a distance, it looks like an ordinary tree bearing pink and white flowers. This tree, however, buds serpents, which grow on the branches until they can detach themselves and hunt for nearby prey. When these little, pink and white snakes coil on a branch and stay still, they look like large buds or flowers. From 20 yards or closer, characters can discern the buds' true nature with a successful (Perception + Awareness) roll at difficulty 2.

Snakebud trees are intelligent and can control the mindless snakes from up to a mile away. A tree waits for prey to come near and sends the serpents out to slay it. The tree then slowly shifts its roots in the soil, causing the dead bodies to slip into shallow ditches, hiding them from casual observation while they rot and nourish the tree. However, a difficulty 3 (Perception + [Awareness or Survival]) roll reveals the unusual number of bones around the tree.

A typical tree carries 100 serpents. These frail, six-inch-long serpents have no attack beside their venom, but attack in swarms of 10, and the tree is intelligent enough to hold off attacking if the prey looks ready to lower its guard. The serpents bleed honey that can be used for many ointments and elixirs. The tree itself has no defenses if all its serpents are slain; but it can regrow from its roots unless it is uprooted or destroyed by fire, salt or magic. The trees detest each other and will not root less than a mile apart. If a tree is slain, the remaining serpents wriggle off in different directions and attempt to root and create new trees. A few wealthy (and foolhardy) people in the Scavenger Lands experiment with training snakebud trees as guards for their property.

See page 154 for snakebud tree stats.

Other Notes: The Mental Attributes listed on page 154 are for the tree, while the Physical Attributes are for the snakes. The snakes are mindless, and the tree can be cut down like any other tree. The tree can attack up to five targets at once, without splitting dice pools.

WINTER ROSE

This hazard of the Far North looks like a normal rosebush perfectly carved out of clear crystal. When someone comes within 50 yards, the leaves brush together as though from a gentle breeze, sparkling hypnotically and creating a soft chiming noise. If a character can both see and hear the roses, her player must succeed at a Willpower roll to resist the glittering, tinkling display. The roll's difficulty starts at 1 and increases by 1 (to a maximum of 5) for each 5 ticks of exposure. Those who block their ears with wax or clay need only roll once, at a difficulty of 1, and characters who both avoid looking at the roses and cover their ears need not roll at all from then on.

Failed rolls means the victims are drawn to the roses, and press themselves against the crystal thorns, fondling the razor-edged flowers in fascination. Each miscellaneous action of this inflicts an automatic level of lethal damage on a victim as the winter rose lacerates her flesh. Each level of damage suffered by a victim enables the patch of roses to grow a foot in diameter, as the blood feeds the roses. When a victim dies, his body falls to dust, leaving only clothes and weapons behind.

Smashing the bush may destroy the winter rose. For a year afterward, however, any blood spilled on the shards and dust will regrow the plant over the course of a day. A winter rose patch shrinks a foot in diameter each month that it goes without blood, though never to less than a yard across. The entire patch of roses can move up to 50 yards per day and leaves a large track in the earth behind it. The roses are entirely mindless and travel in random directions. They would be easy to track and destroy, except Wyld

storms and frozen fog seem attracted to winter roses, and move them about without trace.

See below for rose stats.

Other Notes: This creature should be treated as a construct or automaton for the purposes of effects that do or do not affect such creatures.

CREATURES

Name	Str/Dex/Sta	Per/Int/Wit/Will	Health Lvls	Atk (S/A/D/R)	Dodge DV/S
Bee of Zarlath	1/5/2	3/1/2/4	-1/-2/I	Sting: 4/7/1L + poison (3L/hour, 3, —/—, -2)/1	4/0L/2B

Abilities: Athletics 3, Awareness 2, Dodge 3, Martial Arts 2, Survival 2

Name	Str/Dex/Sta	Per/Int/Wit/Will	Health Lvls	Atk (S/A/D/R)	Dodge DV/S
Earth-Shattering Worm	1/4/4	3/1/2/5	-0x4/-1x4/-2x2/-4/I	None	4/8L/14B

Abilities: Awareness 4, Dodge 3, Endurance 5, Resistance 3, Stealth 3

Name	Str/Dex/Sta	Per/Int/Wit/Will	Health Lvls	Atk (S/A/D/R)	Dodge DV/S
Essence Spider	4/5/4	3/2/3/6	-0x2/-1x2/-2x2/-4/I	Bite: 4/7/5L + poison (4L/hour, 3, —/—, -4)/1	5/5L/7B

Abilities: Athletics 3, Awareness 3, Craft 5 (Wood), Dodge 4, Integrity 3, Investigation 3, Linguistics 2, Lore 2, Martial Arts 3, Occult 1, Presence 3, Resistance 2, Socialize 2, Stealth 5, Survival 3

Name	Str/Dex/Sta	Per/Int/Wit/Will	Health Lvls	Atk (S/A/D/R)	Dodge DV/S
Fire Ants	4/4/4	3/2/2/3	-0/-1x2/-2x2/-4/I	Claw: 6/4/2L, Bite: 5/5/3L/1, Touch: 5/6/2L/1	4/3L/4B

Abilities: Awareness 2, Dodge 5, Martial Arts 4, Resistance 5, Socialize 3, Survival 4

Name	Str/Dex/Sta	Per/Int/Wit/Will	Health Lvls	Atk (S/A/D/R)	Dodge DV/S
Ink Monkey	1/5/1/	5/2/4/2	-1/-2/-4/I	Bite: 5/4/1L/3	5/1L/2B

Abilities: Awareness 5, Dodge 5, Larceny 2, Martial Arts 1, Resistance 1, Survival 2, Stealth 4, War 2

Name	Str/Dex/Sta	Per/Int/Wit/Will	Health Lvls	Atk (S/A/D/R)	Dodge DV/S
Niljake	4/4/3	2/1/3/4	-0x2/-1x4/-2x2/I	Claw: 5/5/5L/2, Bite: 4/8/8L/1, Tail: 4/8/8B/1	4/3L/6B

Abilities: Athletics 4, Awareness 2, Dodge 2, Martial Arts 4, Resistance 2, Stealth 3, Survival 3

Name	Str/Dex/Sta	Per/Int/Wit/Will	Health Lvls	Atk (S/A/D/R)	Dodge DV/S
Serpent of Colorless Fire	1/5/2	3/1/4/6	-0/-1/-4/I	Bite: 4/11/1L + poison (4L, 2, —/—, -4)/3	4/1L/3B

Abilities: Awareness 1 (Scent Firedust +3), Dodge 3, Intimidation 2, Martial Arts 3 (Bite +3), Stealth 3

Name	Str/Dex/Sta	Per/Int/Wit/Will	Health Lvls	Atk (S/A/D/R)	Dodge DV/S
Snakebud Tree	1/3/1	3/2/2/4	-0x3/-1/I	Bite: 5/6/1L + poison (6L, 3, —/—, -5)/5	3/0L/1B

Abilities: Awareness 3, Dodge 3, Intimidation 2, Lore 2, Martial Arts 3, Occult 2, Presence 3, Stealth 3

Name	Str/Dex/Sta	Per/Int/Wit/Will	Health Lvls	Atk (S/A/D/R)	Dodge DV/S
Winter Rose	3/1/4/	2/1/2/1	-0x3/-1x3/-2x3/-4/I	Petals: 6/5/1L (automatic, not rolled)/3	0/5L/7B

Abilities: Awareness 1, Presence 2, Resistance 3

Inanimate Wonders

A number of Creation's natural wonders are inanimate. Many plants and minerals possess unusual powers: some useful, some frightening, some dangerous—or all three at once. Whole industries may depend on a natural wonder, or perhaps the few people who know of the wonder shun it from fear.

Black Ash

Black ash trees rarely grow over 25 feet tall. Their bark, leaves and wood are all dark gray or black in color, with a wood darker and harder than the ebony trees of the Southeast (though not as lustrous). Black ash grows in many shadowlands, but nowhere else. These trees are most prolific in the death-touched forest near Sijan.

Many people regard black ash as unlucky because of where it grows; certainly, few people dare the dangers of a shadowland to cut it. Deathknights, however, can harvest it freely and craft arrows and bow-staves from its strong, flexible branches. Black ash wood resists the necrotic Essence of their Charms and necromancy (but is an otherwise normal hard wood with respect to mundane force, including damaging Charms or sorcery). The wood also decays slowly, if at all, which makes it an excellent wood for coffins.

Cost: Resources ••• (•• in Sijan) for a coffin's worth of black ash wood.

Blood Berries

Blood berry vines grow in Wood-aspected demesnes throughout the outer edges of the Northeast. Since they root in tree branches high above the ground, however, they are seldom harvested outside the arboreal Haltan Republic. In the last months of Descending Fire, these vines produce clusters of tart, red berries, which people who know of their properties then pick and dry in the sun.

These berries owe their name to their curative power as well as their oozing, crimson juice. A character who eats a dozen blood berries a day can halve the time required to heal one lethal wound that caused a great deal of blood loss when it was inflicted. (For instance, the berries help heal gashes but not broken bones.) Dried blood berries keep for a year, after which they lose their potency.

Cost: •• for a basket of 50 berries.

Bright Morning

This purple powder, also known as vision dust, is made from a mixture of various eastern herbs, including the rare skullweed that grows only in shadowlands. It is not alchemical: Given the raw materials and the recipe, any competent apothecary (Medicine rated 2+) can compound the powder.

Smoking this powder produces mild hallucinations and euphoria. It also grants the user the ability to perceive spirits, ghosts and Essence flows. The drug allows an ordinary human to use both the equivalent of the Spirit Detecting Glance and Spirit-Cutting Attack (see **Exalted**, p. 221) Charms without needing to pay any Essence cost. An Exalted user additionally gains the benefits of All-Encompassing Sorcerer's Sight (see **Exalted**, p. 222), without the need to spend Essence. The effects of this drug last three full hours. During this time, the minor hallucinations and disorientation produced by this drug increase the difficulty of all the user's mundane Perception and Wits rolls by 2. However, this penalty does not apply to any magical perceptions.

The Realm forbids the use of bright morning and severely punishes its possession. The Dynasts do not wish mere mortals to imitate any of their powers. The Guild, however, does a brisk trade in other regions, where the drug is both legal and popular among those who can afford it. Bright morning is also addictive: If a character uses it more often than once a week, her player must succeed at a (Stamina + Resistance) roll for the character to avoid addiction.

Once addicted, the character loses one dot off of her Perception due to continual low-level hallucinations. The addict must also take at least two doses a week or suffer chills, bouts of delirium and severe pain: The character loses an additional dot of Perception, two dots of Willpower, and three levels of bashing damage that do not heal until the next dose is taken or the addiction is broken. Kicking this addiction involves going a full month without the drug. Enduring the torments of withdrawal this long when the drug remains available requires a Willpower roll at difficulty 3. When the addiction breaks, however, all lost traits return.

Cost: Resources ••• (•••• in the Realm).

DREAMSTONE

This greenish opal crystallizes at Wyld-charged hot springs. A cut and polished opal records the dreams of anyone who dreams while touching the stone. Acorn-sized stones only record the first dream of the night, while thumb-sized stones record every dream the dreamer has during the night. No stone can hold more than a single night's worth of dreams. After the stone holds one or more dreams, any waking person who touches the stone to her forehead for a minute will dream these recorded dreams the next time she falls asleep. Dreamstone users experience these recorded dreams as if they were their own.

If the holder instead sits quietly while touching the stone, she experiences the dream as a vivid daydream. Dreams can be replayed any number of times, but existing dreams must be erased before these stone can record more dreams. Erasing a dreamstone requires the user to clasp the stone lightly and perform a special meditation. Learning the meditation required to erase a dreamstone rarely requires more than an hour, but learning to have dreams worth recording is an art that can take a lifetime.

Some people become addicted to dreamstones. This is not a physical dependency—merely the lure of escape into wonderful dreams.

Cost: Resources •• for a one-dream stone, ••• for a larger stone.

FIREDUST

Highly combustible and somewhat unstable, brick-red firedust burns both very hot and rapidly. It is a potent explosive if its combustion is contained and a single spark can set it off. Firedust is also one of the most valuable military commodities in Creation, used in firewands, fire cannon and firedust grenades. Travelers in the North and West value it as tinder. Firedust also finds use as an alchemical ingredient and vital addition to some high-temperature metalwork.

Southern Wyld storms often leave patches of firedust behind them. The largest deposits form in the Southern Bordermarches, but firedust also appears in most Southern tainted lands, where it collects in hollows and the lee side of large dunes. Few firedust gatherers brave the dangers of the Wyld when they can collect the dust around its fringes.

Cost: Resources • for a palm-full of firedust in the South; ••, or occasionally higher, in the rest of Creation.

FIRE TREES

Fire trees are medium-sized deciduous trees that bear large numbers of scarlet blossoms around the start of Descending Fire. The blossoms' scent induces mild euphoria in most people who smell it and lowers inhibitions about as much as a mug or two of strong ale. People have transplanted fire trees to the Realm and many other countries. However, the natives of the Republic of Chaya, in the Scavenger Lands, respond more strongly to fire-tree pollen. For the entire month that the fire trees bloom, the inhabitants lose all inhibitions and become wildly passionate. They erupt in extreme emotional outbursts and crazed fits of excitement. The Chayans consider the fire trees sacred and plant them near every habitation, making the hysteria universal.

Most people exposed to the scent of fire tree blossoms lower their Willpower by two points until a half day after this exposure ends. Natives Chayans lose all Willpower for the duration of the flower's season and become wildly emotional and prone to violence. Approximately three weeks after they begin blooming, fire blossom season ends, and the blossoms' effects fade within a day or two.

Cost: Resources ••• to buy a fire-tree sapling from a well-stocked nursery (• in Chaya).

IRON BUSH

These shrubs first grew near the Imperial Mountain. During the First Age, the Exalted planted the shrubs throughout Creation as a biological weapon against the Fair Folk. Today, iron bushes grow in most temperate forests (especially in the Northeast), but do not grow near Wyld areas or demesnes.

The Fair Folk feel burning pain if they touch the leaves of an iron bush—an environmental effect inflicting 1L/action (Trauma 1). The leaves can also be distilled into a liquid that simply tastes foul to humans, but the Fair Folk find deadly. These environmental effects inflict 10L (Trauma 5) to any Fair Folk who so much as sips the liquid, or 4L/action (Trauma 3) on skin contact, until the Fair Folk can wipe it off. Only one iron bush grows at a time within a 20 mile area, and once all the leaves have been plucked from a bush, it does not grow new ones for a decade.

Cost: Resources ••• for three leaves.

Ironwood

Ironwood is a dense, extremely tough deciduous wood with a short, straight trunk. It grows only in certain regions of the East. Ironwood burns slowly and with a noxious smoke, but makes excellent charcoal. Its true value, however, lies in its strength. Ironwood works very well for weapon hafts, siege engines and structural beams for houses.

Certain barbarian artisans can give ironwood almost mystical qualities. A special mixture of herbs and simple thaumaturgical enchantment can give ironwood the resilience and strength of steel. Tribe members sometimes sell these weapons, but the tribal wise men who know how to harden ironwood have revealed this secret only to a few Lunar Exalted.

Bladed weapons made of normal ironwood subtract a point from both their damage and defense values, and are prone to damage and breakage. Ironwood weapons hardened by the proper ritual treatment are not subject to these penalties.

Cost: Hardened ironwood weapons cost one Resources dot higher than their normal counterparts, unless you belong to a tribe that crafts them.

Thaumaturgical Procedure: *Strengthen Ironwood* (1, Intelligence, 2, 3 hours)

Lucky Rock

"Lucky rocks" appear naturally in Wyld-tainted lands around Creation. Their Wyld taint causes them to always wind up back in their owner's possession within a few hours of being thrown or dropped. Some people buy lucky rocks as curiosities. During the First Age, however, Exalted artisans learned how to imbue this power into thrown weapons. Self-returning javelins or boomerangs, for instance, are worth Resources ••• or are considered Artifact •.

Cost: Resources •

Message Seed

These flying seeds come from giant dandelion-like plants that originally grew around an unusually powerful Air-aligned demesne, but have since spread throughout the Northeast. They are most common in the Haltan Republic, where they often spring up in large clearings or around lakes. The plant produces seeds the size of two fists attached to a stalk with a silky "fan" on the top. These seeds float on the wind over the whole of Halta and nearby portions of the East. The message seeds floated in a predictable pattern along the Essence currents of dragon lines. After mapping the path that the message seeds flew along, savants found how to use them to send letters and messages between villages.

Message seeds are not a particularly reliable communication system, since some species of birds eat them, and rainstorms ruin any seeds caught in them. However, they enjoy popularity with secret lovers and others who wish to send messages without needing to trust a courier.

Cost: None within Halta. From Descending Fire to Descending Air, the seeds are everywhere. They have no value outside Halta and nearby portions of the East, but would cost Resources •• to acquire simply as a curiosity.

Mother's Moss

This rust-colored moss grows on the bark of certain trees in Northern forests, particularly in the Haltan Republic. It is rarely exported because it only retains its special properties while still alive or within a few days of harvest. Mother's moss is so called because it holds heat. A few minutes near a fire turn a strip of mossy bark into a soothing hot pack, good for keeping a child warm or easing muscle ache. During the colder months, important visitors to Haltan cities often receive beds with large "sheets" of mother's moss under a thin blanket to keep them warm at night. Herbalists can use a mixture made from dung, crushed beetles and whiskey to preserve the moss for about a year; this requires a weekly (Intelligence + Lore) roll. Fire-aspected Terrestrials can spend three motes of Essence per day to allow the moss to retain its special properties, but Exalts typically have better things to do than transport moss.

Cost: •••• for a three-foot-by-three-foot sheet outside of Halta. It only retains its properties for a week at most without the preparation mentioned above. Much of this expense comes from the cost of these preparations and the fact that the delivery is necessarily rushed. A similar sheet would only cost •• in Halta.

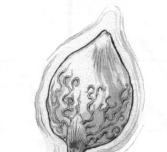

WYLD SEED

Wyld seeds can develop in any tree, bush or root (and even some animals) that grows to maturity too close to the Wyld. Despite their diverse origin, they are easy to recognize—the seeds are swollen and faintly luminescent, and usually brightly colored. The seeds are harmless to handle; their Wyld energy is safely contained within them. If a living thing consumes a seed, though, within a day or two, it develops a Wyld pox or deficiency (equal chances). Also, if any creature eats the now-tainted animal, it too contracts the taint, receiving the Wyld mutation the first magic animal had plus another one of a higher level. For instance, a bird that eats a Wyld seed might develop the Large pox and grow from a tiny songbird into a crow-sized beast. If a hunting cat then ate the bird, the cat would develops the same pox—Large—*and* an affliction or deficiency such as flaps of skin on its side (as the Gliding Wings affliction). Fortunately for Creation, this chain of contagion continues no further.

Fair Folk who eat Wyld seeds or warped animals do not suffer mutations, but remove the need to feed on dreams for three days per seed. Planting a Wyld seed yields a plant that exhibits Wyld traits. A tree might sport mouths instead of knotholes, its roots might bleed, it might "bloom" fur or scales instead of blossoms. Unless planted in a Wyld place, however, the seeds these warped plants bear are not Wyld seeds.

Cost: ••••• for a single seed, but the sale of Wyld seeds is highly illegal in almost all nations.

NATURAL ARTIFACTS

Creation's greatest natural wonders are so powerful they count as artifacts. Such wonders are not usually for sale unless you know the right people, and just as importantly, they know you.

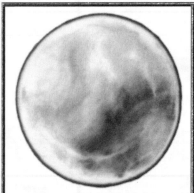

FRESHWATER PEARL (ARTIFACT •)

These fist-sized, snow-white pearls occasionally form in giant oysters that grow in the Western Bordermarches of the Wyld. If a freshwater pearl is placed in a barrel (or lesser quantity) of seawater or fouled water, it instantly renders the water as clear and fresh as that of a mountain spring. It has no effect on larger quantities of water, though ancient legends tell of Solar Exalted (or in the "corrected" versions, the Immaculate Dragon of Water) collecting the magic pearls for a great rite to purify a salty inland sea.

Each pearl works up to five times a day. If placed in a barrel of wine or other alcohol, then the pearl turns the liquid back to grape juice or whatever the appropriate source liquid might be. These pearls has no effect on actual poison.

STEELSILK SAILS (ARTIFACT •)

A few master artisans in the West know how to weave the silk of Essence spiders (see p. 151) into sails as light as canvas but as strong as steel. Captains who possess such sails guard them highly, sometimes only removing them from a well-locked hold when the ship's survival depends on them.

Storms, fire and weapons that would destroy ordinary sails all fail to damage steelsilk sails. The magical sails have 10L/15B soak, take 20 health levels to damage and 40 to destroy. They also suffer only half damage from wind, waves or fire. Their durability makes a ship fitted with them easier to handle, adding +1 to all Sail rolls to control a ship in a storm or for gaining or losing speed. Steelsilk sails also allow a ship to sail closer to the wind. Steelsilk sails requires Charms or thaumaturgical enchantments to mend: ordinary mortal crafts are not up to this task.

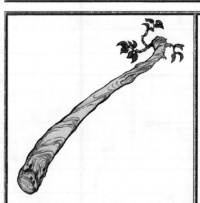

TRAVELER'S STAFF (ARTIFACT •)

This gnarled staff is a branch from an ancient apple tree found in a powerful Wood demesne on the Blessed Isle. The Empress claimed this demesne as a crownland until a few decades ago, when she awarded it to House V'neef. Only tools of the magical materials can cut this tree's wood, and only a master of Lore, Occult and Craft (Wood) can preserve the ageless tree's magic in a staff.

A traveler's staff can be used as a normal quarterstaff in combat, but the staff is more useful as a source of food, firewood and shelter. At sunset, the user may plant the staff into the earth and commit 3 motes. The branch then grows into a full-size apple tree that bears enough ripe fruit to feed five people for the evening. If she needs firewood, the owner can use the tree's branches to provide it—wood gathered this way burns readily. Come morning, she can find a large, straight branch that easily snaps off—and it becomes the original staff. The tree then dies and rapidly rots away. By sunset, no sign of its presence remains, and the Essence is released to the Exalt who caused it to grow.

HORN OF THE WAYS (ARTIFACT••)

In the Middlemarches of the Wyld, space can twist and fray strangely, and that power sometimes inheres in Wyld-spawned creatures. A horn of the ways is made from the horn of any large beast born in the Middlemarches, enchanted and bound in moonsilver. The Lunar Exalted use these artifacts to travel quickly across Wyld regions, but they can also be used to penetrate fortress walls, escape imprisonment and outflank their enemies.

A horn of the ways makes a mournful howling sound, easily mistaken for the wind or perhaps a strange beast. The magical horn opens paths that did not exist before and vanish shortly after the Exalt follows them. Used in the wilderness, a horn of the ways adds four dice to Survival rolls to travel from location to location or simply escape an area. Further, the horn eliminates all terrain penalties to movement speed (see the Complex Travel factors on p. 266-267 of **Exalted**; no matter where the traveler goes on land, treat his movement as on a highway). Used to get past an impassable barrier (a fortress wall, for example), it adds four dice to Larceny rolls to open doors or other passages and eliminates all penalties for the lack of appropriate tools. Using the horn on a journey requires the Exalt to commit 5 motes until he gets where he wants to go. A character can bring no more than 10 people (a combat unit of Magnitude 1) along the horn's secret paths, and if anyone loses sight of the Exalt, they lose the benefits from the horn.

SEED OF THE IMMACULATE BLOOD (ARTIFACT •• OR •••)

If a seed of the immaculate blood is sown and carefully tended, it grows into a pale fern that produces a dozen seeds twice a year, in spring and in autumn. These seeds are dull green and sterile, but may be compounded to create an ointment that restores five health levels to anyone who uses it. This wondrous cure heals bashing, lethal and aggravated damage equally well and always heals the most serious type of damage first. Each green seed counts as Artifact ••.

Once a century, on the last day of Calibration, this ageless fern gives a single scarlet seed, which may be replanted to grow another fern with the same properties. This scarlet seed may also be dried and ground up with the seeds of 25 other types of tree or plant: this produces a small ball of dark thick sap, which smells of fresh woodlands. If this ball of sap is planted in fresh earth, a mature forest composed of all the plants that had their seeds mingled together springs up instantly for a half-mile around the spot. The growing plants topple or shatter buildings and throw humans and animals aside. Elementals of Wood also flock to any location where this ball of sap is planted. (A red seed counts as Artifact •••.)

SILKEN ARMOR (ARTIFACT ••)

This unusual cloth is woven from the silk of Essence spiders (see p. 151) Although the fabric has the weight and texture of silk and can be made into any garment that silk can, it is as strong as steel when struck. Even a light tunic, robe or cloak of the stuff makes effective armor. It is the clothing of choice for those who need its protection but cannot be seen wearing obvious armor.

Unlike other forms of armor, silken armor stacks with other forms of armor. It cannot be detected as magical without the use of some magic-sensing Charm such as All-Encompassing Sorcerer's Sight. Silken armor also can be worn while performing Martial Arts styles that normally prohibit the use of armor. Anyone can wear silken armor, but it remains somewhat stiff unless attuned to the wearer's Essence.

Soak	Hardness	Mobility	Fatigue	Cost	Attune	Tags
+5L/3B	—	-1*	0	••	2	

*Attunement removes this penalty.

BLOOD SEED (ARTIFACT ●●●)

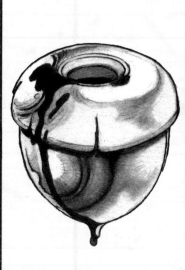

These powerfully magical seeds appear naturally in the Deep Wyld of the East and the Northeast, but a few Exalts know how to duplicate them. The lore of their creation is extremely rare, though. Wyld-spawned or crafted blood seeds work the same way, to create an immediate but temporary military force for an Exalted user.

The seed itself is a fist-sized, hollow acorn with a razor-edged hole on top about an inch across. To use a blood seed, an Essence-user cuts a finger over the hole and fills the seed with blood. This inflicts one level of lethal damage, which cannot be soaked or reduced. The character then spends 10 motes of Essence, which are committed until the soldiers are killed or the scene ends. Once the seed is full, the character sprinkles the blood on the ground. Every five ticks thereafter for 25 ticks, one armed and armored elite soldier (see **Exalted**, p. 280) rises from the blood soaked earth. These five soldiers are never treated as extras, but return to the earth at the end of the scene.

The woody husk of a blood seed is infused with one of the magical materials. A character using such a seed does not harmonize her anima with it—the magical materials involved simply contribute to the effect, rather than forge a supernatural bond with the character. As a result, a character faces no penalties for using a blood seed made with a magical material different than that favored by the Exalt. However, each magical material grants a special benefit to the summoned soldiers.

Orichalcum: Blood seeds that reflect the golden sheen of orichalcum summon stronger soldiers. Add one dot to each Physical Attribute.

Moonsilver: These silver-shimmering seeds summon soldiers with bestial characteristics. Their fists deal one additional point of damage, and that damage it lethal due to the soldiers' long claws. In addition, the soldiers can follow a scent trail with a successful (Perception + Awareness) roll.

Jade: Seeds made of jade summon tougher soldiers. Add 3 to their bashing and lethal soak.

Starmetal: Starmetal seeds summon soldiers with a preternatural sense of their opponents' tactics. Add two dice to Join Battle and all attack rolls, and 1 to both Parry and Dodge DV (final trait, not the dice pool used to calculate them).

Soulsteel: These black, metallic seeds summon the spirits of the dead to animate the bodies. These bodies are not vulnerable to pain and care little about wounding. Such soldiers ignore all wound penalties until they are Incapacitated.

EYE OF THE LIVING EARTH (ARTIFACT ●●●)

The Mountain Folk occasionally quarry these large stones from caverns deep inside the Imperial Mountain. Large as a man's head and clear as the finest diamond, they constantly glow and sparkle with a hundred colors, emitting rays of light that bathe a room in shifting hues. The stone loses its power if it is in any way chipped, carved or polished.

This stone can be used as a potent scrying glass. If an Essence user touches a diamond to the eye, and anoints both the Eye and the diamond with a drop of his blood, he can later use the Eye to scry upon wherever the diamond currently is. He perceives the entire scene as though he were looking down from on high, and can move around the Eye to alter his perspective on events. This works with up to five diamonds at a time: if a sixth diamond is attuned, then the link to one of the others (the owner's choice which) is broken.

HONEY OF THE BEES OF ZARLATH (ARTIFACT ●●●)

This honey comes from the rare bees of Zarlath (see p. 150) that now live deep in the Wyld. It gives speech to the dumb or surpassing eloquence to those born with speech (+3 to all Social Abilities for one hour). The honey can also temper the finest of blades, giving them an edge of great quality (making the creation of a perfect weapon no more difficult than forging an exceptional weapon), and it can be used in the crafting of strings for lyres and harps that provide a +1 bonus to Performance rolls with the instrument.